STAR TANGO

Broken Galaxy Book Two

Phil Huddleston

CONTENTS

Title Page
Note to Readers — 1
Previously Introduced — 2
Prologue - from Book One — 4
Chapter One — 19
Chapter Two — 24
Chapter Three — 29
Chapter Four — 43
Chapter Five — 51
Chapter Six — 60
Chapter Seven — 72
Chapter Eight — 85
Chapter Nine — 101
Chapter Ten — 118
Chapter Eleven — 129
Chapter Twelve — 136
Chapter Thirteen — 145
Chapter Fourteen — 154
Chapter Fifteen — 164
Chapter Sixteen — 173
Chapter Seventeen — 182

Chapter Eighteen	191
Chapter Nineteen	201
Chapter Twenty	209
Chapter Twenty-One	216
Chapter Twenty-Two	226
Chapter Twenty-Three	237
Chapter Twenty-Four	248
Chapter Twenty-Five	259
Chapter Twenty-Six	270
Chapter Twenty-Seven	282
Chapter Twenty-Eight	291
Chapter Twenty-Nine	303
Epilogue	311
Author Notes	315
Preview of Next Book	316
Works	323
About the Author	324

NOTE TO READERS

Heads up! This book contains cursing, mostly around military situations. That's part of military life. You've been warned!

Thank you in advance for choosing to read *Star Tango*, the second book in the Broken Galaxy series. For those interested, the preceding novel in the series is called *Broken Galaxy*.

While it isn't necessary to read *Broken Galaxy* prior to *Star Tango*, there are things that will make more sense if you do. And especially if you like airplanes, Alaska, clones, hand grenades, and a man confused by too many women.

So please enjoy this book - and look forward to the next one in the series, *The Long Edge of Night*.

PREVIOUSLY INTRODUCED

Jim Carter - Former U.S. Marine turned mercenary turned airshow performer turned semi-retired hermit. So far lucky in war but unlucky with women. Lives in an airport hangar in Deseret, Nevada with many expensive airplanes. Frequently treks out into the middle of the wilderness in Alaska or Canada to clear his mind and shake the demons. Doesn't always work. Discovered a damaged sentient AI starship called *Jade* in the Canadian Northwest Territory and restored her to flying condition with the help of Bonnie and Rita - only to discover she was an existential threat to humanity. Fought *Jade* at the Battle of Dutch Harbor.

Bonnie Page - Ex-Air Force fighter pilot and once lover of Jim Carter. Convinced a reluctant Captain Arteveld on the Nidarian scout ship *Corresse* to ambush *Jade*, causing her to crash land at Dutch Harbor, Alaska which started the massive Battle of Dutch Harbor involving *Jade*, *Corresse*, Russia, America, and Canada.

Rita Page - Clone created by the starship *Jade*, who secretly intended to take her back to the enemy planet Singheko as a zoo specimen of humanity. Created with the dual memories, knowledge and feelings of both Jim Carter and Bonnie Page. As a result of her dual consciousness, she is in love with both Jim and Bonnie. Took Bonnie's last name since she didn't have one of her own. Performed the final coup de grace of *Jade* at the Battle of Dutch Harbor.

Arteveld - Captain of the Nidarian scout ship *Corresse*, conducted a five-year mission to monitor Earth and warn Nidaria of any intrusion by the Singheko. Had a secondary mission to collect all possible human historical records from the Web, libraries, and other sources. Was tasked to remain hidden from humanity but broke his orders to prevent *Jade* from revealing Earth's location to the Singheko. After the Battle of Dutch Harbor, allowed Bonnie and Rita to return to Nidaria with him on the *Corresse*.

Florissian (Flo) - Ship's doctor of the *Corresse*, wife of Captain Arteveld. Assisted Bonnie Page in the destruction of *Jade* and became friends with both Bonnie and Rita.

Mark Rodgers - Former U.S. Army General specializing in Intelligence and Weapons Research. Discovered the existence of *Jade*, captured Jim Carter, and tortured him to force him to reveal *Jade*'s whereabouts, but was unsuccessful. Later, upon the advice of Jim's sister Gillian, let Jim escape. Saved Jim's life at the Battle of Dutch Harbor. Fell in love with Gillian.

Gillian Hassell - Former Assistant Director in the CIA Weapon's Directorate. Sister of Jim Carter. Shanghaied by Mark Rodgers to help with her brother, fell in love with Mark and married him.

The Bear - A big male grizzly that attacked Jim Carter in the Canadian Northwest Territories, leading him to discover *Jade* in his attempt to escape. Now a large bearskin hanging on the wall of Jim's aircraft hangar at Deseret.

PROLOGUE - FROM BOOK ONE

Earth. Nevada

The Vietnam-era A-4 Skyhawk attack jet screamed across the desert at low level, barely above the brush-studded surface. Moving at 400 knots, it left a rooster-tail of dust behind it that could be seen for miles.

Perry Barnes sat in front of his hangar at the Deseret Airport, watching the distant dust cloud grow closer.

Pulling on his beer, he pointed.

"Here comes that crazy Jim Carter," he said to his buddy Randy Green, sitting beside him on a couple of old, run-down easy chairs that looked like they belonged in a dump.

"Yep," said Randy. "Still trying to kill himself."

"And he'll do it, too, if he keeps that up," avowed Perry.

Reaching the airport, the Skyhawk pitched and went straight up, climbing like a bat out of hell. Nearing 10,000 feet, it pulled inverted and came back down, rolled wings level, and made a sweeping turn out to the west before turning back into the landing pattern. As it proceeded past the airport, gear and flaps came down and the aircraft slowed dramatically.

Making another sweeping turn, it entered the final approach path, spoilers coming out from the side. Throwing a considerable amount of dirty exhaust behind, it crossed the scrub trees at the east end of the runway and landed firmly on the numbers, rolling out down the runway all the way to the bitter end before the pilot got it slowed to a walking pace.

Turning onto the taxiway, Jim Carter pushed a bit of throttle to keep the jet rolling. He opened the canopy to cool off and waved at Perry and Randy as he went by.

"There goes one crazy son of a bitch," said Randy. "That Air Force gal Bonnie really screwed up his head."

Perry nodded. "That's why I stay away from them pretty ones," he said. "They'll screw you up every time."

"Oh, she wasn't just a pretty one," replied Randy. "She was a stunner. You looked at her and it was like a punch in the gut."

Perry nodded.

"Yep. You are correct, my friend."

Randy lifted his beer and waved it toward the A-4 as it went by.

"How much you think it costs him to fly that thing?"

Perry shook his head.

"Well, let's see. If he burns three or four hundred gallons a flight, then I could make a car payment on what he burns just for a Sunday drive in that thing. But he don't care. He's got money to burn."

"I reckon. Ever since that gal left, all he does is fly and drink."

"Yeah," Perry mused. "And not always in that order."

"Ah, hell," said Randy. "Let's walk down and visit with him. See what he's up to these days."

"Good idea," said Perry. "His beer is a lot better than mine."

* * * * *

Parking in front of his hangar, Jim Carter shut off the engine on the A-4. While it spooled down, he got unhooked from the various tubes and wires that bonded him to the plane. Climbing out of the cockpit, he rested his flight helmet on the windscreen and put the safety pins in the ejection seat to prevent accidents. He grabbed his helmet, closed the canopy, slid off the wing, and pinned the landing gear.

Hooking up a robotic tug, he used a remote control to put

the plane away in the large hangar. It was not typically a one-man job; but he wrestled the jet into position.

Then he grabbed a cloth off the workbench and wiped the sweat off his face. Pensive, he looked across the hangar at his world.

A bunch of expensive airplanes.

Workbenches and boxes full of tools and parts.

A plaque containing some dusty ribbons and medals.

A bearskin hanging on the wall of the hangar.

Not much to show for my life so far.

Looking down the field, he saw Perry Barnes and Randy Green walking slowly down the taxiway toward him. He grinned and went to the front of the hangar, where his overstuffed easy chair - having seen better days - sat waiting for him, next to a beer cooler.

By the time Perry and Randy got to him, Jim had already pulled two Stella Artois bottles out of the cooler and had them waiting. He waved the two towards the extra chairs arranged in a rough circle around the beer cooler and handed each a beer as they sat down. Grabbing his own cold one, he sat down and saluted them.

"Here's to it!" Jim said and took a long pull on the beer.

"And those that do it," said Perry, duplicating the feat.

They relaxed into the chairs. Perry looked over at Jim.

"Jim, you keep flying like that, you're gonna leave a big smoking hole in the desert someday."

Jim grinned.

"Don't you worry about me, Perry. I keep the greasy side down."

Randy chimed in.

"It ain't always about what you intend, brother. Gotta give yourself a little room for error."

Jim saluted with his beer, and they sat silently for a while. There wasn't much more to say.

Finally, Perry couldn't resist. He asked the question both he and Randy had been wanting to ask for a while.

"Have you heard anything about that gal Bonnie?"

Jim shook his head.

"Nope." He took another long pull on the beer.

"So, she just went off into space with them ... what do you call them again?"

"Nidarians," said Jim.

"And that other girl, Rita too, huh," said Randy.

"Yep."

"How long they been gone now?"

Jim gazed out across the airport to the west. It was a beautiful sunset. The sun was easing down, throwing wild colors of every hue back up into the air.

He could barely make out Pyramid Peak and the Funeral Mountains across the state line in California. A few minutes ago, he had been blazing through them at speed, weaving in and out of the mountains, pulling 4G turns to miss the peaks.

Bonnie. Bonnie and Rita.

"Twelve months," said Jim. "They should have arrived at Sanctuary about six months ago."

Perry stared out at the western sunset.

"So, we could hear back at any time, if they turned around and came right back."

"Yep," nodded Jim. "But I don't expect that. I expect they'll have to negotiate with the Nidarians for a while, maybe for six months or a year."

Perry stared at the ground, took another slug of beer.

"Yeah, that sucks. So, it could be another six months before you see her again. Or longer."

Jim set his beer down and got the thousand-yard stare - one Perry and Randy had seen many times since Bonnie left.

"Yep," Jim grunted. "Could be a long time."

Randy looked over at Perry, then back at Jim.

"Is it true what they say on TV? That if we don't get help from the Nidarians, that other bunch of aliens will come and attack us?"

Jim nodded.

"It's possible. That other bunch is called the Singheko. They don't know exactly where Earth is. At least we hope they don't. But they'll find us someday, and when they do, we're in for the fight of our lives, that's for sure."

"Man, that sucks," said Randy. "So if them girls - Bonnie and Rita - don't get some help from the Nidarians, we'll be fighting the Singheko."

"That's about the size of it," said Jim.

It won't be much of a fight, thought Jim. *We're totally outclassed by their technology.*

He didn't say that to Perry and Randy.

Sitting there in his easy chair, watching the sunset, Jim drank his beer, listened to the idle chit-chat of his friends, and thought.

He thought about Dutch Harbor, when he almost died inside the renegade sentient starship *Jade*, who pretended to be Nidarian but was secretly Singheko. She had almost killed him in her last desperate attempt to escape to her Singheko masters and bring flaming hell back to Earth.

He thought about Bonnie and Rita, who had hitched a ride on the Nidarian scoutship *Corresse* to make a desperate plea for help from their government.

Bonnie and Rita, who had left him lying unconscious in hospital, in a coma, while they left for the stars.

They had no choice. They had one chance to go with the Nidarians and seek help for our planet. They did what they had to do. I can't fault them for that.

Jim took another long pull on his beer.

But I miss them. I miss Bonnie. And I miss Rita. And the baby. I wonder if the baby survived. If it did, then it's born by now. I have a child. A son or a daughter.

Jim looked up at the stars coming out in the evening sky.

Somewhere. Somewhere out there, I have a son or a daughter. But I don't know where, and I don't know if I'll ever see them again.

Jim sat quietly as Perry and Randy rattled on. Slowly, he came to a decision.

I can't put it off any longer. I have to get on with living. I can't just sit here and whine about Bonnie and Rita while the damn Singheko conquer my planet. The scuttlebutt is that the Space Force has managed to salvage enough information from Jade's wreck to build some fighters and get a Mars base established.

I guess I'd better make some phone calls.

Planet Nidaria
City of Sanctuary

Rita could see a Singheko walking a couple of dozen meters in front of them. She poked Bonnie.

"See that Singheko?" she said, pointing.

"Yep," replied Bonnie. "Big fucker, ain't he? And don't point; it's really bad manners to Nidarians."

Rita grunted, slapped her forehead gently, and muttered, "Bad Rita! Bad Rita!"

Bonnie laughed. Then she got serious again, staring at the huge seven-foot tawny gold alien walking ahead of them.

The sidewalk was crowded with Nidarians moving to and from Government House. But the small Nidarians parted like river water as the massive Singheko stomped toward the building at the end of the street. His head was thrust aggressively forward, moving neither right nor left as he plowed along.

"Think he knows we're back here?" asked Bonnie.

"Oh, yeah," said Rita. "He's got his earpiece on, see it?"

"Oh. You're right. I see it."

"So, his spooks are telling him everything, I'm sure."

The Singheko reached Government House and started up the steps. He disappeared into the cooler confines of the building.

Rita and Bonnie followed, their nose plugs filtering some of the trace amounts of hydrogen sulfide in the air.

God, I'm tired of the stink, thought Rita. *Please God let us get out of this place sometime soon.*

The atmosphere of Sanctuary smelled like rotten eggs to a human - in fact, sometimes the smell was so strong it could make a human dizzy. They wore their nose plugs for protection.

Especially today. Today, they wanted their wits about them. Today, they were meeting with the High Councilor.

To try and save Earth from the Singheko.

It had been twelve months since the Nidarian scout ship *Corresse* had allowed them - against the better judgment of its Captain, Arteveld - to hitch a ride to Sanctuary, the capital of the Nidarian Empire.

After the battle with the sentient AI starship *Jade* on Earth - a ship that was secretly Singheko - it was clear to them they had no other choice. The technology of the Singheko and Nidarians was so far in advance of Earth's, it was no contest.

They needed help.

Unless the Nidarians intervene - Earth will fall to the Singheko, Rita thought bitterly. *And that'll be the end of the human species as anything except a slave race.*

For six months, they had been cooped up on the *Corresse*, relegated to the status of barely tolerated human cargo.

Flo - their nickname for the ship's doctor, Florissian - and Captain Arteveld were friendly. But the rest of the crew - a bit put off by having their ship shot up by *Jade* - were not. They weren't openly hostile - only sullen and distant. Rita and Bonnie chose to avoid them when possible.

Rita, increasingly large as her pregnancy progressed, had been quite uncomfortable the last month in the single cramped cabin they shared.

Then, six months ago, they finally arrived on Sanctuary.

And had been mired since that day in a web of bureaucratic red tape. It was clear the Nidarian High Council didn't know what to do with them. And it was also clear the High Council was afraid of antagonizing the Singheko, kicking off another war with the nasty creatures.

Week after week went by, and still they could not meet

with the High Councilor, Garatella.

They were given every conceivable excuse.

Garatella wanted to wait until Rita's baby was born.

He was on vacation.

He was ill.

He was off planet on a matter of great urgency.

He was learning English.

Until today. This morning Flo had called excitedly. The day had finally arrived when they could discuss their case, present their argument for the protection of Earth. Flo would meet them at Government House.

So why was the Singheko here? Was the High Councilor meeting with him as well?

Bonnie and Rita knew it was a fragile peace between the Nidarians and the Singheko.

Peace might be too strong a word, thought Bonnie. More like a cease-fire. Based on what Flo has told us…

And were they endangering Earth by being in such proximity to a Singheko? That was the other question Rita had in her mind.

"Crap."

"Crap?" Bonnie queried.

"Crap, we shouldn't be so close to a Singheko. It might give them some kind of clue."

To the best of their knowledge, the Singheko did not yet know the location of Earth. The destruction of *Jade* at Dutch Harbor had prevented the sentient scout ship from reporting back to her Singheko masters. So, in theory at least, Earth had a temporary reprieve.

Unless another Singheko scout ship stumbled across Earth.

"Don't sweat it. I'll bet that bastard knew about us fifteen minutes after we stepped off the *Corresse*. And he knows why we're here."

To ask for a Writ of Discovery. To ask the Nidarian Empire to claim Earth as a protectorate.

And that would allow the Nidarians to share technology with Earth. And allow humans to pull themselves up by their bootstraps to become a star-faring race.

And learn to defend themselves.

But if the Singheko learned the location of Earth before the Writ of Discovery was logged … and got there with a fleet first …

…then it was all over for humanity. That was the way the galaxy worked, Flo said.

The Broken Galaxy. That's what Flo called it.

Flo described to them how a great Empire once spread across the Orion Arm. It had been called the Golden Empire. It had spread for thousands of lights in every direction, a bastion of culture and refinement for more than two hundred centuries.

Then, like so many Empires before it, it grew old and decadent. Jealousy and conflict began to tear apart the unity of society necessary for any high culture to survive. And slowly at first, then with increasing speed, the Golden Empire crumbled and died. Most of the high technology of that age had been lost.

Now it was a free-for-all - a Dark Age. The Nidarians were surrounded by barbarian fragments of the old Empire in every direction, all of them clawing for power and plunder.

And the Singheko were the worst - an aggressive species, glorying in war and destruction. The Singheko made no bones about their ambitions to create a new Empire - with the Singheko in charge.

And they shared a border with Nidaria.

In the last three hundred years, Nidaria had fought two wars with the Singheko. In both, the Nidarians had fended them off, but only by the slimmest of margins.

And it was, Flo said, only a matter of the slightest provocation to start another war.

Thus, the current uneasy truce between the Nidarians and the Singheko balanced on a razor's edge.

And the Nidarians are running scared, thought Rita. They

just about poop their pants when they see a Singheko.

Reaching the top of the steps, Rita and Bonnie moved into the shadowed portico, looking for Flo. Their footsteps echoed as they walked across the flagstones. Finally, they saw her standing just inside the entrance of the large stone building. The little Nidarian doctor was wearing her Naval dress whites.

Bonnie greeted her with a hug and Rita followed. They had few friends in this strange land; Flo was one of the few.

"Did you see that Singheko come in?" asked Rita.

"Yes," said Flo. "But don't worry. He won't be meeting with us."

"Good. That's a relief," said Bonnie.

"Scary looking bastard," said Rita.

"Yes," said Flo. "They are. Follow me, please."

Leading them into the building, Flo took them up an elevator to the top floor and down a long, carpeted corridor. She motioned them through a huge wooden door and into a plush office.

"Sit here," she whispered, pointing to a row of chairs, and went to the receptionist.

Rita and Bonnie sat in the first two chairs in the row. After a few minutes, Flo came back.

"It'll be a while, I think," she said. "He's meeting with the Singheko representative now. It may be a half-hour or even a bit more."

Rita looked at Bonnie with a worried look, then back to Flo.

"Florissian. Why would the High Councilor meet with the Singheko first?" asked Rita.

Are they cooking up a deal? Is he throwing us to the wolves?

Flo reassured them.

"Please don't worry. It will all work out."

Rita nodded. She put her anxiety on hold for the moment.

The office was huge. As it should be, Rita thought - this is the anteroom of the most powerful Nidarian in the Empire.

Flo had told them Garatella was a decent sort, not averse to using power to achieve his ends, but by the standards of

Nidarian culture, a paragon of virtue. And according to Flo, he had taught himself English just for this meeting.

Of course, Flo also said English was relatively simple compared to some of the languages he had learned.

*****

After a long half-hour, the outer door opened. The Singheko stepped out and stalked toward them.

Easily seven feet tall, he had a short muzzle, shorter than a lion but with the same general appearance. Predator ears stood tall on top of his head, the mark of an evolution that had started on four legs. He had short, tawny fur over his entire body.

His hands sported five fingers. On the two largest fingers, half-inch vestigial claws still showed. Flo had told them many Singheko had lost the vestigial claws completely, but some still had them. And those that had them were considered superior, the elite.

Like an appendix, thought Rita. Something left over from earlier evolution. But in this case, it conveys status.

As the Singheko approached them, his lips curled back into a snarl. This revealed his other vestigial artifact - one-inch fangs in the front of his mouth that showed when he smiled. Or snarled. As he came up to them, he paused.

"Sssoon," he attempted in English. "Sssoon you ... slaves ... all your world."

With a last snarl, he stalked away.

Rita looked at Flo.

"What was that all about?" she asked.

Flo shook her head.

"Ignore him. That's the Singheko. They are always ... I think your word, belligerent? Always looking for trouble."

"Well, he can have some from me if he wants it," muttered Bonnie.

"No, no trouble, not good in this place," said Flo. "He knows that too. Just talk."

"But how on Earth does he know English?" asked Rita.

"Not to worry," said Flo. "His spies probably bribed some of your servants to teach them a few English words. Just so he can say that to you. Singheko are much that way. Pay lots of money just to make a small point."

The receptionist motioned to them, and Flo noticed it.

"He is ready for us," she said, pointing to the inner office. "Come."

They rose and went to the door. It buzzed and opened. Down a short hallway, another door stood open, with another receptionist waiting for them.

Entering the second door, they found a large office. A couch and several chairs were scattered around. Behind a large desk was an older Nidarian male, a corona of white hair surrounding his head. He gestured to the couch.

"Please sit, friends," he said in good English.

Rita glanced at Bonnie.

At least that part of the story was true - he WAS learning English!

As they sat and got comfortable, the High Councilor smiled at them. Then he spoke.

"I'm glad we are finally able to get together," he said. "I'm sorry I've been so busy with urgent matters. Of course, your situation is urgent too, and I understand your need."

Rita and Bonnie had decided in advance that Rita would do the talking - her cloning process onboard *Jade* had given her the education and memories of both Bonnie and Jim Carter, the father of her child. Given that she had the knowledge and skills of two people, they thought it wiser to let her speak.

"Thank you, High Councilor," said Rita. "We appreciate your kindness in meeting with us."

"So," said the High Councilor. "Let us dispense with formalities. Call me Garatella. I will call you Rita. Now. You need a Writ of Discovery from the Nidarian Empire. Without such a Writ, you won't survive another year."

"Well," said Rita, "we can survive until the Singheko find us."

"They have already found you," he said. "That's why their representative was here. To let me know they have filed a Writ of Discovery for themselves. Which allows them to attack humans without provocation and enslave you or destroy you as they see fit."

"Oh my God," said Bonnie. Rita heard Flo gasp.

"So, there is no hope for us?" asked Rita.

"I didn't say that," the Councilor replied. "Our spy networks are slightly better than theirs. We knew this was coming; so we have filed our own Writ of Discovery. And we have beaten them to the punch by one week."

Flo relaxed, let out her breath. Rita realized she had been holding her own breath, and slowly let it out.

"So what's next?" asked Rita.

"Next is a battle," said the Councilor. "We race the Singheko to Earth, and then we fight over it. The winner takes all."

Flo objected. "But sir, the law clearly states that if we file a Writ of Discovery first, we have five years of exclusive access to the system before anyone can challenge us!"

Garatella nodded.

"Under normal conditions. But in this case, the Singheko claim we interfered with their scout ship *Jade*, and thus interfered with their primacy of claim. There is only one way to settle this. Either we give in to them and let them have Earth, or we fight."

Garatella leaned back in his chair and looked at Rita.

"So, human Rita. Shall we fight, or shall we give in?" he asked her.

Rita almost jumped to her feet, but reined it in. She had figured out where this conversation was going.

"We fight, sir," she said. "We fight them now, or you'll be fighting them forever."

Garatella nodded agreement.

"Yes, you are wise. For a barbarian."

Garatella smiled, letting Rita know he was joking.

Or was he?

"You state it correctly. If we give in to these damn Singheko on this point, we will be fighting them forever. So … we will draw a line in the sand now. And we draw it at Earth. Your friend Captain Arteveld - and Florissian there - has convinced us you are a most warlike species. Perhaps even more belligerent and aggressive than the Singheko, but currently without the technology."

"So, we've decided to file a provisional Writ of Discovery. It will be good for one year. That is enough time for a fleet to get to Earth and fight the Singheko for possession of the system."

Rita continued to gaze at Garatella, still one step ahead of the conversation.

"And we go along with your fleet, I take it?" she asked.

Garatella smiled.

"I like you, human Rita," he said. "You keep up. Yes. You go along. But not your friend Bonnie."

"What?" asked Bonnie and Flo at the same time.

"I have a different mission in mind for you, human Bonnie," said the High Councilor. "One that will fully test your mettle."

Bonnie looked at him across the desk. "This is all about testing humans for their aggression, isn't it?" she said.

"And their intelligence," replied Garatella. "Of course, you can refuse. In that case, you'll be sent back to Earth as cargo, just as you came."

Bonnie shook her head. "No, thank you. I'll take the job."

"Good," said Garatella. "I think, in the end, you'll be glad you did."

Rita spoke next. "So, I will be an adviser to the Earth fleet?"

"No," said Garatella. "Your world is on the line. This is a test of humanity's ability to fight for their lives. We want to see how effective you can be under that kind of pressure."

He leaned forward in his chair again.

"I understand when you were cloned by *Jade*, you were

given two sets of memories and knowledge - one set from Bonnie here, and one set from a male of your species, an atmospheric pilot from your military. Correct?"

Rita nodded.

"Yes, that's correct. I have the knowledge and memories of two people inside me. But those of Bonnie are much more pronounced than those of - of the male. Perhaps because I am female."

"Yes," said Garatella. "I suspect that is the reason. But in any case, with such a double dose of knowledge, I've decided to assign you as Fleet Commander. We want to see if you are worthy allies. If you successfully defend Earth in this first campaign, then we will extend the Writ of Discovery for another four years. That will allow us to give you access to our technology without limit. You'll have the stars."

Rita wrinkled her brow. She already knew the answer to her next question, but she had to ask it anyway.

"And if we fail?"

Garatella leaned back again, a faint smile touching his lips.

"Then we withdraw and leave you to the tender mercies of the Singheko. Of which there are none."

CHAPTER ONE

Planet Nidaria. City of Sanctuary

Leaving Government House, Rita and Bonnie walked with Flo back toward their quarters. They had been given an apartment not far away, in the downtown area of the Nidarian Empire's capital city.

Now Rita was in a hurry to return. She had left her infant daughter Imogen in the care of her Nidarian nanny, Fallassa. She didn't like to be away from the baby for any length of time. Walking briskly, she soon drew ahead of Bonnie and Flo, who were chatting behind her, walking slowly.

Rita didn't see the knife coming until the last second. She had just enough time to dodge to one side, causing it to tear through her side instead of directly into her chest. She whirled, reaching out a foot to trip the assailant as she herself went down. With a crash, both she and the assassin hit the sidewalk at the same time.

Rita rolled, knowing the knife would be lashing out at her again. As she did, she heard the sharp clang of metal on concrete as it missed her by inches. Rolling again, she came to her feet, facing her attacker at last.

Rita was five feet ten inches tall, towering above most Nidarians by at least five inches. But this one was huge by Nidarian standards, as tall as she. He had scrambled to his feet and was coming at her fast, knife pulled back for another jab. She prepared to dodge, trying to decide which way to go to.

There was a loud crack and the attacker crumpled, falling to the ground in a heap. The knife clattered to the sidewalk.

Bonnie and Flo had rushed forward and now arrived by Rita, enclosing her in a circle of protection, as they looked around trying to understand what was happening.

A voice behind them called out softly.

"You're safe now, humans," said the voice in good English. "He's dead."

"Arteveld!" exclaimed Flo, spinning around.

Sure enough, the captain of the *Corresse* was walking toward them, along with two other Nidarians. Both of his companions had pulse pistols out. The barrel of one was still glowing from a discharge.

"May I introduce your new bodyguards, Raphael and Gabriel," said Arteveld.

"Bodyguards?" queried Rita hesitantly. "What?"

Arteveld gave a big grin.

"The High Councilor knew the Singheko would try something like this. It was inevitable as soon as he agreed to meet with you. He called me and assigned us to protect you. Sorry, we were just a bit late. Are you OK, Rita?"

"Just a flesh wound, I think," said Rita, holding her side. Some blood was leaking out between her fingers. "It'll require a few stitches. Or whatever you use for stitches on Sanctuary."

"Well, come with me," said Arteveld. "Let's get you home. Flo can attend to you there, and we'll be safer than out here on the streets."

Looking behind them, Bonnie pointed vaguely at the body on the sidewalk.

"What about him?" she asked.

Arteveld sniffed.

"I'll call a trash collector," he replied. He started off down the street. Bonnie, Flo, and Rita followed. Raphael and Gabriel brought up the rear, their eyes casting about for danger.

Bonnie turned and looked at the two bodyguards behind them. They were wearing uniforms - Nidarian Marines. And they were big - as tall as Rita and Bonnie. Both had a professional military look about them that exuded reassurance.

"Raphael and Gabriel?" she queried, looking back at Rita.

"Names easy to remember in an emergency," said Rita.

As they arrived back at their apartment, Rita insisted on going into Imogen's bedroom and taking the baby from the nanny. It was a ballet of sorts as she removed her top and started nursing the baby while Flo got her medical bag and dressed the wound, but they managed.

"I can't help but notice your mother's milk looks just like ours," said Flo as she worked. "Convergent evolution, do you think?"

Rita smiled.

"I suspect so. I think the requirements for highly nutritious milk have to be about the same for all creatures with a similar biology, you know?"

Flo smiled.

"This may hurt. You ready?"

Rita nodded. "Go for it."

Flo finishing applying antibiotics to the wound and started gluing it together with something that looked like a pistol, but dispensed glue instead of bullets. When she was finished, she stood back and admired her handiwork.

"Not bad, if I do say so myself," she said.

"You know, your English is really good," said Rita.

Flo laughed.

"It ought to be, after spending five years on station in the Sol system," she said. "Not much to do except watch Earth movies and television."

"Yeah, I guess."

Flo stepped back and smiled.

"You'll be fine, Rita," said Flo.

Rita nodded her thanks. "But the question is, will Earth be fine?"

Flo looked at her.

"We must have faith and hope that it will. And you must fight the good fight to make sure."

Rita looked at Flo, doubt and concern on her face.

"Garatella said I would be assigned the rank of Admiral in your Navy and have sole responsibility for the defense of Earth. Don't you think that's a bit much for an inexperienced human to take on?"

Flo smiled at her.

"Rita. You have the memories, experience and skills of both Bonnie and Jim Carter inside you. I've watched you at work these many months. I've watched as you worked with the functionaries and bureaucrats, trying to put this deal together. And in the end, you succeeded. Please trust me. You can do this."

"But it would be so much better to have a Nidarian Admiral in charge, and me acting as adviser."

"Maybe," agreed Flo. "But Garatella has an agenda. He knows another war with the Singheko is inevitable. He wants to buy more time for preparation. He's told the High Council this is a way to do that."

"There was a program called Lend-Lease in your World War Two history, I believe. It allowed the Americans to give warships to England while remaining neutral on paper. This is similar. He's actually leasing this fleet directly to you, as a representative of Earth. If the Singheko challenge us on the grounds of fighting them at Earth, Garatella will respond that it was an Earth fleet that fought them, not a Nidarian fleet."

"That's why he wants you in charge. He can point to you and say, 'See? It's an Earth fleet.' - and, if you lose the battle, nothing sticks to him. He'll just point out that it was an Earth Admiral that lost the battle, and he had no control over it."

"So I'm a sacrificial lamb," said Rita.

"Only if you lose," responded Flo. "If you win, then Garatella will go to the High Council and say he knew it all along, and we should make you allies."

"Crafty old bastard, isn't he," said Rita.

Flo smiled.

"You don't know the half of it," she said. "He's only giving you old, outdated ships that were headed for the scrap heap anyway."

CHAPTER TWO

Earth. Flagstaff, AZ

Mark Rodgers - General, U.S. Army Intelligence (retired) - turned the horse back toward the ranch house. He let the horse have her head then, and the mare took off like a shot. She loved to run, although you had to watch her around trees - she also loved to scrape an unwary rider off her back under a low branch. A bad habit Mark had never been able to fix.

But he loved to ride the big white mare, and she loved to run. Today they flew across the pasture. Of course, she always ran faster back toward the stables. She knew the ride was over and she would get a good rub down and later, some oats.

As Mark got closer to the house, he saw Gillian on the back patio. She was lying in a chaise lounge, catching the last rays of the sun. She lay down her reader and watched as he came galloping in.

With a strong pull, he got the mare stopped in front of the stables and climbed down. Handing her over to his ranch hand, he walked toward Gillian. She shaded her eyes from the sun with a smile.

"How about a lemonade?" she asked, handing him a glass dripping with cold.

"Oh, you are a wonder," Mark said, taking the cold glass in his hand. He dropped his riding gear beside the other chaise lounge and sat.

"I heard from Jim today," said Gillian.

"Wow, that's news," said Mark. "You mean the caveman came out of his cave long enough to talk to an actual human?"

Gillian smiled.

"Yes, and he said hello. He wants to come down and talk with you about something."

"Well, tell him to come on. I could use the company."

"I already did. He'll fly into Flagstaff tomorrow. I'll go pick him up about four. We'll have a nice dinner in the evening when we get back."

"That sounds great," said Mark. "Any idea what he wants?"

"Maybe a little. I think he's finally getting tired of flying and drinking and pissing his life away. And mooning over Bonnie. I can only guess, but I'd bet he's going to ask for something useful to do."

Mark took a long sip from his glass.

"Well, he knows I'm retired. There's not much I can do anymore."

"But you have connections. You can help him get into something worthwhile."

Mark shook his head.

"He was offered all that right after he recovered from Dutch Harbor. He turned it down. Chance gone."

Gillian leaned over and rubbed Mark's hand gently.

"Chance never gone, love. You can find something."

"I guess. Depends what he wants."

* * * * *

The TBM 940 touched down smoothly at the Flagstaff Airport and angled off the runway. The big turboprop taxied to the ramp, where a lineman waved the pilot into a parking spot. With a descending whine, the engine shut down.

The door popped open, and Jim Carter got out, pulled a flight bag and duffel out of the airplane, and walked into the office.

Gillian was waiting for him. She gave him a big hug and kissed him on the cheek.

"Hi, Jimmy Boy," she said.

Jim grinned.

"Hello, sis. How's things?"

"Things are awesome. Couldn't be better. C'mon, let's get your bags in the car."

Walking out to the front parking lot, Gillian led Jim to a big black SUV. They threw his things in the back and got in. Gillian drove and they headed to the ranch, nearly an hour away.

"And how's Vlad the Impaler?" asked Jim.

Gillian grimaced.

"Mark's fine. You know he's never forgiven himself for … you know."

"Torturing me half to death."

Gillian shook her head. "It was his job."

Jim laughed.

"Oh, don't worry, sis. I've let it go. But I can still have fun with it, you know?"

Gillian reached over and punched him hard in the shoulder.

"I thought you were serious for a second."

They drove in silence for a minute, Jim recalling the days of torture and deprivation he endured at the hands of Gillian's husband.

All in a good cause, he thought. *He had to do his job, and I had to do what I thought was right. I had no way of knowing* Jade *was an impostor. None of us did.*

Gillian pulled into the driveway of the big ranch house southeast of Flagstaff and parked the truck. Popping the hatch, she got out and came around to help Jim get his luggage. Together, they walked into the house, dropping Jim's bags in the hallway.

Mark came out of the den and grabbed Jim in a half bear hug, then shook his hand.

"How are you, son?" he asked. Mark was only ten years older, but he always called Jim "son", much to his chagrin.

"Pretty damn good," said Jim. "Getting stronger every day."

"Excellent," said Mark. "Come in the den, we'll have a cold

one before dinner."

Jim looked over at Gillian.

"Thanks for the ride, sis!" he said.

"Sure thing, Jimmy Boy," grinned Gillian. "I'll be there in a bit."

Mark led Jim into the den, and they relaxed, sinking into two overstuffed chairs by the fireplace.

"It's cooler here than I expected for Arizona," said Jim.

"Flagstaff is a lot cooler than down south," said Mark. "That's what we like about it."

"Nice," said Jim.

"So," opened Mark. "You're fully recovered from Dutch Harbor?"

"Yeah, I'm good to go," said Jim.

Mark took a sip of his beer.

"But?"

Jim smiled.

"You know, it's really hard to slide anything by you or Gillian."

Mark nodded.

"Thirty years in the Intelligence racket."

"Yep. Well, here it is, Mark. I need something useful to do."

"Don't we all," grunted Mark.

"I'm serious. I'm almost forty. I can't spend the rest of my life drinking and flying."

"And trying to kill yourself, from what I hear," added Mark.

"Yeah, that too," said Jim. "Mark, you've got friends in high places. I wonder if you could get me an introduction to someone who could get me back into the fight against the Singheko."

"You were offered that opportunity after Dutch Harbor. You turned them down. I doubt they'd give you a second chance."

Jim agreed. "I know. I screwed up. I was still messed up about Bonnie. I couldn't get her out of my head."

Mark rubbed his chin.

"I'll make a few calls, see what I can do. What area would you want to go to?"

Jim thought about it.

"Surely, they were able to salvage something useful from *Jade*'s wreck. If they are putting up anything in space to defend against the Singheko, I'd like to be in on it. If that's possible."

"Dinner is ready!" came a call from the dining room.

Mark and Jim stood up.

"If there is anything, and if I can get you into it, I'll do it," said Mark. "Maybe a little compensation for the torture I put you through."

Jim grinned. "Not half enough."

CHAPTER THREE

Planet Nidaria. Battlecruiser *Merkkessa*

Rita was buckled in tight to first-class seats in the front of the personnel shuttle. Beside her sat Flo, holding baby Imogen, making baby talk, and feeding her from a bottle.

On the other side of the aisle sat Rita's newly assigned personal aide, Captain Tarraine, and Imogen's nanny, Fallassa.

Behind Rita and Flo sat Rita's Marine bodyguards, Raphael and Gabriel, armed to the teeth. She had learned they were from another planet in the Nidarian Empire - and she couldn't possibly pronounce their real names. So, the nicknames assigned by Arteveld had stuck.

And in front of them was the battlecruiser *Merkkessa* - their home for the foreseeable future.

"I don't think we're in Kansas anymore," Rita said to herself as they came into dock at the huge battlecruiser.

"That's a new one on me," said Flo. "What does that mean?"

"Just an expression similar to "holy shit!""

Flo grinned. "That one I know," she said.

The ship they approached was a bit larger than a wet-navy cruiser from Earth, thought Rita - about 200 meters in length, maybe 60 meters in beam at the rear, tapering in an irregular wedge to less than two meters at the front.

It was black as coal. There was just enough ambient light to see the outline of it, plus the bright light spilling out of the open hangar bay doors.

And just enough light to see the missile tubes and pulse cannon mounted all over it.

Something not to be trifled with, Rita thought.

With a couple of clunks and a bump, the shuttle eased into the hangar bay and landed, sliding a foot or two on the floor as it touched down.

Of course, the *Merkkessa* was an older ship; the Nidarians weren't willing to risk their top-of-the-line equipment to protect a backwater planet like Earth. Nevertheless, walking off the shuttle in the landing bay, Rita looked around in awe.

The hangar bay was filled with personnel preparing for departure, moving around in every direction.

It's like the deck of an aircraft carrier on Earth, thought Rita.

She could see dozens of fighters scattered around the hangar bay. They were mean-looking, droop-snouted, black and wedge-shaped, like smaller versions of the *Merkkessa*. They were called "Devastators". Weapons mounts studded them on both sides. Sturdy landing gear legs stuck out from the bottom.

When the large shuttle that brought her up had left, the *Merkkessa* would be zipped up tight.

And then they would be ready to depart.

As Rita stepped off the shuttle, an honor guard waited in two lines. Her aide, Tarraine, had trained them specially to perform the Earth ceremony. A bosun's whistle sounded, the exact same whistle and tune she would have heard on Earth if she were a wet-navy admiral boarding a ship for the first time. The Nidarian side party saluted her.

Rita was wearing a new uniform, specially tailored for her before she left the planet. It was a Nidarian Admiral's uniform, black with plenty of gold braid. Her hat was not that different from an admiral's hat on Earth.

How funny that such radically different cultures end up with similar designs for impressing others.

Saluting the side party, she stepped past them to a line of officers waiting to greet her. The first was the Captain of the *Merkkessa*, Captain Bekerose - her Flag Captain. He was tall for a Nidarian, only about an inch shorter than Rita. She touched his hand in the Nidarian fashion - not a full handshake, just a touch of the fingers to the back of his hand.

Different strokes for different folks, thought Rita.

Moving down the line, she greeted the rest of the senior officers of the *Merkkessa*. When she had greeted all, Captain Bekerose led the group toward the hangar exit. Leading her to Officer Country, he stopped at a cabin with a flag on it.

"Milady, here are your Flag Quarters. Would you like to get comfortable before the official handover?"

"Yes, thank you, Captain Bekerose," Rita smiled.

Captain Tarraine palmed the door and it opened. Stepping inside, Rita saw her briefing room - a conference room with a large table seating ten, and an office area behind it with her personal desk. A circular staircase in the back corner went up one level to her day cabin behind the bridge.

To the left was a hatch leading to her steward's quarters. A husky Nidarian stood at attention beside the hatch, awaiting her inspection. Rita walked to him and smiled.

"You are Knowelk?" she asked.

"Yes, milady," said the Nidarian.

"Knowelk, please relax, and a cup of *nish* would be good right now, if you could."

"Yes, milady," said Knowelk, bobbing his head as he turned to enter the small galley just inside the steward's quarters.

Turning back to the briefing room and the assembled officers, Rita gave them a smile.

"All, if you would permit me twenty minutes to get settled, I'll see you on the bridge for the handover ceremony."

The assembled officers bowed and departed, all except for Gabriel and Raphael. They made their way through the hatch in the back of the briefing room, with Rita following close behind them.

The next room was her bedroom. In the far-left corner was her bathroom. To the right was her bed, and in the near corner were shelves and storage.

There were two other hatches leading out of the bedroom.

The one on the left led to the Security Office, where Gabriel and Raphael would work. It also doubled as their quarters, containing a small living space at the back.

The hatch in the rear wall led to the nursery for Imogen. While Gabriel and Raphael moved into their Security Office to get situated, Rita stepped quickly through to the nursery and found Fallassa holding Imogen, anticipating Rita's arrival. Rita took the baby and sat in a rocking chair brought onboard for this purpose and fed the baby.

Welcome to the fleet, my baby, she thought.

Twenty minutes later, Imogen fed and put down for a nap, Rita waited in her briefing room for the arrival of Tarraine and Bekerose. The door chimed, and Gabriel opened it for her, revealing Raphael already standing guard outside. Beyond him, Tarraine and Bekerose waited.

"Gentlemen," said Rita, stepping out of the hatch. She turned and headed for the bridge. No way was she going to passively let Bekerose lead her - she had already decided that.

It was time to start showing who was in charge.

With an exchange of glances, Tarraine and Bekerose fell in behind. Gabriel brought up the rear. Together, they climbed the steps to the bridge for the official handover to Rita as Admiral of the Fleet.

Tarraine had briefed her on the protocol. A new Admiral taking a fleet had a specific set of actions to perform. Tarraine had assured her he would lead her through them.

"It'll be fine," he said.

She wasn't so sure.

How strange is it to be a human, taking control of an alien fleet. What must these Nidarians think? Will they resent me? Will they follow me?

Rita had all the memories and knowledge of Bonnie in her brain. Back on Earth, Bonnie had been a Lieutenant Colonel in the U.S. Air Force. So - from a human viewpoint - Rita knew how to lead.

But can I make it work in this situation?

Now Tarraine pointed to the Admiral's station. It was an elevated platform at the back of the bridge, with three small steps leading up to it from the main level. On the platform were three chairs, arranged in a semi-circle, with two more chairs behind them.

Tarraine indicated the first step leading up to the flag bridge. Rita nodded and stepped to the first step. She stopped and faced the bridge.

She knew that cameras were on her - this ceremony was being beamed to every ship in the fleet. It was likely there were ten thousand Nidarians watching her now, if not more. Or maybe the whole planet, if Garatella had decided to broadcast it widely for free publicity.

No pressure, Rita. No pressure at all.

"I am Admiral Rita Page of Earth," she intoned in Nidarian. "I will be faithful to my ship."

Stepping up to the next step, she spoke again.

"I am Admiral Rita Page of Earth," she stated. "I will be faithful to my orders."

Stepping to the last of the three steps, she spoke again.

"I am Admiral Rita Page of Earth," she spoke again. "I will be faithful to Nidaria … and to Earth."

With Tarraine's grudging approval, she had added the last bit for herself.

Finally, she stepped up to the Flag bridge.

"I am Admiral Rita Page of Earth. I take command of this fleet."

Tarraine nodded in approval and joined her on the Flag Bridge, showing her to her chair.

Rita noticed Bekerose did not look happy.

The center chair - her chair - had a perfect view of everything on the bridge below, including the large central holotank and the wide screen spanning the front of the bridge. A pair of consoles mounted to her armrests could be pulled inward to provide her with controls for all the things she would need.

Rita sat down and looked at her new world.

The main holotank was currently off. On the wide screen at the front of the bridge was a real-time view of the outside universe. She could see other ships of her fleet in front of her. Smaller screens around the periphery of the bridge showed various other views of weapons systems and sensors.

A small plastic partition, six inches high, ran around the Flag bridge. Tarraine had explained to her it was a symbolic boundary - separating her Flag bridge from the main bridge of the *Merkkessa*. It denoted that, while she had strategic command of the fleet, Captain Bekerose had tactical command of the ship. This was a line she must never cross in battle.

But the reverse is true as well, thought Rita. *Bekerose must never cross the line of command to my side of things. And I'll have to make sure of that.*

Her aide Tarraine sat down to her left. His job was to advise her and ensure her orders were carried out.

Her Flag Lieutenant, Lieutenant Lirrassa, sat on her right. Her job was to coordinate junior staff, monitor information transfer, and perform general gopher duties.

The Nidarian crew sat at their stations. Bekerose moved to his Captain's chair and took his seat directly below her, in a chair raised above the crew stations on the bridge. This allowed him an unobstructed view of the holotank and the front screen.

Two chairs, also raised, were beside his. The one on his right held his second-in-command - the XO, as Rita thought of it in Earth terms. The one on his left held his Tactical Officer. Both had consoles in front of them.

In front of them, a semi-circle of crew stations curved around the holotank, each with a console containing dozens of controls and indicators. The bridge was fully staffed now. They were ready to get underway.

The thought came unbidden to her mind.

This is where I will probably die. Right here in this chair. The odds are against us.

She shoved the unwanted thought away.

I will not let that happen. I refuse.

I will kick their fat Singheko asses all the way back to their home planet.

But the little voice in the back of her head spoke again.

Or die trying, it said.

Sanctuary. High Councilor's Residence

Bonnie sat in front of Garatella, holding a glass of wine.

She had not been too comfortable about coming to his home. But he had insisted. And he was the High Councilor of Nidaria. The highest office in the Empire.

And she was alone. Rita was gone, on her way back to Earth. Flo was gone, with Rita. Everyone except Arteveld was gone.

She was alone now, on a strange planet, six hundred light years from Earth.

Except for Arteveld - one little alien captain who happened to consider her a friend.

There could be nobody more out of place in this strange land, she thought to herself. *I hope Garatella's not planning an experiment to see if he can have sex with a human.*

But so far, Garatella had been a gentlemen. He had asked her about her trip from Earth, and her time on Sanctuary since her arrival. And he asked about Rita, and how the baby was doing, and generally just made small talk, as his servants came and went with wine and snacks.

Bonnie had grown accustomed to Nidarian wine - weaker than Earth products, but eminently drinkable - and tried to relax, tried to enjoy herself.

But she felt like Damocles - the ancient figure who came to dinner only to find a sword hanging over his head by the thinnest of threads. All Garatella had to do was flick his finger, and her life would be over. Or worse.

A servant came in and whispered to Garatella, and he

looked annoyed. He rose to his feet and bowed to Bonnie.

"My dear human," he said, "I have to go take a call. I shall return shortly. Please be comfortable for a few moments."

Bonnie stood and nodded to him as he departed. She looked around the room, examining the many statues, paintings and other artwork covering the walls.

In the long six months they had spent waiting for an audience with the High Councilor, both Bonnie and Rita had spent most of their time studying the language, history, and culture of this alien empire. Now Bonnie walked around the room, examining the artifacts in more detail. Most she couldn't recognize and had no clue of their significance to the current society that made up Nidaria.

But a few - a very few - rang a bell in her mind.

Here was an ancient sword, the Ranssarrian Sword, said to be wielded by the first Emperor twenty-two thousand years earlier, as he hammered disparate nations into the earliest beginnings of the Golden Empire.

Here was a bell, said to be the bell that hung in the conical roof of the ancient Golden Empire Council, twenty thousand years earlier. The bell which rang when an old Emperor died and a new one was enthroned.

And across the room was a painting of a starship, engaged in battle with others that looked suspiciously like larger copies of *Jade*. Bonnie walked over to examine the painting more closely. Leaning over, she peered at the work.

It was definitely a battle between Nidarians and Singheko, she thought.

"Yes, you are correct. That is the first battle we fought with them, three hundred years ago. We won by the thinnest of threads."

Bonnie turned and smiled at Garatella as he came back into the room.

"But you won," she said.

"Yes," grunted Garatella, taking his seat. "If we had not, none of us would be here now."

Bonnie returned to her chair.

"But why are the Singheko so aggressive and so unrelenting in their push to take over Nidaria?"

Garatella sipped his wine and put the glass back on the table beside him.

"Because we are the last vestige of the old Golden Empire," he said. "Even though it has crumbled around us, we hang on to the old traditions, the old ways. All the other nations look up to us as the last and best memory of that old Empire - the keeper of the flame, you might say."

Garatella waved at the painting on the wall.

"We are somewhat like the Byzantine Empire of your Earth, a last remnant of the once great Roman Empire. And the Singheko are the new upstart barbarians, come to seize the last bit of legitimacy from us and use it to conquer the Arm."

Garatella saw the obvious surprise on Bonnie's face at the reference to Byzantium.

"Yes, I am a historian, dear human. I am a politician of course, but any politician with a hope to success must also be a historian. Of course, I cheated - I referenced the human data files Captain Arteveld brought back on the *Corresse* and placed in our Central Library. I especially liked the history books, I'm afraid."

Bonnie grinned.

"That's wonderful, Garatella. I'm glad you enjoyed them."

"Of course, I had another reason. I wanted to see just how good at warfare you humans really are."

"And?"

Garatella smiled.

"You are particularly good at killing each other. I wonder if you can be that good at killing Singheko."

"Give us the means, and I assure you, we can be."

Garatella looked troubled.

"But where would it stop? That is the question, you see, dear human. Where would the killing stop? If we assisted humanity to take on the Singheko and defeat their ambitions to rule the Arm, would you simply step into their place? Would humans then be the bane of our existence? Would we then have to find an even more aggressive race to protect us from the humans?"

Bonnie stared at the old Nidarian.

"I see your problem, sir."

"Indeed," said Garatella. "It's a dilemma you've brought us."

Bonnie mused for a bit, then spoke.

"I'm sure nothing I can say would convince you either way. So how will you decide?"

"I will conduct two experiments," smiled Garatella. "After all, I have two humans to work with."

"Ah. Rita and me."

"Yes. My experiment with Rita has already begun. She is on her way to defend Earth in command of old ships that would be better sent to the boneyard than a battle. We shall see how that experiment comes out."

Bonnie said nothing. She and Rita had long since understood that part of Garatella's plan. Yet it was the only option they had, so they took it.

"For my second experiment," continued Garatella, "I will send my other human to find something for me. Something which has been lost, and which I want to find again."

"Two thousand years ago the technology of the Golden Empire was far advanced from what we have today. They excelled in areas we can only dream of; for example, their nanobot technology was vastly better than ours. Their reactors were more powerful. They had huge fleets of starships, all of which are gone now - either destroyed in the battles of that era or scrapped for raw materials by the barbarians of the Dark Age."

"Now. Only months before the Golden Empire fell to pieces, it was reported that scientists of that age had discovered a method of making starships go five times as fast as they normally do in six-space. There is a little-known story of a new type of ship which conducted a demonstration of this advanced new engine. It was called the *Dragon*, and it set out to travel to a far planet to prove the concept of the new design."

Bonnie looked puzzled.

"Don't you have records of the discovery? Blueprints? A scientific description?"

"No," said Garatella. "Because the *Dragon* never returned. The last Emperor died, and a bloody war of succession started. The war evolved into a conflagration, involving every nation for two thousand lights. By the time the war was over, the Empire had self-destructed. Only a small remnant remained unscathed here in Sanctuary - hence the name of our city. It took us a thousand years to rebuild our society. And by that time..."

"The ship had disappeared," said Bonnie.

"Exactly," said Garatella. "Not just the ship itself, but even the knowledge that it existed, except for a few obscure references here and there in our records. Which I have found and studied now for nearly twenty years."

"But why do you need me in this search? I know nothing about any of it. And I'm not even Nidarian - how could I possibly help?"

Garatella twirled his wineglass by the stem, a smirk touching his lips.

"Because I believe the wreck of the ship may be in your solar system."

Bonnie sat stunned. Her mouth opened, but no words would come out for several seconds. Finally, she managed to make a sound, somewhat between a word and a squeak.

"Our ... our solar system? Sol?"

"Yes. At the time of the collapse, we had just begun to explore that area of the Arm. We weren't aware of any life on your planet then - this was well before your society developed radio or electronics, so we had no reason to visit your system. But there was a small scout station on a planet not too far from Sol, a system then called Sword. Because that was our farthest outpost at the time, that was the intended destination of the experimental ship."

"What happened?"

"We don't know. According to the records I've reconstructed, it set out on its journey, and was never heard from again. The war started, and in the course of nearly a thousand years of death and destruction, the story of the *Dragon* was forgotten. Survival became more important. When at last we had a stable society again, it was another thousand years before anyone thought to take an interest in that old legend."

"Someone who was a historian at heart," grinned Bonnie.

"Yes," smiled Garatella. "A politician who needs such a ship for the future of his people, but who is also a historian with the means to look for it in the old records."

"And you found something…"

"Maybe. About five years ago, I found an old fragment of a book in a destroyed library, burnt nearly beyond recognition. There was almost nothing left that was legible. But I did find a tiny bit I could read. It was a communication log, which I believe to be associated with the project."

Bonnie couldn't believe she was so engrossed in this story from a completely foreign culture, and yet she was.

Garatella smiled slowly at her.

"I see this story has caught you as it caught me," he said.

Bonnie nodded, afraid to speak. Afraid it would break the mood.

"The log had a statement in it … well, I'll let you read it yourself."

Garatella reached into his pocket and pulled out an electronic tablet.

"I've translated it into English for you."

Bonnie took the tablet. She read the words on the screen.

"…*cannot control …unable to make Sword. Diverting to* …"

"That's all?" Bonnie asked, disappointed. She had expected

more.

"Yes," said Garatella, taking back the tablet. "That's all. Not much to go on, is it?"

Bonnie shook her head. "No. Not much."

Garatella waved his hand, and a hologram appeared over the table. It showed the Nidarian system. He pinched his hands in the air and the hologram compressed to a much larger scale.

"Here is Nidaria," he said, pointing. A star system in the hologram lit up.

"Here is the system then called Sword - the destination of the experimental ship," he said, and touched another system, which also lit up. A line formed between the two systems. "You call this system 36 Ophiuchi A. It's nineteen light years from Earth."

Bonnie looked at the course line on the holo.

"Wow. That course line goes awfully close to our Sol System, doesn't it?"

Garatella smiled.

"Yes, it does. In fact, after some analysis, I've determined that once you get three-quarters of the way to Sword, Sol is the closest planetary system to that course line."

Bonnie started to get it.

"So, if the ship ran into problems late in the trip ...and couldn't make it to Sword ..."

Garatella nodded.

"It would divert to the closest planetary system and call for help. In this case, Sol."

"But help never came," Bonnie said.

"Exactly."

"So you think ..."

Garatella shook his head. "I don't think. I know. Or should I say, I believe. I believe the *Dragon* is somewhere in the Sol system, or lost in the black somewhere between the course line on that hologram and Sol."

Bonnie leaned back, crossed her legs, and took a large sip of her wine. She now understood what was going on.

"And you want me to find it."

Garatella nodded. "Indeed."

"But why me?" asked Bonnie. "And if so, why not send me to Earth with Rita?"

"You, because Sol is your system. No one could be as familiar with it as a human. And secondly, because this is a test, as I said. There are certain things I want to find out about humans, and this is part of that experiment."

"And why not send me to Earth with Rita if I am to do this?"

"Because I keep my experiments separate," said Garatella. "Because Rita may not survive her little run-in with the Singheko. If she fails, I don't wish my other experiment to fail as well. You'll leave three days after her and carry out your mission independently of everything else that will be occurring with the Singheko. Because if Rita loses the battle with the Singheko and they take Earth, you must continue your mission without their knowledge. Even if your planet is destroyed as you do."

Bonnie was aghast. Garatella's indifference to the destruction of Earth caught her off-guard. Her first reaction was to lash out, say terrible things, things she knew well how to say after a career in the Air Force.

But she knew the future of humankind was hanging in the balance here, at this moment, like a child's spinning top dancing on a narrow table. One wrong move would be disaster. With a shudder, she suppressed her anger and frustration.

But she found she couldn't resist one emotional jab to close the conversation.

"You know what, Garatella? You're a cold-hearted son of a bitch," she said. She bit her tongue to stop herself from saying more.

"Indeed," the little Nidarian agreed, smiling. "When it comes to my nation's security, indeed I am."

CHAPTER FOUR

Earth. Quantico, Virginia

"Pick it up, girls!" yelled the drill instructor.

Jim groaned. They had been running for three miles now, and the DI showed no signs of letting up. His body was in the hurt locker.

If I had known, thought Jim. *If I had known I'd have to go through this again...*

He felt the second DI - the woman - run up beside him.

"Come on, Carter. I thought you were an ex-Marine. Pick it up!" she yelled into his ear, jogging along beside him like she was out for a Sunday stroll.

Jim tried to kick a little harder, but he didn't have much left. He was loaded down with full pack and rifle, forty pounds of gear on his back. He slowly struggled back into his place in line, his feet pounding the sand in the heavy combat boots.

The lead DI finally blew the whistle, and the platoon ground to a halt, gasping and coughing as everyone fought for breath. Jim stood, hands on his knees, trying to get his wind back. The female DI came up to him and yelled at him once more.

"Carter! Get your shit together! You want to be an officer in the Space Force? You gotta learn to hump it first!"

Jim waved a hand forlornly at the DI and she stalked away to harass someone else.

It had sounded so good when Mark called him back and gave him the news.

"General Raines in the Space Force is an old friend of mine.

He knows your history and wants to have you on his team. He'll re-instate your commission and put you right where you want to be. You'll be in the thick of things getting ready to fight the Singheko."

"Fantastic," said Jim. "That's exactly what I want."

"Only one catch - you'll have to go through an abbreviated four-week Marine OCS class at Quantico."

"Oh, fuck," said Jim.

"Yeah, I know. But you can tough it out. It's not a full boot camp. Just a re-fam for ex-officers coming back into the military."

"Mark, I'm thirty-nine years old!"

"Sorry, Jim. That's the way he wants it. He has to be sure you can hack it."

Now Jim stood, hands on knees, gasping for breath. He was by far the oldest ex-officer in the re-familiarization platoon. Some of them were in their late twenties, a few in their mid-thirties. But he had at least four or five years on the oldest of them.

I'm gonna kill that damn Mark Rodgers, he thought. *Space Force my ass! All I've done for two weeks is hump mountains!*

The female DI came back over his way, obviously looking for trouble. Jim tried to avoid her gaze, but she stopped in front of him anyway.

"I thought you were the hero, Carter!" she snapped at him, loudly so the entire platoon could hear. "I thought you fought off an alien invasion single-handed!"

Jim shook his head, waved a hand at her in negation.

"It wasn't like that, ma'am," he replied.

"I sure hope not!" she yelled. "If you're all that stands between us and the aliens, we're toast!"

Turning back to the platoon, she yelled at them.

"Form up! Prepare to run!"

Jim groaned anew, tightened his pack straps, and fell into formation.

Corvette *Corresse*. En Route to Sol System

As she sat in her cabin on the *Corresse*, headed back to Earth once more, Bonnie couldn't help but think about Rita.

She shivered at the memory of their last night together. They had made love for the last time - at least, the last time for a long while.

Rita was exceptionally good at making Bonnie crazy in bed - because she had Bonnie's memories and feelings built into her. In a way, it was like making love to another version of herself.

Rita knew everything that Bonnie wanted - everything that drove Bonnie crazy. Rita had taken her to the very limits, driving her so far over the edge Bonnie screamed out loud, waking baby Imogen down the hall and causing Rita's new bodyguards - Gabriel and Raphael - to rush to the room and check on them.

Then they had to explain there was nothing wrong and get the apartment quiet again. And they had laughed, and giggled, and then started all over again.

And afterward, lying in sweaty love, they had talked.

"I love you, Bonnie," Rita had said. "I will always love you. But I love Jim also. You know that. We both love him, and yet we love each other. It's an impossible situation."

Bonnie had thought about it for a moment. Then:

"Love is essentially a miracle, Rita," she had said. "Let's accept the miracle and stop worrying about the who and what and how of it."

And after a long silence, Bonnie heard Rita reply softly - so softly that she almost couldn't hear it.

"Wherever we go, whatever happens - just remember that you are loved, Bonnie. Please…"

A single tear slid out of Bonnie's eye as she remembered.

She was so alone now.

Five hundred twenty-five lights from Earth. Rita and her

rag-tag fleet would be about ten lights ahead of her. They'd arrive at Earth three days ahead of Bonnie.

But even then, Bonnie wasn't sure if she could contact her. Garatella had made it clear that Bonnie couldn't get involved with Rita's mission - and vice versa.

And he's right, thought Bonnie. *If those fat Singheko fuckers find out what I'm doing, they'll move Heaven and Earth to find me and capture me. That's for dead certain. If they could get their hands on the* Dragon, *and the new drive technology could be recovered - conquering the rest of the Arm would be trivial for them.*

With a huge sigh, Bonnie sat up on the edge of her bunk and gazed around the cabin.

So alone.

At least I'm not cargo this time.

The Nidarians had assembled a special VIP cabin for her - one tailored for humans. The bunk was longer, and the chairs taller. The desk had been raised to a human-friendly height. She had everything needed for a comfortable trip.

Except companionship.

Arteveld tried to be friendly - but he was Nidarian. And the rest of the crew, this trip, tried to be supportive. They knew she was now a VIP - not just another alien specimen to be brought back to Nidaria.

I'd trade being a VIP for another human to talk with.

With another long sigh, Bonnie decided to get up and walk around the ship.

On her first voyage, the latent hostility of the crew had kept her and Rita in their cabin, except for the occasional meal with Flo and Arteveld. Now, she had the run of the ship. She was in charge; Arteveld was still captain of the ship, but she was commander of the mission. The crew knew that. Now, when she walked down the passageways, they moved to the side and pressed themselves against the wall, bowing their heads to her.

It was a welcome change.

Leaving the cabin, she walked to the observatory. It wasn't a true observatory - just a large screen on the back wall of the mess room, next to the medical bay. There were no windows or portholes on a starship - but it was a good simulation of one. As the ship progressed on its journey, the artificial reality in the large picture "window" progressed as if they were actually looking out at the universe.

She got a cup of *nish* - a hot liquid the Nidarians drank like coffee - similar, but with a sweeter taste - and sat, looking at the Universe go by.

I miss coffee.

She couldn't tell exactly where they were at first. They had been traveling for three weeks now.

So, we should be about 75 lights from Nidaria. Somewhere around Mirfak.

Sure enough, with a bit of looking she found the star, still well in front of them, approaching slowly.

I wonder if there are any messages.

Arteveld had explained to her no communication was possible over interstellar distances - no instantaneous communication, at least. So, starships would drop message buoys periodically as they traveled.

If Rita were dropping message buoys, the *Corresse* could detect them, drop out of six-space temporarily, and retrieve the messages.

I need to ask Arteveld about that.

Merkkessa. En Route to Sol System

Rita cursed and angrily pushed the keyboard and display away.

The morning had consisted of reports - dozens of reports. It seemed they wanted to keep her inundated with reports, as if that would keep her out of their hair.

And every morning was the same. Day after day.

This is bullshit. They want me to be a symbolic Admiral, not a real one. They're afraid I'll screw things up. Bekerose and his crew are working together to keep me in my cabin doing make-work, so I'll stay out of their way.

Tarraine had set up a staff meeting once a week with Bekerose. The other Captains of the fleet participated by hologram. They had completed three of them now.

Each had been a travesty.

Nobody reported anything of real value. It was all for show. If she asked a question about anything meaningful, the discussion was quickly diverted by Bekerose or one of the other Captains.

If it keeps up like this, when we get to Earth and face the Singheko, this crew will ignore me. They'll do whatever the hell they want and not what I command.

I'm not having it.

"Jimmy Boy, get Bekerose in my cabin immediately," she ordered her AI.

She had named her AI after Jim Carter. She thought it both funny and nostalgic.

She missed Jim so much. She had been in love with him from the day of her creation, of course. Because Bonnie had been in love with Jim already. When cloning her, *Jade* had pre-loaded her brain with Bonnie and Jim's knowledge and memories.

And feelings, she thought. *I got Bonnie's love for Jim, and Jim's love for Bonnie.*

Which left her in the crazy position of loving two people - yet standing between them, the extra woman.

I wonder if Jade *knew the impossible situation she was creating. Did she do it intentionally? To create discord and discontent among the three of us? Or was she just unaware of the impact of it, being an AI and not a biological creature?*

A knock on her door signified the arrival of Captain Bekerose.

"Come!" she said. The Captain entered.

Normally, she would have waved him to sit. This time she

left him standing, which was unusual. She stared at him for a second, gathering her thoughts. Finally, she spoke.

"I will not stand to be pushed into the background and diverted from the command of this fleet," she began.

Bekerose started to speak. Rita held up a hand, stopping him.

"Wait," she said sharply. "Let me finish."

Rita glared at him across the desk.

"Garatella gave me a job to do. And my planet, Earth, is on the line," she said slowly, deliberately.

"I will not let you or anyone else interfere with that mission."

Rita leaned forward and stared him in the eye.

"You have a basic decision to make, and you will make it right now. Either you will accord me the full respect and decision-making authority of my rank as if I were Nidarian; or we turn around and return to Sanctuary immediately, and I report to the High Councilor that you were unwilling to proceed with the mission under my command."

There was a shocked silence from the officer. Bekerose drew himself up to a position of attention.

"I have not interfered in any way with your prerogatives, milady," he said sharply. "If I am deficient in any way, please let me know where."

Rita glared at him. She spun her display around and pointed to a report on the screen.

"Bekerose, I can't believe you think I'm that naive. Are you going to stand there and tell me you didn't have an exercise with the fleet yesterday without my knowledge or input?"

Bekerose looked sullen - if she was reading his Nidarian expression correctly.

"There was no need to bother the Admiral with a routine fleet exercise," he said. "We have done hundreds of them in our careers, and we know how to do them."

"But I have not done hundreds of them!" Rita spoke angrily. "I must learn how this fleet operates, how it responds." She waved at the display, hitting it with the back of her hand. "I cannot learn that sitting at this desk signing off on reports!"

From the other room of her suite, Rita heard Imogen cry.

"The Admiral has many things on her mind. I did not wish to disturb you," Bekerose said with a smirk.

Rita stood up. She was a good inch taller than Bekerose, and now she used it to her full advantage. She glared at him.

"You will engage with me, Captain. You will treat me as any Nidarian admiral. Or I swear to your gods and mine I will turn this fleet around and return to Sanctuary. Am I clear?"

Bekerose nodded, stepped back, and saluted.

"Aye, aye, milady," he said. The rancor in his voice was obvious.

"Dismissed," said Rita. Bekerose turned and left. Rita watched him go, then turned to take care of Imogen in the next room. Walking through the adjoining hatch, she was deep in thought.

I'm going to have trouble with that one.

CHAPTER FIVE

Corresse. En Route to Sol System

Something woke Bonnie up in the middle of the night. Her eyes popped open.

What had it been? Was it a dream?

She lay, thinking, for a while.

Something she had thought of while she slept. It happened sometimes, an unbidden thought coming to her subconscious that snapped her awake. But unable to remember.

But she knew, once awake, there was no going back to sleep. She sighed, swung her legs over the bed, and sat quietly for a while.

What was it? What thought had brought her out of a deep sleep so suddenly?

She couldn't pull it up. It was gone.

Unbidden, other thoughts came into her mind.

Jim. Where are you this morning? What are you doing?

Bonnie hung her head.

I really screwed him over. Leaving him there in a coma and just leaving for the stars. What the hell was I thinking?

I still love him.

Giving up, she got out of bed, slipped into her uniform pants, and threw on a tunic. She stepped into her shoes and went out of the cabin, down the hall to the galley.

To her surprise, Arteveld was there also. She looked at the chrono on the wall. It was nearly dawn, ship's time - two hours to go before Third Watch would go off duty and the Captain would normally take the bridge.

She nodded at Arteveld, grabbed a cup, and got some *nish*. Then she sat down across from him.

"Couldn't sleep?" she asked, speaking Nidarian for the practice of it.

Arteveld nodded. "A lot of things to think about."

"Want to talk about it?" Bonnie asked.

Arteveld was silent. Then, after a space, he responded.

"I think…"

Pausing, he looked over at Bonnie, a troubled look on his face.

"I think Garatella has a hidden agenda," he finally said.

Bonnie nodded slightly. That was it. That was the thought that had woken her, left her unable to go back to sleep. She knew it now.

"I think you may be right," she finally replied.

Arteveld looked relieved.

"Ah…you had the same thought?"

"I do now," said Bonnie. "It didn't crystallize in my mind until you said it first. But now that you've said it, I'm sure you're right."

There was a companionable silence for a while. Finally, Bonnie spoke.

"Any idea what his hidden agenda might be?"

"No," Arteveld said. "But I don't think all this song and dance is for some ancient derelict ship with a unique engine design. Granted, he wants to find it, and he thinks you can do it. But if we do find it - I would be careful with it."

"Yes, I agree," Bonnie said. "And Arteveld - keep reminding me of that as we go along. In case I forget."

Arteveld smiled.

"Not to change the subject, but have we passed any message buoys from Rita's fleet?" asked Bonnie.

Arteveld shook his head.

"No, nothing. So far there is no news of her. We did detect a message buoy from a corvette headed the other way, back to Nidaria."

"Any news of the Singheko?"

"No. If they are on their way to Earth, they are doing it very quietly."

"They are," said Bonnie bitterly. "Trust me, those fat fuckers are on their way even as we speak."

Arteveld grinned at her.

"You know, human, for someone who has only spent a year studying our language you have an exceedingly good grasp of the idioms," he laughed.

Earth. Washington, D.C.

Newly minted Major James Carter, U.S. Space Force, stepped into the office of General Carl Raines at the Pentagon. He snapped to attention and saluted.

"At ease, Major. How are you?" asked the General.

"Excellent, sir, thank you."

"Have a seat," the General said, waving at a chair.

"Thank you, sir," Jim responded, sitting down.

"I was glad to hear you made it through the re-fam course," Raines said. "I could always have given you a desk job if you failed it, but that's not what I had in mind for you. So, I'm glad you toughed it out."

"Yes, sir," replied Jim.

General Raines, a tall, thin drink of water who looked vaguely like the screen actor Jimmy Stewart, leaned back in his chair, picked up a folder and looked through it.

"You have a unique record, Jim. Marine Corps aviation, two tours in the Middle East. Silver Star. Quit the Marine Corps after you lost your backseater in that shoot-down. Went to Africa, mercenary pilot for nearly ten years. Came back a wealthy man."

The General looked up at Jim.

"We won't ask how that happened," he said, with a slight quirk of his lips. He returned to his reading.

"Stumbled across the Singheko starship in Canada,

repaired it, almost let it get away. Discovered its true identity at the last minute, you and Bonnie and Rita Page..."

The General looked up at Jim again.

"I never did fully understand how both of them have the same last name. What's the story on that?"

Jim shrugged.

"I don't know, General. That's just the way things work out sometimes."

Raines looked skeptical. But he returned to the folder in front of him.

"... you and Bonnie and Rita managed to cripple and destroy the renegade ship before it could let the Singheko know about Earth. You were severely injured in the battle ..."

The General looked up at him again, seemed to size him up, looking for damage to his body; then went back to his reading.

"... you recovered, we offered you a position in the Space Force to prepare to fight the aliens, you told us to go pound sand."

General Raines closed the folder, laid it down, and folded his hands on the desk.

"What made you change your mind, Major?"

Jim gave a slight smile.

"Not much to do out in the Nevada desert, General. I realized I better get my ass back in the fight."

General Raines nodded.

"Or become a drunk, I hear," he said.

Jim smiled.

"Or become a drunk. Yes, sir."

"No drinking problem now?"

"No, sir. I'm good."

"OK, Major. Let's get one thing straight. Because of your inside knowledge of the Singheko starship, and your military record, I'm prepared to put you into a responsible position. But so much as one hint of abusive drinking and you'll be sitting on your ass in front of your hangar in Nevada again. Clear?"

"Crystal, sir," said Jim.

"Fine," said Raines. He turned and retrieved another folder from his desk, handed it over to Jim.

"Go study that - on premises, please, not to be removed from my office suite. When you're done, come back and we'll talk."

Outside the General's office, Jim was met by one of the General's aides.

"Sir, we have an office for you down the hall. Right this way."

Jim followed the aide down the hall to an empty office, stepped inside, thanked the aide, and sat down to read the file.

He was more shocked than he had words to express.

They recovered enough of Jade to reverse-engineer a system engine! We can't go interstellar, but by God we can go anywhere we want in the solar system!

Jim read for an hour. He went over the reports in fine detail, making notes in his head.

They had, indeed, recovered bits and pieces of *Jade* from the airstrip at Dutch Harbor where she crashed. And put them back together.

From those reconstructions, they had reverse-engineered a system engine - an engine that could push a spaceship at 255g, while compensating the ship against the massive g-forces to prevent crushing the humans inside.

And at the same time making enough power to provide nearly unlimited life support and weapons...

Jim did some quick calculations.

Enough thrust to make it to Mars in just seven hours when the planet was at maximum distance, including retro braking into orbit.

Enough thrust to make it to Jupiter in 11 hours.

Enough thrust to go anywhere in the solar system in four days.

Finally, Jim stopped reading and sighed, but with a huge smile on his face.

Holy Crap! We have a slight chance of defending ourselves!

Jim returned to the General's office. The aide took the folder, counted the pages, and logged it back into the secure system. Then Jim waited. And waited some more.

After an hour, the General called him back in, waved him to a chair, and leaned back.

"Well?" he asked.

"If we play our cards right, we can put up quite a surprise for the Singheko if they come back into our system," Jim said. "We'll need weapons - missiles that can function in space. We'll need tactics, things we can use against them they won't expect. And we'll need training, lots of it."

General Raines grinned at Jim. He took a piece of paper from the desk and handed it to Jim.

"Major Carter, you just named your own poison. You are hereby assigned to the First Mars Attack Wing, Space Attack Group 15, Black Eagle Squadron as CO. And I'm also requesting that Lieutenant Colonel Webster assign you as the Group Training Officer, with primary responsibility for training fighter pilots to defend Earth against an incursion by the Singheko."

Jim was nearly speechless but managed to stammer it out.

"Mars, sir?"

General Raines grinned.

"Mars, son. Good luck ... you're going to need it!"

Merkkessa. En Route to Sol System

Rita woke in the dark.

Someone was in her bedroom.

She felt it. No, she knew it. It was more than a feeling.

Someone was in her bedroom.

Slowly, inch by inch, Rita moved her hand under the blanket.

Every night since she had arrived on Nidaria more than six months ago, she placed a pistol under her blanket when she lay down to sleep. She never let anyone know because she thought it ridiculous. She had chalked it up to paranoia. She had laughed at herself.

But she did it anyway.

Now it didn't seem so ridiculous.

Slowly, she felt the grip of the pistol under the blanket. She closed her hand around it and carefully, quietly, flipped off the safety. Moving as slowly as she could, she moved it to point outward, toward the room.

Toward a dark figure moving ever so slowly toward her.

"Lights!" she yelled, and the overheads came on, nearly blinding her. She squinted her eyes against the glare to see if she could identify the person. She didn't want to shoot a friend.

It wasn't a friend, and they had a dagger in their hand. They lunged toward her. Rita pulled the trigger.

She was always surprised by how much noise a pulse pistol made. When she first encountered one on the *Corresse*, during their journey to Nidaria, she had assumed such a pistol would be relatively quiet when fired.

They weren't. When a device must generate enough energy to kill, it makes a lot of noise.

The blast left her ears ringing. The Nidarian with the dagger stumbled, fell to one knee, glaring at her with hatred. He made a final lunge, bringing the dagger down hard into her chest just as she fired again.

Her last pulse caught him in the head. It exploded into a spray of brains and blood all over her, her bed, the floor, and the walls of the cabin. With a plop, he fell forward on top of her, pinning her gun hand, the knife sticking out of her chest.

She felt like she had been hit with a cannonball. She was paralyzed - she couldn't move. The door to the Security Office slammed open and Raphael burst in, his pistol at the ready. He took in the picture at a glance. Quickly, he went to the open bedroom door and slid cautiously into the front room of her suite, his pistol up, prepared for anything.

Behind him, Gabriel came through the door, his own pulse

pistol in hand. He took the scene in for a second, then turned to cover the door, backing up toward her, ignoring the gore and blood he stepped in with his bare feet. With one hand, he reached down and pulled the dead body off her, throwing it to one side, and tried to assess her condition with a sidelong glance while still covering the door.

"Clear!" yelled Raphael from the front room.

Gabriel turned and knelt beside Rita's bed, laying his pistol on the bloody floor. He took her still glowing pulse pistol from her listless hand and laid it beside his. Then he carefully examined her wound and the knife sticking out of it. His eyes met hers and he smiled slightly.

"Milady, I'm not an expert on human physiology, but I think he missed all the vital organs. Time will tell."

Rita nodded silently. Things were out of her hands now. It was all up to others. She heard the front hatch slam open and Flo's voice, along with that of Captain Bekerose.

Flo rushed in, her medical bag in hand. She took in the scene - Rita could see the shock on her face. But she hesitated only for a second.

Moving forward, Flo not very gently pushed Gabriel aside and took his place kneeling beside the bed. She examined the wound and the knife. A medical team came in through the door, carrying a stretcher. The room was getting crowded. Bekerose motioned to Raphael and Gabriel and they followed him out into the front room.

Flo spoke gently.

"Is there much pain?"

Rita shook her head slightly, then managed to mutter, 'No, there was at first but now it's mostly numb."

"OK," responded Flo. "There's a lot of blood, but I think he missed the heart and major arteries. So I'm going to take you to sick bay for surgery. I want to give you a sedative first, so you don't feel the pain. Are you ready?"

Rita nodded, once. She looked up at the ceiling as Flo prepared the injection. She thought about her last night with

Jim.

The night we made Imogen…

"Take care of my baby," she whispered as everything faded away.

CHAPTER SIX

Merkkessa. En Route to Sol System

"The *Merkkessa* is noisier than the *Corresse*," Rita thought. It rumbled and vibrated. The deck had a periodic tremor that came about twice a minute, then died away.

Old and tired. That's all they were willing to give me. An old, tired battlecruiser, with an old, tired fleet.

Slowly, she realized she was awake. It was one of those awakenings where she didn't realize she had awakened. She just starting thinking again. She opened her eyes and looked at the ceiling.

This wasn't her bedroom. The light was different, and the mattress much harder than her own. And the vibration wasn't damped by carpet on the floor. That's why it was so loud.

I'm in sick bay, she realized. *There was an attack.*

With some effort, she turned her head. There were electronic displays beside her bed, beeping. Curtains surrounded the bed, and there was a stainless table across the room. There were lots of wires and tubes going to and from her body.

She managed to lift a hand up to her neck and pull the top of her gown up to look underneath. There was a large white bandage circling her chest, just below her breasts.

"Put that down!"

Rita looked up to see Flo arriving beside the bed, and she didn't look happy.

"What are you doing? Put that gown back! Don't be looking under there!" the little Nidarian doctor growled at her.

"Well, it's me under there," Rita said weakly. "Seems like I ought to be able to look…"

Flo bustled about, pulling the gown back in place, checking the displays that were beeping beside Rita's bed, and marking things down on her tablet.

"You have only one job, Admiral, and that is to lie still and get better," snapped Flo. "Can you handle that?"

"Yes, doctor," Rita whispered. "No problem, doctor."

Her eyes closed involuntarily, and she was out again.

* * * * *

The next time Rita woke, both Flo and Captain Tarraine were standing beside her bed. They smiled down at her.

"How do you feel, Admiral?" asked Flo.

Rita thought about it.

"Better, I think," she mumbled.

"Good," said Flo. "You're coming along nicely. You had surgery to repair the damage to your lungs and ribs. There was some initial infection, but we've tamped that down. You're going to be fine."

"How long?" Rita asked.

"Five days," answered Flo. "But you're out of the - how do you say? - out of the trees now."

"Out of the woods," corrected Rita.

Her mind started working a bit better.

"Where's Imogen?" she asked, switching to Nidarian - she knew Tarraine's English was a bit weak.

Tarraine smiled. He reached into his pocket, pulled out a gold coin, and handed it to Flo.

Flo grinned and pocketed the coin.

"Imogen is on the way," she said. "She'll be here in five minutes. Do you think you're up to holding her?"

"Hell, yes," Rita said. "Help me sit up, please?"

Flo reached behind her and helped her move to a semi-sitting position.

"Ouch!" exclaimed Rita. "That hurts!"

"You had a dagger stuck in your chest, Admiral. Of course it hurts!"

Finding a semi-comfortable position, Rita looked at Tarraine.

"What happened? Who was it?

Tarraine grimaced.

"It appears that despite our most careful screening, an assassin managed to infiltrate our crew. He was a cook - or at least, came on board as a cook. His papers were perfect, and he played the part well, right up until…well, you know."

"But why me? What is the purpose of killing me?" Rita asked.

"I'm sure he was paid by the Singheko," Tarraine responded. "It had been my hope they would not be aware of this task force. But it appears they know about it and are concerned enough to try to kill you."

"Do we have any way of knowing if there are more on board?" asked Rita.

Tarraine shook his head. "If so, they'll be in deep cover. We'll do everything we can to smoke them out, but there's no guarantees."

From outside her view, Rita heard Imogen cry. With a smile, she watched nanny Fallassa come into view, holding the baby. She reached for her and Fallassa gently placed Imogen into her arms.

"She's hungry," said Fallassa. "We've been giving her formula, but it's not like Mom's milk. She's very unhappy."

Rita held Imogen, gazing into her eyes. Then she gave a pointed look at Captain Tarraine.

"Oh," he said. "I have some things to do…uh…elsewhere."

The three of them grinned as the Captain scooted away like a scolded child.

* * * * *

Rita finished nursing Imogen and handed her back to Fallassa, who took her away for her nap.

Flo had long since gone back to her duties, and now Rita was alone. She knew she should sleep again, but she wasn't sleepy.

Rita had another problem on her mind.

Since her talk with Bekerose, there had been some improvement in his coordination with her. They had run a half-dozen exercises over the last month with her on the Flag Bridge, monitoring and even making suggestions.

But there was still an undercurrent. She knew she was still thought of as an appendage, or even a nuisance, by Bekerose and the rest of his bridge crew.

But she couldn't follow through on her threat to turn back. And of course, she had never intended to do that anyway, and Bekerose knew it. Turning back wasn't an option for either of them.

There was nothing she could point to as obstruction - nothing that would stand up to scrutiny. He walked a fine line, superficially doing all that was necessary. But still - the resistance was there. She could feel it.

Rita sighed. She had wracked her brain for a solution, but none came to mind. She couldn't think of any approach, any ploy that would get the Nidarian on her side.

And without his active cooperation, she didn't see how they could succeed.

She wondered for a moment if he was part of the conspiracy - paid off by the Singheko, part of the attempt to kill her or block her success.

But she doubted it. He was a career Captain in the Nidarian Navy, and proud of it.

She needed someone to talk to about it. Someone she could trust. But not Flo - Flo had enough on her mind already, plus she was a doctor, not a line officer.

Rita wondered if her AI was still active here in the sick bay.

"Hey, Jimmy Boy, you there?" she asked the thin air.

<I am> she heard in her brain.

"Oh, good. Please ask Captain Tarraine to come see me."

A few minutes later, the curtains at the foot of her bed parted and Captain Tarraine came in. Rita had gone to sleep; his arrival woke her up again.

"You wished to see me, milady?"

"Yes, Captain," Rita mumbled, coming slowly back awake. She was more exhausted than she realized. She pulled herself back up to a sitting position and looked at her aide.

"Captain, I want to know something, and I want to know it honestly. I want you to answer me directly, without sugar coating it."

"Yes, milady," replied Tarraine.

"If we went into battle today, and I gave an order conflicting with Captain Bekerose, would the fleet follow it?"

Tarraine looked uncomfortable.

"Milady, you are injured. I don't think…"

"Answer the question, Tarraine. Don't crawfish."

Tarraine hung his head.

"No, milady, I don't believe they would."

"I see," said Rita. She thought for a few seconds.

"Tarraine, how do we fix this?"

"I don't know, milady. I've never been in this situation before."

"I suppose it's impossible to replace him," Rita mused out loud.

"Yes, milady, that would be a disaster. I don't believe it could be done without turning the fleet around and returning to Sanctuary."

"Very well, Tarraine. Thank you for coming. I'll sleep on this problem. Maybe something will come to me."

Mars. First Wing Headquarters

One week after his meeting with General Raines, in a crater

in Acidalia Planitia in the northern hemisphere of Mars, Jim Carter stepped off the shuttlecraft from orbit.

His head was spinning; he could hardly comprehend all that he saw around him.

Here, a roofed-over gully had allowed the quick build of the First Mars Wing headquarters.

The gully, roughly three hundred feet wide and forty feet deep, had been completely covered for nearly a mile. The west end had been permanently enclosed, with well-hidden emergency escape hatches the only exits from that side of the complex.

At the east end, a huge open-ended portico a half mile long covered an unpressurized parking area. The portico butted up against the Wing HQ building on the other end.

Under the portico, the tarmac contained dozens of fighters and shuttles, parked in rows on both sides. Some designs he recognized - like the A16 fighter - while others were designs he didn't even know existed.

The shuttle from orbit had landed just outside the portico roof. A tug quickly latched on to it and pulled it inside.

Jim had been issued a pressure suit for the journey down from orbit. Now, his newly assigned aide, Lt. Frank Fox, led him down the ramp of the shuttle and over to a small electric cart.

They sat down and the driver took off down the center aisle of the underground parking area, driving like a bat out of hell. Around them other carts zipped to and fro.

Jim slowly saw the system to it. Carts stayed to the right of the centerline, like a highway. If they had to turn left across the opposite traffic, they slowed until there was an opening, then darted across as fast as possible.

It was a madhouse of activity.

"Where are all these carts going?" asked Jim over the suit radio.

Lt. Fox answered, his voice a bit scratchy over the comm.

"We still have massive amounts of construction going on,"

he said. "A lot of these carts are civilian contractors, finishing up construction. Then you have Group maintenance, taking care of the ships. You have pilots, going to and from their birds for training missions. And of course you have personnel transfers, like us, coming in and out."

Jim was puzzled.

"How is it possible the public hasn't heard about all of this back on Earth?"

"We've managed to keep a tight lid on things. We must assume the Singheko will find us. And when they do, it would make sense they'd listen to our TV and radio for a while before they attack. So, the last thing we want to do is have the media shouting about this place over the open airwaves."

Jim nodded in agreement.

"And how come we have normal gravity here? I know the same technology for the system engines can be used to make gravity, but how did you manage to cover such a large area?" he asked.

"I'm not sure of the details, but I know that it involved laying graphite strips beneath this entire complex. They actually laid them as they built - part of the foundation." said Lt. Fox.

"Absolutely freaking amazing," said Jim. "The geeks must have been working overtime on that one."

They approached the end of the portico. In front of them were massive hangar doors, with four smaller sets of doors on either side. The cart pulled up to one of the smaller doors and stopped.

Lt. Fox led Jim out of the cart and through the door, which turned out to be an airlock. They stood inside for a bit as the pressure was equalized, then entered the inner door. Lt. Fox shed his pressure suit and helped Jim with his. Then Fox led him down a corridor to a cross-corridor.

Turning right, they arrived at a stairwell and went up two floors. At the top was a control room. Lt. Fox led him inside and over to a transparent viewing window.

Below them, Jim could see an indoor hangar area, where ships undergoing maintenance were being repaired in a controlled environment. There were four of the fighters inside the pressurized area. Beyond were the two massive double doors.

The miracle of it boggled his mind.

"This was all built in sixteen months?" he queried Lt. Fox. The lieutenant responded with a proud grin on his face.

"No, sir. We didn't have working system engines for two months after *Jade* crashed. This entire complex was built in fourteen months."

Jim was astounded. All he could do was shake his head in wonderment.

Lt. Fox continued.

"You'd be surprised what you can do once you have reliable transportation to Mars," he said. "And a 3D synthesizer that can produce just about anything you want."

"What?" Jim turned in surprise. "I thought *Jade*'s 3D synthesizer was destroyed too!"

"Not quite," grinned Lt. Fox. "It was mostly destroyed. But we re-constructed it. Now we can pour raw materials into the hoppers on one end and have anything we need come out the other end. It's a 3D printer on steroids."

Jim smiled.

"Human ingenuity never ceases to amaze me," he quipped. He turned back to the large window, staring at the fighters two floors below, with men pouring over them like ants.

"What are those called again?"

"The A16 Longsword, sir. The A16 is a fighter/attack platform capable of 255g acceleration fully compensated, and 267g maximum, with six missile stations…"

Jim interrupted with a wave of his hand.

"I just wanted a reminder on the name, Lieutenant. Not the full encyclopedia entry."

Lt. Fox laughed.

"Sorry, sir."

Jim turned to Lt. Fox.

"Lieutenant, let's get one thing straight right from the get-go. We have a tough job to do, and we can't do it if we can't be straight with each other. So never apologize, and never hesitate to tell me I'm full of shit. Got it?"

Lt. Fox bobbed his head with a small grin.

"Got it, sir."

"OK, let's move on," said Jim.

Lt. Fox gestured toward the door. "We should go meet with the CO, sir. He's expecting you."

Jim followed Lt. Fox to the door of the control room and exited. As they walked down the corridor, Lt. Fox couldn't resist asking a question.

"Sir, is it true you destroyed *Jade* with nothing but two hand grenades?"

"Not only is that not true, but it wasn't even me that did that part," said Jim, staring blankly at the floor as he walked. "That was Rita Page. By that point in the battle, I was lying on the deck with a concussion, busted ribs, a broken leg, and a broken arm. It was all Rita from there."

Lt. Fox persisted, not wanting to give up his image of Jim as a hero.

"But you stopped *Jade* from escaping to space, right, sir?"

Jim smiled wanly at the young, eager lieutenant.

"Not even that, Lieutenant. That was Bonnie and Captain Arteveld on the *Corresse*. All I did was blow *Jade*'s cargo hatch open with a shotgun and get the C4 and the grenades. The rest was all Rita and Bonnie."

Disappointed, Lt. Fox led them down two flights of stairs. A few minutes later, they entered the Group Headquarters suite, where an aide showed them to chairs and asked them to wait.

Fifteen minutes later, Jim was called into the Group Commander's office. He entered and stood to attention in front of Lieutenant Colonel Randolph Webster.

"At ease, Major Carter. Have a seat. How was your trip from Earth?"

"Interesting," said Jim, sitting down. "Quite different from anything I've ever done before."

Webster smiled.

"Yes, most of us say that after our first time. But you get used to it."

Webster pulled a tablet over to him and studied it for a minute.

"Per General Raines recommendation, I'm assigning you as CO of Black Eagle Squadron. Also, General Raines has recommended that I take you on as Group Training Officer. He seems to think your first-hand experience with a Singheko starship will help us train to defend against them if they come."

"They'll come, sir," said Jim. "My only hope is that we can be ready for them first."

"Mine as well," said Webster. "So you think you can add value to our training to get us ready for them?"

"I do, sir. I spent many months with *Jade* before we discovered her true identity. There's certainly no way to understand all the technology she had, but at least I got a look at it. So I understand her capabilities, even if I don't understand how they worked. And of course, she was just a scoutship. The Singheko will undoubtedly bring bigger ships when they attack us. But I think the things I learned from *Jade* can still translate to help us fight them."

"Very good, Major. We'll work from that premise for now." Webster laid his tablet down.

"Go get yourself situated, and I'll see you at staff meeting tomorrow at eight."

Jake nodded. Outside, Lt. Fox led him down the hallway, up a flight of stairs to a long corridor, and down a dozen doors to his quarters.

"Here you are, sir," said the Lieutenant. "The door is coded to your dogtags or your palm print, so either will work. Your bags should already be inside."

"Thank you, Lt. Fox," replied Jim. "I appreciate your help."

Jim let himself into the room and watched the lieutenant depart. He closed the door and looked around.

It was sparse. Four walls, a bed, a chest of drawers, a bookcase, and a desk. In the back, a door led to a small bathroom with a shower, a toilet, and a sink.

Jim's bags were on the bunk.

"Welcome back, jarhead," he said to himself, remembering his first quarters as a young butterbar lieutenant more than fifteen years prior.

Corresse. **En Route to Sol System**

The *Corresse* was not a large ship. It was 90 meters long, about 30 meters wide at the rear, tapering in an irregular wedge to a blunt point two meters wide. The shape was designed to help fend off missiles and pulse weapons by deflecting them to the side with a wedge of focused gravity. It sometimes worked, Arteveld told Bonnie. And sometimes it didn't.

There was a crew of twenty on this mission. The lower ranks had four to a cabin, while the junior officers had two per cabin. The three most senior officers and Bonnie were the only ones with a cabin to themselves.

Now Bonnie almost wished she had a roommate. She was so tired of being alone. Besides continuing to study the Nidarian language, and having lunch and dinner with Arteveld most days, she had nothing to do except mull over her mission - which she had done so many times her brain ached.

With a sigh, Bonnie leaned back from the holo she was viewing at her desk.

She had gone over it dozens of times. Based on each point along the *Dragon*'s most likely path within a reasonable distance of Sol, she had mapped out the areas of probability regarding a likely destination. These formed a triangular pattern, with one point at Sol. With a few reasonable assumptions, the probability of the ship being at any point in the triangle could be computed.

Given the sensors of the *Corresse* and thus their ability to search empty space, she had then broken the pattern into search boxes.

There were eighty-five million search boxes. Each search box would take four hours to search.

If they searched each one, it would take 14.6 million days. 38,000 years.

Bonnie shook her head in frustration.

What is Garatella playing at?

Clearly, they couldn't conduct a systematic search of the areas where the *Dragon* could be. It was impossible on the face of it.

So ... Bonnie could only assume that Garatella intended for her to search strictly within the Sol system.

He knows something, she thought. *Or he suspects something.*

Bonnie leaned forward again and put her head in her hands.

I'm on the Dragon, she imagined. *I'm scooting through space, all is good. Then suddenly something breaks. I'm in deep trouble. I can't make it to Sword. I need to divert to the closest system, which happens to be Sol.*

Bonnie thought deeply.

It must be at Earth. Nidarians have the same basic requirements for air, water, food as humans. Their physiology is remarkably similar.

Bonnie raised her head. It hurt her brain to think about it, but she knew it had to be true.

They sent a message drone to Nidaria and made for Earth. They had to. It's the only place that would sustain them.

Two thousand years ago, an ancient Golden Empire ship had made for Earth, hoping to survive long enough for rescue.

Where was it now?

CHAPTER SEVEN

Merkkessa. **En Route to Sol System**

At Rita's insistence, Flo allowed her to move back to her Flag Cabin. She was healing nicely, and she wanted to be closer to baby Imogen for feedings.

She had some hesitancy when she was first wheeled into her bedroom - after all, the last time she saw it, it had been thoroughly covered in blood and gore. But, Tarraine had ensured it was spotless. There was no trace of the mayhem that had occurred there a week earlier.

With a sigh of relief, Rita allowed them to place her back in her bed, with Flo fussing around her fluffing up her pillows and tugging the blankets over her, arranging them until in exasperation, Rita gently said, "Enough, Flo. Let me rest."

Flo sniffed, but stood back and looked down at her. Behind Flo stood Fallassa, Gabriel, Raphael and Tarraine, all with looks of concern on their faces.

And behind them, closer to the door, stood Bekerose. There was no concern on his face; only boredom and irritation.

Rita waved a hand at all of them collectively.

"Everyone, please, let me rest. Except for Gabriel and Raphael. I need to talk to them."

Gabriel looked troubled, as did Raphael. The rest nodded their goodbyes and departed, one after the other filing back through the hatch and out of the suite. Flo went last, taking one last look over her shoulder at Rita.

"No exertions, Admiral!" she flung a parting shot. Then she was gone.

Rita had become good at reading Nidarian expressions. They weren't that different from humans. Now Gabriel and Raphael stood at loose attention before her, concern and shame on their faces. Rita motioned to them.

"Gabriel. Raphael. At ease. Relax. Come closer," she said.

Gabriel glanced at Raphael, nodded, took a step closer, and made an effort to relax. He didn't accomplish it, but he tried. Rita smiled inside - where he couldn't see it. Outside, she maintained a neutral expression on her face. Slowly, Raphael followed suit, stepping up beside Gabriel.

Rita had long since figured out that Gabriel was the natural leader of the two. So now, although she addressed them both, she knew she was talking primarily to Gabriel.

"Gabriel," she said softly. "Raphael. You mustn't blame yourselves. Nobody could have prevented it. The assassin hid in plain sight. He cooked our food. He served us in the Officer's Mess. He was one of us. You must put this behind you and move on."

A lone tear slid slowly out of Gabriel's eye. The big Nidarian's head hung low.

"We failed you, milady," he said, his heart broken.

Rita shook her head.

"No, Gabriel. You did not. Together we are a team. We watch each other, and we take care of each other. But we are not supermen. We are not perfect. No one is asking you to be perfect. That is why we act as a team - you cover my mistakes, and I cover yours. He didn't succeed, and now we learn from our mistakes. All of us - you, me, Tarraine, Bekerose - all of us learn. And we go on. We have a mission to accomplish."

"Yes, milady," mumbled Gabriel. Raphael nodded. But Rita could see their hearts were still troubled.

"Now. Both of you put this behind you," she added. "As I intend to. Put your heart and soul into moving forward with a better security plan. And it occurs to me that I've been unfair to you. You are spread too thin. I want you to recruit two more bodyguards from among the Marine contingent."

"Yes, milady," Gabriel responded, a little more energy in his voice.

"So…go take care of business," Rita smiled at them.

Both Gabriel and Raphael snapped to attention and saluted. It was standard Nidarian Navy practice not to salute on a ship underway - but Rita knew why they did it. She gave them a salute in return, and they turned smartly and departed.

Now. That's taken care of, thought Rita. *Now for the bigger problem.*

"Jimmy Boy, please have Captain Bekerose and Captain Tarraine attend me at their convenience," Rita said to her AI.

<Wilco>

Rita lay back and closed her eyes. She had pondered on this problem for two days now. She had found only one avenue of possible success.

It was a long shot - but on the other hand, the mission was doomed to failure anyway unless she resolved the problem of Bekerose.

Her gut told her that Bekerose had in mind to enter the Sol system, put up a good show of defending it, then cut and run all the way back to Sanctuary as soon as the going got tough.

In fact, she thought that might be his actual orders. This could all be a ploy by Garatella to set her up. Put up a good show, then slink away, leaving Earth to the Singheko. Just to buy more time for Garatella to prepare for his future war.

Subduing Earth would occupy the Singheko for some time, she realized. That was time Garatella could use to his advantage.

We'll see about that.

<Captain Bekerose and Captain Tarraine are on their way>

Rita didn't want to have this meeting lying down in her bed. Groaning, she managed to swing her legs over the edge. She stood up, swaying, holding on to a nearby chair, and shuffled to the door. Opening it, she went outside to her briefing room, and managed to stumble to her desk. She got there just as a gentle knock came on the door.

"Come!"

The door opened. Rita could see Gabriel standing guard outside the room, holding the door open for the two Captains. Tarraine and Bekerose entered the room.

"Captain Bekerose, I have a proposition for you," Rita began.

Bekerose stood up straighter, looking puzzled.

Rita went on.

"I know how much Nidarians like to gamble," she said. "I will make a bet with you."

Bekerose looked even more confused.

Rita glanced at Tarraine. A faint smile tinged the corners of Tarraine's lips. Rita knew Tarraine was quick - certainly quicker than Bekerose. She suspected he already knew where this conversation was going.

I wish he were Captain of this ship, she thought. *But alas...*

"Captain Bekerose, I'll bet I can defeat you in a fleet battle simulation three out of five times," Rita said flatly.

Bekerose had a look of shocked disbelief on his face. Behind him, Rita could see Tarraine trying to suppress a smile, his lips working.

Bekerose stuttered.

"But ... but ... Milady ..." was all he could get out at first.

"Well?" Rita asked. "Do you take the bet?"

Bekerose slowly began to get his bearings.

"But ... Milady ... three out of five? What conditions? What stakes?"

Rita knew she had him then. She had been sure he couldn't walk away from such a challenge - especially not with Tarraine there to spread the word around the ship if he had refused. Not that Tarraine would do that - until she forced him to. But Bekerose couldn't be sure of that.

There was no way he could walk away from this. To refuse a bet with the Admiral he disparaged and disrespected - he couldn't do it. Not if he hoped to maintain any respect among his officers at all.

"The conditions are that we'll set up the simulator to be an exact copy of the Sol system. I will have one copy of this fleet; you will have another. We will alternate simulating the Singheko fleet. Each of us can have three crew members to assist. Five iterations. First person to win three simulations is the winner."

Bekerose began to smile. Rita could see his mind working. He felt there was no way he could lose.

"And the stakes, milady?" he asked.

"If you win, I will step down as Admiral. I'll record a message to Garatella for the ship's log that my injuries prevent me from completing the mission and I've turned over command to you. You will have full and complete control of the fleet."

"I see," Bekerose.

Rita continued, glancing at Tarraine as she did so. Tarraine was her witness to the bet.

"If I win, you will give me your complete and unconditional support, and unwavering obedience in the rest of this mission. No more undercutting, no more behind-the-back muttering, no more second-guessing my orders."

Bekerose stood straighter, anger on his face.

"Milady, I do none of those things."

"Nevertheless, that is the bet. Take it or leave it," said Rita sharply. "Captain Tarraine will be our witness. And may I point out, Captain Tarraine will also be the judge of compliance to the bet - regardless of who wins. If either of us renege on the outcome, Captain Tarraine has my authority and permission to take any action he sees fit to ensure compliance."

Bekerose drew himself up even straighter if such was possible.

"That will not be necessary," he said haughtily. "There will be no issue with compliance."

"So you accept the bet?" Rita asked.

"I do," answered Bekerose. "When do you desire to begin?"

"Tomorrow morning," said Rita. "0800 hours, in the main

simulator room."

"Very good, milady," said Bekerose, his voice dripping with anger and contempt.

"Tarraine. See to the setup, please," said Rita.

"Aye, aye, milady," Tarraine responded.

Corresse. En Route to Sol System

Bonnie punched the heavy bag hard, working up a sweat.

Arteveld had been puzzled when she asked for a punching bag before their departure, but he accommodated her - finding someone who could make it to her specifications and having it mounted in the back of the common room of the *Corresse*.

Now she punched it over and over, working out her irritation and frustration, until her hands were sore, and she couldn't go on.

With a final reverse high kick at the bag, she removed her gloves and headed for the shower. She peeled off her workout clothes and stepped in, luxuriating in the hot water that seemed to be plentiful on the *Corresse*.

Bonnie had once asked Arteveld how they were able to provide such large amounts of water on a spacecraft. He had looked at her in puzzlement as if the question didn't make sense; he then replied that the reactor could generate as much hydrogen and oxygen as they needed, and all they had to do was combine it. As if she had failed basic chemistry.

Bonnie had sighed and decided not to pursue the question further. Nidarian technology was just too far above her engineering knowledge.

Stepping out of the shower, she toweled off and dressed. Since coming onboard, she had been directed by Arteveld to wear a military uniform, with the rank of a Marine Colonel. Arteveld explained it was necessary to ensure that the crew took her seriously and would obey her orders in an emergency.

She would have preferred to be a Naval Captain, but there could only be one Captain on a ship, Arteveld explained.

Completing her dress, she put away her workout clothes in a locker, checked her hair - cut short now that she was a pseudo-military officer in the Nidarian Marines - and left to go back to her office. On the way, she passed Arteveld's XO, Dallitta, who waved at her gaily.

"Good morning, Colonel!" said Dallitta gaily. "Anytime you want to spar, let me know!"

Bonnie smiled and nodded. The rumor around the ship was that Dallitta was quite a good fighter. She would have to find out sometime.

But not now. While she had been at the bag, she had been thinking about the *Dragon*.

It had to be on Earth. The more she thought about it, the more she realized that was the only logical place for the *Dragon* to be.

Garatella had dispatched the *Corresse* to Earth five years ago. The *Corresse* had spent five long years in the Sol system meticulously collecting every scrap of information they could intercept from Earth. They had a complete history of virtually everything available to a human researcher on Earth. Every encyclopedia, every Wiki, every reference.

Why? Why would Garatella have done that five years ago?

Because he already knew the Dragon was on Earth. He sent the Corresse there to collect records to help him find it.

He's a slimy bastard. But he's the only slimy bastard I've got.

Focus.

Focus on the problem. Locating the Dragon.

There had to be some way of finding it. Two thousand years ago, there was at least some writing. Records were made, chronicles were kept. A starship descending from the skies would have caused someone, somewhere, to make note of it and write it down.

Yet Garatella couldn't find it, even with the resources of his entire government.

Crap! Bonnie suddenly realized. *That's the reason he delayed us for six months. It wasn't any of the reasons he stated. He was*

searching for the Dragon *in the records the Corresse brought back.*
And he couldn't find it.

Bonnie went through all the major civilizations of that era in her mind, thinking through each one.

Rome. The Empire was highly literate, at least among the nobility.

Surely any hint of an alien spaceship would have been well-documented in that environment.

China. Literate, well-documented.

No chance that a starship from the heavens would have gone unrecorded there.

And Antarctica - if the ship had any control left at all, the crew would never land in the freezing hell of that continent.

I'm ruling areas out, but that still leaves an enormous land area to cover. Assuming they had enough control left to make a soft landing and didn't crash into the ocean or burn up completely on re-entry.

Once again, Bonnie decided to go back to her process of imagination.

I'm on the Dragon, she imagined. *I'm scooting through space, all is good. Then suddenly something breaks. I'm in deep trouble. I can't make it to Sword. I need to divert to the closest system, which happens to be Sol.*

Somehow, I make it to Sol. Assuming I still have some remote sensing capability, I realize that Earth is my only viable option - temperate climate, compatible atmosphere, water, potential food. I get closer. I realize there are lifeforms there, sentient creatures who might be able to help me repair the ship. Now what decisions would I make?

Bonnie arrived at her cabin, threw her gym bag in a corner, and fell on her bed, pounding her pillow in frustration.

Damn it! There are so many millions of square miles to cover. This task is impossible!

But she couldn't give up. She had to think this through, make the best possible decisions she could make, and keep trying.

OK. I'm approaching Earth. It's two thousand years in the past - roughly 179 A.D. What can we know about this period?

<*Corresse*, give me a summary of the major civilizations of the year 179 A.D. and their notable accomplishments>

<The year 179 A.D. per the Earth Common Era. The Roman Empire was well established. Emperor Marcus Aurelius was the Emperor. It was the last year of the Pax Romana. Han Dynasty China had created a golden age of cultural and scientific enlightenment but had entered their last long decline under Emperor Ling. King Sindae of Korea died and was succeeded by King Gogukchean, his second son. An early form of Christianity was introduced to the city of Edessa in Mesopotamia. In India and Bactria, the Kushan Empire was ruled by Emperor Huvishka. The Persians were fighting the Romans as usual. Do you want more?>

"No," sighed Bonnie.

That was no help.

Merkkessa. En Route to Sol System

At 0800 hours, Tarraine accompanied Rita as she walked into the simulator room of the *Merkkessa* - still hurting, still in pain, but walking. The room contained several smaller simulator stations, including several copies of the Devastator fighter cockpits. But it also contained two larger simulators that duplicated a simplistic version of the bridge of the *Merkkessa*. These allowed full fleet-level battle simulations.

Rita should know. Other than Tarraine, Gabriel and Raphael, few knew she had already spent dozens of hours in the simulator since they departed Sanctuary. Since leaving, she had spent more time in the simulator than anywhere else.

She hoped Bekerose had not noted that in the logs.

With Tarraine's help, she entered the sim cabinet assigned to her and settled herself in the captain's chair.

"Tarraine, thank you for setting this up," she said to him.

He nodded. He took the XO position beside her. Behind

him, two additional officers came into the simulator. One was her Flag Lieutenant, Lt. Lirrassa. Tarraine had advised her that Lirrassa was an excellent Weapons Officer and would be a good addition to the team.

The other she knew only by sight - the Second Watch Tactical Officer, Naditta. Tarraine said he was an up-and-coming young officer with a good grasp of tactics. Lirrassa and Naditta took their seats and prepared for battle.

"Just a quick recap of the ground rules," said Rita. "We alternate being the Singheko. This time around, that's Bekerose. We have stipulated his fleet is already present in the Sol system and has been there for one week, giving him ample time to prepare an ambush of his own design. Any questions?"

"No, milady," came a chorus of responses.

"Alright, then," said Rita. She looked at Tarraine. "Ready."

Tarraine nodded. The sim booted up. The front viewscreen, the holo and the side screens initiated. Rita found herself in the Sol system. A horn hooted, signifying the sim was underway.

Rita assessed the holo quickly. She had directed Tarraine to translate the fleet into the Sol system at a point midway between the orbits of Uranus and Saturn, which was the closest possible translation point given the gravity well of the Sun.

Now she found her fleet in battle formation, 14.35 AU from the Sun - 2.15 billion miles from the star. The planets were arranged as they would be when she arrived at the Sol system in a few weeks. Uranus was behind her, and Saturn directly in front of her. Beyond Saturn, Jupiter was slightly off to her relative left, almost - but not quite - in conjunction with Saturn.

Much farther in, Earth was also slightly to the relative left of her course line. It was a somewhat unique configuration of the solar system that happened only once in a long while, with Earth, Jupiter, Saturn, and Uranus in rough alignment.

Bekerose and his fleet were nowhere in sight. Either he was

so far away that light from his fleet had not yet reached her, or...

"Perhaps hiding behind one of the planets or behind the star, milady?" said Naditta.

Rita realized Naditta was likely correct. If Bekerose had placed himself so far away that light speed distance prevented her from seeing him, she had nothing to worry about for quite a while. But the most likely place Bekerose could be was behind one of the larger planets or the other side of the Sun.

She had to scout the battlefield before she committed to a course of action.

"Scout One Alpha to Saturn, Scout Two Alpha to Jupiter, Scout Three Alpha to Mars, Scout Four Alpha to Earth," she called out.

The AI recognized her voice and crafted the order to both her console and Tarraine's for authentication. She checked the command on her verification screen and hit the Execute button - the order went out. The four corvettes of her fleet advanced their throttles to 255g and streaked for their destinations.

"Fleet advance at flank speed to Saturn," added Rita. "Advance the clock to next communication."

Given the incredible distances of the solar system, it would take the scouts 16 hours in real time to get to Saturn. With no sign of Bekerose's fleet nearby, she could skip ahead in the sim. The clock jumped ahead by 16 hours.

"Scout One Alpha reports nothing at Saturn, milady," called out Naditta.

As Rita expected.

"Fleet advance at flank speed to Jupiter. Advance the clock to next communication," Rita called.

A few seconds later, Naditta reported. "Scout Two Alpha reports nothing at Jupiter, milady."

Now Rita was surprised. She had been sure Bekerose would try to ambush her at Jupiter.

That's what she would have done.

But he wasn't there. So that left Mars, Earth, Venus, or behind the Sun. Mercury was too small - he couldn't hide a fleet behind that tiny planet.

"Scout One Alpha to rejoin formation. Scout Two Alpha to the Sun," she said. "Fleet advance at flank speed to Mars."

Now she had some decisions to make.

"Tarraine." Rita began. "Assume he's behind the Sun. What do you recommend?"

Tarraine scratched his chin, a very human gesture to Rita.

"Well, we could split the fleet and try to flank him. Send TF1 to the left, TF3 to the right, hold TF2 in reserve. But of course, there's the danger he would anticipate that and come orthogonal to us, say over the top, end up taking TF2 in detail."

Rita thought about it.

"Or we could just go en masse around the star and make a direct frontal attack," added Tarraine.

"Or we could hold in a good position, say at Earth, and wait for him to come to us," said Rita.

"True," said Tarraine. "That's actually the best idea, I think."

"Tarraine, I think we go to Earth, wait it out. Make him come to us."

Tarraine nodded.

"OK," decided Rita. "Put that movement plan together, but don't execute until we have all the scouting reports."

Tarraine bent to his console. Rita continued to watch the screens and the sensors. She could advance the clock now; the enemy was nowhere in sight, and it would take 8.2 hours for her scout to report at Mars.

But something held her back.

They were passing Jupiter now, starting their accel toward Mars. The big gas giant was to her relative right. She looked at the moons of Jupiter in the holo. They had passed Io; they were nearly to Ganymede. Because they had decelerated before entry into the Jupiter system to allow for adequate scouting, they were only just now building speed for the leg to Mars.

Something was bothering her.

Ganymede was passing beneath them relative to her position.

You couldn't hide a fleet behind a moon that small…

"Missile launch!" cried Naditta. "I have multiple missile launches from the surface of Ganymede! Twenty-four missiles coming right at us!"

"Countermeasures!" yelled Tarraine. "Evasive! Shredders!"

"Working," called Lirrassa. "We're targeted. They're on us!"

Tarraine was working madly at his console.

"He took missiles off his ships and put them on the surface," yelled Tarraine. "That son of a bitch launched them remotely!"

"Damn it all to hell," cursed Rita.

Her chair started to rock violently as the simulator imitated the high g-forces of a starship exceeding the compensator limits, trying to avoid the missiles.

And then it was too late. With a loud crash imitating a major hit on the ship, the lights went out. All the consoles and screens went dark. The flagship was down.

Rita sighed. Per prior agreement with Bekerose, if the flagship went down, the battle was over.

She had lost Round 1.

CHAPTER EIGHT

Merkkessa. **En Route to Sol System**

Rita had taken a large chance with the second simulation. Tarraine was not happy.

"Milady, this goes against all precepts of fleet ops. If you have guessed wrong, we are lost!" complained her aide.

"Understood," acknowledged Rita. "Thank you, Tarraine. I value your opinion, but I want to take this chance."

After losing Round 1 of the contest with Bekerose, Rita had spent several hours in the simulator alone, banging her head against the wall of tactical limitations.

There were just not that many ways to fight in space. You could hide behind a planet or a moon. Or the Sun. You could wait in open space, engines quiescent, hoping to ambush the enemy before they detected you.

Sure, you could do crazy things like put missiles on a moon to ambush the enemy as they went by - that had cost her the first round, but only because Bekerose got lucky and took down the flagship in the first volley. Realistically, she knew that if the flagship had survived, she might have won that sim.

But the rules were the rules, and there was no going back.

In Round 1, Bekerose had taken the Singheko part. Now it was her turn. She would be in-system first; Bekerose would have to enter the system blind to her disposition of forces.

After hours of experimentation in the sim, she had noted something.

The key to success was timing - if she had some way to know when and where Bekerose would enter the system, the number of ways she could ambush him went up exponentially.

But how could she know that?

He's an arrogant, impatient asshole, thought Rita. *That's how I can know it.*

She had thought about it for a long time, working in the sim through various configurations.

She had made a decision.

Bekerose would have a low opinion of her skills. After all, she had never commanded a fleet, never even been the captain of a ship before.

It wasn't certain he knew about the knowledge and memories of being a fighter pilot she inherited from Bonnie in the cloning process - she didn't know how much Garatella had told him. But even if he did, he would discount that experience.

He'll assume I'm stupid, thought Rita. *So, what would I do if I were stupid?*

I'd wait behind the sun. I'd make some assumption about where he'll enter the system, and I'd wait directly behind the sun from that position. Because that would give me the maximum amount of time to prepare for him, and there's no way he could sneak up on me.

He'll expect me to be behind the Sun waiting for him.

So, Rita had done something unorthodox. She had violated Rule Number One of battle. She split her fleet.

TF1 - Task Force One - consisted of the *Merkkessa*, the two cruisers and the four destroyers. She had set their initial position at 14 AU from Earth, above the ecliptic, at a forty-five-degree angle to the plane of the planets. A spot where there was nothing - no planets, no moons, not a damn thing.

And her fleet had been accelerating for a while now - they were already moving at more than 8,391 kps - more than 18 million miles per hour. They had completed their acceleration and their engines were off.

They were a silent arrow winging for Earth - from the middle of nowhere.

TF2 was the four corvettes. They were right up against

the Sun, in line with the three planets that were in near-conjunction right now - Jupiter, Saturn and Uranus. They were the bait for the trap.

Rita was certain Bekerose would assume she was hiding behind the Sun.

Because a stupid commander would assume Bekerose would come in on the ecliptic, in line with the three planets in conjunction, hoping to screen behind them.

Which meant a slightly less stupid commander would assume Bekerose would come in directly opposite the three planets in conjunction, to throw her off.

Which to Rita meant Bekerose would do neither of those things. He would come in from directly above the ecliptic, or directly below, and head straight for the Sun, disdaining any attempt to screen behind the planets. He would give away his position instantly because he didn't care. He would care only about charging directly at Rita, and he would believe she would be right up against the Sun, waiting for him.

Which was where the corvettes were, simulating her entire battle fleet. In Rita's hours of study of the tactical manuals, she had noted a little-used electronic warfare function that allowed ships to emulate the engine signatures of larger vessels.

And in a position that close to the Sun, a fleet couldn't turn off their engines and lie doggo. They had to keep adjusting their positions constantly, or the Sun would pull them off orbit.

So her four corvettes were sitting right up against the Sun, as close as they dared go, emulating the signals of the battlecruiser, the two cruisers and the destroyers, as well as their own. The fierce radiation of the Sun contributed to the deception; the signals coming off the corvettes were intermittent, noisy.

From her vantage point - now only 10 AU away as she raced toward Earth - it looked completely realistic.

The timing was the real issue. Even if she had guessed

correctly how Bekerose would enter the system, how could she know when it would occur?

His arrogance, thought Rita. *He'll waste no time, brook no delay. He wants to end this quickly. He can already taste the moment when he has full command of the fleet and can relegate me to my Flag Cabin for the rest of the mission. He's drooling over it.*

Rita was sure Bekerose would enter the system within a relative hour after his side of the simulation started, either directly above or directly below the ecliptic, as close to the Sun as possible. He would translate in and immediately boost hard for the Sun. He might send a couple of scouts ahead, but he would be pushing in right behind them, trying to minimize the time Rita would have to re-deploy her assets once she realized he knew where she was.

I hope I'm not over-thinking this. Maybe he's smarter than I think, or more cautious.

But I don't think so.

"Translation!" called Naditta. "14.35 AU, down 90 degrees. He's coming in from below, right as expected, milady."

Thank God, breathed Rita. *Thank the ever-loving God of us all.*

She heard a whoosh of breath come out of Tarraine beside her.

"Vector? ETA?" she asked.

"Umm ..." replied Naditta. "Direct vector for the Sun. Pushing hard. Given the light delay, I estimate ETA of ...47.5 hours."

"And our current ETA to Earth?"

Naditta turned and looked at Rita, a huge smile enveloping his face.

"49.5 hours, milady."

Rita grinned.

All I have to do is fox the bastard for an additional two hours, and his ass is mine.

"He's advanced the clock, milady. That means he's detected

TF2 at the Sun and doesn't want to waste any time."

"Very good, Naditta. What's the new position?"

"2 AU out from the Sun, milady. Still on track for an ETA as expected. No sign that he's detected us."

"OK, have the corvettes start their run for Earth, show him their panic, and accept the clock advance."

"Roger, milady."

On the holo, the simulator advanced the clock to show Bekerose just 2 AU out from the Sun. Rita's corvettes at the Sun turned to flee, headed directly for Earth. As she watched, Bekerose adjusted his vector to chase them down, giving him an intercept position near Earth.

Two hours later than his original ETA.

Tarraine looked over at her.

"Mum, ignore everything I said earlier."

Rita smiled at him.

"It's not over yet, Tarraine. As the corvettes move away from the Sun, their signal will clean up. He may figure out he's not chasing the entire fleet. There's a lot that can still go wrong."

Tarraine shook his head.

"I know, milady. But I think you've got him, either way."

"Milady, Captain Bekerose has advanced the clock to 5 minutes before intercept with the corvettes," called Naditta.

He's anxious to get it over with, thought Rita. *He wants the end game to start now. He's getting cocky.*

Rita studied the holo. That would put the corvettes just short of Earth, only a few million miles from the planet. She would be lagging the intercept by one minute.

That gives him one minute to figure out he's been foxed. I would rather he had no time. But I'll take what I can get.

"Accept the clock advance, Naditta."

"Roger, milady. Clock advanced. We are one minute from intercept."

Rita sat on the edge of her seat. Her muscles clenched from the tension.

Would he see it? The closer he got, the more likely he would detect the false signals from the corvettes. But there was a point where it wouldn't matter anymore. Once he was in the missile envelope of her fleet, it didn't matter what he did. She had him.

"He's gone to maximum decel, milady! 260g negative! He's figured it out!"

"Will he stay in the envelope?"

"Umm ... yes! He's gone the wrong way! If he had accelerated, he might have been able to get out of it, but now - he's toast, milady. He'll be right in the center of the envelope!"

That means he hasn't seen us yet, thought Rita. *He figured out the corvettes were broadcasting a false signal, but he still doesn't know where we are.*

Tarraine at his console started a countdown. It wasn't necessary - the AI would take care of the coordinated missile launches on their own - but it felt good to hear it. Everyone hung on his words as he counted.

"Five. Four. Three. Two. One. Launch!"

Rita felt the simulated *Merkkessa* shudder as twenty simulated missiles left twenty simulated tubes. In the holo, she saw the two cruisers and the four destroyers sending another forty missiles out.

All of them directed at Bekerose's flagship.

It was over in seconds. At their passing rate, her fleet flashed by Bekerose' fleet so quickly they were already 25,000 klicks beyond it by the time their missiles struck Bekerose.

It was a long three seconds of waiting. Rita stared at the holo like her life depended on it.

And Bekerose's flagship disappeared.

Mars. First Wing HQ

"Hey new guy," called a voice.

Jim lifted his head and looked at the woman approaching his mess table.

Tall, with gypsy dark eyes and black hair, she was muscular - an athlete of some kind - with a blinding smile that lit up the room. She was in civilian clothing and wearing a nametag on her shirt.

Jim cocked his head and looked at her.

"Are you talking to me, ma'am?"

"Yes, and don't call me ma'am, I'm not from the South like you, Major," she said, sitting down in front of him. "How's the chow today?"

Jim gazed at her. "Not bad, I guess."

He looked closer at her nametag.

"Caroline Bisset," he spoke as he read it. "AirBoeing Space."

"Yep. I'm the tech rep for the A-16 Longsword," she replied. "I understand you are the new Training Officer for SAG-15."

"That's me," said Jim. "What can I do for you?"

"Nothing at the moment. But I thought I should introduce myself. Anything you run across in Training that translates into a change order for the Longsword, bring it to me. I'll take care of validating it and transmitting it back to Toulouse."

"Ah," said Jim. "So, you're the gatekeeper of all things between us and the factory."

Caroline smiled.

"Yep."

"You don't sound French," said Jim. "You sound English."

"Yeah," said Caroline. "I grew up in both France and England. That helps when working with a multi-national force like this."

"Well, nice to meet you," said Jim. "I'll keep you in mind when I decide to change the paint scheme on the Longsword."

Caroline grinned hugely. "It comes in any color as long as it's black."

She rose to leave but paused.

"You interested in going out to see the Perseverance, Major?"

"What?"

"The Perseverance Rover. It landed at Jezero Crater in 2021, remember? I'm going to take a two-seater Longsword on a test flight this afternoon. If you want to go along, I'll even let you drive for half the mission."

Jim thought about it, but not for long.

One - he was a space exploration buff.

Two - he needed stick time in the Longsword.

Three - she was a beautiful woman - the kind you look at and your knees go weak and your heart jumps in your chest and your brain stops working.

"Sure, I'll go along. What time?"

"1400. That work for you?"

"It does," Jim smiled. "See you then."

At 1415 hours, Jim was dressed for flight, waiting by the airlock leading to the outside parking apron. He drummed his fingers on a nearby maintenance bookcase, fiddled with his helmet, and wondered if he had been stood up.

But just as he was about to call Caroline, she stepped out of the ready room, helmet in hand, and walked toward him.

God, even in a damn pressure suit, she takes my breath away.

Caroline came up to him and stopped, a half-smile on her face.

"Female prerogative to be late. Sorry," she said.

"No problem," Jim responded.

"Shall we?" Caroline pushed her helmet on and walked to the technicians standing by the entrance to the airlock.

One of them checked her helmet, stuck an oxygen hose into her suit and pressurized it, then removed the hose and did a final check on her suit. He tapped her on the shoulder, and she stepped into the open airlock door.

Jim followed, standing patiently as the techs did their work. When he was tapped on the shoulder, he followed Caroline into the airlock. The door closed behind him. He felt his pressure suit moving around him as the pressure dropped. In a minute, the outer door opened, and they stepped out.

"We won't need a cart, just follow me," said Caroline over

the comm.

"Roger," Jim acknowledged. Caroline led him to a two-seater TA-16 positioned just outside the huge double doors of the pressurized hangar. Two crew chiefs waited - Jim's own personal crew chief Sergeant Baines, and another one he didn't recognize. Two ladders placed beside the fighter gave access to the cockpit.

While Caroline climbed into the front seat of the Longsword, Jim climbed the back ladder to the rear seat. Settling himself in, he buckled in and let his crew chief connect him to the oxygen, electronics, and other systems of the fighter.

Sergeant Baines gave him a tap on the shoulder and Jim gave him a thumbs up. He heard the avionics come on and his comm beeped, letting him know it was ready.

"You ready back there, Nuke?" Caroline asked him.

"Nuke?"

"New Kid. Nuke."

"Oh. Yeah, ready."

With a loud whine, the cockpit closed around them. There was no clear canopy on the Longsword; space was not a place for thin plastic between a pilot and death.

Instead, once Jim was fully connected to the ship, he had a VR - virtual reality - display of his entire environment. No matter which way he turned his head, it was like there was no canopy on the ship at all.

A few minutes later, Jim was wondering if he had made a terrible mistake.

Caroline Bisset was flying the Longsword through the hills and rills of Mars like it was a fighter jet.

Jim had spent most of his life in aviation on Earth, but this was different. In the thin atmosphere, the Longsword could reach Mach 8 before the outer skin started overheating, and Caroline was flying every bit of it right now as she streaked toward Valles Marineris, the largest canyon in the Solar System

- larger than the Grand Canyon on Earth.

"Uh ... Caroline?" Jim finally broke in, as the canyon loomed directly in front of them, a giant gash in the ground that lay for hundreds of miles across the planet's surface.

If she goes down in that fucking canyon at this speed, we won't survive.

"Relax, Nuke," said Caroline. "You'll be fine."

With that, she pitched and went straight up, accelerating even more. The Longsword was in space in a few minutes. Jim breathed a sigh of relief. At least they were away from the terrain.

What the hell have I got myself into here? Is this woman nuts?

Still accelerating, in a few more minutes, Mar's largest moon Phobos loomed in front of them. Caroline spun the Longsword around expertly and started a hard decel, exceeding the compensators for a few seconds, slamming Jim back against the seat with a force of 6g as they came close to the moon. At closest approach, Caroline spun the craft again and accelerated hard, performing an Oberth slingshot around Phobos and heading back for Mars.

"How you doing back there, Nuke?" Jim heard over the comm.

"Oh, fine," said Jim. "Sorry, I nodded off there for a second."

He heard a laugh from the front.

"Yeah, I'm sure."

With another burst of deceleration that exceeded compensation by 3g, slamming Jim forward against his harness, she re-entered the atmosphere, plasma streaming off the front of the Longsword.

As the temperature on the outside of the Longsword reached a critical number and the overheat alarm went off, the Longsword finally decelerated enough to fall back below normal re-entry speed. After a few seconds, the overheat alarm stopped.

"Well, Nuke, I pronounce this bird ready for operations," he heard from up front. Jim saw the sidestick shake.

"Your bird."

"My bird," he said, taking the sidestick.

"Jezero is at your two o'clock."

"Roger."

Jim located Jezero Crater on his moving map and set a vector for it. He let the Longsword continue to decelerate until they were moving at a leisurely Mach 2 - upwards of 1,100 miles per hour in the thin Martian atmosphere.

Soon the walls of the crater were in front of them. Jim slowed, cleared the walls, and looked for the old rover they had come to see.

"Over to your right, about ten klicks," Caroline said over the comm.

"Got it."

Jim found the glint of light in the distance and maneuvered over to it, setting the Longsword down about fifty meters from the rover.

"Opening the cockpit," Caroline called.

"Roger."

With a whine, the cockpit opened, and Jim looked out on Mars.

The view was spectacular. Although the VR in the cockpit was almost indistinguishable from the real thing, there was always a little bit of loss from reality.

Now, seeing Mars - the real Mars, not down inside a roofed-over gully full of spacecraft and soldiers - Jim was in awe.

"It's incredible," he said.

"It is that," Caroline agreed. "I'm shutting down."

Jim heard the engine whine down and the avionics go off.

A stray thought crossed his brain.

They were well over 4,000 klicks from the base. If the batteries in the Longsword failed, such that they could no longer start the engine or comm back to base...

Don't think about that. We filed a flight plan. If they don't hear from us in another two hours, they'll come.

"Well, c'mon, Nuke. You wanted to see a dead rover,"

Caroline said over the helmet comm.

Jim worked his way out of the myriad connections to his suit and stood up, stepped out of the cockpit into the small hidden steps on the side of the ship, and started to climb down. It was not as easy as using one of the crew ladders, but it could be done. Halfway down, he came to the stub wing which normally held missiles. From there, he could slide off to the ground.

Caroline was already standing there waiting for him.

"Damn, you're fast," he said.

"I've done it a lot more than you have," she grinned at him through the helmet. "You'll get there. C'mon, let's go."

Then she turned and walked briskly off toward the rover.

Jim followed, having a little difficulty in the light Martian gravity, just 38 percent of Earth normal. It was like walking on a trampoline. But he adapted, slowly catching up to Caroline.

Finally, they came to the old rover, which had been gathering dust on Mars for so many years.

"Poor thing," said Caroline. "It looks so forlorn."

"Yes, it does."

"How long did it last, again?"

"Incredibly enough, even though every mechanical thing on it had long since quit working, it kept taking pictures right up until last December," said Jim. "More than 57 years after launch."

"What happened then?"

"Its third replacement RTG - its power source - finally gave out," said Jim. "It reached a point where the folks at JPL knew it had only a day or so left, and they didn't want to replace the RTG again, so they shut it down. It died a hero's death."

"What do you mean, a hero's death?"

"It confirmed the existence of microbial life on Mars. In the distant past, of course. All gone now. But it made folks realize we're not unique in the universe."

"Oh. Yeah, I guess that would change people's worldview."

Caroline leaned over and patted the rover's mast camera,

which was covered in red dust.

"Bye, Perseverance. See you later."

Turning back to Jim, she motioned toward the Longsword.

"Why don't you take the front cockpit and I'll take the back for this leg," Caroline said, smiling sweetly. "And you can scare the shit out of me for a change."

Merkkessa. **En Route to Sol System**

Today was the fifth and last sim session. Today it was winner take all.

Bekerose had won the third sim, besting Rita by destroying her entire fleet when she came into the Sol System. She found him right behind her at entry - a power play on his part, to show her he could turn the tables on her, predicting her system entry just as easily as she could. Within seconds after she translated into the system, his fleet behind her cut her to pieces.

Rita had won the fourth bout. Once again playing the part of the Singheko, she dispersed her ships in the asteroid belt and let Bekerose pass her by on his way in from Saturn. Then her entire fleet erupted out of hiding and chased him down, catching him before he could get to Mars. He turned and they slugged it out, but she had the advantage of speed in the first pass and decimated his fleet. After that it was just mopping up until only his flagship remained, while she still had her battlecruiser, two cruisers and one destroyer. She pounded him into simulated scrap metal and the computer declared her the winner.

Today was the decisive round. If Bekerose won this sim, Rita would be relegated back to her cabin, no longer an active player in this drama, just a passenger along for the ride.

Stepping outside her cabin with Gabriel, she found her new bodyguard Uriel on duty. Gabriel had gone through the Marine contingent on board and selected two additional bodyguards to protect her. Both were big for Nidarians, and both appeared to be cut from the same cloth as Gabriel and Raphael.

And in keeping with the tradition already established by Arteveld, Gabriel had given them the pronounceable names of Uriel and Sariel.

Four angels to watch over me, Rita thought bitterly. *Would that I did not need them.*

Now Gabriel walked ahead of her, and Uriel fell in behind her. She walked into the sim room stiffly - her chest wound was still healing and had become sore and tender. Tarraine was waiting for her.

"Lirrassa and Naditta are inside, ready to go," he smiled. "How do you feel?"

"Stiff. Sore. Pissed off," replied Rita.

"Good," smiled Tarraine. "You'll fight better."

Rita grunted and entered the fleet simulator, taking her seat in the captain's chair. She greeted Larissa and Naditta and waited while Tarraine got his console situated. When he was satisfied with it, he turned to her.

"Ready, milady."

Rita nodded grimly.

They had briefed on the strategy for the final battle.

There was none.

Rita had decided to take Bekerose head-on. One final duel to the death.

Today, I let Jim Carter take the lead in my head. Today the ex-Marine comes out in me. To hell with Bonnie's finesse and fighter pilot skills. To hell with my own unique self.

Today Jim Carter is in charge.

The sim started.

Bekerose played the part of the Singheko today.

And she was sure of his tactics this time.

He'll want a straight up duel to the death. No tricks, no deception. He'll be waiting for me just outside the orbit of Saturn, ready for a fight.

She could feel it in her bones.

Sure enough, as she translated into the system at the 14.35

AU point, there he was, right in front of her, just over 100 million miles away.

"Straight at him and kill the son of a bitch," she said, waving a finger at the holo.

They charged at Bekerose, and he charged at them. 50 million miles later, the two fleets entered engagement range.

The missiles started flying.

Rita had placed her ships in an unusual formation. The four corvettes led the way, sacrificial lambs for the slaughter. Today she didn't care about losses, only victory.

Right behind them, tucked up close, came the battlecruiser, with all four destroyers surrounding it as a screen.

And behind her battlecruiser came the two cruisers, one behind the other, almost like an afterthought.

Bekerose was in the standard formation dictated by Nidarian protocol. His flagship - the battlecruiser - was at the rear. Two destroyers screened it - standard practice, and predictable. In front of his flagship were his two cruisers, with two additional destroyers screening them.

And like Rita, Bekerose had no qualms about sacrificing his corvettes - all four of them were directly in front of his battlecruiser, cannon fodder to obstruct Rita's fleet as they came together.

As Rita had expected and predicted, Bekerose expended all his missiles at her battlecruiser. Every ship in his fleet fired every missile tube they had at the simulated *Merkkessa*. Sixty-eight missiles came at her battlecruiser from his fleet.

Rita's four corvettes and four destroyers fought well. Their point defense shredders took down fifty of the missiles. Only eighteen of the dangerous shipkillers got through.

The *Merkkessa's* own point defense shredders took care of ten of those.

But eight of the big missiles blew the *Merkkessa* out of the black.

Bekerose jumped from his seat in jubilation.

"Yes!" he crowed, watching in his holo as Rita's battlecruiser exploded in the sim, breaking into three large chunks, spinning in space. One of her engines detached from the g-forces, spitting fire and vapor as it tumbled away.

"We've won!" Bekerose yelled. He turned to his XO, Biddaresse, thumping him wildly on the arm. "We beat the bitch! Now we have full control of the fleet!"

"Uh... Captain," said his Tactical Officer.

Bekerose ignored him. He turned his face to the ceiling, lifting his arms in triumph to the heavens, dancing a jig in his happiness.

"Uh ... Captain. You need to look at this," called his Tactical Officer, much louder this time. Bekerose thought he heard a note of alarm in his voice.

"What?" he yelled, looking at the officer.

The Tactical Officer pointed to the holo.

"The computer hasn't terminated the sim, sir. I don't understand it, but the sim is still running."

"What?" Bekerose was dumbfounded. "What?" he said again.

Looking, he realized the sim was still active. Rita's fleet was now right in among them. Her destroyers were well behind him now, and her two cruisers just passing him.

And they fired every missile they had at his battlecruiser.

Bekerose suddenly got it.

She changed her flagship. One of the cruisers is her flagship. She sacrificed the battlecruiser!

Forty-eight shipkillers came at him from point-blank range.

"Point defense now!" Bekerose yelled, but he knew it was too late. He had no time to react. They were on him in seconds.

And the lights went out.

CHAPTER NINE

***Merkkessa.* En Route to Sol System**

In dealing with Bekerose, Rita had two choices.

She could humiliate him. She could crow in public, making it known she had bested him in the simulator, that she was now in complete charge of the fleet.

Or she could downplay it, make it just another day at the office.

Sitting in her briefing room, she made her decision. There was no point in humiliating him. She needed him.

A gentle tap came at the door. Bekerose.

"Come!" she called.

The door opened and Bekerose entered. He came in front of her and assumed a position of attention.

Rita smiled at him, waved him to a chair.

"Please sit, Captain Bekerose."

He sat stiffly, ill at ease. She knew his ego had taken a beating, being bested by a human female in front of his officers.

But it was something she had to do. She had to have full and complete control of the fleet.

Rita's steward Knowelk came out of the tiny galley with two cups of *nish*, placing one in front of each of them. He retired back to the galley, closing the door behind him.

Rita smiled inwardly. Knowelk probably knew every detail of her business. But he never spoke a word, to her or to anyone else, about anything except his duties.

Now Rita sipped her *nish*, waiting Bekerose out. Nidarian

emotions were remarkably like those of a human, she had learned. She waited patiently. This was a final test, and she had to win it.

After a long, excruciating silence, Bekerose finally spoke.

"Milady. My congratulations on your victory. And I assure you I will live up to the terms of our bargain," he said.

Rita gave him a big smile.

"I know you will, Bekerose. You are one of the most honorable people I've ever met. But thank you for saying that."

Bekerose nodded.

"Captain, let's be honest. I was incredibly lucky in the sims. If it had been four out of seven, I'd be sitting in my cabin now with nothing to do."

Bekerose managed a slight smile.

"Thank you for saying that, milady."

"Captain, you are certainly my better at handling the fleet. There is no doubt in my mind on that score. But my planet is on the line here. That is why I did this. I am responsible for the future of my people. Put yourself in my position. If you were responsible for the future of your people, would you not feel the same?"

Bekerose nodded again.

"I suspect I would, milady."

Rita leaned forward.

"Then help me, Captain Bekerose. Work with me. Support me. Give me the advice and counsel I need to succeed."

There was a long silence. Bekerose gazed at her.

For the first time on the entire voyage, Rita saw respect in his eyes.

"Milady, you have my word. I will be there for you," said Bekerose. "You need have no more doubts on that."

"Thank you, Captain Bekerose. That means a lot to me."

Rita stood up and reached her hand forward. Bekerose stood up as well, and they touched hands in the Nidarian fashion.

"We need to start our strategy meetings for entry into

the Sol system, Captain. Can we start over a nice dinner this evening?" Rita said.

Bekerose smiled.

"That would be ideal, milady. See you then," he said, and departed.

Rita sat at her desk quietly for a moment, drinking her *nish*.

It had been a long week. She had solved one problem. Now she had to start thinking about her other problems.

One - I must assume the worst at Sol, that the Singheko are already there waiting for me. I need to do final planning for that scenario.

Two - someone wants me dead.

"Gabriel," called Rita, knowing her AI would transmit the call to her chief bodyguard. Sure enough, in a few seconds the door to the Security Suite opened, and Gabriel stepped into her room.

"Milady?"

"Is there any progress on detecting the person or persons who want me dead?" she asked.

Gabriel shook his head sadly.

"No, milady. We haven't found anything at all. If there are more of them, they're keeping their heads down."

"There are more of them, Gabriel, trust me. OK, keep looking. Let's try to find them before we get to Sol."

"Yes, milady. We're doing our best."

Gabriel departed and the door closed behind him.

Now for the strategy at Earth, she thought. *I must assume the Singheko are there when I arrive. And I must assume they expect the Nidarians to send a fleet and thus they are ready for me.*

She intended to sort this all out with Bekerose, Tarraine and others in attendance. She certainly didn't intend to come up with a plan on her own.

But still, she wanted to start going over options in her head before the first strategy meeting tonight at dinner.

She could translate into the system so far out there was little chance of immediate detection - say, 50 to 60 AU outsystem. That would be the safe bet. Then she could slowly coast into the system, scouting as she went. Sooner or later the Singheko would detect her. Then a straight up battle would undoubtedly ensue.

But that approach might put her in a bad position tactically. If she translated in on the wrong side of the system, for example.

Not knowing where the Singheko were before she translated in was a problem.

So, she needed to sneak a scout into the system, one lone corvette, to map things out and report back to her.

That meant they would have to translate into three-space well before they got to Sol, far out in the black, and send a corvette forward to scout.

So far so good.

Mars. First Wing Headquarters

"Am I to understand, Lt. Vickers, that you accidentally spun out your Longsword while reaching for the missile arming switch?"

Jim voice was neither quiet nor loud, neither harsh nor sarcastic.

"Yes, sir," responded Lt. Vickers. "I'm sorry, sir."

"No apologizing," said Jim. "We acknowledge our mistakes, and then we fix them. So, what did you learn from this?"

"It's a tight cockpit, sir, and the sidestick is really sensitive. You have to be careful not to bump the stick when you reach for things."

"Did everybody hear that?" asked Jim, looking around the room.

A chorus of voices went up. "Yes, sir!"

"OK, I have only one more thing to go over."

Jim pointed with a laser pointer to the holo at the front of the room, which showed a mock-up of the Singheko starship *Jade*.

"In the battle with the *Corresse*, here ... and here ... are the points where the Nidarian missiles struck *Jade* and disabled her. We're still not hitting these areas accurately enough in our simulations. If you don't hit your targets, then expect the rear-facing missile tubes here ... and here ... to remove you from the universe."

"Everybody - trust me - the universe would not be nearly as much fun without you. So do a better job of hitting these target areas - or go update the beneficiaries on your wills."

Muttering around the room showed the young pilots got the message.

"OK, good debrief. Everybody hit the showers and see you tomorrow morning at 0700," said Jim, closing out the meeting.

The assembled young pilots filed out, talking and laughing, as Jim turned off the display and collected his things.

"Hi there, sailor," said a voice.

Jim looked up to see Caroline standing in the doorway of the Ready Room.

"Ah, just the woman I wanted to see," said Jim. "And I'm not a sailor."

"Oh, you will be someday," said Caroline. "It's just a matter of time until the Space Force recognizes the error of their ways and moves to a Space Navy org chart."

Jim smiled back at her.

"I need a change order on the sidestick on the Longsword. It's set too far to the right. We need to move it one half inch to the left."

"Yeah, I heard about that. They said that boy looked like a spinning dart. And no. We're not going to move the sidestick placement for the A-models. We're deep in the production run."

"That's fine," Jim said. "But let's get it in queue for the B-models, at least."

Caroline sniffed.

"OK, send me the specs, I'll forward them to Toulouse. Are you running tonight?"

"Of course," said Jim.

"Good. See you at six," said Caroline, and with a backhand wave, she was out the door and gone.

Jim finished collecting his materials and left, heading back to his quarters. As was his habit, he stopped at the Intel Shack on his way and checked in.

"Anything?" he asked the young Captain in charge of the Shack this evening.

"No, sir. No detections from the Kuiper belt inward."

"How about deep space?"

"No translations detected. We're clean."

"OK, thanks," said Jim, leaving.

A young sergeant turned to the Captain, curious.

"Sir, why does he stop by every evening and ask the same questions?"

The Captain turned to the sergeant and smiled sadly.

"His fiancée was Bonnie Page. She went with the Nidarians when they left. I think he keeps hoping she'll come back."

"Do you think she will?"

The Captain sat back down at his desk and shook his head.

"I don't know, Sergeant, but I doubt it. They say when she left, she gave him a note saying she wasn't coming back."

"That sucks."

The Captain gazed at the closed door.

"Yes, it does."

* * * * *

Changing into his jogging gear, Jim left his cabin and walked down two flights of stairs, then down a long hallway to the gym. He entered and saw Caroline already stretching at the running track, a balcony circling the room on the second level. He climbed the stairs and joined her.

After stretching, they began their run. The pounding of their feet was a gentle song for Jim's soul. They ran slowly for the first six minutes, giving Jim's knees time to warm up - a routine they had followed for six weeks now.

"Can I ask you something?" Caroline finally said as they ran along.

"Sure," Jim answered.

"Are you still carrying a torch for that Bonnie Page?"

Jim ran silently for a while.

"That's kind of a personal question," he finally said.

"I'm kind of a personal girl," Caroline responded.

After a bit, Jim spoke.

"No. I know she's not coming back to me."

"Good," said Caroline.

They ran in silence for another ten minutes. Then Caroline looked back over at him.

"What are you thinking about?"

"Your body," said Jim.

"Ooo," said Caroline. "That put a tingle in my jingle."

Jim grinned.

"And what would you do with my body if you had it?" she asked.

"I think we both know the answer to that," replied Jim.

Caroline looked back over at him again.

"Jim…" she began, then paused.

He looked at her.

"Let's not start anything if you're still hung up on her."

Jim put his head down, ran for a while. Finally, he spoke.

"I'm not. We're good to go."

Running alongside him, Caroline smiled.

Later - two miles later - they walked down the stairs together. Caroline grasped Jim's arm and paused on the stairs.

"Hit the showers, then meet me in the mess hall?"

"You got it," said Jim.

Entering the men's showers, Jim stripped and showered, dried off and dressed. He left the gym and went to the Officer's Mess. Caroline wasn't there yet, so he got his meal and found an empty table. She soon came in, got her tray, and joined him.

"One of these days I'm going to beat you to the mess hall,"

Caroline said.

"Not as long as you have hair and makeup," said Jim.

"True," admitted Caroline. "Maybe you should do more on yours," she laughed. She reached over and smoothed out Jim's hair.

An electric tingle went through Jim's body at her touch. It was all he could do not to jump in his seat.

Damn, I didn't realize how bad it was, he thought.

Caroline, oblivious, turned to her meal. She took a bite, then looked at Jim.

"I want to ask you something," she said.

Jim gazed at her.

"Can we stand against the Singheko?"

Jim shook his head.

"Nobody knows, Caroline. *Jade* was the only Singheko ship we've ever encountered. She was just a scout ship - the smallest ship they have, we think. And she pretty much kicked our ass, until the *Corresse* stepped in to help."

"Of course, we've learned a lot since then. We've managed to copy her missiles, for one thing. But who knows? For all we know, they'll come with a fleet of battleships. Or they may come with a small squadron of scout ships like *Jade*. We just have no way of knowing."

"But what do you think? Really, deep down?"

"I don't think we can stop them, Caroline. We have three squadrons of Longswords now. Forty-eight ships, with two spares. But I think the Singheko will come with a fleet. Just to clear away any resistance before they bring in their drop ships, or whatever they'll use to subdue the planet. So ... no, Caroline. I don't think we can stand against them for long."

Caroline looked down at her plate.

"So ... we'll go down fighting, but we'll go down. That's what you're saying."

"Caroline. I'll never give up. I'll go down fighting, and all the other pilots as well. We'll hope for help from the Nidarians until the very last. But we have to face reality. If the Singheko come with a fleet, and the Nidarians don't come to help ... we simply won't be able to stand against them."

Caroline sighed. "I've lost my appetite, I think." She looked up at Jim.

"Take me to your room, please?"

* * * * *

The artificial sunlight that marked Martian dawn started to lighten the fake window in Jim's cabin. He never turned it off as some did; he liked waking with the dawn, even if simulated.

Caroline stirred in his arms and he carefully disengaged from her, got up and left the bed. He moved to the bathroom, took care of business, then started coffee brewing in the pot. He pulled his uniform out of the locker and started to dress.

Caroline moved, grunted, threw an arm over the empty spot in the bed where Jim had been, and opened her eyes.

"My God, it's still night! Why are you up?"

Jim smiled at her.

"Sorry, I'm an early bird. Coffee?"

"God, yes."

Jim made her a cup and brought it to her. She sat up in bed and turned sideways, leaning against the wall. Her t-shirt was all she was wearing.

"Wanna try for Round 3 before you leave?" she asked him, a twinkle in her eye.

"No, I don't think I have Round 3 in me this morning," said Jim. "Catch me later."

"OK. I take it you're off to the simulators again?"

"Yeah. It's our best chance. I keep working up new ship designs for the Singheko. I throw them at my guys and see what happens."

"And what has happened so far?"

"We get our asses kicked most of the time," said Jim.

"Not good," said Caroline.

"Yeah, but not bad either. That's how we learn. We're

getting better every day. I can see a day when we can win as much as we lose."

Caroline leaned over and kissed him.

"Then go do your thing, Jim Carter. I'll see you tonight."

Jim grabbed his gear, blew a kiss to Caroline, and went out the door. He started up to his training area on the top floor when his comm pinged in his ear.

"Major Carter, report to Wing Command Center ASAP."

"On my way," Jim acknowledged. He turned and trotted back the other way, down the stairs and along the corridor to the Command Center, buried deep in the east end of the complex.

Entering, he found a buzz of activity. Lt. Fox was waiting for him and gestured him to follow.

At the far end of the room was the office reserved for Colonel Decker, the Wing Commander. Entering, Jim found Colonel Decker, his XO Dominic Couture, Group Commander Webster, and Intel Chief Frank Carpenter huddled over a display on the Colonel's desk.

Decker looked up at him.

"We've got company," he said. "Come look."

Jim walked around the desk and looked at the display. He read the sidebar notes and recognized it immediately - it was a remote sensor array out in the Kuiper Belt, 40 AU from the Sun, roughly on a line past Uranus. He had seen it before in the Intel Shack.

A dozen ships were evident on the display, all heading in toward Uranus.

Decker looked at Jim.

"Frank analyzes them as one big fucker - at least 180 meters, maybe 200 - two slightly smaller ones, in the 100-meter range - four in the 75-meter range, and the rest support ships of some kind."

Jim looked over at Frank Carpenter.

"Can you classify them at this range?"

"It's shaky, but I'd classify the big one as a battlecruiser, the two slightly smaller ones as cruisers, then four destroyers, maybe three corvettes and I think two supply ships."

Carpenter pointed to the sidebar of the display, where statistics on the movement of the distant fleet could be seen.

"They're moving slow. They may be trying to slip up on us. Or maybe they just want plenty of time to monitor our signals, figure out what's going on with us. Either way, unless that changes, it'll take them a bit over twelve days to get to Earth."

Colonel Decker moved to sit behind his desk and faced the assembled officers.

"But we're going to fight them long before they get to Earth," he said.

"In fact, we're going to fight them at Saturn. That will be …"

Colonel Decker looked at the display again.

"That will be 9.7 days from now. By then, I want to know everything about them, right down to how many hairs their mother's maiden aunt has on her chin."

Decker looked at Jim.

"Jim, that's where you come in. I need eyes on these bastards. I want you to take your Red Flight and go scout them. It's gonna be a bitch mission - day after day sitting on your ass in a fighter. But I've got to know what kind of ships they've got, what their armaments look like. Have a scouting plan to me in two hours, then get going. And Jim …"

Decker paused. Jim thought he was going to say something melodramatic.

Like, try not to get yourself killed.

But evidently Decker thought better of it.

"Good hunting," he finished.

Jim nodded and trotted out of the Command Center. As he went, he used his comm to call Flight Operations.

"Scramble Red Flight to the Ready Room, and stage all Red Flight fighters with live weapons and a full load out for max range intercept, this is not a drill. And Captain Rickard to the Ready Room, stat."

Even from this distance, Jim could hear the klaxon going off in the Ops Center, and the PA in the pilot barracks as his commands were executed. He trotted to the Ready Room and already had a solar system display up in the holotank by the time the first of Red Flight's pilots started to trickle in. His wingman, Captain Angel Flores, was the first to arrive.

"What's up, Major?" he asked.

"Big trouble, Angel," Jim said. "Hang loose a minute until everyone is here."

Jim sat on the edge of the desk and waited until the other two pilots of Red Flight came hustling in.

"Have a seat, guys," he said, pointing to the chairs. They sat. He looked out at them.

Red Flight was made up of himself, Angel, Hank "Spanky" Smith and Roberta "Bobber" Houseman.

Angel was his wingman, and a hot pilot. And knew it. He never let anybody else forget it, either.

Spanky was a good pilot, solid, dependable. Jim liked having him in his flight.

Bobber was green and inexperienced. Jim was worried about taking her on this mission. But he didn't have time to switch her out, and he knew it.

Let the chips fall, I guess.

Just then Captain Rickard, his squadron XO, came in and sat down, a question on his face.

I have to give it to them straight, he thought. *There's no sugar coating this one.*

"Boys and girls, we've got an incursion. About 40 AU out, coming in slow, taking their time. I'm not gonna lie to you guys, it's a big fleet. A big ass battlecruiser, two cruisers, four destroyers and five other ships. Intel thinks they'll maintain their current vector and try to sneak up on us. That would give them an ETA to Saturn of 9.7 days, ETA to Earth of 12.5 days."

The look on the faces of his pilots said everything. Their faces went white. Jim saw Bobber's hands start to shake.

"We've been tasked to scout them. We'll take Red Flight out

and try to nip in behind them if we can. Captain Rickard, you'll be Squadron Commander in my absence."

Rickard objected immediately.

"Jim, I should be taking the scout. You need to stay here and command the squadron," he protested.

Jim smiled.

"Decker told me to go, Chuck. Sorry."

Before Rickard could protest again, Jim turned to the display and used a laser pointer to outline the position of the enemy on the display.

"There they are, guys. 40 AU out."

He turned back to the pilots.

"We've got Saturn and Uranus in conjunction right now, and Jupiter not far out of alignment with those two. So my thought is they're trying to screen behind Uranus, then come in on a Uranus - Saturn line so they can screen behind Saturn as well. Then nip over to Jupiter and use that as their final screen. If we hadn't seeded the outer system with sensors already, they could've gotten all the way to Jupiter, maybe Mars, before we picked them up. It's a good plan on their part. The only flaw in it is that we've managed to reverse-engineer *Jade*'s system engines and so we've got a Space Force in place. I doubt they know that. So that's our edge."

Jim turned back to the four pilots.

"Any thoughts so far?"

Angel pointed at the display.

"Take a vector out past Jupiter to the middle of nowhere, then curve back in, slingshot around Uranus and come up behind them," he said.

Jim paused to see if anyone else had a better thought, but the others in the room just nodded, so he continued.

"Good. That was my thought as well. But you guys realize what that means. We'll be sitting on our butts in a Longsword for something like a week - or more."

A groan went up in the room like someone had died.

"I know. But we've no choice. Our best chance to get intel

without getting shot to pieces is to nip out past Uranus as quietly as possible, get in behind them, and come up on them slowly. We'll work that plan and try to catch up to them shortly after they pass Uranus - roughly 6.7 days from now."

"We'll load up and go immediately - they could change their acceleration or vector at any time, so I want to be as close to them as possible if they do. I want us to launch in ... two hours."

Jim looked around the room somewhat grimly.

"That gives you time to make sure your will is up to date, write one last letter to your loved ones, pack your pogey bait into your flight bag, and haul your ass to the flight line."

Jim looked at the clock on the display, which read 0728.

"We launch at 0930 hours. I'll have a detail flight plan ready by then. Don't be late. Dismissed."

The three pilots got up and left the room. Rickard came up to Jim and faced him.

"Tough mission, Jim," he said. "You ought to let me take it."

"Here's the rest of it, Chuck. Decker says we'll fight them at Saturn. So I'll be coming up from behind, and you'll be coming in from the front or side. Make sure you drill the guys continuously between now and then on those scenarios. And for God's sake, don't shoot us blue on blue when the balloon goes up!"

"We won't. I'll make sure of it. Be careful, Jim."

Rickard extended a hand and Jim took it. They shook solemnly, then parted. Jim headed back to his cabin.

Entering, he found Caroline just dressed, still buckling her belt. She looked at him in surprise.

"What's going on?" she asked.

"Incursion," said Jim. "They're coming. Caroline..."

Jim went to her and put his arms on her biceps, held her.

"You need to get out of here. Take the next shuttle to Earth, and don't let the door hit you in the ass. Understand?"

Caroline face twitched.

"You mean..."

"I mean you are in the second most dangerous place in the solar system right now, and you need to get the hell out of here."

Caroline reached out for him, embraced him. She kissed him gently.

"Just when we were getting something going," she whispered sadly.

"Don't I know it," said Jim. "Sucks."

They held each other for a space. Finally Jim pulled back and looked at her face.

"I launch in two hours," he said. "I'm sorry, but I need to get my flight bag and go."

"And I guess I know where the most dangerous place in the solar system is gonna be, huh?"

Jim grinned.

"Yep. Wherever I am."

Caroline grabbed him again and pulled him in for one more kiss. Then she let him go and stood back.

Jim grabbed his flight bag, opened a desk drawer, took out a paper bag and stuffed it into the flight bag, then turned to look at her.

"Pogey bait," he said, pointing to the bag.

"What?" Caroline looked puzzled.

"Candy bars," Jim laughed. "I'm about to be stuck in a fighter for a week or so. I'll be wanting those."

Caroline went to him one more time.

"Please, please be safe," she said. "Just try to come back to me."

Jim kissed her.

"I will do my utmost."

And he was out the door and gone.

* * * * *

Entering the pre-flight locker area, Jim shed his uniform. As he worked to put on his pressure suit, the rest of Red Flight came in and began dressing for the mission.

Jim was first out of the locker area and walked to one of the four crew airlocks leading outside to the parking apron. He crammed his helmet on and sealed it, walked to the technician near the door. The technician pressurized his suit, performed a safety check, and tapped him on the shoulder.

Jim entered the airlock. He had to wait for thirty seconds while another dozen personnel came in, including Angel and Bobber. Then the door closed, and the lock cycled.

When the outer door opened, he went to the nearest in a long row of electric carts lined up outside. The driver hit the pedal and they ran to Jim's bird, the last Longsword in line at the far end of the apron.

Jim's crew chief was waiting. He assisted Jim up the ladder.

Getting himself secured in the cockpit, Jim let the crew chief hook him up. When he was done, he tapped Jim on the shoulder and gave him a thumbs up.

Jim returned the gesture, closed the canopy, powered up the engines and systems, and got clearance from the tower to depart. As soon as he was cleared, he carefully levitated the ship off the landing skids and moved it out of the covered area. Once outside, he headed for space, retracting the skids as he accelerated up and out of the Martian atmosphere.

Jim didn't wait for the rest of his squadron - they would form up on the way. Instead, he headed for Jupiter. His navigation display had already locked in the course sent to his fighter by the Intel Shack.

6.77 days to intercept, he saw in the display. Nothing in space was fast. Even with a max accel of 255g, it took forever to get anywhere.

First, 3.6 hours of accel and a 10.8-hour coast on a vector to nowhere. This would bring them to a point well off the line of the inbound Singheko fleet - to mask them from any sensors that might be pointed toward Earth.

This would be followed by 4 hours of tangential burn to curve the trajectory into a long parabola toward Uranus.

And then an agonizing 3-day coast to Uranus, and another 3-day coast to catch up to the enemy. Jim shuddered just thinking about it.

Six long days coasting through the black. Nothing to do but listen to the electronic fans whir; and the sound of the life support system pushing air through the ducts.

Of course, given the immensity of the solar system, it had been obvious in the planning of the Longsword that some missions would be incredibly long.

So thanks to some farsighted design nerd in Toulouse, a pilot could loosen his straps, lay the back of his seat down, and slide backwards into a tiny bunk nestled behind the cockpit.

It certainly wasn't fancy, but it was a bed. And there were two small compartments there containing food, a cold box with drinks - and even a tiny coffeemaker.

And Jim's pogey bait, which he had transferred from his flight bag.

Now, in his VR display, Jim saw Angel come up and slot into travel formation beside him, ten miles to his right. The other members of his flight slowly caught up to them.

When all were formed up, Jim gave a command via his computer, and all four ships went to max accel simultaneously.

In the far distance on his enhanced VR view, a tiny point of light marked Uranus, 3.8 days away.

If they timed things correctly - and Jim certainly intended to do that - then by the time they arrived at Uranus, the enemy would be just a bit past the planet, on their way to Saturn. When Red Flight performed their slingshot around Uranus, the planet would screen them from the Singheko.

And this would put Jim and Red Flight behind the enemy. They would not even have to accel again after the Uranus slingshot - they would just coast up behind the enemy and slowly pass by, there in the black between Uranus and Saturn.

And hopefully live long enough to report back to Wing.

It was going to be one hell of a long mission.

CHAPTER TEN

Merkkessa. **En Route to Sol System**

Sitting in her briefing room, Rita looked at her staff. Bekerose sat on her left, Tarraine on her right. Down the length of the table sat the remainder of her senior officers. Surrounding the physical table, the various Captains of her fleet were present via hologram.

They had just completed a long two-hour meeting. Everyone was tired.

"All, thank you for your hard work and excellent results. The plan is finalized, and we are ready to enter the Sol System in a bit over three days. Good job by all concerned."

"Now. We have three days to drill for this entry. I want the crews rested, but not too rested," she smiled. "Let's ensure we drill hard every day until system entry. Any questions?"

"No, milady," came a chorus of voices. Rita stood.

"Then dismissed, and happy hunting," she said, closing the meeting.

Now, as the assembled staff departed and the holos of her distant captains clicked off, Rita thought about the next most troubling thing on her mind.

"Gabriel," she called. Almost instantly, the door to the Security Office opened and Gabriel stood before her.

"Yes, milady."

"Any progress on the conspirators?"

"No, milady, I am sorry to say, they are lying low. I anticipate they will come out of the woodwork as we translate into the Sol System, as we will be most distracted at that time.

So we are making every preparation for that."

"Thank you, Gabriel."

With a bow, Gabriel departed back to the Security Office.

Rita went to the nursery and fed Imogen, then sat rocking her for a while until she slept. She placed Imogen into her crib and watched her for a few minutes.

She was feeling guilty now - bringing a baby on a warship. But she was never going to leave her behind, either.

It was what it was.

Retiring to her bedroom, Rita readied herself for bed. Then she lay down with a tablet and read for a while. But her mind wasn't in it. After a bit she put the tablet away, turned out the light, and lay in the darkness.

She was thinking about Jim again. It had been happening a lot lately.

Maybe as I get closer to him, I feel his presence more.

But it wasn't exactly his presence she was feeling. She closed her eyes and could feel his body on hers, that last night they had together. She could remember everything about it. The feel of his skin, the sound of his voice. The love she felt for him as they made a baby.

But was it real? Or was it Bonnie's memories and feelings that she had felt then?

How could she tell?

The hell of it was, she couldn't. She could never know how much of what she felt was her own, and how much came from the memories of Bonnie and Jim implanted into her when she was cloned by *Jade*.

I wonder where you are, Jimmy Boy. What are you doing now? Will I ever see you again?

Sol System. 19.18 AU from the Sun

As Red Flight approached Uranus, Jim's AI woke him. He had slept for the fourth time during the long, 3.8-day mission. Now, as he slid from the tiny bunk back into the cockpit, his AI gave him a status report.

<Good morning, Gunner. There are no messages. You are thirty minutes from initiation of the slingshot maneuver at Uranus. All systems are nominal. All pilots report their systems nominal. Your health status indicates a deficiency of Vitamin C and D as well as a lack of hydration. Please address these issues>

Jim sighed, pulled the seat back into place, and tightened his belts. He reconnected the tubes and wires that married him to the Longsword. Then he scratched his itchy growth of beard.

Wing had already informed him that the Singheko were keeping to their initial approach as expected. The enemy was still on plan for arrival at Saturn just under 6 days from now - if they maintained present vector.

And there the battle would begin. They were planning to catch the Singheko in a crossfire. As Jim's flight came in from the rear, the rest of Jim's squadron under Captain Rickard would come in from the side. Then the other squadrons of the Wing would attack from the far side of Titan, Saturn's largest moon.

With a bit of luck, the Singheko would be confused by the various elements attacking from three different directions and would make mistakes.

And any mistake would be welcome, when forty-eight small fighters went up against a battlecruiser fleet.

Decker at Wing HQ had sent all civilians back to Earth - Jim was thankful for that. He had gotten a short message from Caroline, just a short "I'm home in London, be safe." Of course he couldn't reply; except for highly directed tightbeam laser blips to a relay satellite out past Jupiter, he was under total comm blackout for long distance communication.

He could still talk to his flight, though. The Longsword used a separate low power tightbeam laser to have comms in flight. Now Jim checked in with his pilots.

"Lead to Red Flight, everybody check in."

"Two is good."

"Three is good."

"Four is good."

Jim smiled. There was something about a mission. Despite the discomfort, the monotony, the danger - there was something about the professionalism and camaraderie that let you know you were doing what you were made to do.

"Angel, how ya doin'?" he asked.

"I'm out of pogey bait," complained Angel. "Does anyone have any they can lend me?"

Jim laughed. There was no way any of them had any candy bars left at this point.

"Sure," said Spanky. "Just slide over here and open your canopy, and I'll pitch something in for you."

Bobber chimed in.

"It's gonna be brown. But maybe not chocolate."

Jim groaned. He knew they were getting punchy when the outhouse jokes started.

Although the Longsword had provision to dispose of bodily wastes, that didn't mean it smelled nice. Especially after 3.8 days in a space the size of an automobile seat.

Jim was glad the slingshot around Uranus was coming up. At least that was something to take their mind off the monotony.

And after that, the enemy would be in front of them. By his flight computer, they would intercept the Singheko fleet in another 3 days.

Then the fun begins, thought Jim.

"Bobber, you doin' OK?" Jim asked.

"Peachy-keen," replied Bobber.

All three of them laughed at that. "Peachy-keen" was the mission code word that indicated a pilot had been taken prisoner and was being tortured.

"Nice, Bobber," said Jim. "We'll send a rescue party! How about you, Spanky? All OK?"

"This is such fun," replied Spanky. "Can we do it again next week?"

"Absolutely," Jim responded. "I'll call the Singheko fleet and ask them if we can all go back to our starting positions and do the whole thing over again."

There was a long silence at that point. Jim realized what he had done. By mentioning the Singheko, he had reminded them they would enter combat soon.

They might not be alive next week. Or tomorrow. Or six hours from now.

Jim tried to change the mood back.

"Bobber. How'd you get your handle?" he asked.

There was another long silence. Finally, Angel came back.

"Uh, Major? I don't think you want to know."

Jim thought about it.

"Oh, one of those, huh?" he asked.

"Yep," said Spanky. "Same way I got mine."

Jim laughed silently.

Some people got handles because of the way they flew. Some people because they were excellent shots - like Jim, with his handle of 'Gunner'. Some handles were just a variation on the person's name because it fit - like Angel.

But God forbid if the squadron ever managed to find out something unique or embarrassing about a person's sex life. Jim suspected he now knew where Bobber had got her handle - and he didn't want to ask any more questions about it.

Changing the subject, he checked his display and noted the time to the slingshot around Uranus.

"15 minutes to go, ladies. Everybody do final checks and make sure your computer sync is tight."

"Two."

"Three."

"Four."

Looking out front, Jim saw Uranus coming up. The big blue planet filled the sky in front of them. The thin, white ring that surrounded the planet glistened in the faint sunlight that made it out this far. It was a beautiful sight, and it made Jim think.

Why does war seem to take place in such beautiful

environments? Or is it just that there are beautiful environments everywhere, and sometimes war must come to them?

Or is it because creatures want to live in beautiful environments, even if they must take them by force...

Deciding he had just enough time to hydrate and take his vitamins, Jim pulled out a water tube, took a good long drink, and swallowed his pills. He decided to wait until after the maneuver to crunch down a meal bar.

He put the water tube away, cleaned up his cockpit, and tightened his straps one last time.

Then he was starting around Uranus in a long slingshot, the rest of his flight tucked in tight beside him. As they reached closest approach to Uranus, their engines fired hard, changing their outbound vector. It didn't take long, and soon they were out the other side, their path curved back toward the inner solar system.

Now was the test. This new vector would take them high above the Singheko fleet and across their rear, just clipping across their path. No more engine burns would occur until they had completed their recon pass. They would be cold and dark now for three days.

If the Singheko were looking behind them, and if their instruments were sensitive enough, they might pick up the flight as they approached. And if they did, Jim was quite sure they'd send back a couple of destroyers to police up their rear.

Soon Red Flight would know if they would live or die.

***Corresse.* En Route to Sol System**

"Arteveld, do you have time for a brief chat?" Bonnie spoke to her AI.

<I do, Colonel. I'll meet you in the galley>

Bonnie stood from her desk, brushed off her uniform, checked her hair in the mirror and left the room. Walking to the galley, she arrived before Arteveld and grabbed a quick cup of *nish*, then sat down and waited for the Captain.

Arteveld came in, poured a cup of *nish* from the coffee bar, and sat across from her.

"How can I help, Colonel?" he asked.

"Arteveld. You spent five years in the Sol System, collecting every conceivable record from Earth. Don't you have any idea where the *Dragon* might be?"

"I do not, milady. But I was acting as Captain, not as a researcher. It may be that my XO, Dallitta, would know more. She is cross-trained as a scientist and historian and was in charge of all data collection."

"Could we speak to her now?"

"Absolutely." Arteveld closed his eyes as some did when communicating over their implant. Then they drank their *nish* quietly for a minute until Dallitta swept into the room, her bright happy smile lighting up the place instantly.

"Good afternoon, Captain and Colonel. How can I help you?"

"Dallitta. You were in charge of the data collection effort during the five-year mission on Earth?"

"I was," smiled Dallitta.

Bonnie frowned. "And do you have any idea of the possible location of the *Dragon*?"

"Well...no, not really ..."

Dallitta hesitated. There was something in her manner that showed she was reluctant to speak. At last, she replied.

"We never found anything definite," she responded. "Nothing we could point to with credible evidence."

"But?" asked Bonnie, trying to draw her out.

Dallitta looked at Arteveld, somewhat reluctant to proceed. Arteveld gave her a nod of encouragement.

"There was one legend ... from Tibet ... which had some strange correlations ..."

Dallitta's voice died out. It was obvious to Bonnie that she was uncomfortable.

"Dallitta. At this point, we're grasping at straws. I'll take anything. What is the legend?"

"It's probably a hoax, cooked up to get publicity or sell books," said Dallitta.

"What?" asked Bonnie and Arteveld simultaneously.

"It's called the Dropa Stones. All reputable sources, both past and present, call it a hoax. One author even wrote a book about it and later admitted his entire book was a hoax, just a way of making money on the legend. So it has no credibility at all."

"So why bring it up?" asked Bonnie.

"Because..." Dallitta was hesitant. "Because the description of the stones is similar to the description of certain recording devices used in that era of the Golden Empire," she finished hurriedly. "Even though it's probably just a coincidence."

Bonnie leaned forward.

"Dallitta. You'd have not brought it up if you didn't think there was something there. Tell us about it."

"Well," Dallitta started, obviously still ill at ease. "Shortly before the collapse of the Golden Empire, there were magnetic recording devices that used a tiny circular disk, less than an inch in diameter. They had relatively low capacity for the time - something like 1 terabyte per disk - but they were useful in small devices that had limited space, for example in spacesuits, handheld radios, things like that."

"Go on."

"Well, the thing that caught my eye, they used a somewhat unique pattern for the tracks. They used a double spiral, starting from the center, which spiraled out to the edge. I'm not sure why they selected that pattern, but they did."

"Strange," muttered Bonnie, looking at Arteveld. "Doesn't seem very efficient."

"Exactly," said Dallitta. "Not efficient at all. It seems to be based on some historical precedent that we're unaware of, but that's what they did. There are several of these ancient disks in museums on Nidaria."

Arteveld was now getting impatient.

"And?"

Dallitta grew a bit more animated.

"The Dropa Stones were supposedly large stones that had a similar pattern. Two grooves excised into them starting from the center, spiraling out to the edge. They were large stones, up to one foot in diameter. There was a legend associated with them."

Bonnie nodded, gestured at Dallitta to continue.

"What was the legend?"

"That a spacecraft crashed in the Bayan Har Mountains of Tibet and that the ship contained small people who were hunted down and killed by the locals, except for a few survivors."

Arteveld let out a long, slow breath. He was clearly shocked by such a story. Perhaps his worst nightmare during the long five years he had been assigned to monitor Earth - crashing into the planet and being hunted down as a monster.

Dallitta continued.

"No evidence was ever found that any of this was true. The stones, if they ever existed, disappeared sometime after 1938. Most likely, it was a complete hoax. But it is the only tiny clue we've ever found that made any sense at all, given the facts."

"What did Garatella think about it?"

Dallitta hesitated.

"He discounted it. He thought it was grasping at straws. He said, if the *Dragon* had landed on Earth, they would have had enough weaponry to defend themselves indefinitely and would never have been overcome by the weak tribes of that era. Plus, he was convinced the *Dragon* was lost in the Sol System somewhere and would never have landed on Earth. He said the Captain of the *Dragon* would have found a safe place to repair the ship in the Sol System, but would have never landed on Earth once he realized it was populated by ..."

"By savages," Bonnie finished for her, seeing her embarrassment.

"Yes. So he completely discounted it."

"But you don't," said Bonnie pointedly.

"Well. It's just a tiny possibility, I admit," said Dallitta. "But I keep thinking about them. The crew of the *Dragon*, I mean. What if they worked to repair the ship for months, or even years, thinking that rescue could come at any time? But rescue never comes - because the Empire has collapsed. They don't know that - but they know something is wrong because help never arrives. Sooner or later, they run out of resources. They decided to go down to the planet as a last resort."

"Hmm ..." mused Bonnie. "And if I were going down to a strange planet under those conditions, I would want two things. I would want to be reasonably close to a civilized society, so I could obtain the resources I need to repair my ship."

"Yes," nodded Dallitta eagerly. "Exactly. And China was one of the most civilized and scientifically advanced cultures of that era."

"But I wouldn't want to be so close to them that a powerful culture could immediately capture my ship and crew and take my technology - or make us into specimens."

Bonnie looked at Dallitta, and they both said it at the same time.

"Tibet."

"Right," Dallitta nodded eagerly. "Not so close to China that I would immediately arouse the curiosity of the powerful culture there, but close enough that I could trade for the things I needed to repair my ship."

"So carrying this crazy hypothesis a bit further, what do you think happened to them?" asked Bonnie.

"The mythology says almost all of them were killed by the native tribes, who thought they were some kind of monsters. A few survived to make the stones."

"But no chance of finding the stones now?" asked Bonnie.

"No. If they ever existed - which is not certain - they have all disappeared by now. If they were real, they were probably destroyed during the Cultural Revolution in China in the 1960's and 1970's."

"Still," Bonnie thought out loud. "If there is even a tiny shred of truth in this…"

She looked over at Arteveld.

"What do you think, Captain?"

Arteveld shrugged. "We've got nothing. We have to start somewhere."

Bonnie slapped the table with both hands.

"Fantastic! We have a plan! Tibet here we come!"

CHAPTER ELEVEN

Sol System. 9.64 AU from the Sun

Red Flight was coming across the rear of the Singheko fleet, high above their line of flight, and crossing at an angle.

It had been a long, hard three days of coasting since Uranus.

Jim dared to hope they were undetected. There had been no response from the enemy. No change in the vectors of the ships, no ripple of radar or lidar back in their direction.

"Lord, please let them be as arrogant and stupid as they seem," prayed Jim.

Red Flight couldn't use active radar or lidar themselves - it would give them away. But they could see the Singheko clearly now on passive sensors.

And it was just as bad as Intel Officer Frank Carpenter had estimated back on Mars.

The battlecruiser was huge. Jim's sensors estimated it at 200 meters. It bristled with weapons - eight missile tubes in the rear, and by his best estimate, twelve in the front. There were four pulse cannon on top and four more on bottom - a total of eight of the devastating weapons.

Jim had seen *Jade* use two of those at Dutch Harbor. He knew the power they had.

Finally, there appeared to be a half dozen anti-fighter defenses - point defense shredders - on the top of the ship, and another half dozen on the bottom.

A hard nut to crack. This is gonna be hell.

The battlecruiser was screened by two cruisers. These

were 125 meters long and carried half the armament of the battlecruiser - six missile tubes in front, four behind - and two pulse cannon top and bottom.

Four destroyers were arrayed in a protective screen around the capital ships. Jim's sensors showed the destroyers had four missile tubes front and back and eight turrets of point defense shredders top and bottom. Clearly the destroyers were focused on defense, not offense.

The remaining five ships consisted of three corvettes with two missile tubes front and back, guarding two large, unarmed transports - supply ships or troopships.

Jim had a barely controllable itch to send missiles into those two big fat transports - but he resisted. He knew a better opportunity would come soon enough.

When they got to Saturn.

His passive sensor scans finished their work and Jim sent the results via tightbeam laser to the relay buoy near Jupiter.

"Red Lead is scan complete, transmitted," he sent over tightbeam to the other ships of Red Flight.

"Two is scan complete, transmitted."

"Three is scan complete, transmitted."

"Four is scan complete, transmitted."

Jim smiled. Their main mission was a success now. Wing would have all the data needed to fine-tune the attack at Saturn.

Now all Jim's flight had to do was sit tight, hope they weren't detected, and angle off past the Singheko fleet into the black. When they were far enough away, they'd turn back and start coming up behind them again.

They'd catch up to them and come into missile range at Saturn.

And then the brown stuff will be liberally spread on the mechanical cooling device, smiled Jim grimly.

It would be another 3 days before the battle started. Another long, hard, grinding 3 days.

He had a lot of time to reflect now. He tried not to - but he kept thinking about Bonnie and Rita.

Where are you, girls? What happened to you? What are you doing out there? We're about to get our asses kicked by these fat bastards and you're nowhere in sight.

When will I see you again?

Corresse. En Route to Sol System

Dallitta and Bonnie sat in the galley, planning their mission to Tibet. A large holo hovered over the table, taking up almost the entire galley space, showing the globe of Earth, with Tibet facing them.

"Right here are the Bayan Har Mountains," Dallitta pointed out. "It's rugged territory. Not much there."

"That's good for us," countered Bonnie. "Gives us at least some chance of slipping in and out without a hassle from the Chinese."

"I wouldn't be too sure about that," said Dallitta. "They run a pretty tight ship."

Bonnie sighed.

"Well, we'll just have to do the best we can. Now tell me about this cave that was supposedly found with these mysterious stones in it."

"Ah. Well, actually, nobody knows where the cave is. The legend is that a man named Chi Pu Tei found a cave in 1938 in the Bayan Har mountains, on the border between China and Tibet. The cave contained the strange stones I mentioned. Then around 1958 supposedly, a Chinese scholar named Tsum Um Nui studied the stones and declared he could see microscopic writing in the two spiral grooves that came out from the center. He was ridiculed and soon disappeared, along with the stones. They've not been seen since, at least not by the public."

"Um. That doesn't help much."

Dallitta smiled.

"We have much better sensing equipment than the people

of the past. If there is a cave around there, we can find it."

"Yes," agreed Bonnie. "But in order to find it, we have to be in orbit over it, right?"

Dallitta nodded.

"And if the Singheko are already there, that could be a big problem. Not to mention the Chinese shooting missiles at us if they detect us."

Dallitta's smile disappeared.

"Yes, I see."

Bonnie continued. "So we will need to come up with a plan for finding this cave in the face of those challenges."

"I think ... I think I can come up with something," Dallitta mused out loud.

"Please do, Dallitta."

"I will work on it," the XO responded. She stood up and left.

Bonnie adjusted the holo to zoom in on the Bayan Har mountains.

Somewhere in there, she thought. *Somewhere in there might be the wreck of the Dragon. Or at least a clue.*

But getting to it is the problem.

Sol System. Saturn

"That is one big-ass planet," Angel said over tightbeam.

"Yep," agreed Spanky.

Jim was silent. To one side of their flight path, Saturn loomed, a huge, colorful interruption of the black. The rings made it appear even larger; a storm bloomed magnificent in the gas giant's atmosphere, leaving its mark on an otherwise pristine surface. On the bottom of the planet, a ring of light in Jim's enhanced VR image encircled the south pole - an aurora.

So much beauty. And soon so much death, he thought. *It doesn't seem fair.*

The Singheko fleet was just nipping past the big gas giant, barely missing the rings - trying to use it as a screen to hide their entry into the solar system.

Red Flight was well above the Singheko fleet's vector, closing on them slowly. The enemy still had not reacted. Jim was finding it hard to believe any military force could be so ignorant of a potential enemy in their rear.

But, on the other hand, until ten months ago, Earth had zero capability for space warfare.

So, if the Singheko were working from outdated intel, maybe they simply didn't realize there could be any danger to their fleet.

We'll bring them up to date, he thought. *They've screwed with the wrong species this time.*

Jim could see the moon Titan, on the far side of Saturn from his position. And he knew lurking behind Titan were the rest of the Longswords, thirty-two more fighters, counting down for the attack.

And off to his relative left, the other twelve ships of Black Eagle Squadron under Captain Rickard were poised.

Jim checked his chrono. Ten minutes to go.

Jim had learned from countless battles one important thing - to check, re-check and then check again.

"Red Flight, confirm targeting."

"Red Two, I put two missiles into the big honker on the right side." Angel replied.

"Red Three, I put two missiles into the big honker on the left side," responded Spanky.

"Red Four, I put two more missiles into the big honker on the left," said Bobber.

"Roger that," acknowledged Jim. "Everybody stay frosty."

His chrono beeped.

Five minutes to go.

"Red Flight, arm weapons and check in," he called over tightbeam.

"Two armed."

"Three armed."

"Four armed."

They were in tactical combat spread now, twenty miles

133

apart. They could only see each other because of their VR. At that range, the coal black coatings and anti-radar wedges of the Longsword provided no visual feedback, and little radar cross-section. They were as nearly invisible as it was possible to be.

Above and left of him in the VR, Rickard's three flights stood out like a sore thumb - the twelve friendly fighters like blue diamonds in the sky, blazing brightly in his virtual reality due to their IFF transponders.

Against his will, a picture of Rita came into his mind.

How confusing it had been. Knowing he was in love with Bonnie, but thinking Bonnie was dead. He and Rita needing someone, anyone, just a body to hold tight. Then finding out Bonnie was alive. And Rita was pregnant.

And both of them leaving him to try and save Earth.

It was Bonnie, in the beginning. Then it was Rita. Now who do I love? Neither of them, after all this time? Both of them?

Does it matter?

Jim heard a beep from his onboard computer. His display showed a message from Rickard.

Have you on scope with solid lock, don't shoot me and I won't shoot you.

Jim grinned. He responded.

You take all the fun out of it!

One minute.

The soft whine of electronics and the whisper of the life support system faded away in his mind. Jim's whole awareness was focused on the job he had to do. He saw Rickard's three flights off to his left fire their first volley of missiles, then immediately boost to max accel and head for the battlecruiser.

He saw the other squadrons of First Wing come boiling out from behind Titan, accelerating at 261g toward the Singheko. The pilots in those ships would be experiencing 6g against their bodies as they exceeded the ability of the compensators to offset the extra accel above standard.

Then his AI started his own countdown. An orange light

started flashing. It turned red, the AI asking for permission to launch missiles.

Jim punched the button on his sidestick.

The Longsword gave a lurch as two of the big missiles fired off the side of the ship. The missiles accelerated so quickly they were out of sight in seconds.

And all hell broke loose.

CHAPTER TWELVE

Sol System - Saturn

Per plan, Rickard and his three flights in Black Eagle Squadron fired four missiles each at the battlecruiser, roughly ten seconds before Jim Carter's Red Flight fired.

Instantly accelerating at 261g, Black Eagle Squadron headed directly for the battlecruiser, to get in knife-fight close with the huge warship. At 6g over compensation, they were pressed back into their seats so hard it was tough to breathe. Grunting with the effort, they aimed directly for the rear of the big capital ship.

There was nothing else they could do. Attempting to conduct a long-range battle of attrition with the behemoth would only ensure their destruction, with little chance of hurting the battlecruiser. They were too few and too lightly armed for such a slugfest.

But if they could get in close…if they could get right up to the damn thing, prevent the screening ships from firing on them for fear of hitting the battlecruiser…then maybe they had a chance of scoring some real damage.

Before they died.

Rickard was a realist. He knew there was no survival from this battle. All they could hope for was to sting the Singheko hard enough to give them second thoughts, buy some time for Earth. Maybe make them turn back, decide to fight another day.

Maybe.

At their accel, it didn't take long. The battlecruiser got

bigger and bigger in Rickard's VR, and then they were there.

Firing their missiles, they targeted the pulse cannons of the battlecruiser. It was those weapons they were most concerned about.

Based on Jim Carter's reconnaissance, Wing Headquarters had formed a battle plan on the theory that the battlecruiser - and the other ships - would have a limited supply of missiles. So once they fired their onboard missile supply, they would have to reload from the supply ships.

And if Jim Carter could take out the supply ships, there would be no reloads. Once each Singheko ship had exhausted their onboard missile supply, they would have only the pulse cannon left.

So Rickard's assigned objective was to ignore the missiles and take out the pulse cannon. It was a calculated risk - a decision to let the Singheko fire all the missiles they wanted - just concentrate on the pulse cannon. Ignore the short-term problem and focus on the long-term problem.

Suddenly the point defense weapons of the battlecruiser came online. The space around Rickard's squadron filled with flak.

Now they were forced to bob and weave, trying to race past the battlecruiser while not being ripped to shreds.

With glee, Rickard saw one of his missiles hit home on a pulse cannon, tearing the emplacement completely off the battlecruiser. He yelled with delight as another of his squadron got a similar hit, knocking a big hole in the enemy directly under a cannon emplacement, causing it to tilt and fall into the crater in the hull.

Then he started taking hits from the point defense that was pouring at them like rain. His ship rattled and shook as he desperately jinked, jerking on the sidestick, trying to find someplace to be where the shrapnel wasn't.

Rickard saw two of his squadron disappear in silent explosions as they failed to avoid the flak. Then another one.

God help us all.

It was his last thought.

* * * * *

In front of Jim, the supply ship on the right disappeared in a huge explosion that looked like a nuclear weapon going off. It was so bright the VR automatically darkened the image. One second the big honker was there - next minute, it was just gone.

"Yes!" Jim yelled, pumping his fist.

Then the four missiles from Spanky and Bobber hit the one on the left. Four big holes appeared in the enemy ship. Two of them belched out fire, fed from atmosphere inside the ship. They rapidly puffed out and disappeared, leaving soot marks on the side. The ship swerved to one side, and started a slow spin, clearly no longer in control.

"Spanky and Bobber, give them two more each, let's see if we can take him out completely."

Immediately Jim saw four more missiles come off the rails from Spanky and Bobber on his left. They ran true to the target. Spanky's two missiles made more big holes in the side of the ship, but aside from the holes there was no obvious damage.

Then Bobber's two missiles impacted into the engines of the supply ship. There was a large puff of vapor, then a tremendous explosion tore off one of the engines, leaving it hanging crazily from the severely damaged rear of the ship.

"Yes!" Jim said again, pumping his fist for the second time.

"Incoming!" yelled Angel.

Jim glanced at the display and saw a dozen enemy missiles headed toward them from the destroyers and corvettes.

"Break into them!" he yelled. All four of them accelerated to 260g, directly at the incoming missiles. The excess g forces slammed Jim back into his seat, but he grunted it out. It was life or death.

Jim had briefed his pilots in advance; although space warfare was totally different from the air warfare he had spent fifteen years learning, there were certain principles that held true. You couldn't run away from missiles. They were too fast. You had a choice of trying to fool them or trying to break into them so quickly they couldn't turn fast enough to follow you. Or both.

In this case, Jim had briefed his flight to go directly at the missiles at max accel, jinking at the last second to confuse them.

Based on the designs they had copied from *Jade* it was believed the enemy's missiles would use a combination of radar and lidar to track. So as they approached the missiles, they launched radar and lidar chaff. And just in case there was an infrared component, they launched flares.

At the last instant, Jim jinked and spun to the right - there was a tiny hole between the two missiles closest to him, and he went right into it. Both missiles turned hard, trying to follow him, but they couldn't make the turn.

And then he was through, and coming up on the next line of ships, the corvettes. He had briefed his flight to ignore them, get past them as quickly as possible, and take on the cruisers. As they went by the corvettes, a wall of flak and shrapnel came at them, but they were still at long range. Jim heard some shrapnel rattle off the side of the Longsword, then he was in range of the cruisers.

He fired four missiles at their pulse cannon as he went by, then vectored off to the right toward Saturn, letting the gravity of the big planet help pull him away from the enemy.

Finally, he thought he was out of range of the point defense systems.

"Red Flight, check in," he called.

"Red Two is good," called Angel.

There was a silence that lasted a little too long.

Then:

"Red Four is good," called Bobber.

Got one missing.

"Red Three, check in," called Jim.

Another long silence.

"Red Three, check in," called Jim.

No answer.

"Did anyone see what happened to Spanky?"

"Red Two, I didn't see anything."

"One minute he was right beside me, the next minute he was gone," called Bobber. Jim could hear the shakiness in her voice.

"OK, Bobber, you are now wingman to Angel. I'm solo. Back at them for another pass."

"Two."

"Four."

"Take the near cruiser. Focus on the pulse cannon. Here we go."

Jim turned and selected his target, punched the throttles. The Longsword began an initial acceleration at 255g. As soon as Jim was certain of his vector, he punched it up to 261g - six over compensation. The g-force slammed him back into his seat, trying to push his chest into his backbone. He grunted out the breaths, barely hanging on to consciousness.

I'm too old for this shit.

Then, as the enemy cruiser began to come into range:

I'm gonna kill that son of a bitch.

Flak started exploding all around him as he came into range of the cruiser. The red *Ready* light on the AI came on and he pushed the *Authorize* button on the side stick, allowing the AI to fire when it decided it was at optimal range and position. A second later, he felt the missiles depart their tracks on the side of the Longsword, the fighter giving a slight shudder as they left.

Pulling hard away from the cruiser, Jim tried to escape the flak that was coming at him from every direction. There was no time to think, no time to plan, it was just twist, turn and run. The Longsword was now lurching as it was impacted by indirect hits. Then a much closer explosion rolled the fighter, and he almost lost control, but somehow brought it back to an escape vector.

Then there was a loud crash. The engine quit cold. He was thrown forward hard into the straps, then back again as the compensator stuttered and quit with the engine. Everything in the cockpit went dark. All the displays, all the nav gear, the computer, everything.

Then another loud crash and Jim was knocked unconscious.

Merkkessa. Outer Kuiper Belt

Rita's fleet translated down into three-space 50 AU from Sol, in the outer edges of the Kuiper Belt. Rita was on the bridge, sitting quietly in her chair. All had been planned; Captain Bekerose was in charge.

"Dispatch the *Wesker*," he called.

"Corvette *Wesker* dispatched," responded Lt. Tinnippi at Comm.

Bekerose turned to Rita.

"Now we wait," he said.

Rita nodded. "Thank you, Captain Bekerose. I'll be in my briefing room."

She rose and stepped down from the Flag Bridge, walking to the hatch in the back corner of the bridge that led to her day cabin. Raphael followed quietly behind her. Gabriel's team were on high alert - they were convinced the next attempt on her life would happen now, as they were entering the Sol System, and so they were staying close to her.

Entering the day cabin, she went down the circular stairs to her briefing room and looked around at her domain in thought.

It had been a long mission. Six months to get to Earth. Everyone on the ship had frayed nerves, most of all herself.

Any action would be welcome. She never thought she would feel that way, but she did. She wondered if that was Jim Carter rising to the fore in her consciousness.

Jimmy Boy is certainly a man of action, she thought. *Maybe he's taking over my brain.* Rita smiled at the thought and sat at her desk while Raphael took his place outside her door. As much as she trusted Raphael and the rest of her bodyguards to keep her safe from the unknown assassins, that had become the least of her concerns right now.

Where are the Singheko? Will they be at Earth already?

She was certain they would be. She assumed they had not gone to Garatella to notify him of their intention to claim Earth unless they already had a fleet on the way to back up their claim.

But she would soon know. That was the reason she had dispatched the scout.

The corvette *Wesker* would up-translate back into six-space. It would travel to a point directly over Saturn, but 30 AU above the ecliptic. There it would return to three-space for a look-see.

It would take the *Wesker* less than a half hour to reach that spot; but given the light-speed delay from its scouting position, it would take 5.9 hours for the first data to start coming back via tightbeam laser.

Rita and Bekerose assumed the Singheko would have their own scout presence in the system. But the vastness of space precluded scouting every possible approach to Sol. While it was possible a Singheko scout might be stationed close to the *Wesker*'s scouting location, it was so unlikely as to be a safe bet for an initial look at the system.

With a sigh, Rita scratched her head.

I need a good long workout to get rid of some of this tension. I'll go to the gym while I'm waiting.

Rising, she headed for her bedroom to get her workout clothes.

"Jimmy Boy, I'm headed to the gym for a workout," she called. Her AI would automatically notify her bodyguards, Tarraine and Bekerose of her plans. In her bedroom, she grabbed her gym bag and went out through the other door to the nursery. Fallassa was there, reading, while Imogen slept.

"How is she?" asked Rita.

Fallassa smiled. "She is sleeping quietly, Admiral. You have plenty of time to work out before the next feeding."

"Good," Rita said. "I'll be back in a couple of hours."

Leaving the suite, Rita headed downship toward the gym. Raphael automatically went ahead of her, while Uriel fell in behind guarding their rear. They reached the gym in a few minutes, and Rita went into the female locker room to change.

Convergent evolution, she thought, smiling. *Nidarians have two sexes, and they roughly correspond to male and female. That makes it somewhat easier. Thank God they didn't have three sexes - choosing a locker room would have been a bit harder!*

Coming back into the gym proper, Uriel was waiting for her, also dressed to work out. When she went to the gym, one of her bodyguards worked out with her. She was never sure if that was to facilitate protecting her or just for their own benefit. Either way, she preferred it to working out alone.

Rita smiled at him and they got started, stretching for a bit. Then they started on weights. She finished five sets of upper body weights, then rested for a while, wiping the sweat from her face with a soft cloth. Then she did five sets of lower body and leg weights. Then she ran for an hour in the corridor outside the gym, which had been made into a small circular track with a padded floor for that purpose. Uriel ran with her, keeping pace a few strides behind her. Although most Nidarians were only about five feet tall, Uriel was a monster by Nidarian standards - her height - and had no trouble keeping up with her.

After an hour, they quit and hit the showers. Rita took a good long one. There was no way to know what was coming, but it could be a week-long battle. Best to ensure she was clean at the beginning.

Finished with her shower, she toweled off, dressed, and brushed her hair down. She had thought so many times about cutting it short; but it had grown long and curly by this time, black as night, and she loved it. When she was cloned, she had only short fuzz on her head, almost bald. It had taken forever for her hair to grow out. She hated to cut it now, even though it was a pain to take care of.

Finally done, she packed up her gym bag and headed out of the locker room, expecting to meet Raphael and Uriel outside waiting for her.

They weren't there.

Rita opened her mouth to yell into the men's locker room, thinking they were in there still; but something - some sixth sense - stopped her.

She froze, listening. There was no sound.

It was not right. Neither Raphael nor Uriel would ever leave her alone outside of the locker room.

Slowly, she faded back into the women's locker room, peeking around the corner.

Something clunked in the men's locker room. Someone was in there; but who?

Who knew where she was? Only Bekerose, Tarraine, Fallassa, her bodyguards. No one else should even know she was here.

The sound of footsteps came from the men's locker, and around the corner came a figure.

Fallassa. She was holding a weapon, which Rita realized was a traditional Nidarian weapon, a rotary crossbow. They were deadly, firing six short bolts with great efficiency. And quiet. That's why she hadn't heard anything from the men's locker room. With an automatic cocking mechanism, they could fire almost as fast as a pulse pistol.

Rita pulled back, wondering if she had been seen.

CHAPTER THIRTEEN

Merkkessa. Outer Kuiper Belt

"I know you're in there, Rita. You can come out or I can come in. Which do you want?"

Rita looked around the corner of the women's locker room. Fallassa was walking toward her, the rotary crossbow held up and aimed straight at her. Behind Fallassa, another figure came out of the men's locker, also holding a rotary crossbow.

Her personal steward, Knowelk.

<Gabriel. In the gym. I need help>

She heard a laugh from Fallassa.

"Trying to call for help? It won't work. I've got a blocker on you."

Stepping out, Rita faced them. Fallassa pointed to a device on her belt which was blinking red.

"Nobody is coming to help you, human bitch. I've got all your comms blocked."

"You, Fallassa? You of all people?"

Fallassa sneered. "Yes. Me of all people. And it gives me great pleasure to finally end you, human bitch."

"But … why?" asked Rita. "Why do this, Fallassa? What do you have to gain?"

"The end of Garatella, you stupid donkey. He's a traitor to our ancient Empire. Giving a barbarian bitch command of a fleet! It's an insult to every loyal Nidarian!"

"And of course the Singheko will make you wealthy, I suspect. Right?" asked Rita.

Fallassa sneered. "Of course. But that's a secondary

consideration."

"Of course," agreed Rita. "Money means nothing to you."

"Shut up and kill her," growled Knowelk. "Someone will come."

"No," snapped Fallassa. "I've got Fadderria and Jillattee guarding the door. They put up a cleaning sign. Nobody will come in."

Out of the corner of her eye, Rita saw movement at the entrance of the men's locker room.

A bloody hand slowly came into view on the floor, moved forward, stopped.

I must distract them, she thought. *I have to buy time.*

"Will you spare Imogen, please?" she asked.

Another bloody hand came into view. The first hand moved forward another few inches and stopped, then the second moved forward again.

"Forget it," snarled Fallassa. "I've taken care of that baby bitch for six months. She's going straight out the airlock as soon as I leave here, you stupid cow!"

With another pull, Raphael's head came into view at the entrance of the men's locker. His hands left a trail of blood on the floor as he pulled himself forward another three inches. Wearily, he laid his head on the floor, looking at the scene. Rita realized he was badly injured, maybe dying. Raphael took in the scene for a second. Then he reached out and pulled again, dragging himself another six inches out of the locker room. His right hand went back and disappeared.

I have to buy more time.

"I'll pay you well to let her live, Fallassa," said Rita.

She saw Raphael's right hand slowly come back into view. It held his pulse pistol. Slowly he aimed it at Knowelk, who was closer to him and slightly behind Fallassa. He looked at Rita and gave a slight nod.

Then he fired, the crack of the pulse pistol deafening in the gym. Fallassa involuntarily jerked and turned to look as Knowelk fell dead, a smoking hole in his back.

Rita was half-deaf from the pulse pistol discharge as she dove and rolled directly at Fallassa. She felt a crossbow bolt go through the edge of her clothing, tearing at it, but missing flesh. Then she hit the floor hard, knocking the breath out of her as she crashed into Fallassa's legs, bringing her down. As Fallassa fell to one side, the crossbow clattered to the floor between them.

Both grabbed for it at the same time. Rita got her hand on the arched bow, while Fallassa had the pistol grip handle.

Grunting, they fought over the weapon for a second. Rita was still partly stunned from her impact with the floor. With a hard wrench, Fallassa jerked the bow out of her hand. But the effort caused Fallassa to fall over backwards.

Rita rolled toward the body of Knowelk a few meters away, grabbing for the other rotary crossbow lying beside his body. She heard the twang of Fallassa's rotary. A bolt went past her head by inches and embedded deep into Knowelk's body.

Then Rita had her hand on Knowelk's crossbow and rolled again, bringing the bow around to face Fallassa.

Another bolt from Fallassa's weapon came at her, hitting where she had been an instant before, glancing off the floor and flying past her cheek, drawing blood as it zipped by her face.

Then Rita was shooting. She fired the rotary as fast as she could, pulling the trigger over and over. Six bolts left the rotary in the space of three seconds, until it clicked and clicked and clicked and she realized she could stop pulling the trigger.

Fallassa stood in astonishment six meters from where Rita knelt on the floor. Her eyes were wide in disbelief. She looked down at her chest, where three of the bolts protruded, buried up to their feathers.

"You human bitch," were her last words. Her eyes rolled back, and she collapsed into a heap on the floor.

A noise outside reminded Rita this was not over. Fallassa had said there were two more. The loud crack of Raphael's pulse pistol would bring them running.

Rita dove for Raphael, sliding to a stop beside him on the floor, and pulled the pulse pistol out of his nerveless hand. She didn't know if he was unconscious or dead, but he was out. Scrambling, she grabbed his ankles and pulled him back to get him out of sight of the front entrance. Then she went forward, leaned around the corner, and looked.

Two Nidarian crewmen entered the gym, both carrying pulse pistols. Rita slowly slid her own pistol around the corner and fired. She missed her target, and both of the crewman dove for cover behind a desk. The crack of the pistol left her ears ringing, half-deaf again.

Return fire started coming at her, the pulses punching holes in the wall and door jamb around her as she pulled back into cover. The two kept up a steady fire, preventing her from looking around the corner again. She knew they were advancing on her, leapfrogging one at a time to keep up a covering fire while they worked their way toward her.

But there was little she could do. Rita realized they were probably ex-military. They knew their business.

Rita stuck her pistol out and fired blindly. She pulled the trigger as fast as possible, at least a dozen times, and the pistol beeped loudly, letting her know it was overheating. She pulled it back.

There was a lull in the shooting. She thought about peeking out around the corner to see, but then decided that was exactly what they were hoping for. She guessed they were set up in good sniping positions, and as soon as she poked her head out, they'd have her.

So she waited, pistol ready in case one of them came around the corner at her.

Suddenly there was a flurry of loud cracks from outside. Now Rita did peer around the corner. She saw the two enemy gunmen turned away from her, firing at the gym entrance, as a flurry of shots came back at them. One of them fell, and Rita quickly fired at the other one. She hit him square in the back, and he fell also. Gabriel peeked his head around the front hatch of the gym, and Rita yelled out to him.

"I think they're both down but be careful!"

She saw Gabriel nod. Rita pulled herself forward a bit more to get a better view.

There was no movement from the enemy.

Sol System - Saturn

Jim came back to the universe with a slow kind of awareness. There was no pain, and no thought. He just became aware that he was still in the universe.

Still breathing, he thought.

Still in the Longsword.

Instinctively, Jim glanced at the cockpit pressure gauge in the instrument panel. He knew it was mechanical and didn't depend on the electronics for an accurate reading.

It read zero. The cockpit had lost pressure.

I need to see if the pressure suit is holed...

Carefully, he lifted his arm to look at the gauge on the left wrist of his pressure suit. It read normal.

The suit's OK. Now to see how long I've got...

He turned his head to glance at the suit's external oxygen feed indicator on the side of the cockpit, which was currently connected to his suit, feeding him air.

Thirty-six hours...

He looked back at the instrument panel. It was completely dark. Not a light anywhere.

Reaching for a switch, Jim flipped the emergency battery pack on to see if he could at least bring up communications.

Nothing. Not a blip of a light anywhere.

He toggled the switch back and forth several times to see if it would change anything.

It didn't.

OK. I've got no power for comms. No power for Nav. No power for the VR to see where I am. But it seems like nobody is shooting at me right now. That's a good thing.

Jim thought for a moment. His most immediate problem was to find out where he was, and what the ship was doing. For all he knew, he could be falling directly toward Saturn, with only minutes to live.

It would be nice to know that. I think...

There was an emergency unlock lever for the canopy. Since he had already lost pressure in the cockpit itself, it didn't matter if he opened the canopy or not.

Reaching for the emergency lever, he lifted the safety cover. With a hard pull, he broke the safety wire that held it down to prevent accidental activation. The lever clicked into the upright position.

With a slight vibration, he felt the canopy unlatch. He reached up to push it away from him. The canopy was heavy - it was a thick cover with electronic visual arrays and instruments mounted all over the inside - but he managed to push it up several inches.

All he could see were stars. It wasn't open quite far enough to see around him.

Unstrapping his lap and shoulder belts, Jim was able to lean forward and partially stand up, using his back and helmet to push the canopy open a bit more.

Returning to his seat, he re-attached the straps and looked out at the universe.

He was a long way from Saturn, pointed away from it. It was impossible to tell his actual path without instruments, though. He could be on a decaying orbit that would come back and intercept the big gas giant in hours.

Or days. But that won't matter to me, because after thirty-six hours I'll be dead.

He watched Titan, the largest moon, for a good ten minutes. Finally he decided he was indeed moving away.

Good. If I have escape velocity, then at least I won't be crashing into that big son of a bitch anytime soon. They can come pick up my body and treat me to a decent burial someday.

Merkkessa. **Outer Kuiper Belt**

After the battle in the gym, it took nearly two hours to get everyone settled down and back to work.

First Gabriel took charge and firmly ushered Rita out of the gym back to her quarters, while Rita repeatedly asked about Imogen.

Bekerose met them as they came into Rita's quarters, rushed to Imogen's room, and quickly reported back that Imogen was fine, sleeping quietly in her crib.

Rita breathed a huge sigh of relief and finally let Gabriel sit her down on the edge of her bed. Then Flo rushed in, making a huge fuss, putting antibiotic on the cut on her cheek where the arrow clipped her, and in general driving her crazy.

Gabriel departed to check on Raphael, but Rita already knew the results. She had performed a quick check of them before departing the gym. Uriel was dead, and Raphael just barely alive.

It hurt. She had grown close to the big Nidarians of her bodyguard over the months, but most of all to Gabriel and Raphael.

Gabriel and Raphael, along with Tarraine and Flo, had become her family. And Bekerose, too, she realized slowly. He had become important to her, too, as he melded into a calm, supportive Flag Captain that she could rely on in tough times.

Please God, please don't let Raphael die.

Rita knew people died in war. It was part of the price to be paid for defending your homeland.

But not like this, thought Rita. *Not like this, with four arrows stuck in your gut.*

Finally, she grew tired of the fussing and stood up. She looked at Bekerose, who was standing nearby.

"Captain Bekerose, I believe we have some scouting reports coming in soon?"

"Yes, milady, if all is well with the *Wesker*, we should hear something in about an hour."

"Very well," Rita replied. She looked around the room.

"Everybody out, please. I thank you for your concern and your support, but give me an hour with Imogen before the scouting reports come in. Please."

Flo fussed about it, but gave in, and headed for the door. Bekerose, amused by Flo's antics, winked at Rita and followed. Tarraine was the last, and as he departed, he turned back to her.

"Thank you for not dying, milady," he said. "We need you."

What a strange feeling. That's the first time anyone on this ship has ever said anything like that.

Moving to Imogen's room, she sat in the rocker, watching her sleep.

My baby, my baby, she thought. *We're headed for the place where your father lives. I hope you get to meet him.*

After feeding Imogen, Rita put her down for a nap and called Flo to watch her. Then she went to the bridge. Bekerose rose from his chair and gave a slight bow as she came in.

How times have changed, thought Rita.

She stepped to her station on the Flag Deck. Tarraine and Lirrassa were already there.

"Anything yet?" she asked, sitting in her chair between them.

"No, milady," responded Tarraine. "But any minute now."

"Very good, Captain."

Rita sat and waited. It didn't take long. Within five minutes, she heard the Comm Officer.

"Receiving data, Captain!" he called to Bekerose.

Rita glanced at Tarraine. He smiled at her; but she could see his own nervousness under the surface.

This was a make-or-break moment - either the system would be clear, and they could enter unopposed; or the Singheko would already be there, and it would take a battle to enter the system and protect Earth.

If Earth could be protected at all.

The holo came to life, showing the disposition of everything in the system.

There was the Singheko fleet, in orbit around Earth.

It was going to be a fight.

CHAPTER FOURTEEN

***Merkkessa*. Outer Kuiper Belt**

The comm officer spoke again, troubled.

"Captain, there's evidence of a recent battle near Saturn. Much debris in the black, and at least one abandoned ship showing hot spots."

Rita sat up straighter. She punched in keys on her console and brought up her own holo. Zooming in, she saw what the scout corvette had sent from its position high above the solar system.

Definitely battle debris, she decided. *One large ship, pieces of another. Junk everywhere.*

Some of the junk looked like it might have been fighters at one time.

So they managed to recover some of Jade's technology. They put together some kind of defense. Not enough, but something. Good on them...

"Tarraine. How long ago do you think that battle occurred?"

"Um...just a guess, milady, but taking the lightspeed delay into account, and with one ship still showing hot spots, I think no more than 24 hours."

"Right. Send another corvette in to the closest translation point and have them boost hard for the battle area, look for survivors. Inform them we'll relocate to the high overhead point with the *Wesker* and to join us there after the scout. And tell them to keep us well informed!"

"Aye, milady." Tarraine issued the orders via his console to the next corvette in the scouting order, the *Kaimina*. A few minutes later, Rita saw the *Kaimina* disappear from local space in the holo.

"OK, let's go join the *Wesker*."

Tarraine nodded and passed the order on. Rita watched her holo as the fleet set a course for the *Wesker*. With the typical slight shudder, she felt the *Merkkessa* translate back into six-space for the transition.

"Tarraine. Let's assemble everyone in the briefing room for a conference, please."

Rita strode to the briefing room, sitting at the head of the table. Tarraine, Lirrassa, Bekerose and Biddaresse came in shortly. The holos of the remainder of her fleet leadership came up in short order. When everyone was seated and the holos were stabilized, Rita began.

"Everyone, you've seen the holo from the *Wesker*. The Singheko are in orbit around Earth. I don't think they've been there long because the battle debris at Saturn is still glowing hot in some cases. So we estimate about 24 hours since the battle. That means they have only just now arrived at Earth, probably within the last few hours."

"My intention is to attack them immediately, before they have a chance to get organized or cause significant damage to the planet, and certainly before they know we are here."

Rita gave a wry smile.

"I'm sure all of you have taken the time to review the sims of the recent fleet exercises between Captain Bekerose and myself."

There were a couple of suppressed snickers, which both Rita and Bekerose were careful to ignore. Rita and Bekerose had promoted a rumor that the sims between them were just for practice. Of course nobody believed it. And of course, every officer in the fleet had reviewed all five of the sims.

"We'll use the same basic strategy that I used in the second of those sims. We'll call this the "Silent Arrow" plan for ease of discussion. We'll boost hard to near 10% light, shut down our engines and coast in on them, hitting them before they realize they are under attack. After the attack, we'll not slow down, but keep going, just in case something goes wrong and we don't damage them sufficiently to gain a significant force advantage. Once we assess the results of the attack, we'll choose one of two options."

Rita nodded at Tarraine, who took up the thread of the briefing.

"Option One - if our initial attack doesn't do sufficient damage to the Singheko fleet to obtain a leveraging force advantage, we'll boost to the mass limit, translate, and rendezvous at a designated point in the black. From there, we'll plan our second attack."

"Option Two - if we determine we've accomplished our mission to significantly damage their fleet and have a strong force advantage, we decel and return to mop them up."

"Any questions so far?"

"What about survivors, if a ship goes down?" asked Lirrassa.

Rita shook her head grimly.

"There's too much at stake right now. No stopping for survivors until we know more about the results of our attack. Let me say that a different way, to be perfectly clear. No ship will stop for survivors unless they clear it with me first and I give definite, formal permission. Is that clear enough?"

Heads nodded, although expressions were grim. But Bekerose jumped in, his expression troubled.

"Milady, what if the flagship goes down?"

Rita smiled. "Good question, thank you Captain Bekerose."

She gazed across the assembled officers.

"If the flagship goes down, the order of command is clear, and everyone here should know it. Captain Teollutt of the cruiser *Daeddam* is next in line for command. Captain Teollutt, you will continue to execute the plan as we have outlined it here; namely, if the Singheko battlecruiser is down and you have a force advantage, you will decel, return and mop up.

Otherwise, you will boost out, translate to the rendezvous point and regroup."

Rita moved her gaze around the room, covering every one of her senior officers.

"You will not, under any circumstances, stop for survivors, unless the mopping up operation is clearly successful."

"Aye, milady," Captain Teollutt spoke over his holo link. "But milady...if the *Merkkessa* is down and the Singheko battlecruiser is still operational, there is no plan that can succeed with only two cruisers. What should we do then?"

Rita looked at Bekerose. He shook his head. Rita understood what he meant.

There's no solution to that question.

"In that case, Captain Teollutt, you are authorized to use your own discretion. You may return to Nidaria if that is your best choice. You may also make clandestine contact with Earth and seek their advice regarding how to proceed. I will leave each Captain with a file regarding my suggestions for making such contact."

Captain Teollutt nodded. "Thank you, milady."

Rita looked around the room.

"What else?"

Commander Lirrassa gestured a hand for attention.

"Yes, Commander?"

Lirrassa had a look of deep thought on her face.

"Milady, why don't we use the other ploy from that second simulation? We could send a corvette outsystem below the ecliptic and have them broadcast a fake fleet signature to distract the Singheko at the last minute."

Rita thought about it for a bit.

"Bekerose? What do you think?"

"I'd be concerned that we unnecessarily give away our presence in the system," said Bekerose. "If the corvette brought up the signal even the slightest bit ahead of schedule, the Singheko would go on full alert. That would not help us at all. The potential for mistakes is too great, in my opinion."

"I agree," said Rita. "No, we won't try to be that clever. What else?"

No one spoke. Rita waited a decent amount of time, then smiled at the group.

"Captain Tarraine will release a detail plan to you within two hours. We'll attack in six hours. I'm sorry for the short notice but every moment we sit here is another opportunity for the Singheko to discover us."

Rita rose, and the assembled officers in the briefing room rose with her.

It was not required in a ship underway - but Rita did it anyway. She gave her people a slow, sharp salute.

They returned it and held it until she dropped her own.

"Good luck people - and good hunting."

Sol System. Saturn

Jim grunted, realizing he had fallen asleep.

He had tried to stay awake for his last few hours of life. He wanted to experience every drop of life, right to the bitter end. It was a promise he had made to himself after he returned from Africa.

Flying as a mercenary in some of the bloodiest conflicts in the history of that continent, Jim had seen death in every possible form. It had changed him; the young Marine officer of his youth had long since disappeared, replaced by a harder, more cynical man who flew hard, spoke little, and drank much.

But somehow, against all odds, when he returned to the States, he had brought his demons under control. Mostly.

Part of that process had been his sister, Gillian. She had looked up to him, worshiped him as the big brother knight in shining armor. Somehow, that had pulled him back from the brink. He felt he had to live up to her image of him, even if it was distorted from the truth. And slowly, ever so slowly, he had dragged himself back to sanity.

Somewhere along the way - he couldn't remember just

when, but he did remember he had been flying at the time, in some airplane somewhere - he had made a life decision. He had thought the words at first, then spoke them out loud so he would remember them.

"I will never again give in to fear. I will live every day, every hour, every minute, every second of my life, without fear. And I will enjoy my life - right up to the very last hour. The last minute. The last second."

Now, remembering those words, Jim cursed himself for falling asleep.

Not doing a good job of sticking to that mantra.

On the other hand...

If I go to sleep, I won't know it when I run out of oxygen. Maybe that's the way to go after all...

Jim wanted to turn and check the ox gauge again, but he resisted.

It didn't matter. He knew he was down to hours, maybe minutes.

Better to just make the best of it. Sit here and enjoy the view. Think about the good things in your life.

Rita.

Now why did I think of her first? Bonnie's the one I love...

Wait a minute. I gave up on both of them and started up with Caroline. Why the hell am I thinking about Rita again?

Jim, you are hopeless. What an idiot.

Smiling, Jim looked out at Saturn, now only about half the size it had been thirty-plus hours ago.

At least I didn't fall back into the damn planet. Maybe someday they'll find my body and give me a decent burial on Earth. If Earth is still around.

A small shadow passing across the face of Saturn caught his eye. It was tiny, just a bit larger than a dot.

Another piece of junk from the battle, Jim thought.

Then something about the outline caught his attention.

That wasn't a piece of junk.

That was a ship.

His mind adjusted some more.

Not a Singheko ship.

With a start, Jim jerked upright in his seat. He slammed the quick release on his harness, knocked the back of the seat down and reached into the bunk area for the emergency kit. Pulling it forward, he restored the seat back to an upright position and quickly rummaged through the kit.

There was a handheld laser designator in the kit.

Where is it? Dammit!

He found it. He looked back toward Saturn, where he had seen the shadow passing across the planet's face.

It was gone.

Desperate now, Jim placed the laser designator on the sill of the open canopy and turned it on. He set the adjustment to wide angle and pulled the trigger.

"Yeah, I'll live every second, but if I can add a few more, I'm all for that," he mumbled to himself. He held the trigger down and began to pray.

* * * * *

Captain Pojjayan of the corvette *Kaimina* had traversed the debris field near Saturn several times, looking for information and survivors.

So far it was clear. The humans had caught the Singheko here in an ambush. But their ships were small and carried little firepower compared to the Singheko. The Singheko had taken out the fighters without even slowing down their advance into the system.

But surprisingly, the humans had destroyed two supply ships. Pojjayan was impressed by that. They had been smart enough to know that without the supply ships, the Singheko couldn't rearm their missile launchers.

They did a great job for what little they had to work with, he thought. *But it was pissing in the wind.*

His tactical officer called.

"Captain, I have a weak signal coming out of the debris field. Weak laser, intermittent."

Pojjayan leaned over the tactical officer, looking at his screen.

"Any targets there?"

"Tons of debris that general area, all broken up and scattered around. Nothing large."

"OK, let's scoot over there and take a look."

"Signal disappeared, sir."

"That's OK. We'll go take a look anyway."

Jim had kept his finger on the trigger of the laser designator for a full hour, waving it gently around in the direction where he had last seen the shadow of the ship against Saturn. His arm was getting tired; he had to hold the pistol-shaped designator up to the sill of the canopy, which was higher than his shoulders. There was no comfortable position he could find. The strain was wearing on him.

I should give up. It's been an hour. If they haven't seen it yet, they're not going to see it.

Ten more minutes. Just ten more minutes, then I'll stop.

The oxygen gauge on the bulkhead behind him had gone to zero minutes earlier.

Slowly, Jim's head sank down, and he went to sleep.

Captain Pojjayan was staring at the holo. They had moved to the general area of the intermittent laser signal. There were wrecks of the human fighters all around. Most of them were smashed, exploded, broken into dozens or hundreds of pieces. There were only a few that were even semi-intact.

They had checked two of them now. In both, they had found dead bodies. They left them in place. It would be up to the humans to come find the bodies after the war. If there were still humans to do it.

There was one more wreck that was almost intact. The back was sheared off, the engine half-in and half-out of its mounts. As they approached it, he saw the nose had a large hole punched all the way through it, with wires hanging out. It was coasting at a good clip away from Saturn.

The canopy was open. That was interesting. Either the pilot had abandoned the ship or had stayed alive long enough to open the canopy.

As they pulled up to the fighter, Pojjayan saw the figure of the pilot slumped in the seat. They oriented directly over the ship, opened the bottom sally port, and a two-man team went down to investigate. A few minutes later, he heard a report over his internal comm.

<Pilot is alive but unconscious. We are removing him into the ship. He was holding the laser designator in his hand, so this is the one>

<Understood. Take him to sick bay>

Merkkessa. 30 AU Above the Ecliptic.

"Execute," said Rita.

And it was just that simple.

One simple word, and her fleet went into battle.

How easy it is to send people to their death, thought Rita. *Just one word.*

The *Merkkessa* and the other ships of her fleet went to 255g acceleration. Given their initial velocity, it took only ten minutes for them to be moving directly at Earth at 1,000 miles each second.

3.6 million miles per hour.

And still accelerating.

At the three-hour point, they had already traveled 1 AU.

149,597,871 kilometers.

192,955,779 miles.

They were moving now at 27,353 kilometers per second.

61,187,247 miles per hour.

Three and half hours later and moving at 20% light speed, they shut off their engines and began their long coast to meet the enemy. The "Silent Arrow" was on its way.

Rita stepped down from the Flag Bridge and made her way back to her Flag Cabin. It was seventeen hours to intercept; there was no point in hanging around the bridge making people nervous.

She checked on Imogen. The baby was awake, but happy, smiling, playing with Flo's fingers.

She looked like Jim. Rita had to catch her breath.

"We're close to him, baby," she said out loud. "Close to Daddy."

Flo smiled at her.

"I've assigned one of my junior aides to be here during the intercept," Flo said. "I'll have to be in sick bay in case of injuries."

"Understood," said Rita. "Thank you for being here with her now."

"No worries," replied Flo. "Happy to do it."

While Flo disappeared back to her duties, Rita took the baby and sat in the rocking chair. She fed the baby, knowing it would be the last time before the battle. She had instructed Flo to change over to bottle feeding from now on, so that she would be rested and able to make good decisions once they reached intercept.

Imogen cooed and Rita smiled.

What am I doing? I could send Imogen to a corvette and take her to safety before we intercept. Why am I not doing that?

Because I must be with her. We live or die together. I don't know why. I just don't.

CHAPTER FIFTEEN

Sol System. Earth

Jim, wherever you are, I'm coming.
The thought jumped into Rita's mind.
I'm coming, Jimmy Boy.
WHY? Why am I thinking about Jim right now?
Put it out of your mind, girl.

They were approaching intercept. Rita had returned to the bridge and was sitting in her command chair, waiting, just as everyone else on the ship waited.

If the Singheko detected them in time to get their defenses up, they were screwed. Everyone knew that.

The dice were cast and were bouncing.

"Milady, we are twenty minutes from intercept," called Lt. Larissa.

"Thank you, Lieutenant."

Rita's thoughts wandered back to Jim again. She tried to ignore them. But she thought about Jim's body on hers. She thought about his hands on her. She tingled all over.

My God, why am I thinking this now? Of all the times to go down that rabbit hole...are these truly even my own thoughts? Or is Bonnie's consciousness taking over?

I should be focused on this battle.

But I've got nothing to do now. Everything is planned, everything is delegated, everything is in motion.

Maybe just a few seconds. To remember him in bed...one last time. In case I die today...

His hands on me.

His lips on me.

"...Milady?"

Rita abruptly came back to awareness. Someone was talking to her.

"Yes?" she answered, not sure what the question was.

"We are approaching point of no return, milady. If we are to break off the attack, we must do so now. Do we continue?"

"Um. Yes, continue, continue," Rita blurted out.

Did the Nidarians notice my distraction?

I need to get focused.

Rita looked at the holo. They were close now - two minutes from intercept. In another minute, they would have them. It would be too late for the Singheko battlecruiser to get out of their way, even if it tried.

And based on their own experience and the best intelligence the Nidarian Empire could buy, beg, or steal about Singheko fleet capabilities, it took at least one minute for a Singheko battlecruiser to bring up weapons.

One more minute. If the Singheko took no action in the next minute, she would have them, regardless of what happened after that.

Rita bit her lip. Like everyone else on the bridge - and probably everyone in the entire fleet - she started counting down. The countdown timer in the holo was right in front of her, but she counted anyway. It made her feel better. She noticed everyone else on the bridge was also counting down silently, their lips moving.

Tarraine beside her couldn't resist anymore. He started counting out loud.

"Sixty-five."

"Sixty-four."

"Sixty-three."

"Sixty-two."

"Sixty-one"

"Battlecruiser is powering up!" yelled the Tactical Officer. "They've spotted us!"

"Fifty-nine!" said Tarraine beside her. "I don't think they can do it! I think we've got their ass!"

Rita nodded.

"God willing," she muttered.

Corvette *Kaimina*. Near Saturn

What the hell is that stink?

Jim's awareness came back, but the stink came first. It smelled like rotten eggs. It was like having smelling salts held under his nose. He snapped his eyes open and looked up.

There was a bright light over his head. For a second, he wondered if was dead. Had he walked into the light?

But he didn't feel dead. Surely being dead didn't require a headache of this magnitude. It felt like a hundred little elves with a hundred little hammers were pounding away in his skull.

"Oww," he muttered, reaching up to touch his forehead. "What hit me?"

"A Singheko battlecruiser," said a voice in heavily accented English. "Pardon if my English not good, but I am still ... a studar, I think is the word?"

"Student," muttered Jim.

"Yes, ah, a student," said the voice.

Jim managed to turn his head to see the speaker. At the foot of his bed was a small creature. It was roughly like a human, but had a squarish head, not as rounded as a Human. It was no more than four feet tall. It appeared to be female, based on the upper chest which showed obvious mammary glands of some kind. A white uniform made him think of the similar white uniforms of the nurses in the Space Force.

"Where am I?"

"Ah. You are on... ah, let me think of the word ... a corvette. A corvette of the Nidarian Navy."

Jim looked at the creature more closely. When the *Corresse* had left Earth those many months ago, Bonnie had beamed back a couple of videos as they left the system, showing the people of Earth the Nidarians who were taking her away to their home planet. One of them, called Flo by Bonnie in the videos, had looked like this one, albeit a good bit taller.

"You look like Flo," he muttered. "Can I sit up?"

"Yes, yes, I am Flo for this corvette. A medical. Yes, please, sit up. That is good."

Jim managed to drag himself to a sitting position on the bed - which was too short for him. His legs hung over the end. He looked around. It was clearly a sick bay.

If you've seen one sick bay, you've seen them all.

"Are we still at Saturn?"

"Yes, for the moment. Soon we will be en route to a ... a place to meet. With the rest of the fleet. We are ... we are waiting for the fleet to attack the Singheko in ... let me think, in your measure ... in one minute."

"One minute!" yelled Jim. "Get me to a holo!"

"Oh, no, honored human. You must rest. You..."

"Get me to a holo!" yelled Jim again. "I have to see this!"

Merkkessa. **Nearing Earth**

"All weapons free and targeted," called the Tactical Officer.

"Very good," Bekerose responded. He turned and gave Rita a small smile.

Rita smiled back at the Captain.

No more waiting. No more doubt. No more planning, no more thinking.

Just fight.

"Three," she heard Tarraine beside her, not able to keep his countdown silent.

"Two."

"One."

The *Merkkessa* gave a rumble that could be felt throughout the ship as twenty missiles left the tubes. In the holo, she saw the rest of the fleet launch everything they had at the battlecruiser.

There was no point in shooting at the other ships in the Singheko fleet. If they didn't take down the battlecruiser, it was all over. But if they did, they could come back and finish off the others at their convenience.

Or so the plan said.

Then they flashed by Earth, moving so fast the planet went by like a film in fast motion. The missiles would have to decelerate to hit the Singheko ship, but that was OK. That was part of the plan. The missiles had the capability, and it would make it much harder for the Singheko to defend themselves.

Another countdown timer started on the holo. Rita watched it desperately.

It told them when they would be able to see the results of their attack.

There was the flight time of the missiles, plus a small light speed delay. The counter started at four seconds and counted down.

It reached zero.

In the holo, magnified to maximum range, Rita saw the Singheko battlecruiser in orbit around Earth.

It looked undamaged.

"Crap," she muttered.

It didn't work.

Then the enemy battlecruiser came apart. Like a flower blooming in the springtime, the main hull opened like a can opener had been taken to it. Parts flew off in every direction.

Then a magnificent explosion removed it from the universe.

Nobody said anything. There was no celebration, no cheering. Nobody raised their hands in the air in triumph.

That could just as easily have been them.

"Captain Tarraine, please give the signal to execute plan Alpha-2."

Tarraine nodded and keyed the command into his console. Rita confirmed it and it was relayed to the rest of the fleet.

As one, the ships began decelerating, to return to Earth and mop up the rest of the Singheko fleet. Without their battlecruiser, it should be a relatively straightforward operation. Rita stood up to go to her day cabin. At their speed relative to Earth, it would take hours to slow down and reverse course.

"Oh no," Rita heard from the Tactical Officer. "Oh, by the gods, no, please!"

She spun to look.

At the magnification they were using to see the battlecruiser clearly, Earth was huge, a big brown and blue ball nearly five meters across in the holo. Europe was facing them.

London was a huge orange glow.

Moscow was a huge orange glow.

Just on the very edge of the horizon, another glow could be seen. Rita knew where it was.

Beijing.

Tarraine whispered it out.

"They nuked your planet. Those godforsaken unholy bastards nuked your planet."

Bekerose turned and looked at Rita, a grim expression on his face.

She shuddered, looking at the holo.

I miscalculated. I thought we could just drive them away, make them go back to Singheko. I never thought...

Rita was frozen. She couldn't think. She couldn't speak.

I killed them. I killed all those people.

Bekerose stared at her. He could see the impact this event had on her. He could see her sanity exposed like a raw wound.

His instincts told him this was a moment that could destroy any living, thinking creature if it went the wrong way.

And somehow - against all rational probability - he had come to like this human creature in the Admiral's uniform.

He thought about what he would say to a Nidarian Admiral in the same situation if he wanted to re-focus them on living and pull them back from a precipice of despair.

"Admiral. Let's go kill some Singheko."

Slowly, Rita came back. She brought her gaze down from the holo and stared at Bekerose across the bridge.

I still have a job to do.

"Let's do that, Captain," she finally said. "Let's go kill them all."

Corvette *Kaimina*. Near Saturn

Caroline.

Jim thought it slowly, as he sat stunned by the image on the holotank in front of him.

Caroline.

She was in London.

She's dead.

Jim bowed his head. The pain in his head became nothing compared to the pain in his heart.

Caroline is dead.

He wanted to jump up, throw off the blanket the Nidarian doctor had wrapped around him, scream and rage at the universe.

But it was pointless. All he would accomplish would be to scare the crap out of the Nidarian bridge crew. And the Captain - Pojjayan - had graciously allowed him on the bridge to watch the attack by the Nidarian fleet against the Singheko battlecruiser.

And for a few minutes - for a few precious minutes - he had thought his world was saved.

Then the nukes hit.

The filters in his nose that were supposed to keep the stink out were now choking him to death. He reached up and ripped them out, throwing them on the deck. Then he shook his head.

She's gone forever.

Slowly, Jim rose to his feet. He looked around the bridge.

Every one of the Nidarian crew avoided his eyes, except for Captain Pojjayan. The Captain gazed at him steadily. Pojjayan walked over to him.

"I am so sorry for your loss, Major. May I escort you back to sick bay?"

His English was much better than the medics. Jim nodded dumbly.

Caroline.

He let the Captain and the doctor lead him back to sickbay. With a sigh, he lay down on the too-short bed again. The doctor put a needle in his vein, but he didn't care. He closed his eyes.

Caroline.

Earth. Flagstaff, Arizona

Earlier in the day, Gillian had received the bad news about Jim going missing in the Battle of Saturn. A Space Force Lieutenant pulled up in the driveway and knocked on the door.

Mark had spent most of his life in the Army. He knew instantly, as soon as he answered the door, what it was about. He invited the man in and called Gillian.

She came to the living room, took one look at the officer, and knew as well. Like Mark, she had been around the military most of her career.

"Jim?" she had said quietly, and the Captain had nodded.

"Yes, ma'am, I regret to inform you that your brother is missing in action. Unfortunately, I cannot give you any details. But we will keep you informed."

Gillian nodded dumbly, and Mark thanked the Captain, showed him out of the house.

Now, this evening, he had to ride. It was the only way he could work it all out in his mind. He rode the mare hard, until both were tired. Then he came back to the house, put the horse away, rubbed her down and fed her, and walked slowly in through the back patio. He decided he might take a shower.

Gillian was standing stock still in front of the television. She was as white as Mark had ever seen her. She turned to look at him slowly.

"They nuked Washington," she said.

Mark thought he misunderstood.

"What?"

Gillian shook her head slowly.

"They nuked Washington."

Mark realized she was serious. He stepped over to the television.

She had turned the sound down low, but the picture was unmistakable. A large mushroom cloud, dissipating, the view taken from a helicopter. The crawl under the picture stated that Washington was gone.

Mark turned up the sound.

"It's just gone," said a reporter's voice. The man talking was clearly distraught. His voice shook.

"It's all gone, all gone," he repeated.

Mark turned the sound back down and went to Gillian, held her. By reflex, he smoothed her hair down. He looked out the window at the patio, at the paddock, at the pasture in the distance.

If I had stayed in the Army, I'd have been in the Pentagon today. Gillian would have been at CIA Headquarters at Langley.

Gillian whispered tearfully, her voice breaking with emotion.

"All our friends. Everybody we knew. Gone."

Mark held her.

"Some will survive. Some would have been on trips, on vacation, elsewhere. Some will survive."

"Not enough," cried Gillian, losing control. "Not enough!"

Mark held her, staring out the patio door, while she cried.

CHAPTER SIXTEEN

Merkkessa. **Returning to Earth**

It took the fleet 6.7 hours to decel back to zero relative to Earth, and another 9.4 hours to get back to the planet. But the Singheko had fled long before they got back, taking a vector directly away from them to exit the system. Rita would not get the satisfaction of killing the rest of them.

She let them go; she had to go to Earth.

She had to face the music.

She expected the governments of Earth - the survivors, at least - to court-martial her, and then hang her, or lock her away in prison for the rest of her natural life.

I killed millions upon millions. I deserve whatever they do to me.

As they returned, the news became even worse. The Singheko had nuked Washington, Beijing, London, Moscow, New Delhi, and Tehran.

"Why Tehran?" asked Rita, sitting with Bekerose and Tarraine in the briefing room, looking at the planet on the holo and watching news from Earth on video.

"Who knows?" said Tarraine. "Probably more of an intimidation tactic than anything. Just to put every part of the planet on notice."

Bitter, Rita slammed her palm down against the table.

"And then they slink away like a snake in the night!"

Bekerose nodded.

"They knew they couldn't stand against us without their battlecruiser."

"God, I wish we could catch them and smoke them all," Rita said.

Bekerose stared across the table at Tarraine.

"No one more than we do, Admiral. But it's not possible. They'll be at the mass limit and translate out of the system long before we can catch them."

"I know. But still…"

"Yes."

<Incoming message from the corvette *Kaimina* for the Admiral> Rita heard over her implant. She could see from the faces of Bekerose and Tarraine they had received the message as well. Only private messages were not copied to them.

<Go ahead> responded Rita. She drummed a pencil on the tabletop, a nervous habit.

<Captain Pojjayan reports he has rejoined the fleet and has rescued one human survivor. He will transfer the survivor to the flagship shortly>

<Thank you, *Merkkessa*>

She lifted her gaze to look back at Tarraine and Bekerose.

"Captain Bekerose, upon arrival at Earth, I'll go down to the planet to meet with the governments. I'll take Captain Tarraine and Lieutenant Lirrassa with me. You'll be in command of the fleet until … if … I return."

"Very good, milady."

"Fine. Then we arrive in …"

Rita looked at the chrono on the wall.

"… thirty minutes. I'll prepare to depart. Oh, and you can bring the survivor from the *Kaimina* on board my shuttle, I'll take them down to Earth with me. If they are ambulatory."

"Very good, milady."

"Thank you, Tarraine. I need a word with Bekerose before I go."

Tarraine rose and nodded, turned, and left the briefing room.

"Captain Bekerose. I may not be able to return. The government of Earth would be completely within their rights to hold me responsible for the millions of deaths that have occurred. And they would be right. I am responsible."

Bekerose began an objection, but Rita held up her hand.

"Please. Let me finish. If I am not able to return, you are in charge of this fleet. I have posted that in my orders. You are to do what you think is right."

"Yes, milady. I understand."

"Please remember that Garatella - at least in theory - leased this fleet to Earth. You may therefore do either of two things if I am no longer in command. You may return to Nidaria, leaving Earth to fend for herself. Or you may stay and work with the governments of Earth to establish a defense. If I am no longer in command, that choice is up to you. But I would hope and even pray that you would consider staying to protect Earth."

"Milady, if it is within my power, I will defend this planet."

"Thank you, Captain Bekerose. I am proud to have served with you."

"And I with you, milady."

Rising, Rita saluted the Captain. With a small smile, he rose and saluted her back.

It was a gesture neither could have imagined six months earlier.

Bekerose left, and Rita went to Imogen's room. Flo was there, packing up Imogen's things for the trip down to Earth. Rita gave the little Nidarian doctor a hug - she couldn't resist. Flo looked at her strangely. But Rita just took Imogen out of the crib and held her for a while, looking at her, thinking about her future.

If they lock me up, who will take care of Imogen?

I've tried to reach Jim, but I can't find him. I've called and called, but nobody knows where he is.

She thought about it.

Gillian. Jim's sister. I'll go to Gillian, ask her to take care of Imogen.

<Admiral, we are in orbit over North America. The shuttle is ready>

<*On my way*>

On the nine-hour return to Earth, Rita had given much thought to where she should go, who she should report to. She had established communications with the U.S. military via the Deep Space network, and had been provided access to a General Raines, a senior commander in the Space Force. He had evidently been out of Washington when the nuke hit, and as a result had become the most senior member of the Space Force in an instant.

Raines told her to meet him in Colorado Springs, at Petersen Air Force Base, the headquarters of the Space Force.

Quickly, Rita recorded a brief message to Gillian, Jim's sister.

<*Hi Gillian. This is Rita Page. I have never met you, but I am the mother of Jim Carter's child, Imogen. I have just returned from Nidaria and I am on my way to Petersen Air Force Base in Colorado Springs. I need your help. I need to find Jim and I can't get in touch with him. I may need him to take care of his child. Could you possibly have him meet me there? Contact General Raines at the base for coordination. Thank you*>

Rita sent the message and sighed. At least that was done. If they imprisoned her, at least Gillian would know what to do.

Rising, she walked to the door of her Flag Cabin, and turned to look back one last time.

I might never see this place again.

Opening the hatch, she stepped out. Gabriel was there to escort her. She smiled at him and started the walk to the shuttle bay. On the way, she passed several crew members. They did the traditional "Attention on deck" call and slammed themselves back against the passageway wall, as they always did when she passed.

But this time, there was something different. Each one snapped to attention and saluted her as she went by.

That's different, she thought. *I wonder what this is all about.*

Coming to the shuttle bay, she stepped through the hatch and pulled up short.

A goodly number of the ship's crew stood in ranks as an honor guard. The flags of both Nidaria and various countries of Earth were arrayed on both sides of the path to the shuttle door. At the front of the path was a small podium, and behind the podium stood Captain Bekerose and Captain Tarraine.

"What's this?" Rita asked, coming to a confused stop in front of the two of them.

Bekerose spoke, and his words were amplified over the ship's comm, coming through the speakers overhead. She knew that meant they were also going out via comm to the rest of the ship, and probably to the entire fleet.

"Rita Page of Earth, Admiral of the White," Bekerose began speaking.

Rita, puzzled, didn't know how to respond. She knew what an Admiral of the White was. It was a new Admiral who had never fought a battle. Never been blooded. It was the rank assigned to her by Garatella upon her departure from Nidaria.

Bekerose continued, his voice loud over the loudspeakers.

"By order of the High Councilor Garatella of Nidaria, I hereby inform you of your promotion to Admiral of the Black and the title Defender of Nidaria."

Rita was stunned.

"How...what is this all about?" she asked.

Bekerose smiled.

Tarraine leaned over to Rita and whispered in her ear.

"Garatella provided us with secret instructions, not to be opened until after the battle. We opened them a few hours ago."

"As of this moment," Bekerose continued, his voice echoing around the hangar, "all personnel in this fleet will accord Admiral Rita Page of Earth the respect due an Admiral of the Black. Any person failing in their duty to this charge will be severely punished."

Bekerose reached out a hand and placed two new shoulder boards in Rita's palm. She looked at them in wonder.

Admiral of the Black. A full admiral in the Nidarian Navy. A blooded admiral, one who had fought the enemy.

Rita looked up at Bekerose. Impulsively, she stepped forward and gave him an awkward hug. Stepping back, she turned to Tarraine and gave him one also.

The assembled crew began cheering.

Rita felt her face grow hot. She had never experienced anything like this.

"I am humbled, and don't know what to say."

"Then we'll say it for you," said Tarraine. "Thank you for being our Admiral. Thank you for not getting us all killed. And thank you for reminding us where honor lies."

Rita wiped a tear from her eye and shook her head.

"You guys need to get back to work," she said.

"Aye, milady," said Bekerose, grinning.

Rita gave him one last hand-touch and then followed Tarraine and Dallitta toward the shuttle, Flo, Gabriel, and Raphael bringing up the back of their little parade. As she walked down the aisle between the ranks of assembled crew, they snapped to attention and saluted. Her eyes still full of tears, she stepped on to the shuttle, with Flo right behind her holding Imogen. Moving to the front, Rita started to sit down when she noticed another human sitting in the front most seat, right behind the cockpit.

Oh yes, the survivor pilot rescued from the battle at Saturn, she remembered. *I should say hello to him.*

Stepping forward, she came up beside him and looked down to speak to him.

Earth. Flagstaff, Arizona

"What?" asked Gillian, puzzled.

It was strange. Someone had called from Petersen Air Force Base in Colorado Springs and said they had a message for her. Then they asked her to hold for a moment.

She turned to Mark, watching the news on TV. There was nothing but bad news since the nuke strikes. It was all about digging people out of rubble and evacuating the few survivors before the radiation got them.

"I don't know anyone in Colorado Springs, do I?" she asked him.

"No," he grunted, never taking his eyes off the television.

The line clicked and a voice came on, a voice she had never heard before.

"Hi Gillian. This is Rita Page. I have never met you, but I am the mother of Jim Carter's child, Imogen. I have just returned from Nidaria and I am on my way to Petersen Air Force Base in Colorado Springs. I need your help. I need to find Jim and I can't get in touch with him. I may need him to take care of his child. Could you possibly have him meet me there? Contact General Raines at the base for coordination. Thank you."

"Oh my God," whispered Gillian. "She doesn't know."

"What?" Mark asked, finally turning around to look at her. "Who doesn't know what?"

Gillian put down her phone and started at Mark helplessly.

"That was Rita Page. She asked if we could get Jim to Petersen to take care of the baby. She doesn't know."

"Oh, God," said Mark. He stood up. "Can you call her back?"

"No, it was a recorded message. She said she is on her way to Petersen, and she needs Jim to take care of the baby."

Mark shook his head.

"She'll be with General Raines. I'd better call him."

"Yes. Call him. Then throw some clothes in a bag. We have to go to Petersen, Mark. Other than Rita, we're the only family that baby has. If Rita's in some kind of dust-up, she'll need us there."

Mark stood silent for a second, then nodded slowly.

"Not that I want to go, but you're right, of course. We have to go."

Merkkessa. Shuttle Bay

Stunned, Rita looked down at Jim Carter in the shuttle.

How can this be?

It ran through her mind two or three times as she stood beside him in shock. Then the man looked up at her.

It was Jim, alright. He looked a little the worse for wear. But it was Jim.

"My God, Rita!" he exclaimed. He sprang out of the seat and grabbed her in a bear hug. Gabriel and Raphael ran to Rita's side, hands on their weapons…

But then Rita grabbed the man's face and kissed him full on the lips. Puzzled, they hesitated.

Discreetly, they faded back again.

"Oh my God, Jim. Oh my God. How can you be here?" Rita sobbed, tears running down her cheeks. She held on to him as if she would never let him go. "Oh, Jim! Oh God, I needed you and here you are! How can you be here?"

Jim just held on to her, swaying her from side to side, never wanting to let her go. Tears ran down his cheeks as well. The two of them stood, the emotions raw, while the rest of the people in the shuttle waited quietly. They weren't sure what they were seeing, but it seemed something good for their Admiral. So they waited.

Flo was the only person on the shuttle who had seen Jim Carter before. Now she stepped forward; Jim looked over Rita's shoulder, and Rita turned to see Flo standing there with Imogen.

Shyly, Rita Page, Admiral of the Black, turned and took the baby from Flo. She turned back to Jim.

"Jim, meet your daughter. This is Imogen."

Earth. Flagstaff, Arizona

Mark had talked to General Raines on the phone, and Raines had arranged for a plane to pick them up at the Flagstaff Airport and bring them to Petersen AFB.

They were just pulling into the Flagstaff airport when Gillian's phone rang.

"Yes? What? What? Oh my God, oh my God. You're sure? You're sure? Oh my God, thank you. Thank you so much."

Mark looked over at Gillian as she put down her phone.

"What?"

Gillian looked at him.

"Jim's alive. They rescued him."

"No!"

"Yes. General Raines confirmed it. And get this - he was rescued by a ship from Rita's fleet. He's on the shuttle with her right now, coming down from her flagship to Petersen!"

"I swear, that brother of yours has nine lives," Mark grinned. He pulled over for a moment.

"So do we go back home?"

"Hell, no!" exclaimed Gillian. "We're going to Petersen to see my new niece!"

CHAPTER SEVENTEEN

Earth. Colorado Springs

Rita's shuttle touched down at Petersen just at dusk. She was surprised to see an honor guard awaiting her here as well.

I guess they want to observe the traditions before the court-martial.

It was easier to go through a ceremony the second time. Having Jim at her side helped a lot. Rita and her party filed off the shuttle, a band played, people saluted, and a lot of officers introduced themselves, most of whose names she would never remember.

Then they were inside a building, walking down a long corridor, and into a conference room. General Raines was standing at the middle of the conference table.

"Welcome, Admiral Page," he said warmly. He reached out a hand and shook hers, gestured to a chair across from him.

"Won't you sit down?"

Rita nodded. She walked around the table and stood behind her chair, waiting for the rest of her staff to filter in and find their places. General Raines had recognized Jim and was over pumping his hand, congratulating him on surviving the Battle of Saturn - so far, the only survivor.

Some protocol had been exchanged between the two groups before the meeting; even before her shuttle left the *Merkkessa*, the two groups had exchanged basic rituals and taboos to prevent misunderstandings.

As a result, the humans in the room knew not to shake the Nidarian's hands, but instead to touch them on the back of the hand in greeting. And the Nidarians knew that, if a human was carried away and grabbed their hand in greeting, to handle it gracefully.

Now, finally, everyone took a seat. Rita wanted Jim beside her, for moral support, but she knew it would be a breach of protocol - he a mere Major - so he sat at the far end of the table, well away from her. But he kept his eyes on her and a strong, supportive smile on his face.

She could get through this. If Jim were there for her to look upon in times of trouble, she could get through this.

General Raines finally sat, and the meeting could start. Rita felt like she should make an opening statement.

"General Raines, thank you for greeting us so warmly. Of course we are devastated by what has happened. We never expected the Singheko would react the way they did. Had we known, we would have taken a different strategy."

General Raines looked surprised. He glanced sideways at his protocol officer, whose name Rita had forgotten, and then back at her.

"Admiral Page, you have won a great victory. You have driven off the most dangerous enemy humanity ever faced. Quite frankly, I fail to understand what you have to apologize about."

Rita sat stunned. She looked over at Tarraine, who gave her a smile.

"General Raines, because of our attack, millions upon millions of people have died. That tragedy is on me. I am so sorry for my error in judgment."

General Raines looked at her.

"Admiral Page, you seem to be operating under a misunderstanding. Let me clarify the situation for you. Before your arrival, the Singheko communicated an ultimatum to Earth."

Raines turned to his aide.

"Colonel Garth, will you please read the ultimatum sent by the Singheko upon their arrival?"

"Yes, sir," said the woman next to General Raines, a full bird Colonel in the uniform of the Space Force.

"I quote:

Lesser beings of this planet, you are now our slaves. You have no chance of resistance. All who resist will be killed. You will immediately collect 120,000 healthy able-bodied persons between ages twelve to forty for transport to Singheko as the first shipment of slaves. We will take only five million slaves per year. This is very generous on our part. You will agree to these terms and surrender, or we will destroy one city every two hours as the Earth turns beneath us until you surrender your planet."

Colonel Garth finished reading and looked up. In the background, Flo was just completing her translation to the Nidarian contingent whose English was not yet good enough to follow in real time. The group was quiet.

General Raines continued.

"Admiral Page. The first nuke was launched at Washington. This occurred before your attack - before the Singheko even knew you were attacking. You didn't see that because the planet was turned away from you as you approached."

Rita swallowed. Her emotions ran wild. It was all she could do to control herself in front of this crowd. In fact, she did not completely succeed, as a tear slid slowly down her face. She lifted a hand and wiped it away. She realized she was not the only one around the table wiping away tears now.

"Admiral, you did not cause the Singheko to nuke our planet. They had already started that process before your attack saved us from slavery by these animals. Yes, you may have caused them to hurry things. But you probably saved many of the world's cities, even if you don't know it."

Rita wiped away another tear.

"I don't see that, General. If I had not attacked, you would have had time to negotiate a surrender, or at least negotiate with them."

General Raines shook his head.

"I think humanity has more backbone than we suspected,

Admiral. The consensus had already been reached among the nations of the world that we would not surrender. Thus, you changed nothing, except to drive the bastards away before they could nuke any more cities."

Rita sat, stunned.

General Raines continued.

"By the time of your attack, the decision had already been made. We had already decided to tell them to go pound sand. We had started emergency evacuations of all the major cities."

Rita just shook her head. She couldn't speak at the moment. Beside her, Captain Tarraine reached over and touched the back of her hand, the ultimate sign of support from a Nidarian in public.

"The plans were coming together to conduct guerrilla operations against them as they landed. I think you may have underestimated humanity, Admiral. We weren't going to go quietly."

Rita finally found her voice. She looked over at Tarraine, smiled to thank him for his support, and then looked back at General Raines.

"You need to keep moving forward with those plans, General. This is a temporary reprieve, we think. The Singheko will not give up this easily. They'll be back in force, and with a lot more ships. We don't know how long, but it could be soon. It's possible this was just an advance party. A larger fleet could be right behind them."

"I agree," said Raines. "We need to form a strategy for fighting them when they come back." Raines turned to Jim Carter.

"Major Carter, you fought them at Saturn. Can you give us any insight into tactics that would be more effective against them?"

Jim nodded. "I'll try, sir. The main thing we learned at Saturn is that small, unarmored fighters have a tough time penetrating their point defense. The flak took down all our fighters; we destroyed none of their capital ships. The

Longsword can't penetrate that flak. Worse, our missiles were largely taken out as well. We need bigger, tougher missiles, with more evasive capability, and those can't be carried by small fighters."

"What are you recommending, Major?"

Jim perused the table, his brow furrowed. "I'm not sure exactly, General. We need a task force to come up with a new approach, and quickly. But one thing is certain, we need to start on new missiles immediately. Missiles with much more AI capability, better maneuverability, and bigger payloads. That much is certain - we can start on that today. Then we have to figure out how to deliver them to penetrate the flak and hit the targets."

Sol System. In the Black

The *Corresse* translated into three-space 20 AU below the ecliptic, off-center of the Sun, in the middle of nowhere. Bonnie and Arteveld felt it was the safest place to be in case the Singheko were already dominant in the system.

They studied the holo carefully. The information there would be two and a half hours out of date, but that was close enough for their purposes now. It didn't take them long to get the lay of the land.

"Nidarian battlecruiser in orbit around Earth, along with the rest of Rita's fleet. Lots of debris, though. Looks like the remains of a Singheko battlecruiser. Good for Rita," said Arteveld.

"Another swarm of debris out by Saturn," said the XO, Commander Dallitta. "The wreck of at least one ship there, and what looks like lots of wrecked fighters."

"Agree," said Arteveld. Then Arteveld looked a bit closer at the holo.

"Colonel," he said quietly.

"What?"

"Look at the major cities on the planet."

Bonnie leaned forward, stared at the holo. She ran the magnification up a bit.

"Oh, sweet Jesus."

Arteveld was grim.

"They nuked a bunch of cities," he said.

Bonnie retched, gagged, nearly puked. She threw her hand over her mouth, trying to fight it off. Regaining control of herself, she leaned back in her chair, wordless. Together, the three of them sat for a long while, staring at the blue planet in the holo with the dark craters on it.

After a long while of bitter thinking, Bonnie spoke.

"We can't let this stop our mission. That problem is in the hands of Rita and the Earth governments. They have a job to do. And we have a job to do."

Arteveld nodded silently.

Bonnie turned to him.

"We will find that damn starship."

"Aye, Colonel."

Bonnie was still not used to that title. She ducked her head, thought for a bit, then looked up and responded.

"I don't want to be detected when we come in. I don't want to have to explain to the Earth governments what we're doing here or go through a lot of red tape. Can you put us on the backside of the moon without being detected?"

"That would be difficult, with the Nidarian fleet there. Their sensors would pick us up the minute we boosted for the moon. But..."

Arteveld dipped his head, as if in apology.

"...Garatella anticipated this situation. He briefed Bekerose and Tarraine in a set of secret orders to be opened only when they arrived at Earth, and only if the fleet was still intact. I assume they have read those orders by now."

"Really?" asked Bonnie. "And what do those orders say?"

"They let Bekerose and Tarraine know we are coming. They identify us as a courier boat from Nidaria, come to check on the status of the mission. We can drive right in and park in orbit, just like we own the place."

"Damn. That Garatella is scary good," said Bonnie.

"You don't become High Councilor by being stupid," Arteveld smiled weakly.

"OK. Take us in, park us in orbit at some convenient place to Tibet, and let's prepare to go looking for some hidden caves."

Nineteen hours later, the *Corresse* settled into orbit over Afghanistan, behind the corvette *Kaimina*.

Bonnie and Arteveld convened in the briefing room to plan next steps.

"Can you get us to Tibet without detection?" she asked Arteveld.

"I think so," he said. "You'll remember we have that little shuttle you used at Dutch Harbor - the one that looks like a smaller version of a normal blended-wing airliner. From a distance, it's hard to tell the difference. We used to do this all the time when we were here on our research mission. You have no idea how many times we landed on Earth to dig out information and were never detected. We can drop into the atmosphere over an uninhabited area - Antarctica probably - then fly like a normal aircraft to our destination."

"Could we drop in over Mongolia or Siberia instead? That would be a lot closer."

"Maybe. Let me check their radar coverages. If I can find a gap in their radar, we can do that. But the last thing we want is to trigger a Russian or Chinese alert and have a bunch of their fighters come up in our face."

Bonnie was somewhat bitter as she spoke.

"Sad to say, they may have other things on their minds right now."

Arteveld nodded. "Still, we can't take chances. Let me check it out. I'll know within the hour where we can come in. Why don't you and Dallitta get ready for the mission, prepare everything you need, and stage it on the shuttle? I'll prepare the flight plan."

"Done."

Bonnie got up and left to her cabin.

It'll feel good to get out of this ship for a change. I love the Corresse, *but still ... six months cooped up on this damn thing. Let me out of here!*

An hour later, Bonnie stood with Dallitta just outside the shuttle. Arteveld had found a spot where he was reasonably sure the shuttle could slip into the airspace over Siberia without detection. From there, they could make it safely to Tibet. It involved a lot of low-level terrain following once they got down, but he assured them the AI could handle it.

"Let's do this, Dallitta," Bonnie smiled.

"Let's!" replied Dallitta. The little Commander was excited. She had been on previous missions to Earth during her last tour, and she loved it. She thought the planet was wonderful - although she said the atmosphere lacked flavor, as it had no rotten egg smell.

Buckling into the shuttle, they prepared for the drop into atmosphere. The clamshell doors beneath them opened, and with a lurch, they were pushed away from the *Corresse* by large springs. The AI took control and the little blended-wing shuttle decelerated rapidly. A few moments later, the ship had become stationary relative to their entry point and they descended into the atmosphere like a hawk stooping on a kill.

Earth. Colorado Springs

Mark and Gillian arrived at Petersen Air Force Base well after midnight. Gillian had kept in touch with General Raine's staff, so she knew the lay of the land. She had even talked to Jim, and he assured her he was alright. He told her he would be waiting for them to arrive.

"Jim, you should sleep," she said.

"I slept in the Longsword when I was on mission," Jim laughed. "I'm good, sis."

Now they passed through the gate and followed an escort sent by General Raines to lead them to Jim and Rita. Rita had been given a four-bedroom house on base for her use; their guide pulled up in front. Mark and Gillian parked and got out.

Coming out to meet them, Jim grabbed Gillian first, giving his sister a big bear hug, and then kissing her on the forehead.

"I'm glad to see you, Jimmy Boy," Gillian said, trying not to cry. She held on to him a bit longer, then she looked over at Mark. Gillian released him, and Mark grabbed him roughly.

"You look like shit," he grinned at Jim.

"Thank God I don't feel as bad as I look," Jim shot back. Although he had showered and shaved and changed into uniform, Jim's face still reflected his ordeal. He had lost ten pounds during the mission.

"Come in the house and meet Rita and the baby," Jim said. He led them inside. Rita was waiting for them, with Flo beside her holding a sleeping Imogen in her arms.

Mark had met Rita at Dutch Harbor, briefly, before she left with Bonnie on the *Corresse*. But Gillian had never met her. Jim introduced them, and Gillian gave Rita a hug.

Then they introduced Gillian to Flo - her first glimpse of a Nidarian in the flesh. Gillian immediately reached for the baby, taking her gently and cradling her, cooing at her even though she was sleeping.

Jim glanced at Mark.

"I think this conversation is about to degenerate into baby talk, so maybe we should adjourn to the den," he smiled.

Mark nodded, gave Gillian a quick kiss, and Jim and Mark left for the den. Gillian, Rita, and Flo headed for the baby's nursery.

Their peace and happiness would last exactly twenty-four more hours.

CHAPTER EIGHTEEN

Earth. Colorado Springs

The first day after the holocaust was spent digging out, re-forging connections to foreign governments, and getting used to the new normal of the world. All the countries impacted declared new capital cities. Shanghai, St. Petersburg, Mumbai, Birmingham, Isfahan - all became the new capitals of their respective nations.

And Philadelphia. Once again it was the capital of a nation at war, as it had been in 1776.

There were survivors of the government - the Secretary of State had been on a trip away from Washington. She assumed the role of acting President under the Presidential Succession Act. She immediately declared martial law, to allow the executive branch to do the things necessary to re-create a viable government.

The only other senior member of the Executive branch to survive, the Attorney General, assumed the role of Vice-President.

The Senate and House had been completely decapitated - they had been in session when the bomb struck, with only a half-dozen of them out of the Capital for various reasons. The President issued a second Executive Order that the six remaining elected legislators constituted a quorum and could propose and enact temporary laws until new elections were held.

There were few survivors in D.C. Those few that were pulled out of the outskirts of the city died of radiation sickness soon after. It had not been a clean bomb. The consensus was that the Singheko didn't care how many people they killed, because there were plenty of slaves available for them on Earth anyway - far more than they could carry off the planet in any reasonable amount of time.

In the face of this mounting horror, Rita and Jim went their different ways - Rita for a conference with General Raines on the defense of the planet, and Jim to meet with technical staff on a full debrief of the Battle of Saturn.

General Raines had also sent Mark to an Intelligence meeting; although Mark was retired, it had only been two years. Since he had been a participant at the Battle of Dutch Harbor, Raines wanted his input.

Captain Bekerose, in orbit, sent out corvettes and destroyers as pickets, each one posted 10 AU from Earth and in position to give early warning of any Singheko movements.

The rest of the planet went on about their business, for the most part. There was a sudden surge of marriages, as people all over the world realized how short life could suddenly become in this new reality. The battles and wars that were ongoing mostly sputtered to a stop that second day, although there were a few combatants that just couldn't stop killing each other, even in the face of a greater menace.

And after working all day, Rita, Jim, and Mark came back together in the evening, exhausted, and with no better answers than when they had left in the morning.

"They'll be back, and in greater force," said Mark. He had reviewed records of both battles, Saturn as well as Earth. "There's no doubt in my mind. And we are totally unprepared for a large fleet."

Rita nodded. "I know."

"I think the only solution right now is to prepare for guerrilla warfare. Both in space and on the planet. And hope the Nidarians have mercy on us and send reinforcements."

"Agreed," said Rita. "And General Raines also agrees. I talked to Bekerose this afternoon, and he is in complete agreement with us. So now the question is how to implement that approach."

Mark went quiet, thinking. Then he spoke.

"Do you think there's any possibility Garatella sent a fleet right behind yours? You've said he's a tricky bastard. What if you are the stalking horse - the bait - and he has another, larger fleet right behind you to smash the Singheko reinforcements?"

"That would be just like that clever SOB, but we have no way to know," replied Rita. "The *Corresse* arrived a little while ago with some dispatches, but there was nothing in them that gave any clue to Garatella's thinking. Just routine stuff."

"Yes, I heard. But why do you think he sent a courier boat just three days after your departure? Doesn't that seem a little strange?"

Rita nodded. "It does. Captain Arteveld said Garatella ordered him to assess the situation and report back to Sanctuary. But it does seem a bit strange to me."

There was a long silence as they withdrew into their own thoughts.

Jim's thoughts wandered to Caroline. So far, he had been too busy to think about her. But now, with the meetings over for today, his mind kept returning to her fate.

And he realized he needed to mourn her. Their relationship had been short - a few weeks, only a day if you counted the intimate part.

But he needed to mourn her.

"If you guys will excuse me, I'm going to take a short walk," he said.

Leaving them, he walked outside and down the street, trying to clear his head. The air was crisp, not cold but not warm, just that perfect temperature that makes you glad you're alive.

But Caroline is not alive. Dear God, please let it have been so quick for her that she never knew it. Please don't let her have suffered.

Jim wondered if God listened to such prayers. Jim

considered God a distant, aloof entity, who had created the Universe and then moved on to other priorities, letting the gears turn and the chips fall where they may.

But if you listen to us, he thought, *please hear my prayer. Take good care of Caroline. And Angel. And Spanky, and Bobber. They gave everything. Please hold them in a special place in your heart. And protect my baby Imogen. If you can find it in yourself to keep her safe, I would gladly give you my life in exchange for hers. Please protect my baby.*

To his surprise, Jim realized he had made the block and was back at their quarters. He started up the driveway and went into the house. There was a commotion going on; he could hear Rita talking, and her voice sounded grim. He walked into the den. Mark and Rita were standing. Rita was on the phone, and Mark looked pale.

"What?" Jim asked.

Mark looked over at him.

"They're back. A much larger fleet. Two battlecruisers, four cruisers, eight destroyers, six corvettes. Ten big fat freighters."

Jim nodded in understanding.

"The freighters are for the slaves," he said. "The first fleet was just their test, to see what our defenses were like. Now they know exactly what it takes to defeat us."

Mark agreed. "The first fleet was expendable. They wanted to draw out the Nidarians."

Jim spoke bitterly.

"They're not as dumb as they look."

Earth. Over Siberia

The shuttle with Bonnie and Dallitta on board didn't reenter the atmosphere with heat and flames like a capsule, or with a long streak of disturbed air behind it. It had been designed specifically to allow the Nidarians to sneak down to the planet with a minimum risk of detection. At night - like tonight - it was virtually invisible.

As they entered the atmosphere, wing extensions unfolded up and out and oriented the shuttle in a stable position. Their inertial system engine fired nearly continuously, keeping their speed down.

After a while, the air became thick enough for the extended wings to bite. In a few more minutes, the air was thick enough for the blended wing configuration to provide lift, and the wing extensions folded back out of sight.

They became an aircraft.

Bonnie took manual control, not because she needed to - the AI could fly the plane better than she could - but because she was a fighter pilot, and it had been two years since she had been behind a stick. She gave a yelp of joy as she twisted and turned the little shuttle, bleeding off speed. Dallitta shared her enthusiasm - after a few minutes, Bonnie handed control over to Dallitta, who also twisted, turned, and generally abused the shuttle as they coasted down to the lower atmosphere.

Finally they got serious, as the ground came up and they fell below 25,000 feet. They turned control back to the AI and let it resume their flight plan.

"Where are we, *Corresse*?" Bonnie asked the AI.

<We are 120 miles north of the Tunguska State Nature Reserve. We are on a course to the Abakan Mountains of southwestern Siberia. From there, we will enter Mongolia over the province of Zavkhan, and make our way to the Bayan Har mountains of Tibet. The entire trip will take nearly six hours, so you may want to sleep>

"Why so long?" asked Bonnie. "It's only about 3,200 klicks, right?"

<Yes. But to perform terrain following at night without detection, I cannot fly faster than 300 knots, or roughly 555 klicks as you say in your language>

"Fine," grumbled Bonnie. "Wake me when we get there."

And with that, she settled into her seat and closed her eyes.

Earth. Colorado Springs

Rita finished up her phone call and looked at Jim across the den.

"I'm going back to the *Merkkessa*. I'm going to fight them from there."

"I'm going with you," Jim responded.

"I'd rather you stayed here with Imogen. I'm leaving her with Gillian and Mark. Please stay with her and keep her safe."

"I can't, Rita. My place is in the fight. Mark and Gillian will take good care of her."

Rita looked down, accepting Jim's decision.

"Get your things together, then. I'm leaving in a half hour."

"On it," said Jim. He left to their room.

Rita turned to Gillian and Flo, who were standing in the doorway to the kitchen. Their faces reflected the utter sadness in their hearts as they realized Rita and Jim were headed back into harm's way.

"Gillian, please take good care of my baby," Rita said. A tear glistened on her cheek. "If I don't come back…"

Gillian shushed her. "Don't talk like that, Rita. You'll come back. And in the meantime, know in your heart that Mark and I will do everything in our power to keep Imogen safe. Don't even think about fretting about that. Flagstaff will be one of the safest places on this planet."

Rita nodded, wiping the tear from her cheek. She turned to Flo.

"Flo, you've stood by me through thick and thin. I'll never forget it. But I'd like you to be with your husband now. We don't know what will happen. But at least you'll be together."

"Thank you, Admiral."

"You can ride up with us on the shuttle, then transfer over to the *Corresse* from there."

Flo nodded.

"OK. Then that's that," said Rita. She stood. Walking to Gillian, she gave her a good long hug.

"I'll go kiss my baby goodbye and we'll head for the

shuttle."

"Take care of yourself, Rita. I'm proud to have met you. I think Jim is lucky to have you," Gillian whispered.

Rita blinked back the tears.

"Thank you, Gillian."

Rita went to Imogen's room and stood over the crib. She looked down at the sleeping baby. Carefully she leaned in and kissed her on the cheek.

"Goodbye, little one. I may not see you again. If I don't make it back, know that I loved you very much."

Quickly, before she started crying again, Rita left. She grabbed her bag and walked outside with Jim and Flo. Tarraine and Lirrassa were waiting with a vehicle. They drove to the shuttle pad, and in a half-hour, they were launching for space.

The plan was for Flo to remain on the shuttle after Rita and her party debarked on the *Merkkessa*, then the shuttle would take Flo over to the *Corresse*. But just before they docked into the shuttle bay of the *Merkkessa*, Flo got the closed eye look of someone receiving a private comm. Suddenly her eyes flew wide open, and she stared at Jim.

"Jim, we have a problem. You need to go back to Earth."

"What?" Jim looked puzzled. "Why?"

"You need to trust me. Arteveld has something to tell you, and it's for your ears only."

Jim looked at Rita.

"There's nothing he can tell me that can't be for the ears of the Admiral also," Jim said firmly. "Rita is in charge of the entire fleet."

"No. The *Corresse* is on a detached mission, not part of the fleet."

Rita figured it out, the conclusion coming into her brain instantly.

"Bonnie," she said suddenly. "Bonnie's on the *Corresse*."

Flo sighed. "I knew you'd figure it out sooner or later."

Jim was stunned.

"You mean Bonnie's on the *Corresse*? Right now?"

"Not exactly," said Flo. "She's on her way to Earth in a shuttle right now. But here's the problem. The *Corresse* was supposed to be the support system for her mission. But Arteveld can't stay here with the Singheko coming back. Like the rest of the fleet, he must find someplace to hide. That leaves Bonnie with no support and no comms back to the rest of us."

"So Arteveld wants Jim to go back to Earth and be Bonnie's support system," said Rita.

"Exactly."

"What's Bonnie's mission?"

"I don't know. Something Arteveld is holding close to his vest. But it must be important, or Garatella wouldn't have sent her separately."

Rita looked at Jim.

"I don't want you to go. I just got you back. Send someone else."

Jim gazed at Rita, sadness in his face.

"You know I can't do that, Rita. Bonnie is us, and we are Bonnie. The three of us are a team. We can't leave her alone in this."

"Dammit!" cursed Rita. She threw a half-full coffee cup against the wall of the shuttle, shocking those around her. "Just for once, can't you choose me over Bonnie?"

Jim tried to say something, but Rita cut him off.

"Just go. I don't give a shit anymore. That's fine. Just get your ass back to Earth and do whatever."

Very gently, Jim spoke.

"Rita. This is not choosing one over another. This is about where I can add the most value. On the *Merkkessa*, I can do little. I know nothing about your ship or your processes. I could fly one of your fighters - but not as good as your own pilots can. I can support you emotionally, yes. But I will be of more value helping Bonnie complete her mission. Whatever it is, Garatella thought it important enough to send her here."

With a crunch, they arrived in the shuttle bay. Silently, the rest of her staff left the shuttle, knowing they needed to give

Rita and Jim time to sort through their emotions.

In a moment, they were alone, with only Flo remaining behind.

Rita heaved a long sigh. Staring at the coffee dripping down the shuttle wall, she turned to Jim. She gave him a long, deep kiss - a goodbye kiss for two people who knew they might never see each other again.

"Alright. Go. I'll give you one of the *Devastator* fighters. The AI can teach you to fly it as you go."

Jim held Rita close, not wanting to let her go. But he had no choice. In his world of honor, he couldn't leave Bonnie to fend for herself without support.

Rita pulled back from him. The bitterness was gone from her voice now. Only sadness lingered.

"Go take care of the woman we both love, Jimmy Boy. And try not to die."

Earth. Bayan Har Mountains, Tibet

Bonnie and Dallitta were a long way from anywhere. They were in the middle of an inhospitable mountain range, with nothing for miles in any direction.

The ends of the Earth.

Arteveld had spent the entire night doing remote sensing from the *Corresse*. Now he transmitted his data down to them. He had found three caves in the area which were possibilities.

"We'll start with the one which is the most accessible to civilization," Bonnie told him, and Arteveld gave her the coordinates.

Bonnie and Dallitta selected a likely looking area to hide the shuttle and put it down into a deep rocky hollow just as dawn was breaking. Completely surrounded by rocks and trees, it would be difficult to see unless someone fell into the pocket by accident.

Then Arteveld gave them the bad news.

"The Singheko are back, a much larger force," he told them.

"Rita is taking the fleet to hide in the Kuiper belt and conduct guerrilla warfare against them. I can't stay here, so I'm going with them."

"Understood," replied Bonnie. "Good luck to you."

"One more thing," added Arteveld. "I couldn't leave you there without support. I notified Jim Carter of your location. He's coming to help you."

"What?" Bonnie was shocked. "How did you get in touch with him?"

"It's a long story. I'll let him tell you when he finds you. In any case, he has your coordinates. How he gets to you is his problem. Oh, he said you'd know the frequency to monitor."

Bonnie smiled.

"Yes, I know the frequency. Thank you, Arteveld."

"*Corresse* out. Good hunting."

"Good hunting to you, *Corresse*."

CHAPTER NINETEEN

Merkkessa. **Leaving Earth Orbit**

Rita felt cut in half.

First, she had failed to protect Earth, and millions of people had died.

Now the Singheko were coming back - so it was all in vain.

And lastly, the absence of Jim, Flo and Imogen tore her soul apart.

But she couldn't show it.

"Captain Bekerose, take us out of here. Find us someplace to hide," Rita said crisply as she walked onto the bridge with Tarraine and Lirrassa.

"Aye, milady," Bekerose acknowledged. He motioned to the Tac Officer, who entered a command. Within seconds, the *Merkkessa* was moving, clearing Earth orbit.

They were on the opposite side of the planet from the incoming Singheko fleet. The Singheko were 20 AU out, coming much faster than the first incursion. They had nothing to fear now; they knew the humans couldn't stop them.

"Dammit all to hell!" Rita cursed, looking at the holo.

Beside her, Tarraine nodded in silent agreement. He was getting quite good at cursing in English, just as Rita was quite good at cursing in Nidarian. They found it a useful talent.

"Private comm from General Raines, milady," said the Tac Officer.

"Give it to me," called Rita.

The comm came over her implant.

<*Admiral Page, the decision has been made by the United*

Nations. We'll make a show of surrendering to them for now, to prevent any more nukes dropped on civilian populations. But we'll fight them on the ground everywhere. Every time they land, every time they set foot on this planet, we'll fight. We'll stay coordinated with you using the codes we've established. Good luck and good hunting>

Rita had expected it. There was no use killing more millions of people, when it was clear they couldn't stand against the Singheko. A token surrender, followed by guerrilla warfare, was the only answer that made any sense.

With a big sigh, she looked at the holo. They were headed directly away from the Singheko, into the Kuiper Belt. The Earth was between them and the incoming fleet, hiding them for the moment.

By the time they came out from behind the planet's radar shadow, they would be coasting, cold and dark. The Singheko would play merry hell following their path. Getting to the 14.35 AU point where they could translate into six-space and make their escape should be no problem for her fleet.

But then what? How could she fight the Singheko from there?

It required more thought than she could bring to bear for the moment. All she could do right now was run - run away, and it hurt like hell. It hurt like hell to leave behind the people of Earth, leave them to face the Singheko and Lord only knew what kind of retribution.

But she had to preserve the fleet. That was her first and foremost responsibility. It was the only small chance they had to fight another day.

"Captain Tarraine. As soon as we are safely away, convene a meeting in the briefing room. We need to start planning some dirty tricks."

"Aye, milady," acknowledged Tarraine.

Rita got up and left the bridge. She went to her day cabin and down the stairs to her Flag Cabin, and into her bedroom.

There she threw herself on the bed and stared at the

ceiling.

She pushed all thoughts of Jim, and Bonnie, and Imogen out of her mind. She focused on one thing, and one thing only.

How to kill Singheko.

Earth. Bayan Har Mountains, Tibet

"I give up. It's a fools' errand," said Bonnie, slumped on the side of a slope only a mountain goat could love.

Dallitta lay beside her in the rocks and scree.

"It's only two miles back to the shuttle, Colonel," said Dallitta. "Let's just rest a bit and then keep at it. We need to get back there before nightfall, or we might not find it in the dark."

"I can't move another inch, Dallitta. I'm gonna lay right here and die."

Dallitta managed a weak smile. They had trekked out at dawn, trying for the first cave on the list provided by Arteveld. It took them six hours to find the cave; and except for bear excrement, it was empty. There was nothing in the vicinity; no signs of habitation, no artifacts, no graves, nothing.

Dallitta had brought a handheld sensor along. It could detect a Nidarian starship reactor, even after two thousand years, if they were within a mile or so. Or so Dallitta claimed.

But it had registered nothing.

The trek back was supposed to be easier. But it wasn't. They had now been walking on the return for five hours, and it was getting dark.

And two miles still to go.

Dallitta rose to her feet. Just in case of an inadvertent sighting by a human, she had disguised herself in a hooded jacket with a face mask and goggles. Now she pushed the goggles up on her forehead.

"Come, Colonel. We have only two miles to go. You can make it."

Bonnie sighed and pulled herself to her feet. They had fabricated walking poles with the 3D synthesizer on the

Corresse before they departed. Now they started down the slope again, using the poles and working their way at an angle to maintain their footing. Bonnie reached out a hand behind her and pulled Dallitta's hand onto her shoulder, to help them balance.

"This is a waste of time, Dallitta. There's nothing in these mountains but rock, scree, bears, goats and batshit."

Dallitta laughed. "It amazes me you still have a somewhat limited vocabulary in our language yet can curse like a sailor in it."

Bonnie grunted, slipping on a rock and catching herself.

"One has to keep one's priorities in order, you know."

Dallitta giggled, slipped, and said a Nidarian curse.

"See what I mean?" quipped Bonnie.

Finally they reached the end of the slope and some relatively flat ground. It was getting on toward twilight now. They stepped out, trying to make the shuttle before full dark. After a half hour, tired and focused on putting one foot in front of the other, they were walking head down, not looking ahead of them. That was how they came upon the man without seeing him until the last second.

Abruptly Bonnie realized there was someone standing in front of them. She slammed to a stop, holding out her arm to stop Dallitta behind her.

Before her stood a figure, indistinct in the dusk, but clearly human. It was a man, she decided, even though his clothing looked like a skirt. He had a heavy load on his back, which appeared to be made up mostly of sticks.

Bonnie and Dallitta stood silently, and the figure before them also stood frozen in the dusk. Finally, the man spoke.

"Tashi delek," he said. He stood, seemingly waiting for an answer.

Bonnie turned sideways to Dallitta, who had come up beside her.

"Any idea what he said?" she asked in Nidarian.

"Not a clue," said Dallitta. "But I learned a little Chinese when I was here for five years. Let me try that."

Dallitta spoke in Chinese. But the man did not immediately reply. Instead, he backed up in great fear, and turned, as if he would run away. But he seemed to get his fear under control, and stopped, turning back to them. He stepped forward again and looked hard at Dallitta in the dim light. He took another step forward, and another, until he was only a few feet from Dallitta, staring at her intently.

Then he spoke to Dallitta, in crude and heavily accented Nidarian.

"You too far from home, Dropa."

Earth. In Orbit

The AI had taken control of Jim's Devastator fighter and flown it out of the hangar just minutes before the *Merkkessa* departed. For the first hour, Jim was content to let the AI continue the flight, as it taught him the rudiments of controlling the black, wedge-shaped Nidarian fighter. The AI had walked him through basic maneuvers using the throttles and sidestick, then moved on to the weapons and comm systems.

A fighter is a fighter, thought Jim. *There are only so many ways you can ergonomically design it for a humanoid.*

He felt comfortable now with the nasty-looking beast and was hand-flying the ship, getting to know it better. He was still in orbit.

"Devastator, I can't keep calling you by that clumsy name. Can I rename you?"

<Of course. You may choose any name you like>

<Good. Then henceforth you shall be named Angel. After my former wingman. He was a good one>

<I am now "Angel" and will respond to that name>

<Excellent. Angel, compute a deorbit maneuver to put me at the coordinates Arteveld provided for Bonnie's shuttle while minimizing the likelihood of detection by any Earth entity>

<I have computed a re-entry over Antarctica which will put you at Bonnie's location in twenty-two hours with 2 percent chance of detection."

"Oh, hell, no. That's too long. Compute another one that's shorter and doesn't involve Antarctica."

<I have computed a re-entry over the Arctic which will put you at Bonnie's location in twelve hours with 6.8 percent chance of detection."

"Damn, Angel. Can't you find something that will get me there sooner? We can accept a little more risk."

<I have computed a re-entry over Siberia and Kazakhstan which will put you at Bonnie's location in seven hours but carries a 12.2 percent chance of detection by Russian Air Defenses."

"That's fine, do that one. If they detect me, I think they'll leave me alone once they catch sight of me."

<Anticipate an initial deorbit acceleration of 2.1g in 90 seconds. Please ensure you are strapped in and your life support systems are attached and functional>

"Everything is checked, you're good to go, Angel."

Ninety seconds later, the Devastator broke orbit and headed down into the atmosphere.

Jim was in no mood for interference. He rode a black angel of death and was prepared to use it. The Devastator was fully loaded with six missiles and a laser cannon that had a range of a thousand miles in space and ten to twenty miles in atmosphere.

Jim was quite sure that was enough.

Earth. Bayan Har Mountains, Tibet

"You too far from home, Dropa."

The man spoke again. Dallitta was stunned, as was Bonnie.

"That's...that's some kind of Nidarian!" said Dallitta.

"Yes," said the man. "I speak ... little. Why you far from Dropa place? You die here."

Bonnie was stunned; she couldn't think of anything to say. Dallitta recovered more quickly.

"We are lost," she said. "Can you help us get back to Dropa place?"

The man paused, clearly thinking about it.

"No. I don't go. Too danger. But I show," he said. He turned and pointed in the distance.

"That mountain," he said.

Bonnie and Dallitta turned and squinted in the gathering dusk. In the direction the man pointed were several mountains, but the largest was a distinct, snow-capped one at least a thousand feet taller than the others.

"The big one?" asked Dallitta. "With the snow?"

"Yes," said the man. "You go there, other side. At snow. Behind snow. You don't come back here. You die here."

Then, the man turned suddenly and started moving off, quickly.

"Wait!" called Dallitta, but the man never paused, never looked back. He was clearly troubled, fearful to be in their presence.

Bonnie watched him go and turned to Dallitta.

"Well, that was special."

Dallitta nodded. "How is that even possible? How could a human in the middle of Tibet know Nidarian? And his words were crude - I could hardly understand them."

"Well, let's not worry about that now. Let's get our asses back to the shuttle."

Dallitta nodded and they started out again. Trudging along, they moved as fast as safely possible in the deepening night, but their speed was limited by their need to watch out for rocks, potholes, and slippery patches of snow. It was slow going.

Finally, after another fifteen minutes of hard trekking, they found the depression hiding the shuttle. They had climbed out via ropes and now they took them from their hiding place, threw them back down into the hole and climbed down, exhausted.

Inside the shuttle, they collapsed into the tiny galley and prepared food, almost too tired to eat.

"That was one of the hardest days of my life," said Bonnie.

"Mine as well," said Dallitta. "And remember, I take three steps for every two of yours."

Bonnie smiled grimly.

"Sorry about that."

They ate their meal mostly silent. They were too tired to talk. But finally, they finished, rose from the table, and headed for the small bunks in the back of the shuttle.

"We'll go check out that big mountain first thing in the morning," said Bonnie.

Dallitta nodded. She fell into a bunk and her eyes closed. She was asleep in seconds.

Bonnie smiled. Despite her exhaustion, she paused for a second before climbing into the other bunk.

She loved working with the happy-go-lucky Commander. Dallitta always had a joke or a quip to make the time pass. And she was smart, prepared, and effective at her job.

Sometimes you just get lucky, she thought. She was asleep before she knew it.

CHAPTER TWENTY

Earth. Bayan Har Mountains, Tibet

Next morning, Bonnie and Dallitta crawled out of bed, groaning, their bodies sore from the previous day's exertions.

"Primates are not designed to climb mountains," grumbled Bonnie, putting together a breakfast in the galley.

Dallitta smiled.

"I'm not a primate, but I agree," she said.

"Oh, that's right," said Bonnie as she sat down to breakfast. "Nidarians are not evolved from a primate-type of ancestor. You come from what we humans would call a type of marsupial, I think. Or something close to that."

"Yes, I suspect that would be the closest Earth-approximation. It's surprising, though, that after millions of years of evolution, a marsupial and a primate grew so close together in terms of appearance."

Bonnie ate, thinking, then responded.

"I think it's convergent evolution, as we've talked about before. The need for an intelligent creature to free up their hands for toolmaking. The need for a large brain case. The need for speech. All these things coming together to drive the body pattern in a common direction."

Dallitta agreed. "And don't forget the need for sex to ensure a more rapid evolution and more diversity," she giggled.

Bonnie smiled. In her time on Nidaria, she had learned that Nidarian sexual evolution had also converged in the same general way as humans. Even though they started as marsupials millions of years prior, they had long since lost that aspect of their body plan and were now virtually identical to humans in their reproductive systems.

Which had caused no end of jokes among Nidarian females as they realized human males would be much bigger than Nidarian males. Bonnie had lost count of the times Nidarian females had asked if all the areas of human males' bodies were proportionately larger than Nidarians.

A question she had steadfastly refused to answer, merely inviting the questioners to find out for themselves.

Finishing breakfast, they adjourned to the cockpit and plotted a course to the other side of the big snow-covered mountain.

"Is one of the other caves that Arteveld gave us over there?" asked Bonnie.

"No, doesn't seem so," responded Dallitta. "It's not on the list."

"Hmm. Interesting," said Bonnie. "OK, let's go check it out."

With a hum, the shuttle lifted off into the dawn light. They moved carefully through a low saddle across the ridge in front of them and over into the next valley, then up that valley until they were at the foot of the big mountain. They slowly moved up the face of it, past the trees until they were approaching the snowline.

They were letting the AI fly the shuttle while Dallitta ran sensors. Bonnie was monitoring the visual environment on the screens.

Suddenly Dallitta jumped.

"I've got a hit on residual radiation," she called. "Ten o'clock, one-half mile."

They moved to that point and stopped, hovering. They were just slightly above snow line now, about a hundred meters past the nearest trees below them.

"No place to hide here," said Bonnie. "We'd stand out like a sore thumb. Let's mark this spot and then go down into the trees and find a hiding place."

"Roger that," responded Dallitta. Marking the spot on

their inertial nav system, they turned and went down the mountain. About a kilometer down, they found a small meadow, surrounded by rocks, which would make a good hiding place for the shuttle. Landing, they put on their parkas, gathered their packs and walking poles, and headed out.

It was hard going uphill. The slope was steep, and they spent as much time crawling as they did walking. It took them a full hour to make the kilometer back to the site.

Entering the snow, they slogged through it until they arrived at the location they had marked. Dallitta frowned at her sensor.

"According to this..." she said, paused, then continued.

"According to this, we're standing right on top of it. Something directly beneath us is showing residual radiation of the type I would expect to see for a two-thousand-year-old Nidarian reactor."

Bonnie nodded, and started punching her snow pole into the hard-packed surface. She walked in a circle, starting at Dallitta's location and spiraling out, punching a hole about once every foot as she went outward. Dallitta moved over about ten feet from Bonnie and started a similar search. The two of them worked for fifteen minutes but found nothing.

Bonnie stopped, disgusted.

"Nothing," she said.

Dallitta stopped and looked at her sensor again. She adjusted a small knob, looked again, and looked around at the holes they had punched in the snow. There were two well-defined circles of holes, one circle punched by Bonnie and one circle punched by Dallitta.

Dallitta walked over to a point right in between the two circles, and then turned and walked up the mountain a few meters. She looked at her sensor, and then down at the snow. She punched her snow pole down hard into the snow.

There was a solid thunk.

Dallitta looked at Bonnie. Then she dropped to her knees and began digging in the snow. Bonnie rushed to her side, and they started digging together, trying to get down to the bottom of the pole, which seemed to be about three feet down. It was slow going, as the snow was packed. It took them a good minute to gain sight of the bottom of the pole.

It was resting against a black metallic plate. As they pulled more and more snow away from it, the outline of it became clear.

It was an antenna, not that different from the one on the outside of their shuttle.

And it was solidly connected to something underneath.

Earth. Russian-Kazakhstan Border

The two Russian fighters finally gave up the chase as Jim crossed the border into Kazakhstan. He had played with them a little. It was cruel - but he couldn't resist.

The Russians had picked him up somewhere over Siberia. He could tell they were having trouble tracking him, so he turned off the stealth to help them. The two fighters came up on him fast then as he cruised along a few hundred feet over the terrain. His AI - Angel - warned him when they were getting close, and he sped up just enough that they started to fall behind. After a minute, they started to catch up again as they went into afterburner. He let them get a little bit closer. Then, just as they were almost into missile range, he sped up again.

It was cruel, but he was bored.

Finally, the Kazakhstan border came up, and they dropped off. He was sure they would call the Kazakh to intercept him, but he didn't plan to make it easy for them. As soon as the Russians were out of range, he turned his stealth back on, kicked his speed up to Mach 5 and headed for Tashkent.

He wanted to disguise his true destination as much as possible. Had he turned directly for Tibet, it would have been obvious, and the Chinese would be waiting for him.

Instead, he continued south, crossing the border into

Kyrgyzstan west of Tashkent and then down into Tajikistan. He did pick up a couple of Kazakh interceptors coming at him out of Almaty, but they couldn't find him with his stealth on and never got close.

Finally, after passing the Pamirs, he turned a bit more southeast and flew just north of the Karakoram range, sticking to the Chinese side but low - he didn't think they had much chance of spotting him. The Devastator was designed for space combat; it was black as the devil and heavily stealthed.

Finally, shortly after dawn, he arrived at the Bayan Har mountains. Arteveld had sent him the coordinates for Bonnie and Rita; he found the site and circled over it. It was a deep depression, almost invisible except from directly overhead.

They weren't there.

Earth. Bayan Har Mountains, Tibet

It took Bonnie and Dallitta three hours to dig enough snow away from the object to find a hatch. But long before that, Dallitta had identified the object.

"This is an ancient Nidarian shuttlecraft," she said, panting, as they dug. "It's not the *Dragon*. It's too small. It's more like our own shuttle."

"Damn. I knew it was too easy," Bonnie said, gasping for air in the high altitude as they worked. Her gloved fingers were near-frozen. She had to stop and warm them every few minutes.

"But it's something," said Dallitta. "It's a lead, at least. We know they made it to Earth."

Breathing hard, Bonnie kept digging.

"Do you think any of the shuttle's log would still be readable?"

"Who knows?" said Dallitta. "If the maintenance microbots survived, then yes. But two thousand years in this environment? Hard to tell."

"Then...what good is it? We still won't know what

happened."

"Don't give up hope, Colonel. There's always hope," smiled Dallitta, digging away in the snow. Suddenly she stopped and stared. Then she gave a whoop.

"A hatch!" she cried. "Look! Here's the edge of it! And there's a hinge!"

"Damn straight," said Bonnie. She turned to help Dallitta. In another five minutes, they had cleared a space of snow around the hatch. There was no doubt of its nature; it was nearly identical to the top hatch of their own shuttle.

They squatted back on their heels, breathing hard, trying to catch their breath, as they stared at the closed hatch. Finally, able to breathe again, they looked at each other.

"You go first, Dallitta," said Bonnie. "It's your people."

"Thank you, Colonel," smiled Dallitta. She reached out, pulled on the lever, but it wouldn't budge. It was frozen solid.

Bonnie reached into her pack and pulled out a snow hammer, giving it to Dallitta. Dallitta pounded gently on the hatch handle, trying to shake loose two thousand years of ice, snow, and neglect without breaking the handle off.

The handle moved a tiny bit. Dallitta kept up her gentle thumping. A few more strokes and the handle moved again, this time by a quarter of an inch.

Dallitta put the hammer down and pushed on the handle. With a groan, it moved a full inch, then stopped. She pushed again, harder, and it moved another three inches. With one last effort, she pushed as hard as she could, and the handle moved all the way around to the stop. A soft sigh of air came out of the hatch as it popped open.

Bonnie helped Dallitta pull the hatch open, and they looked inside. It was dark inside, but it appeared to be an airlock, with a ladder leading down to another hatch. Dallitta looked at Bonnie.

"Here's goes nothing," she said, and put her feet over the edge onto the rungs of the ladder. She climbed down into the shuttle to the bottom of the ladder and stepped off beside the lower hatch.

"There's another hatch. I'm going in."

Bonnie heard a creaking sound from below, then another exhalation of stale air pulsed up from below. She saw the top of Dallitta's head disappear into the lower hatch.

"It's what I thought," called Dallitta. "It's an old shuttle. You can come down if you want to."

Bonnie stepped into the hatch and went down the ladder, through the lower hatch, and down another ladder. She found herself on the deck of an ancient shuttlecraft. Everything was covered with dust and cobwebs.

Dallitta looked sad.

"It's a derelict," she said.

Bonnie nodded. She walked to the front, where the cockpit was. There she found everything smashed. Screens, controls, seats, even the walls had been destroyed, hammered, and punctured by blunt force and something that looked like axe damage.

"This was no accident," she said to Dallitta. "Someone intentionally destroyed this shuttle."

"Yes," Dallitta agreed. "Such a waste. Such a hideous waste."

They investigated for an hour, but nothing in the wreck helped them. It was a mess. It had been systematically and thoroughly destroyed.

Finally they gave up. Hearts broken, they climbed the ladder back to the top, shut and sealed the hatch, and covered it over with snow again. Then they started the long walk back to their own shuttle. Slipping and sliding on the snow until they got back down to the forest, they moved into the shade of the trees, lost in their own thoughts. Neither of them saw the welcoming party waiting for them at their shuttle until it was too late to run.

CHAPTER TWENTY-ONE

Earth. Bayan Har Mountains, Tibet

Bonnie froze. Dallitta, confused, bumped into her from behind, then stopped and stepped to the side to see.

Ahead of them was their shuttle, tucked away in the meadow, surrounded by tall trees on all sides.

In front of the shuttle stood a dozen men. They were dressed much like the man they had seen the night before on the mountainside. They wore traditional Tibetan garb; but the AK-47 rifles they carried were modern.

And those rifles were pointed directly at Bonnie and Dallitta.

The men stepped forward, advancing on them. It was too late to run. They were trapped.

The man in front - she assumed he was the leader - came up to within a few feet of her and motioned with the rifle. He pointed toward the ground and said something in Tibetan. She shook her head.

"I don't understand."

One of the men came forward, pushed her roughly on the shoulders down to her knees. Another did the same to Dallitta.

I guess they shoot us right now, thought Bonnie. *No candy, no dinner, no foreplay.*

But the man behind them pulled rope out of his robes and started binding their hands behind them. He was efficient but very rough doing it. When he was finished, the leader said something else in Tibetan, and gestured with his rifle for them to stand.

They stood, and the men started off, leaving the clearing. Half of them went ahead and the other half stayed behind Bonnie and Dallitta, pushing them forward. They pushed hard with the gun barrels if they slowed down even for a minute. They seemed to be in a hurry.

They walked for hours. It was soon twilight, but the men slowed only a little in the dim light, keeping up a hard pace. Then it was night, but they kept moving. Dallitta was having a hard time; her short legs were the limiting factor of the march, and the men were angry that she couldn't keep up. The third time she fell and one of the men jerked her roughly back to her feet, Bonnie had reached a breaking point. She turned and yelled.

"No!" she screamed at the man pulling Dallitta hard to bring her back to her footing. She advanced toward him. He lifted a rifle, but she didn't stop. She walked to Dallitta and stood beside her, defiant.

"No more!" she yelled. "She can't move any faster!"

The man slammed the rifle butt into Bonnie's stomach, dropping her like a poleaxed steer. She lay in the rocks groaning, gasping for breath. She felt Dallitta's hand on her, trying to help her, but there was nothing the little Nidarian could do. Only time could bring her breath back. She gasped for what seemed like minutes before she could breathe again. Finally, she was able to open her eyes and look up.

The leader of the group stood over her. He wore a red cap. Now Red Cap looked down at her and said something in Tibetan, but she couldn't understand it. Then he said something in Chinese. Dallitta jerked her head up, then said something in return to him. He spoke again in Chinese, and then stalked off back to the front of the group.

Dallitta helped Bonnie to her feet.

"What did he say?" Bonnie asked Dallitta.

"He said, you get up, but no more yelling. If no more

yelling, they slow down a little so I can keep up."

"OK, that sounds like a deal," moaned Bonnie. "I couldn't yell right now if my life depended on it."

Together, the two of them started off again down the trail. They had been trending down the entire trip. They continued downward for another two hours. Then they came out of the forest into a clearing. There were three small cabins arranged around the clearing. The men herded them into one of the cabins. It had a small table, four chairs and a tiny kitchen area.

They were forced to sit at the table. One of the men roughly removed their ropes, and the men left, slamming the door behind them.

"Well, here's another nice mess you've got me into," muttered Bonnie in English, rubbing her wrists to get the blood flowing again.

"What?" asked Dallitta, not following.

"An old expression I picked up from Jim Carter," said Bonnie, switching back to Nidarian.

"Oh, the lover you left behind," said Dallitta.

"That's the one."

"What do you think they want with us?"

"Nothing good, I suspect," said Bonnie.

They sat for an hour. Bonnie got up once and tried the door, but it was locked from the outside. She tried to peek out a window, but a rifle barrel on the outside waved at her, so she returned to her seat.

The door opened. Red Cap came in, followed by another man, a tall ugly one they didn't recognize from the earlier group. He was wearing a yellow cap. Yellow Cap stopped and stared at them, mostly at Dallitta. He walked around her, looked at her, pulling back her hood. He muttered under his breath as he inspected her. They heard the word "Dropa" a couple of times.

Finally he turned back to the leader by the door and spoke a long string of Tibetan to him. Then he left.

Red Cap smiled at them and spoke to Dallitta in Chinese.

Then he departed. Bonnie heard the lock fall into place from outside.

"What did he say?" Bonnie asked.

Dallitta looked glum.

"He said I am a blasphemy to humans, and they will kill us tomorrow at dawn."

* * * * *

The next morning dawned cold and cloudy with spatters of showers occurring from time to time. Bonnie had been unable to sleep; it was hard to do when your execution time had been set. Dallitta as well had sat up all night, staring glumly into space. They tried to talk a bit, but there was really nothing to talk about.

Men had come back into the cabin and re-tied their hands, and then tied them to the chairs, ensuring they could not escape. They gave it the old college try; both spent several hours trying to work the bindings loose. But all they succeeded in doing was wearing sores on their hands until they were bleeding.

When the light coming in through the windows was bright, the door opened again. Red Cap came in, followed by three other men. The men grabbed them roughly and hustled them out of the cabin into the clearing.

Off to one side, they had erected two posts. Now they tied them to the posts, yanking the leather tight enough to cut off the blood flow.

Then Red Cap walked off a dozen meters and turned back to them. Six of the men came forward with their AK-47 rifles at the ready and placed themselves in a line. The leader started a long harangue in Tibetan. Although Bonnie couldn't follow it, she could guess.

These evil witches must die, or they will contaminate the village, she thought. *Or something like that.*

The laser fired across the men so quickly, Bonnie had no

concept of what was happening. Red Cap was cut completely in half; the other six standing in line with their rifles sustained slightly less gruesome wounds, but just as devastating. All six of them fell dead, one of them without a head.

The rest of the men standing around screamed and ran, throwing their rifles to the ground as they vanished in seconds.

Bonnie and Dallitta found themselves alone, tied to posts in the middle of a clearing in the Bayan Har mountains, with no idea of what had just occurred.

Out of the corner of her eye, Bonnie saw figures approaching from the forest. They were small, dressed in hooded cloaks, and carried long, thin weapons that looked like rifles, but without stocks or triggers. There were four of them; they came up and stood in front of Dallitta, ignoring Bonnie. Although they were clearly men, they were no more than five feet tall.

One of them spoke to Dallitta. It was in Nidarian, but so heavily accented that Bonnie could just barely make it out.

"Are you of the people?" asked the man.

Dallitta looked at him in shock.

"I am Nidarian," she said. "Is that what you mean?"

Upon hearing her voice, all four of the men fell to the ground and prostrated themselves before the Nidarian officer.

Dallitta, at a loss how to proceed, looked at Bonnie.

"Ask them to untie us," suggested Bonnie.

Dallitta nodded and made the request. The man who appeared to be the leader jumped up and made haste to remove the ropes binding them to the posts, and then untied their hands.

Bonnie stood, rubbing her wrists, while Dallitta carried on a conversation with the leader of the group. Bonnie could follow most of it, although his language was broken and heavily accented.

The gist that Bonnie got was that these men were called the Dropa, and were hated by the local Tibetans, who viewed them as witches. The man suggested they should leave while they had a chance.

Dallitta agreed and the six of them trooped off, back up the mountain.

At least we're going in the general direction of the shuttle, Bonnie thought. That helps.

They walked for an hour, then called a stop for rest. Bonnie and Dallitta hadn't eaten since breakfast the day before and were hungry. Dallitta communicated this to the Dropa leader, and he rummaged around in his pack and pulled out some bread cakes for them.

After a short break, they started out again, climbing the mountain higher and higher. Bonnie was starting to get concerned they would bypass the shuttle completely, and she was right. Before long, the men turned and took a different path. Another three hours of walking and they were well around the mountain, the shuttle far behind them.

Then they came to a large rock escarpment, forming a natural terrace. They started up it. It was hard climbing, and Bonnie and Dallitta slipped many times, the men helping them as necessary.

They came to a dead end. The way was blocked by a large boulder. The men halted and milled around, waiting for Bonnie and Dallitta to catch up. At last the two females were standing at the boulder, looking at the men in confusion.

The leader and two of his followers grabbed a smaller rock that was standing between the boulder and another one, and grunting, pulled it out of place. In the space it left, a dark cleft could be seen between the two larger boulders. The first two men got down on their bellies and crawled into the cleft, one at a time, leaving one man on guard outside and the leader with Bonnie and Dallitta. He gestured to the cleft.

"Cave," he said. "We go inside."

Dallitta nodded, got down on her stomach, and crawled into the cleft. Bonnie shook her head.

"I guess I go inside," she said. Getting on her stomach, she wriggled through the cleft into darkness.

After a few feet, the space widened out considerably. Bonnie was able to see dim light. She got to all fours and crawled forward. The space got wider, and the light brighter. In another few meters, she could stand up and look around.

She was in a large cave, with flickering torches in holders around the walls. Racks on the walls contained a dozen of the laser weapons, and the two men who had entered ahead of her were replacing their weapons in the racks. The leader of the group came up behind them; he gestured to the back of the cave and led Bonnie and Dallitta to something that looked like a small altar.

In the center of the altar was a large stone, about twelve inches in diameter. It had a two-inch hole in the center. Two lines curved away from the hole, spiraling out to the edge of the stone.

"What is that?" Bonnie asked Dallitta.

"It is a stone as I described on the way here," said Dallitta. "But I don't know its meaning."

The leader of the men smiled at them.

"It is the Waiting Stone," he said. "It waits for you. We have kept it for your arrival for two thousand years."

Bonnie and Dallitta stared at the large round stone on the altar.

"Waiting Stone?" asked Dallitta in Chinese. "What does that mean?"

The leader of the Dropa shook his head, replying in Chinese.

"We do not know. We have preserved it and guarded it for 2,000 years. But over the centuries, the meaning of it and the reason for it have been forgotten."

Dallitta translated for Bonnie, who just shook her head.

"Who were those people who tried to kill us?" she asked Dallitta in Nidarian.

Before Dallitta could translate into Chinese, the leader replied in broken, heavily accented Nidarian.

"You speak. Is good. Enemies of Dropa. Those men."

Bonnie nodded.

"But why enemies?"

"We do not know. They kill us, we kill them. We hide from them all times, but sometimes they find us."

"But you're human - not Nidarian!" said Bonnie. "Why do they kill you?"

"We ... guard stone. They know stone. They want stone. They think ... evil. Much evil. From old days, they hunt us. But we know stone not evil. It is Waiting Stone."

Bonnie looked at Dallitta, who had walked over to the stone and was bent over, examining it.

"What is the purpose of the Waiting Stone?" asked Bonnie.

"Save Earth," said the leader of the small band. "Waiting Stone here to save Earth from demons."

* * * * *

A half-hour later, Bonnie sat leaning against the wall of the cave, exhausted from the ordeal of the capture, near-execution, and escape.

And the uncertainty and frustration of their present situation.

The leader of the men had sent away the rest of his band. He had produced more food from his pack and offered it to Bonnie and Dallitta. It seemed to be some kind of rice cake, hard but edible. Barely. Bonnie was so hungry, she wolfed it down regardless.

Dallitta was still examining the stone. She had walked around it for minutes, looking at it from every angle. Then she had squatted down and stared at it for at least ten minutes now.

"Anything?" called Bonnie across the cave.

"I think ..." Dallitta began, but then she hesitated.

"What?"

"I think there is writing in the spiral grooves, but I can't make it out. It's tiny. It could be ancient Nidarian, but I just can't be sure."

"So what can we do?"

Dallitta stood up and turned to Bonnie.

"We have to get it back to the shuttle and let the AI scan it."

Bonnie looked at the leader.

"We need to take the stone to our ship," she told him. "Can you help us?"

"Yes," said the leader. "We have a way to carry it. The others are coming just now with a harness."

Bonnie wearily climbed to her feet.

God, I'm not looking forward to another hike on this mountain.

But there was no choice. She watched as the other three Dropa came back into the cave, carrying a leather harness with slings and ropes attached. Deftly, they opened the harness, placed the large stone into it reverently, tied it in place and carried the entire assembly to the cave exit. One of them crawled out of the cave, then the other two pushed the stone through the opening.

The leader pulled four of the laser weapons off the rack and held them bundled in his arms. He gestured to Bonnie and Dallitta to leave. Dallitta crawled through the opening followed by Bonnie, and they were outside again.

The sun had come out and the day was getting better. It wasn't as cold as earlier. Bonnie looked up at the sky.

What am I doing? How did I come to be here in this place, with these people, and this craziness? I should be in Deseret, curled up with Jim in his bed, watching the sunset over the mountains and drinking wine...

The leader came out of the cave and passed two of the laser weapons to his companion. Then the other two men arranged the harness between them and started on the trail, back the way they had come earlier in the day. They seemed to know where they were going.

"Do you know where our ship is?" asked Dallitta.

"We know," said the leader.

Bonnie looked at Dallitta and shrugged. They started off following the two with the stone. The other two Dropa fell in behind, carrying their weapons.

CHAPTER TWENTY-TWO

Merkkessa. **Kuiper Belt, 35 AU from Earth**

"It won't be as easy this time," said Bekerose.

Rita and her staff were gathered around the conference table in the *Merkkessa*'s briefing room.

"No, it won't," agreed Rita. "They'll be ready for us."

Tarraine pointed to the holo. "They've put out plenty of pickets. The two battlecruisers and one of the cruisers are in orbit around Earth. The slave ships have all landed now, near the largest cities. But the rest of their fleet is scattered around the system, set up to be pickets - early warning systems. They've got the corvettes out the farthest - 10 AU from Earth. They're not taking any chances this time."

"Once burned, twice shy," said Rita. "They've learned."

"But," Bekerose thought out loud, looking at the plot, "that actually gives us an opportunity. Look here," he pointed to the holo with a laser pointer.

"… right here, they've got one of their destroyers a bit overextended if you ask me. I'd have to run the numbers, but I don't think they can get reinforcements to it before we can take it out. It's just a bit too far away from support."

Rita studied the holo.

"Good eye, Captain Bekerose. I think you may be right. Lt. Lirrassa - have Tactical run the numbers on that destroyer out by Jupiter. See if we can take it out in a "Silent Arrow" attack and get away before they can get reinforcements to it."

"Aye, milady," said Lt. Lirrassa. Her eyes crossed a bit as she went into a comm session with the tactical team.

Rita looked around the room at the assembled officers and staff.

"It's going to be guerrilla warfare now, folks. For a long while, I expect. We'll have to pick them off one at a time, when they make a mistake. And if they don't make a mistake, we must be patient. We can't force the issue. If we get in a rush, they'll have us for sure."

Lirrassa came out of her cross-eyed comm session with Tactical.

"Tactical says we can do a "Silent Arrow" on the destroyer at Jupiter and make an escape back into six-space before they can catch us or reinforce. It'll be close, but just barely doable. We'll have to hit them when they're on the far side of their orbit, and the timing will have to be perfect, but it can be done. Also, they pointed out that if we hit the one at Jupiter, we might as well hit the one at Mars too. They're both on the same side of the system, so we can get a double."

"Excellent. We'll take what we can get. Two destroyers are better than nothing. Put it together, please, Tarraine."

"Aye, milady," answered Captain Tarraine.

Rita rose, and the group rose as one.

"Thank you everyone and keep up the good work. We've got a long road in front of us, but we'll get there." She turned and headed to her suite. As the rest of the group departed, Tarraine caught up to her.

"Milady, a word please?"

"Yes?" said Rita, pausing to turn to him.

"Milady, I request to go on the mission."

Rita stared at him.

She understood what he was saying; and she understood why. He was a Flag Aide; he supported her, translated her wishes into actions, stood by her side as she decided the fate of her fleet.

But he was a full Captain in the Nidarian Navy. He wanted

to fight. He wanted to return to Nidaria with his head held high, a mission command patch on his jacket.

And she couldn't let him. He was too valuable.

Just spit it out, just tell him.

"Tarraine. If there was any way I could succeed without you, I would let you go. But I cannot. You are my right hand. I can't afford to lose you. I simply cannot. I'm sorry."

Tarraine looked disappointed, but he accepted it with a good heart.

"Thank you, milady. I had to ask."

"I know."

"I'll report back when we have the attack plan finalized."

Earth. Bayan Har Mountains, Tibet

"God, my feet hurt," said Bonnie.

Dallitta nodded agreement. They had been walking for two hours. The sun was high, and it was getting hot on the mountain. Their escorts seemed to be following a faint trail, but it wasn't an easy walk.

"We should be almost there," said Dallitta.

Bonnie could just grunt. From walking most of the day yesterday, and all this morning, and now again back to the shuttle, they had spent most of two days on their feet. She was too tired to speak anymore.

The Dropa leader, who had moved ahead to the front of the column, dropped back and joined them.

"Five more minutes," he said.

"Thank God!" exclaimed Bonnie.

She trooped along, head down, thinking.

If the AI in the shuttle can scan the stone and get useful information out of it, then maybe this wasn't a wasted trip after all. But... if not, then I have totally wasted my time coming to Tibet. I'll have to go back to the Corresse *and start over. Dammit.*

Suddenly rifle fire came from all around them. The sound was deafening. She hit the dirt, as did Dallitta. She looked up to see what was happening.

The two Dropa carrying the stone were already crumpled on the ground, and they looked very dead.

The leader and the other one had pulled their laser weapons out and were firing into the trees beside the trail, but Bonnie couldn't see what they were firing at. And she didn't think they could either. With a groan, the leader fell over, hit hard. Seconds later, the other Dropa also fell, blood spurting from holes stitched down his stomach.

The rifle fire stopped. Bonnie and Dallitta lay in the dirt, uncertain what would come next.

Out of the trees in front of them, ugly Yellow Hat from the day before came slowly out, rifle at the ready, along with a half-dozen of the others from the camp where they had been held prisoner.

Yellow Hat prodded the bodies of the Dropa to make sure they were dead, then turned to Bonnie and Dallitta. He gestured with the rifle and yelled a command. This time, Bonnie understood it. She got up, and stood, swaying in shock and anger.

Yellow Hat gestured to the stone, half-hidden under the dead bodies of the two Dropa who had fallen atop it and yelled again in Chinese.

"We are to carry the stone," said Dallitta.

One of the men pushed his rifle barrel into Dallitta harshly. She moved over to the dead Dropa covering the stone and pulled one of them out of the way. Dazed and moving like a zombie in shock and horror, Bonnie went and pulled away the other one. Together, they fitted the rope and leather harness around themselves and lifted the stone off the ground. The leader stepped off down the trail and someone behind them poked them with a rifle barrel.

They started walking. The stone was heavy, but with the two of them and the harness, it was possible to maintain a normal walking pace. If they slowed, the man behind poked them with the rifle barrel. They followed the faint trail for a few minutes, and suddenly they came out into the meadow.

There was the shuttle, right where they had left it. The leader of the men marched over to it, and waved at his men, gesticulating wildly and screaming orders at them. Two of the men put down their packs and started pulling something out of them. Bonnie knew what it was instantly - C4 explosive.

They were going to blow up the shuttle.

No!" Bonnie shouted, dropping the stone with a thunk. "No you cannot!" she screamed again, charging at the leader. The speed and suddenness of her rush bowled him over, and he hit the ground on his back. Bonnie smashed her fists into his face, over and over, until a rifle butt hit her in the back of the head, and all went dark.

* * * * *

"Where can they be?"

Jim was frustrated. He had arrived at dawn the previous day. Bonnie and Dallitta were not at the coordinates Arteveld had provided. Jim had found the rocky hole where they were supposed to be, and it was empty. The shuttle was gone. He had called on comms, but there was no answer.

Arteveld had also provided the coordinates of three caves which they planned to investigate. He assumed they had already completed the check of the first cave, returned to the shuttle, and left for one of the others.

He had flown to each of the three sets of coordinates but found nothing. Then he orbited the area for a while, again finding nothing. He was concerned the Devastator - a strange black craft with no wings and little sound - would attract too much attention. The last thing he wanted right now was to have the Chinese Air Force on his case.

After a few more minutes of futile searching in the general area, he gave up and went back to the depression in the mountains, putting the Devastator down in the empty spot.

He exited the ship and climbed out of the cockpit,

examining the depression. It was really almost a hole, with sides so steep he wasn't sure he could climb them without assistance. He rummaged through the small cargo compartment on the Devastator but found nothing that would help him scale the sides. Then he walked around the perimeter of the space.

On one side he found a spot where he could scale the wall. Slowly, he made his way up the rocks, working his way out of the hole until with a gasp of relief, he reached the top.

Knowing it was a waste of time, he trekked to the first set of coordinates Arteveld had given. But his instincts were correct. There was no sign of Bonnie and Dallitta there. By the time he returned to the Devastator, it was late in the day. He thought about lifting off and searching for them in the dark, but the risk of running into a mountain was so great, he talked himself out of it.

Better to be sighted by the Chinese Air Force in the air tomorrow and outrun them, than to smash the Devastator into the side of a mountain tonight and leave the wreckage for them to find later.

Jim climbed back into the Devastator. Like the Longsword, it had a small bunk behind the seat for the long missions a space fighter could make.

Rummaging around, he found a food compartment and broke out some rations. It wasn't bad - his first Nidarian food - and afterward he lay back in the bunk, staring out the open canopy at the sky. The Milky Way was overhead and in the darkness of the mountains, it was magnificent.

A little closer to home, he could see Jupiter and Saturn, near each other in the night sky.

Somewhere out there is Rita and the fleet. I wonder where they decided to hide. I'm sure they're in the Kuiper Belt, but that doesn't narrow it down much. Or they might have gone high and be sitting 50 AU above the ecliptic. Or 50 AU below it. Or at some random point 50 AU in any damn direction at all.

Jim sighed.

Bonnie and Rita. I love both of them, both of them love me, and it can't go on like this forever. And I will be the one that has to choose. I know that. Bonnie and Rita will never choose. They'll force that decision on me. And I guess that's right. I guess it has to be that way.

But it sucks.

Finally, he slept. And while he slept, the stars turned above him in the night sky, and the planets whirled in their races around the sun.

The sun hitting Jim in the face next morning woke him up. He grimaced, holding his hand over his eyes, then managed to get up on one elbow and look around.

Where the hell am I?

It took him a few seconds to get oriented. Then he remembered.

Gotta find Bonnie. She's around here somewhere.

Getting out of the cockpit, Jim took care of his morning business, then returned to the cockpit and tried to contact Arteveld. But it was no use; he couldn't raise the *Corresse* or any of Rita's fleet. Likewise, there was no response to his attempts to contact Bonnie in the shuttle.

Breaking out more of the rations, he had breakfast, then settled himself back in the cockpit and strapped in.

"OK, Jimmy Boy, then we'll just go look for them," he said. He powered up the Devastator, closed the canopy, and slowly lifted out of the depression until he was several thousand feet in the air. He started moving around the mountain, searching every possible clearing and depression for any sign of the shuttle.

He spent most of the morning working the mountain but found nothing. Then he moved on to the next mountain, which was directly west. But again, a thorough search of the entire mountain found nothing.

By early afternoon, he was losing all hope that he would find them.

I think they've left the area. But where would they go? They knew that Arteveld was leaving with Rita. So they know he's gone. They can't go back to the Corresse. *Would they go to Philadelphia? Colorado Springs? Back to Deseret looking for me?*

"Angel, I'll search one more mountain. Then I'm leaving," Jim announced to his AI, who really didn't care.

<Very good, Jim>

Jim smiled and turned the Devastator toward the larger mountain to the northwest. He started a search pattern around it, about halfway up the side, circling the mountain slowly, moving up after each complete sweep to the next higher level. He was getting plenty worried about the Chinese Air Force now; he had been up at altitude in broad daylight for six hours. The day was bright and sunny, and he had to be standing out like a sore thumb in the black-as-night Devastator.

He tried once again to call Bonnie in the shuttle on comms, but there was no response.

With a sigh, he reached the snow line and made one last circle of the mountain. But there was nothing.

"I give up, Angel," he announced to the AI. "Let's go to Nevada, I guess. That's the only place I can think of where she would go."

Turning the fighter to the south, Jim started a slow descent back to the valley between the mountains. A glint of light off to one side flashed; his eyes unconsciously turned to see what it was. In a small clearing several miles away, something flashed again.

Curious, Jim made a slight turn and headed toward the clearing. Approaching it, his heart leaped. There was the shuttle, tucked in among the trees in the edge of the clearing. As he got closer, he turned the Devastator, trying to see into the clearing.

And saw Bonnie lying on the ground, with men pointing rifles at her. Even from this distance, he could see blood on the back of her head. Dallitta was a little distance away, with two men guarding her as well.

Spinning the Devastator around, Jim got it pointed directly at the men and dropped it over the edge of the trees, planting it firmly on the ground with the nose pointed directly at them. The big black fighter with the droop snout had a huge laser cannon mounted on the front, and the barrel of the cannon was pointed directly at them. Now Jim hit the arming switch for the cannon, and a loud howling noise came from it as it started building up a charge. He toggled the auto-tracking radar, and the cannon barrel twitched and jerked as it tried to find a starship target in this strange environment.

That was enough for the men with the rifles. They broke and ran, as fast as they could go, and disappeared into the trees. Jim turned off the laser, popped the canopy and unstrapped. He hopped out of the fighter, slid down the stub wing, and ran to Bonnie. Dallitta beat him there; she was cradling Bonnie's head in her arms, and she looked up at Jim.

She said something in Nidarian, but Jim couldn't understand her. But she pointed to the shuttle and then gestured for Jim to take Bonnie. Quickly, he picked her up. Dallitta went to the shuttle and opened the airlock hatch. They carried Bonnie inside; just behind the cockpit were two small bunks. Jim placed Bonnie on one of them and Dallitta shooed him back, began examining the wound. She got up and ran to a compartment on the wall, took out a medical kit, and returned to Bonnie. From the medical kit she took a cloth and handed it to Jim.

"Water," she said in English. "Hot. There." She pointed to a door in the back of the shuttle. Jim opened the door and found a small restroom. He ran hot water over the cloth and returned it to Dallitta. She gently cleaned the wound, then sprayed antiseptic into it. Finally, she stood up and turned to Jim.

"We go. Quick. They return maybe."

Jim nodded.

"Where?"

"I don't know," said Dallitta. "You decide."

Then she knelt back at Bonnie's side and started strapping

her into the bunk.

Jim nodded. He thought hard.

The Singheko were in orbital position by now. He knew from his AI that the Singheko had positioned three capital warships in equidistant geocentric orbits over the Earth - one battlecruiser over the equator slightly west of Central America monitoring North and South America, one just north of New Guinea to watch Australia, China, and the rest of Asia, and one cruiser over Africa to keep an eye on that continent as well as Europe. The slave ships had landed at various locations around the Earth near major population centers.

"We go to Antarctica. Do you know Antarctica?" asked Jim.

Dallitta stood up.

"Yes. I know Antarctica. We go quick."

"OK. Antarctica it is. I'm Jim, by the way."

The little Nidarian stared at him, a bemused expression on her face.

"Oh, the lover left behind. Jim Carter."

Jim nodded. "Yep, that's me."

"I am Dallitta. We go now. Go quick now."

Jim turned and headed for the airlock.

"Wait!" Dallitta yelled. "Bring stone! We must have stone!"

"I'll get it," said Jim. He ran out the hatch and looked on the ground. There he saw a large stone, tangled in a rope and leather harness. He ran to it, lifted it with a grunt, and carried it back inside the shuttle. He laid it on the other bunk and used the straps to tie it down. He could hear Dallitta up front in the cockpit, already throwing switches. He heard the engines start to whine in the rear.

Running back out the airlock, he slammed the hatch shut and started for the Devastator. Suddenly AK-47 fire started coming out of the forest to his right; he ran faster, dodging and weaving as bullets smacked into the ground around him. He reached the Devastator and slammed his feet into the emergency steps on the side, climbed to the top and threw himself into the cockpit as bullets pinged off the side of the ship. He hit the canopy switch and as it closed around him, he toggled the arming switch for the cannon.

I don't have to worry about hitting Bonnie this time, so no bluff, you bastards. This time I'm sending it.

The cannon barrel twitched, and the ready light came on, and Jim pressed the trigger on the stick. The laser was designed to punch a hole in a starship from a range of a thousand miles in space; here on the mountain it cut a swath two meters wide and five miles long, cutting the trees to bits, crashing them down into smoking, flaming piles.

The rifle fire stopped and was replaced by screaming. Jim turned off the cannon and lifted, translating backwards to cover the shuttle as it also rose out of the clearing.

<Message from Dallitta> said his AI, automatically translating into English. <There is no sub-orbital path to Antarctica which will keep us from direct line-of-sight of the Singheko. We will have to go nap of the earth. You have better terrain-following, so please lead, I will follow>

"Acknowledged," replied Jim.

He turned and once more headed down into the valley to the south. The shuttle turned and fell in behind him. In tight formation, they started their long journey to the bottom of the world.

CHAPTER TWENTY-THREE

Earth. McMurdo Station, Antarctica

It took them twelve hours to get to Antarctica. By the time they arrived, both Jim and Dallitta were running on pure nerve. Neither of them could talk anymore - they were just too tired. Jim made his approach to the airstrip at McMurdo without a word, and Dallitta followed silently behind him. When the Devastator was finally safe on the ground and the engines whined down, Jim decided to close his eyes for a moment. He was unaware when he went to sleep.

He woke up when someone started pounding on the side of the canopy. He hit the switch to open the canopy. The cold air hit him like a knife, taking his breath away and hurting his throat. A man wearing a huge parka, with a face mask and goggles, stared down at him.

"Well, at least you're human!" he said.

Jim managed a weak smile. The man handed him a face mask and goggles. Jim put them on, then the man helped him out of the cockpit. He had placed a ladder beside the Devastator, which helped. Jim climbed down, shivering, and the man handed him a parka.

"I guess you came from the Nidarian fleet?" he asked.

Jim nodded.

"Yes. Indirectly."

"Should we go to the other one - the airplane looking thing? Or do you want to go to McMurdo Station?"

"Let's go to the other shuttle. It's closer. We'll talk there."

The man led Jim to the shuttle, which was parked forty meters away. The cold bit into him and he shivered. The man turned back to him.

"Lucky for you we're having a warm spell today," he said.

"Yeah. Lucky."

Reaching the shuttle, Jim opened the hatch and they entered the airlock. Dallitta had closed the inner door; now she opened it, waiting for them.

The man paused at the sight of Dallitta. Videos of the Nidarians had been common on Earth before the arrival of the Fleet, and even more had been posted afterward. But the first sight of one still took humans by surprise.

Dallitta waved them in and shut the hatch behind them. It was warm inside the shuttle. They shed their parkas, masks, and goggles. Jim turned to his guide, now revealed to be a gray-haired man of indeterminate age, and pointed to Bonnie, still unconscious in the bunk beside them.

"We have an injured officer here. Do you have a doctor available?"

"Yes, absolutely," said the man. He pulled out a walkie-talkie and talked to someone briefly.

"They're on their way," he said. "It'll take about thirty minutes for them to get here."

"OK, thank you for helping us," Jim said. "I'm Major Jim Carter of the Space Force. This is … uh, Dallitta."

"Commander Dallitta," Dallitta added in English. "Pleased to meet you."

"Greetings and welcome to McMurdo," the man said. "I'm Lieutenant Ken Johnson, the Operations Officer here today. What brings you to Antarctica, and how can we help?"

Dallitta turned away to attend to Bonnie. Jim thought about how to respond, finally decided the truth was best.

"We need a place to hide from the Singheko for a bit. I'm not sure how long. It could be a few hours, or it could be days or weeks."

Ken nodded. "We heard 'bout the invasion. It just doesn't seem real. Especially to us, stuck way down here. It's hard to believe."

"It's real, all right. Have you heard any recent news? In the last two days?"

"Well, let's see. Earth surrendered, you know. No possible way we could fight them. At least not in space. The Singheko appointed the U.N. as a World Government - they said they weren't going to deal with hundreds of countries, so we had to accept it. Or else. Then they landed those big-ass ships all over the planet, and now they're collecting up slaves to load them up."

Jim looked at Dallitta. She shook her head grimly, then continued working to change the bandage on Bonnie's head.

"I think we'll need some time to sleep first," said Jim. "We've been airborne for hours. We're out on our feet. I think it best if we sleep here in the shuttle, though. In case we have to make a quick departure."

"Understood," said Ken. "Just tell us what you need, we'll take care of it for you."

Jim swayed.

"Sleep," he muttered, and then crumpled to the bunk.

Sol System. Backside of Mars

Rita watched on the holo as her detached task force of three Nidarian destroyers slashed past the Singheko destroyer orbiting Jupiter. The Singheko never had a chance. The Singheko warship had about sixty seconds warning and did manage to fire two missiles at the Nidarians as they flashed by. But it was far too little, and far too late. Before they could fire again, Nidarian missiles smashed into the enemy destroyer, leaving an expanding cloud of gas, starship parts and Singheko bodies.

"Scratch one destroyer," said Tarraine, watching the holo. Then the three attacking Nidarian warships accelerated as they tried for the mass limit to escape.

Unfortunately, the Nidarian ships had seemingly miscalculated. Although they clearly had enough velocity to escape pursuers closer in to Sol, there was one Singheko cruiser farther out they had apparently overlooked.

The Singheko cruiser had recently changed her picket location to be inside the orbit of Saturn and was perfectly positioned to catch them before they could make the mass limit. The Singheko, pissed at the loss of their destroyer, gave immediate chase with the cruiser.

The Nidarian destroyers, detecting the engine signature of the Singheko cruiser, vectored away, trying to escape, but it seemed to be hopeless. The Singheko cruiser was soon making ground on them and would catch them before they could reach the mass limit.

However, in the event, all the Singheko cruiser did was catch the rest of Rita's fleet, lying in the black directly in its path, engines off and cold, just waiting for the cruiser to waltz into their trap. It was another ambush.

The cruiser picked them up a half-minute before intercept. It was far too late for the Singheko cruiser to reverse course or to even veer off at a tangent. The enemy was caught like a fly in a spider's web.

With no other option available, the Singheko cruiser attempted to accelerate through Rita's fleet, firing every missile tube she had at them as she entered engagement range. But in terms of missile capacity, she was outnumbered by better than five to one.

The Singheko cruiser survived just long enough to watch one Nidarian destroyer take a direct hit in the nose, knocking the front of the ship completely away, spilling flame, debris and crew into space, and her counterpart - one of the other Nidarian cruisers - take a hit in the engines, knocking one of its four engines out of action.

Then the Singheko cruiser became a large ball of expanding junk in the black, on a long orbit to nowhere.

And suddenly, at Mars, another two Nidarian destroyers flashed past the Singheko picket in orbit there, while its attention was focused on the battle going on by Saturn. Before its crew even knew there was another attack occurring, they were all dead.

"And scratch two more of those assholes," muttered Tarraine grimly.

On board the *Merkkessa*, Rita gazed at the holo, then turned to Captain Bekerose nearby.

"Congratulations, Captain Bekerose. Your plan was much better than our original one. You are a devious fellow, Bekerose, has anyone ever told you that?"

"Thank you, milady," replied Bekerose. "I think. But we took some losses, I'm afraid."

"Yes," stated Rita. "We did. But it is what it is. This is war. Any movement from the rest of the Singheko ships?"

"None so far, milady. They're holding position. I think they've had enough for one day."

"Very good, Captain. But I think we should get out of here and back to never-never land as soon as possible."

"Aye, milady," agreed Bekerose. "We're leaving now."

Rita turned back to Lt. Lirrassa. "Lieutenant, please send a message to General Raines on Earth. Give him the results of the battle, tell him we'll disappear for a while, and warn him of almost certain retribution by the Singheko."

"Aye, milady," responded Lirrassa.

Rita rose from her chair.

"Captain Tarraine, I'll be in my day cabin if needed."

"Aye, milady."

She went to her cabin and closed the hatch behind her.

Then Rita Page, Admiral of the Black, sat on her couch. She let one tear slide down her cheek for the lives lost - and the more lives that would be lost on Earth because of her actions. She knew the retribution would be horrible.

Please forgive me, she whispered. *You who are innocent. Please forgive me. But I don't have the luxury of choosing. I must fight them and kill them as long as I draw breath. That is my job.*

Earth. Petersen Air Force Base, Colorado Springs

"How many?"

"Ten thousand, sir. In retaliation for the attack on their ships."

General Raines hung his head, moisture flashing into his eyes. It was all he could do to speak.

"Where?"

"The collection point outside Los Angeles. They just slaughtered them. They told them to assemble for loading into the slave ship. When they were gathered, they brought down a squadron of fighters and killed them all."

The officers of his staff sitting at his conference table were silent.

Raines took a deep breath.

"We expected it. We knew they would retaliate. But I didn't think it would be this bad."

"It's going to happen every time we attack them," said his aide, Colonel Garth. "We either accept it as the cost of war, or we give up for real and submit to them."

There was a growl of dissent around the table. Giving in to the Singheko wasn't a concept they could tolerate.

"Well, we're not giving in." spoke Raines. "We're going to have to accept the cost of war. As painful as it is, as much as it hurts, we will not give in to these bastards."

"So we proceed with Operation Pearl Earring?"

"We proceed. You have a green light," said General Raines. "Go kill some Singheko."

Earth. Teterboro, New Jersey

The slave ship was huge. It was shaped like a pentagon, remarkably like a smaller version of the famous building in Washington, D.C. Each side was 450 feet in length and 35 feet tall. The Singheko had taken over Teterboro Airport to park it.

It sat in the middle of the runway and taxiways, a black symbol of humanity's surrender.

Each side of the pentagon had two hatches. From each hatch, ramps led down to pens that looked remarkably like the cattle holding pens in a stockyard.

The busses left from the Port Authority Bus Terminal in downtown New York City. Each bus contained fifty manacled and shackled convicts, with ten heavily armed guards watching them. It took 45 minutes for the convoy of buses to make the trip to Teterboro, sandwiched between four armored cars.

Upon arrival at Teterboro, each bus went through a human checkpoint. The name of every prisoner was double-checked against a master list, and their fingerprints and iris scans were taken one last time. Then the bus passed through to a second checkpoint.

The second one was a Singheko checkpoint. The human guards left the bus, glad to be away from an onerous and horrible duty. Big burly Singheko guards came on board, the smallest of them six and a half feet tall. Waving laser rifles, they glared at the prisoners, yelling at them in an unintelligible language, growling, slapping any prisoner who made eye contact.

It was then the convicts knew they were truly and completely forsaken by humanity. They had known it logically much earlier; the day after the surrender, the U.N. had announced that the first bodies to fill the Singheko slave ships would come from prisoners sentenced to death or life imprisonment. It was a brutal kind of logic. Those who had no say about it would be the first to go.

Now the bus would be driven to the holding pens, and the prisoners would unload directly into the pens. There, they would be stripped naked and their hair shaved, forced through a disinfectant dip like cattle, and pushed up a ramp to disappear into the ship.

No one knew what happened inside the ship after that.

Operation Pearl Earring began before dawn, two days after Rita's attack - and after the first day of loading had completed. 4,000 prisoners had been loaded on the slave ship that first day. There were two more days to reach the quota of 12,000 slaves demanded for each slave ship.

Two hours before dawn, a small Delta Force team slipped onto the field. They killed all the Singheko guards around the ship, most of whom were asleep at their posts - the Singheko had no concept the humans would attack after surrendering.

Working quickly, the Delta Force team moved to the hatches around the perimeter of the ship and prepared for entry. They breached the hatches and attacked into the ship, killing every Singheko they encountered. They found the prisoners in huge cages, stuffed in like livestock; they freed them as they came to them.

Each Delta Force member carried an extra rifle and two extra pistols; as they freed the prisoners, they handed the weapons to them. The so-called prisoners - now revealed to be fellow Special Forces volunteers, naked and unafraid - joined the hunt for the Singheko. In an hour, it was all over - there wasn't a Singheko left alive on the ship or on the airport.

By dawn, the area had been evacuated of all personnel, and charges went off throughout the ship, enough ordnance to render it a pockmarked crater that couldn't be recognized as a once-terrible symbol of their conquerors.

They knew the retribution would be terrible. There was no doubt.

But this war had just begun.

Earth. McMurdo Station, Antarctica

Bonnie came to her senses in the dispensary at McMurdo Station.

Her first thought was that she was dead, because her head hurt so badly, she was cold, and it was eerily silent.

But after a few seconds of looking up at the white ceiling

over her head, with its long fluorescent bulbs in a rusty fixture and a pockmarked faux ceiling that had seen its better days, she decided heaven wouldn't be nearly this tacky.

"Hello there," said a voice she would recognize anywhere. She lifted her head to see Jim sitting in a chair past the end of her bed, a reading tablet in his hand.

"About time you got here," she mumbled, her mouth not working quite right.

"You've been pretty doped up, so don't do anything strenuous - like badmouth me," said Jim.

"Ha. The day I can't find the strength to badmouth you, I'll be lying in a pine box."

Jim, serious for a moment, got up and walked over to her, took her hand.

"Well, you almost made it this time. Don't scare me like that again, OK?"

"I'll do my best. Where the hell am I? And why is it so damn cold?"

"We're at McMurdo Station in Antarctica. I found you guys right after that creep bashed you in the head. Dallitta and I loaded you in the shuttle and made a break for Antarctica. It's the only place we could think of to give us some quiet time for analyzing the stone."

"Oh. I hope you smoked that yellow hat son of a bitch."

Jim grinned. "I'm quite sure I did. Last time I saw him, he was the brightest spot in a forest fire."

"Good," Bonnie said. Her eyes started to close. "Good. Wake me when we get there."

And she was out again.

Hours later, Bonnie woke up again. Someone - a doctor, she decided - was checking her blood pressure and raking a thermometer across her forehead to get a temperature.

"Are you a doctor or just a stray pervert?" asked Bonnie.

The man laughed.

"Possibly both," he smiled. "I'm Dr. Riza. How are you feeling?"

"Like someone peeled back my head and filled it with rocks," said Bonnie.

"Oh, good, you can feel the rocks," said the doctor. "I wasn't sure we put enough in."

Bonnie laughed, then groaned. "Oh, shit. That hurt. Don't make me laugh."

"OK, fair enough. You don't make me laugh; I won't make you laugh."

"Deal," said Bonnie. "Where's my crew?"

"They're in that strange aircraft, the one that looks like a fat black miniature space shuttle. They are working on something which is top secret."

"Ah," said Bonnie. "So everybody knows…"

"Of course," replied Dr. Riza. "We are a small community here, and there isn't much to talk about. They are trying to decipher the writing hidden on the stone."

"Are they having any success?"

"Ah, that you would have to ask them directly," smiled Dr. Riza.

"May I get up?" asked Bonnie.

"You may get up and walk around a bit, but please don't overdo it."

A few minutes later, Bonnie had managed to walk weakly down the hallway to a small waiting area. There, she sat in an overstuffed chair and watched the news on a television.

According to the news, guerrilla forces outside the control of the U.N. had attacked one of the Singheko slave ships in Teterboro, New Jersey, killing 317 Singheko, freeing 4,000 prisoners, and destroying the entire ship.

The Singheko had retaliated by killing another ten thousand humans in Chicago, Illinois.

The U.N. had protested they couldn't be responsible for every underground guerrilla movement in the world.

The Singheko had declared that any more attacks on their ships or personnel would result in double the retribution.

Meanwhile, the loading of the other nine slave ships

scattered over the world continued. The ship in LA was now three-quarters full, with 9,000 convicts loaded aboard. Ships in Europe, China, and Australia were half-full.

And the one in Russia was full and ready to launch. The Singheko announced it would depart Earth tomorrow.

It was an ugly day all around.

CHAPTER TWENTY-FOUR

Earth. McMurdo Station, Antarctica

A day later, Bonnie felt well enough to go to the shuttle and join Jim and Dallitta. She found them huddled over their screens, trying to decipher the stone.

"OK, I'm here now," she announced, coming into the shuttle. "You're saved from a lifetime of failure trying to figure out that stone."

Jim and Dallitta both jumped up from their chairs and embraced her, one on each side. They hugged together for a bit, until Bonnie, blushing, pushed them back.

"Hey, give a girl a break! We've got work to do!"

Laughing, Jim and Dallitta led her to a workstation they had set up in the shuttle. It was a tiny shuttle compared to most - about the size of the average corporate jet - but in addition to the two bunks behind the cockpit, it had six large first-class seats and a decent galley. Bonnie settled into one of the plush seats with a screen and keyboard before her and looked at the pictures on the monitor.

"What have you got so far?" she asked.

"The AI scanned the stone and as I suspected, there are tiny, almost invisible characters in the spirals. The AI has identified them as archaic Nidarian. But the problem is that when we get to the key part, the stone is damaged."

Dallitta pointed to a part of the image where the stone showed some intense weathering. The line of characters in the bottom of the spiral disappeared for a space.

"Tell me what you've deciphered so far."

Dallitta pointed to a translation on the other screen.

"Here it is. They begin by saying that the *Dragon* is damaged. They just barely made it to the Sol system before the interstellar engine quit. In fact, it quit nearly 100 AU from Sol, and they had to make it the rest of the way on their standard system engine. They parked the *Dragon* and came down to Earth in the shuttle to obtain the materials for repairing the interstellar drive. They were ambushed by the locals and most of the party killed. Here…"

Dallitta pointed to a highlighted part of the translation:

"… it says the survivors were captured by a different tribe of locals, who looked upon them as gods and refused to let them go back to the shuttle. They were kept for many years, until they were old. The last two survivors prepared this stone, along with several others, to leave behind in case anyone ever came looking for them."

Dallitta leaned back and gazed sadly at Bonnie.

"That's all," she said.

"What?" croaked Bonnie. "Where's the *Dragon*? Where did they park it?"

Dallitta shook her head sadly.

"That's the part that's damaged."

Jim leaned over and pointed to the translation.

"See? Right here. It says, 'we parked the *Dragon* at …" and then the rest is gone. The stone is too damaged for the AI to read the characters until the next sentence picks up with, 'Then we came down to this place in the shuttle to get the iridium.'"

Bonnie cursed, slapped the table, and cursed again.

"Not fucking iridium again! After *Jade*, I hoped I'd never see those damn words ever again in my life!"

"Yeah, me too," Jim agreed. "But it is what it is. They needed iridium and came down here to get it. They left the *Dragon* somewhere else. But we don't know where."

"The most logical place would be the Moon," said Dallitta.

"Yep, but that doesn't narrow it down much," said Jim. "The moon may be only a quarter the size of Earth, but it's still a big place. And hundreds, maybe thousands of rills and valleys and holes where you could hide a ship."

"Well, we've extensively explored the near side. So it would have to be somewhere on the far side," responded Bonnie.

"Yeah, I agree - if it's on the moon at all. But what if it's on Mars, or one of the Galilean moons of Jupiter? Or Titan? Or one of the dwarf planets, Ceres or Eris?"

Dallitta objected. "They wouldn't leave it so far out. It must be inside the orbit of Saturn, I think. It would be a long trip on the shuttle to go much farther."

"Fine," agreed Jim. "Even so - it would take us years to search everyplace it could be."

Bonnie had been quietly studying the image of the stone on her screen. Now she jumped back into the conversation.

"What's in the other spiral?"

"What?"

She turned to Jim and Dallitta.

"What's in the other spiral?"

"Oh. Nothing that we can see," replied Dallitta. "We've examined it very carefully, and it appears to be blank."

Bonnie shook her head.

"Why make another spiral and then leave it blank? If they were trying to make sure their message passed down through the years intact, they had to provide some level of redundancy."

Dallitta pointed to the magnified image on the screen.

"But there's nothing there. You can see it. The second spiral is blank. We think maybe they never got a chance to finish it."

Bonnie shook her head.

"No. I'm not buying it. They completed the first spiral. How likely is it they would be interrupted exactly when the first one was complete and the second one not yet started?"

She looked up at Jim and Dallitta standing beside her chair, looking down at the images.

"We're missing something here. We need to look at alternatives to written characters. They did something else for redundancy. But they didn't use the second spiral, for some reason. Maybe they were being threatened by that time. So they did something besides writing into the second spiral."

Dallitta looked puzzled.

"What else could they do in a primitive setting like they were in, except writing?"

Bonnie leaned back and thought.

"We know they had some of the technology out of the shuttle, because the Dropa had their lasers. Which still worked after two thousand years, so good tech."

She looked over at Dallitta.

"What could you do if you had a small laser? A handheld one?"

Dallitta shook her head. "I don't know - cut some kind of pattern into the stone?"

Bonnie looked back at the images of the stone. Incised around the entire rim of the stone were regular ridges, almost like the patterns on the edge of a coin.

Dallitta and Jim had assumed they were decorative only. Bonnie looked up at Dallitta and pointed to the pictures of the rim pattern.

Dallitta snapped to the possibility instantly.

"*Corresse*, analyze the rim of the stone for any patterns that could be interpreted as communication."

<I am analyzing. I have completed my analysis. The spacing between the ridges on the rim of the stone is not regular. It varies from ridge to ridge. Taking the variations into account, the spacings appear to fit an ancient Nidarian communications code similar to the Morse code of this world."

"Bonnie, you are the cat's meow," smiled Jim. Dallitta was beside herself.

"*Corresse*. Can you translate the rim? Specifically, the section pinpointing the location of the *Dragon*?"

<Yes. Translating from archaic Nidarian. Translation complete. The sentence reads: 'We parked the *Dragon* on Mars, in a canyon just east of Candor Chasma'>

"Yes!" exclaimed Jim, pumping his fist in the air. "Mars! Candor Chasma! We can find it!"

Jim and Dallitta started dancing around, laughing gaily. Bonnie couldn't help but smile at the incongruous sight of the big, six-two Jim Carter dancing like a madman with the little five-foot Nidarian.

Finally, as the celebration started to die down, Bonnie said dryly, "Perhaps we can celebrate after we get to Mars?"

* * * * *

"We have two main problems," said Bonnie. "One - we have to get the iridium to repair the *Dragon*, and - two - we have to get by the Singheko before we can get to Mars."

"We can get the iridium from General Raines," said Jim.

"Who's General Raines?" asked Bonnie.

"The new head of the Space Force at Petersen. If we get in touch with him, he can get it for us."

Bonnie agreed. "OK. So he gets the iridium for us. How do we get our hands on it?"

Jim was lost in thought for a bit.

"That's a problem, all right. Let me think on that. But while I'm thinking, we have a bigger problem. We can't get to Mars without the Singheko detecting us."

"Sure we can," piped up Bonnie. "You go up in the Devastator and distract them, while Dallitta and I escape in the shuttle."

"Distract them? How?" asked Jim.

"Attack the cruiser that's parked over Africa," replied Bonnie. "That should get their attention."

Jim looked astonished.

"Attack a cruiser with a single Devastator?"

"Well, you don't have to actually attack it. Just make a run at it. Pretend to attack it. Then sheer off at the last minute and make a run in the opposite direction."

"Sure," said Jim. "Just sheer off in the opposite direction. With twenty or thirty of their fighters on my ass."

Bonnie winked. "I'm sure you can handle it, Mr. Carter."

Jim glared at her.

"That's Major Carter to you, Colonel."

"Oops, not, sorry," said Bonnie. "No longer active reserve. So it's just Miss Page, thank you very much."

Jim shook his head, but he was smiling.

"OK. Let's say, just for the sake of argument, that some idiot was crazy enough to go attack the cruiser with a Devastator and distract the Singheko. Then what?"

"We'll go straight out the south pole of Earth to about 1 AU. That should give us sufficient distance to lose any pursuers."

Jim grunted. "If one of their fighters comes after you, it won't matter how far you go. They'll catch you in a heartbeat."

Dallitta demurred. "Not so, Major. The shuttle is deceptively fast in three-space. I venture to say we can hold our own with any fighter."

"Yeah," rebutted Jim, "but even if they can't catch you, they can still stay with you until you've got no place left to go."

Suddenly Bonnie jumped to her feet. "Hey, that gives me a hell of an idea! We need to contact Rita!"

* * * * *

It took a week to get the iridium. The AI translation of the stone revealed they required thirty pounds of it. Using McMurdo's encrypted satphone, Jim was able to reach General Raines in Colorado Springs and outline their plan.

"Excellent idea!" he told Jim over the phone. "Let's do it! I'll have the iridium to you within a week. That's enough time for us to plan the rest of the mission. Call me again tomorrow night and we'll do a status!"

"Roger, sir, call you tomorrow night," said Jim, signing off.

He turned to Bonnie and Dallitta, standing nearby in the comm shack.

"Done," he said. "We have a 'go' from Raines. Let's work out the details and be ready when the iridium comes in."

The next two days were spent fine-tuning their plan. When they were satisfied with it, they communicated the last details to General Raines. Raines assured them he had found the required quantity of iridium and it was on the way to McMurdo via a drone A400D routed through New Zealand. Since it was a normal supply flight, they saw no reason for it to arouse any suspicions with the Singheko.

Then they waited. Bonnie's head healed up and she was back to her normal, acidic personality. She baited Jim unmercifully, but he loved every minute of it. They had been separated for more than eighteen months; now it was like they had never been apart.

Yet a deep sadness still permeated Jim's soul, one he was having difficulty shaking off. Bonnie noticed, and finally on the last day she came and sat beside him in the cabin of the shuttle as he was working on his screen.

"Jimmy Boy, I think it's time you tell me about her," she started out. "I can see it in your eyes. Who was she?"

Jim looked at her. He had expected this conversation, sooner or later. He pushed his keyboard away, put his head down, and thought for a few seconds.

"Her name was Caroline," he said. "I met her on Mars when I went to the First Space Wing. We got together."

"And?" asked Bonnie.

"She's dead," said Jim.

Bonnie was silent for a bit.

"Washington?" she finally asked.

"No. London," said Jim. "They evacuated all civilians from the base when the first Singheko wave entered the system. She got home just in time to die."

"Was it serious?" asked Bonnie.

Jim shook his head and looked down at the table in front of

him.

"Not really. We didn't have enough time to know if it was going to be serious or not. It was just a few weeks, then she was gone."

"It didn't take you and I long," said Bonnie. "I knew it was serious after the first night with you."

Jim nodded. "Yeah. So did I."

"We had a good thing, you and I."

Jim looked back up at her.

"Yeah. We did. Until you decided to go off and explore the universe without me."

Bonnie closed her eyes, hurt.

"I know," she whispered. "But I had no choice. It was either you or all of humanity. I had to make a decision."

"I know that," admitted Jim. "But that didn't make it hurt any less."

Bonnie opened her eyes and looked back at Jim.

"I do still love you, you know."

"I know," said Jim.

"Not like before. Not the hot and heavy. But still strong."

"I know. Me too."

"And exploring the universe isn't all it was cracked up to be, you know?"

Jim laughed.

"You mean spending six months coercing bureaucrats on a stinking planet, getting chased around by Singheko, getting your head bashed, and freezing to death in Antarctica?"

Bonnie smiled. "Yeah. Jim, when this is over - or mostly over, whenever we get a breathing spell…"

"Yeah?"

"You need to make a decision. You need to let us know."

"Yeah. I know."

"You have to choose between Rita and me. And you must be clear about it. As much as the three of us love each other, this can't go on forever. I know that as far as you and Rita go, it could. You two would be happy if the three of us were together forever. But I can't do that. I'm a different breed of cat. I have to have resolution."

"I know," Jim admitted. "I know I have to decide. But it's like cutting off an arm or a leg."

"Even so," said Bonnie. "When we are at a good point, you decide, and you make it clear to us. So we can go on with our lives."

Jim nodded. "I will."

"OK," said Bonnie. She rose from her chair.

"I think I hear the drone coming in. Let's get our iridium and get the hell out of here."

* * * * *

The drone A400D came in from New Zealand with the iridium in a crate. They unloaded it and strapped it into the cargo bay of the shuttle.

Then they were ready.

Their plan required Jim to leave seven hours ahead of Bonnie and Dallitta. They went to McMurdo Station and said their goodbyes to Lt. Johnson and Dr. Riza and others who had helped them, then returned to the shuttle. Jim said goodbye to Dallitta, who was wise enough to disappear into the cockpit for a while. Bonnie held him tight in the cabin, and they kissed goodbye, and embraced; an embrace they both knew might never come again if things went south.

Then Jim went out and strapped himself into the Devastator, and Bonnie and Dallitta buttoned up the shuttle and prepared to wait for their own departure time. After Jim's departure, they would take a sleep cycle, then depart when Jim had sufficiently diverted the Singheko.

If it worked.

Jim, alone now in the cockpit of the fighter, said the standard fighter pilot's prayer as he finished his pre-start checklist.

"God, please don't let me fuck up."

Then he hit the engine start switch and listened as the system engine came to life. With the help of the AI, he did his post-start checklist and was ready to depart.

"Angel One is ready to go," he called to Bonnie, who was working comms for the shuttle.

"Angel Two copies. Good hunting," called Bonnie. "Let's do it."

Lifting off, Jim translated to his outbound vector and slowly accelerated. Before all else, he needed to ensure his diversionary attack on the cruiser didn't lead back to McMurdo. So his first destination was Amsterdam Island, a small island in the middle of nowhere in the vast reaches of the Southern Indian Ocean, 3,500 miles from McMurdo.

Flying at 100 meters over the snow, the AI piloted the Devastator expertly, rising and falling with the terrain to maintain a precise altitude. Jim started out at Mach 1, feeling that he would be largely out of sight and range of any Doppler radar coverage by the Singheko in orbit over the Earth. As he left the continent and came out over the ocean, he dropped down to 75 feet and increased his speed to Mach 2.

Then he settled back in his seat, relaxed, and let the AI fly.

Three and a half hours after departing McMurdo, Jim roused himself and watched Amsterdam Island pass off to his left. Now it was time to change course. He turned slightly to the northwest, heading for Abu Dhabi on the Arabian Peninsula, another 4,500 miles away, and kicked his speed up one more notch. Once again, Jim leaned back in his seat and dozed off.

Three hours later, passing over Abu Dhabi at six in the morning, Jim was finally ready.

"Well, Angel, here goes nothing," he said to the AI.

<Understood, nothing is going>

Jim grinned.

"Not exactly, but close enough. Give me manual control."

<You have control>

Jim turned and took a vector directly for the Singheko

cruiser in an equatorial orbit above Libreville, Gabon. He accelerated steadily as he cleared atmosphere.

It didn't take long for the Singheko to notice him. Within a minute, the AI reported the Singheko cruiser was launching fighters.

"Yippie ki yi yay, motherfuckers!" Jim yelled as he saw two dozen blips appear on his display. "Let's tango!"

Jim hit the master arm switch and the AI beeped an error - target out of range. He hit the override switch and fired four missiles at the cruiser. There was no way any of the missiles would survive the point defenses of the cruiser from such a distance.

But that was not the object of the attack.

Jim vectored hard now, turning away from the cruiser and the oncoming fighter squadrons to escape. He gave every appearance of a frightened rabbit as he jinked madly, even though none of the enemy fighters had fired at him yet.

This is a real head game, he thought.

Behind him as he sped away, he saw all four of his missiles taken down by the cruiser's point defense.

No surprise there.

Jim pushed his accel up to 257g - two g over compensated limits - and headed for Jupiter.

Now we'll see how long these fat fuckers want to chase me.

His long day was just beginning.

CHAPTER TWENTY-FIVE

Earth. McMurdo Station.

Bonnie and Dallitta lifted off from the snow-covered apron at McMurdo and headed out on a vector straight away from Earth, right out the South Pole of the planet. As they cleared atmosphere, they accelerated to 255g. In twenty-five minutes they were 2.9 million klicks from Earth, traveling upwards of 13.7 million kph.

There was no pursuit, at least none they could see. They dropped their accel and held their course for another two and a half hours. With still no signs of pursuit, they breathed a sigh of relief.

"I think we got away clean," said Dallitta. "Nothing coming after us, no sign they noticed us."

"Thank the Lord," Bonnie exclaimed. "Can you spot Jim?"

"Yes, he's blazing a bright path. I can still track him from here. Without stealth mode turned on, that Devastator stands out like a sore thumb. He's got a couple dozen fighters on his tail, and he's about a quarter of the way to Jupiter. But like you predicted, they've backed off on the accel. They're only pushing 10g right now. Too much danger of hitting a rock - hell, at the speed they're moving, even a grain of sand would take out a fighter. So they had to drop off the hard accel. But they're still keeping on his tail."

Bonnie leaned over and looked at the display.

"What's his ETA at Jupiter?"

Dallitta peered at her display.

"If they don't change accel again, he'll get there in 28 hours."

Bonnie sighed.

"I feel for him in that damn fighter. At least we have a full galley and nice bunks."

Dallitta nodded.

"Yeah. But he drew the short straw." She turned to Bonnie. "Let's head for Mars."

Sol System. Nearing Jupiter

<Time to wake up, Major Carter>

Jim ignored the alarm. He was exhausted.

<Time to wake up, Major Carter>

Dammit.

"I'm awake, Angel," he finally grunted.

<We are approaching the Line of Departure, Major>

"Very good, Angel. Thanks for waking me."

Jim pulled an orange juice out of the tiny fridge in the back of the fighter and slammed it down, then ate two of the protein bars he had brought from McMurdo. He washed them down with a bottled water and inched his way back into the cockpit, pulling up the seat back and locking it into place. Then he strapped in, hooked up, and put his helmet back on.

"How long, Angel?"

<Twenty minutes to intercept, Major>

"Are they still chasing me?"

<Yes. As you instructed me, I have let them draw a bit closer, as if I were not paying attention. They have boosted quite subtly to 10.05g, but I did not respond. As a result, they have been closing the gap quite nicely and will catch up to us exactly at the intercept point>

"Angel, you are an angel," said Jim. "How about the destroyer?"

<Exactly as you hoped for, the destroyer that had been

replaced at Mars has come out to intercept and is almost upon us. That ship will also catch up to us as we pass Ganymede. In nineteen minutes and four seconds, we will be shot to pieces by the combined forces of the destroyer and the fighters behind us>

"Excellent work, Angel. My compliments."

<Thank you, Major>

Sol System. Surface of Ganymede

Rita had learned well from her simulations with Captain Bekerose - especially the one where she got her ass kicked at Ganymede. Now the two destroyers and forty-eight fighters of the Nidarian raiding party lay on the surface of Ganymede, engines idling. Rita could see Jim Carter's ship coming over the top of the moon's horizon. With his stealth turned off, his fighter was easy to spot in the black.

The two dozen Singheko fighters were almost on him; and the Singheko destroyer lured away from Mars was going to catch him in about two minutes.

"Sixty seconds, everyone," said Tarraine from the lead destroyer. "Good luck and good hunting."

Rita had finally relented and let Tarraine lead a mission. It was a risk; but everything in war was a risk, and she couldn't say no to him anymore.

Of course, she negotiated the deal such that she got to fly a fighter herself. Which Tarraine was not happy about and had made his objections known with an uncharacteristically raised voice for the normally quiet and efficient Captain.

Even Bekerose had objected, telling Rita it was an absolute breach of regulations for an Admiral to take an operational part in a mission.

All of which Rita had ignored.

<Thirty seconds, Admiral> said Rita's AI.

"Thank you, Jimmy Boy," Rita replied. She always named her AI helpers after Jim. It was part of her good luck ritual.

I hope it works this time too.

There were four squadrons of Devastator fighters in position on Ganymede, ready to ambush the approaching enemy. Each squadron consisted of twelve fighters.

Rita had been forced to join Green Squadron, which was the reserve squadron. It would be the last to launch and the last to engage.

But Bekerose and Tarraine would have it no other way. They put their foot down at the end, threatening mutiny if she tried to lead the attack. She finally gave in, happy just to get off the ship and take part in the mission, even in the reserve squadron.

She was assigned as wingman to the Green Squadron leader, Major Willedda. She had met him before - he was also the Wing Intelligence Officer for the *Merkkessa*.

<Twenty seconds, Admiral> said Rita's AI. <Arm weapons and set engine boost to max>

"Roger," acknowledged Rita. She toggled the necessary switches and all the lights on the panel turned green.

<Green board, Admiral. You are ready for combat>

Rita took another look at the range scanner. Jim was past Ganymede now. The fighters were coming over the horizon. The destroyer would be about ten seconds behind them. It was going to be a bit close for Jim, but they had no choice - they had to wait until the destroyer passed in order to catch it in the rear.

"Hang in there, Jim," Rita breathed under her breath as the first of the Singheko fighters launched missiles at Jim's Devastator.

<Ten seconds, Admiral>

Then things started happening fast. Rita watched Jim suddenly go into stealth as the missiles started climbing up his backside. Because of his coded IFF transponder, he was still visible to her and the rest of the Nidarian ships, but not to the enemy.

But not completely invisible. Another couple of Singheko

fighters launched missiles at him. The first pair of missiles was almost on him and the second pair not far behind.

"Jink!" Rita yelled involuntarily, as the missiles got too close to him. Then suddenly he did, jinking hard, accelerating to 265g and vectoring right into the missiles, radar and laser chaff spraying out behind him as he turned. He went right in between two missiles and was a bit past them when they both exploded.

"Shit!" Rita yelled. Then the Singheko destroyer was past, and all hell broke loose. The two Nidarian destroyers sitting on the surface of Ganymede launched their missiles from the ground, not even bothering to take off first, then both of them accelerated off the moon and made chase on the enemy destroyer, firing more missiles as they went.

<Launch, launch, launch> her AI spoke, and Rita was busy launching off the surface of Ganymede, the other fighter squadrons accelerating away in front of her, she trying to stay attached to her flight lead, a crazy world of missiles and lasers coming to life in front of her. She saw at least two hundred missiles in her battlefield display, everybody shooting at everybody. But the advantage held by the Nidarians, coming from behind and by surprise, was overwhelming. Fighter after fighter of the Singheko went down, blasted to bits.

Suddenly Rita saw Jim's Devastator go by her at incredible acceleration, heading away from the battle.

She couldn't resist.

"Where you going, Jimmy Boy?" she called out to him on her private AI channel.

"The hell away from here, baby. My job is done and I'm out of missiles. I'm not hanging around. Y'all have fun!"

And with that he was gone, and Rita didn't even have time for a snappy comeback because a missile was coming at her and she had to jink. She elected to use the same tactic Jim had used. She waited until the last second, then vectored away at 265g, throwing chaff and flares behind her, moaning under the crush of the incredible g-forces. Without her g-suit she would have been unconscious long before. The missile exploded nearby, and shrapnel pinged off her fighter, but all her status lights stayed green. She checked pressure and engine, and all were good, so she looked for her element lead again.

There!

Major Willedda was nearby, but in trouble. He had two of the Singheko fighters on him. Rita vectored back toward him, pushed it up to 265g again, and grunted with pain as her trajectory slowly moved back toward his. When she was close, she dropped it back to standard, breathed in to catch her breath, and settled her targeting pipper on the tail-end Charlie of the two Singheko fighters. She got a red "locked" light and fired two missiles at the Singheko. Both went right up the fighter's engine cone, and it disappeared in a flash of high explosive and engine parts flying in every direction.

The other enemy fighter, realizing she was on his six, bugged out and tried to make a run for it. She left that one to Major Willedda, who chased it down and dispatched it near the surface of Ganymede while she hung on his wing, protecting his rear.

"Good job there, Green Two," she heard from Willedda.

"Thank you, Major."

Rita checked the display. All the enemy fighters had been destroyed or disabled. The Singheko destroyer had its engines knocked out and was on a slow decaying orbit into Jupiter. Unless it surrendered and allowed them to rescue the crew, they were goners. Rita decided to leave that decision up to Tarraine - it was his mission.

Staying tucked in close to Major Willedda's wing, Rita felt the adrenalin slowly leave her body, and started working to calm her breathing and get back to a state of semi-normalcy.

"Not a bad day's work, Captain Tarraine," she finally sent over her private AI channel.

"Thanks, Admiral. We're talking to the destroyer crew. They are so far refusing to surrender, so we're just letting them fall into Jupiter. But I'm keeping a couple of our destroyers nearby in case they change their mind."

"Thanks for the status, Captain, but this is your mission. I'm headed back to the *Merkkessa* with Major Willedda. Be safe out there."

"Roger Wilco," came back from Tarraine. "And thank you, Admiral, for letting me do this."

"Likewise," grinned Rita.

Sol System. Mars

Bonnie and Dallitta hovered over a small canyon in the surface of Mars.

The shuttle's AI had identified this location as the one consistent with the coordinates recorded on the stone.

From the air, it looked like any small canyon, separated from the much larger Candor Chasma to the west by a few miles.

"We need to run a subsurface survey before we land, Bonnie. If we land on something unstable, we could collapse it and fall in."

"Roger," said Bonnie. "I'll monitor the ship while you do the survey."

Dallitta acknowledged and began running a radar survey on the bottom of the small canyon, while the AI held the ship in position and Bonnie monitored, ready to take control if anything went wrong. It was standard procedure for planetary operations; no matter how good an AI was, it could make mistakes, and there had to be a human in the loop for safety.

"OK," said Dallitta, finishing up. "There's a good solid surface."

She pointed to the display, which showed shades of color, with one oblong gray area highlighted near the center of the canyon floor.

"Alright, let's do it," responded Bonnie.

Dallitta issued the commands and the AI moved them to

the designated coordinates, then settled them gently to the canyon floor. With a descending whine, the system engine shut down.

"Mom, I'm home!" yelled Bonnie in English, unable to resist.

Dallitta looked at her strangely.

"You humans have a very warped sense of humor," she said.

"That's been said before," Bonnie grinned at her. "So now what? Do we wait for Jim?"

"Hell, no," replied Dallitta. "He won't be here for a while. Let's go take a look."

"But where do we look?"

"Ah. That. Well, remember I have a sensor to detect residual radiation from a system engine. If there is a Nidarian spaceship in this canyon, we can find it."

"I'm not sure I want to find it now," said Bonnie. "If it's a piece of junk, I'm going to be so disappointed."

"Cross fingers," said Dallitta.

An hour later, Bonnie and Dallitta stood on the floor of the canyon outside the shuttle. Bonnie was pulling a small cart with tools and equipment. Dallitta scanned with her handheld device.

"I have something," she said. She pointed to their left. "Over there somewhere."

They started walking. The direction was toward the center of the canyon. Bonnie was a bit surprised.

"I would have thought it would be toward the sides of the canyon," she said.

"Too much danger of a landslide coming down and hitting the ship," replied Dallitta. "If it's here, they parked it in the center of the canyon."

They walked for a hundred meters, until they were in the center of the canyon. Finally Dallitta stopped, looking down.

"It's here," she said, pointing to the ground.

Bonnie looked down.

"I don't see anything but regolith."

Dallitta muttered under her breath, turned around a couple of times, then returned to her starting point.

"It's here," she insisted. "It's under us."

"OK," Bonnie muttered. "I guess we dig."

Taking shovels from the equipment cart, they carefully started digging into the soil. The ground was a bit hard. They got down about five inches when Bonnie's shovel hit something.

"Whoops," she called out, the shovel clanking on something. "Found something."

Carefully, using their hands and a trowel, they brushed away the loose soil until a black surface could be seen. Kneeling, with the hole between them, they looked at each other.

"That's a starship hull," said Dallitta.

"Yep."

"That's the *Dragon*."

"Yep."

Then they went crazy. They jumped up, screamed, hit each other, raised their arms to the sky in a prayer of thanksgiving, then danced and jigged until they were both out of breath.

Then they kneeled beside the hole and looked down at the black hull beneath them.

"Any idea where the hatch might be?"

"No. We don't have any idea of the design of the ship. It was two thousand years ago. It could be anything."

Bonnie sighed.

"OK. Let's dig some more."

Sol System. Mars

Jim came into the atmosphere of Mars at a screaming Mach 20, letting the Devastator heat up until the overheat alarms went off and he had to use the system engine to slam on the brakes.

That was for you, Caroline.

Coming down over Valles Marineris, he located Candor Chasma and the little isolated canyon to the east of it. Making a pass over, he saw the shuttle sitting in the canyon. A hundred meters away, he saw Bonnie and Dallitta standing beside a hole in the ground.

A black surface could be seen at the bottom of the hole.

"Hey ladies, what y'all doing down there?" Jim transmitted as he made his pass over them.

They waved at him and shaded their eyes to watch the fighter go over.

"We're just sittin' here waitin' for you, big boy," he heard Bonnie say.

"On my way down," Jim called, and made a fighter break over the canyon, just for the hell of it. Then he slowed, settled into a space right next to the shuttle, and shut down the fighter.

By the time he got the Devastator powered down and the canopy open, Bonnie and Dallitta were standing beside it. He unhooked, got out and stepped down onto the surface of Mars. Overcome with emotion from his exhausting journey, he took a step forward and embraced Bonnie, holding her as close as he could through the spacesuits they both wore. Then, on impulse, he turned to Dallitta and embraced her gently as well, trying to be careful not to hurt her. Dallitta hugged him back.

"Sorry, Dallitta, I hope I didn't break any Nidarian taboos."

"No problem, Jim, although now you have to give me children for the rest of my life."

Jim choked and turned red, but both Bonnie and Dallitta started laughing, so he realized it was a joke.

"I deserved that," he said. "I should have asked first."

"No worries," said Dallitta. "Would you like to take a look at *Dragon*?"

"God, yes," said Jim. He followed them to the excavation. Standing on the edge, he looked down.

They had dug out about a five-by-five square foot area.

There was a black hull showing, the same type of surface he remembered from *Jade* - a composite-looking material formed by nanobots that was common to both Singheko and Nidarian ships. Jim had a sudden feeling of deja vu, remembering a similar sight beside a river in Canada more than two years earlier.

"That looks familiar," he said. He glanced over at Bonnie. "Remember?"

"Yes, I know. It looks like *Jade*'s hull. But this is *Dragon*, not *Jade*. Don't let it throw you."

"Do you want to dig some more today?" asked Dallitta to Bonnie.

"No. Jim's tired, probably way beyond tired. Let's call it a day and pick it up tomorrow."

"OK by me," shrugged Dallitta. "My shoulders and back are killing me."

The trio trudged back to the ship and entered the airlock, shedding their suits into an autocleaner.

Entering the shuttle proper, Jim collapsed on one of the bunk beds and was out like a light. Bonnie and Dallitta looked at him and smiled.

"Guess I'll sleep on the floor tonight," said Bonnie.

"Not necessary," said Dallitta. "I'll go sleep in the Devastator. There's plenty of room in the flight bunk behind the seat, and I'll see if Jim left me any food."

"Better take some with you," said Bonnie. "I know Jim. There won't be any food in there."

CHAPTER TWENTY-SIX

Sol System. Mars

Jim woke up like coming back from the dead. It was dark. Someone was taking off his pants.

"That better be you, Bonnie," he whispered.

"Would you care who it was at this point?" Bonnie whispered back.

Jim smiled.

She's got me there.

* * * * *

Next morning, Dallitta came in through the airlock and found exactly what she was expecting.

Two naked humans together in one bunk, entwined with each other like a couple of Terran octopuses.

"Ahem," she cleared her throat loudly. There was no reaction.

"Ahem Ahem," she tried again.

Bonnie stirred, lifting her head.

"Oh, shit," she said, realizing Dallitta was standing in the cabin.

"I'm going to the galley to make breakfast," Dallitta said pointedly. She turned and went into the small galley and started preparing food. She could hear the two humans just outside, sorting clothes and dressing.

"Here, this is yours," she heard Jim say.

"Got it," she heard from Bonnie.

In a few minutes, Bonnie came into the galley.

"So how's your morning going?" she asked brightly.

Dallitta smiled at her.

"Not nearly as good as yours, I think."

Bonnie grinned and poured herself a cup of *nish* and sat down at the small table. Dallitta continued working on breakfast but talked over her shoulder.

"You know I'm a xenologist too, right?"

Bonnie shook her head, then said, "No, I didn't know that."

"Yes. In addition to my naval duties, I have what you would call a Doctorate in Xenology."

"That's the study of aliens, right?"

"Yes. The study of alien culture, history, language, habits, and all that."

"Oh. Good."

"So you realize what this means…"

"Not really."

"I'll have to write a university paper on this when I get back to Nidaria."

There was a silence from Bonnie.

Dallitta looked at her mischievously just as Jim came into the galley.

"I think I'll title it *Mating Habits of the Human Under Stress*," Dallitta added in English.

Jim stopped, looked astonished at Dallitta.

"What?"

Bonnie just shook her head.

"Never mind, Jim. You're going to be a star in the annals of Nidarian science."

An hour later, the three of them were digging in the excavation. They had decided to dig in a common direction. If they guessed right, they would come up to the hatch sooner. Of course, if they guessed wrong, they'd come out at the engines and have to start over.

Thirty minutes after they started, Dallitta's shovel hit

something solid.

They stopped and stared as Dallitta got down on her knees with the trowel and carefully began to move dirt away from the raised lip of a hatch. When she had cleared enough away, they stood and looked down at it.

It was clearly the hatch of the ship's top airlock.

Bonnie looked over at Dallitta.

"It's your people," Bonnie said, as she had on the mountain in Tibet. "You go first."

Dallitta nodded. She knelt, grabbed the manual handle, and pulled it hard. It moved a bit, stopped, moved again, then with a sudden rush it went to the stop and the hatch cracked open.

It was virtually identical to the top airlock on their shuttle. Dallitta gave Bonnie and Jim a thumbs-up, then descended the ladder into the airlock.

At the bottom was a separate hatch. Dallitta looked at the telltale on the hatch.

"Oh, wow, it still has pressure!" she said. "At least according to this gauge!"

"How is that possible?" asked Jim.

Bonnie elbowed him in the ribs. "Think about it, Jimmy boy. This ship was built by nanobots and uses nanobots for maintenance. If the nanobots are still functional…"

"Oh. Right. If the nanobots are healthy, then the ship is healthy."

Dallitta pulled the lever on the hatch. It moved to a halfway position and stopped. A safety valve let out a huge rush of air as pressure equalized between the interior of the ship and the Martian atmosphere. It took five full minutes before the safety valve released and the hatch lever would move again to the fully open position.

"So it still has power," said Dallitta. "If it didn't, the safety systems wouldn't work."

She lifted the hatch cover and entered the ship. Bonnie and Jim followed, working their way down the ladder, through the second hatch, and into the ship proper.

It was huge.

"Oh my God, I had no idea," said Bonnie, looking around. "I was expecting something small, like the shuttlecraft."

Dallitta was walking around, examining things.

"I knew it would be big," she said. "After all, they launched a shuttle to Earth from this thing. I think this is a destroyer," she added.

"Where's the cockpit?" asked Jim.

"This way," said Dallitta. They walked toward the front of the ship. They crossed three side passages before they arrived at a heavily fortified door.

"Bridge," translated Bonnie, looking at the sign on the door.

The door was locked. There was no keypad or visible means of unlocking it.

Dallitta mused on it for a few seconds.

"If the AI is still active, it'll be a voice lock," she said. She raised her voice.

"*Dragon!*"

<I am here> said a voice.

Dallitta turned to them. "It's an archaic form of Nidarian. I can just barely understand it."

She turned back to the bridge hatch.

"*Dragon. What is your status?*"

<I await orders>

<Please open the bridge hatch>

<Authenticate, please>

"Crap," said Dallitta in perfect English. "I was afraid of that."

<That is an incorrect authentication>

"Any ideas?" asked Bonnie. She was having great difficulty following the Nidarian words because they were so archaic.

"Think, Dallitta," said Dallitta, mostly to herself. "What authentication would they leave, knowing it might be any random Nidarian who found the ship?"

"What's the oldest word in your language?" asked Bonnie.

"Crap," said Dallitta in Nidarian.

<That is an incorrect authentication>

"What?" asked Jim.

"She said, 'crap'" Bonnie interjected in English.

Dallitta ignored them. She was thinking.

I'm in a strange, alien solar system. I must leave the ship and I might not return. I want only a true Nidarian to be able to open the ship. What code word would I put on it?

My destination. Only a Nidarian would know that.

"Sword," said Dallitta.

<That is an incorrect authentication>

They wouldn't make it quite that easy, thought Dallitta. *But maybe...*

"My destination is Sword."

<Authentication accepted>

The bridge hatch clunked as the locking mechanism tripped open. Dallitta turned to Bonnie and Jim.

"After you, o humans of mine," she said gaily. Bonnie grabbed her and gave her a hug. Then she pulled the hatch open and stepped inside, Jim behind her and Dallitta behind the two of them.

It was a pristine bridge, and not a small one. All the screens and consoles were dark, but there were a couple of little lights blinking here and there. So clearly there was at least some power.

"*Dragon*, please report ship status."

"Main reactor is shut down. Standby reactor is running at 1% of rated power. System maintenance records show the star drive is inoperable due to a lack of iridium catalyst. All other systems are operable but in an off state>

"I've really got to learn Nidarian," muttered Jim. "What did she say?"

Dallitta looked thoughtful.

"*Dragon*. Are you able to link to our internal comm units?"

<Yes, I can link to them>

"All of them? All three of us?"

\<Yes\>

"Good. Link to our comm units, please, but use Nidarian for my language. For the other two, use English."

\<English is an undefined language for me\>

"Damn, I forgot about that," said Dallitta.

Bonnie was looking at her with eyebrows raised. Jim was just looking puzzled.

"How about the English translation routine on the shuttle?" asked Bonnie in Nidarian.

"Oh, of course," said Dallitta. *"Dragon* - can you access the shuttle parked nearby?"

\<I can partially access it. It is using a strange format. It requires a code word\>

"Oh, right. Use code word Dallitta-Corresse-two-two-four-two-nine."

\<I have obtained read-only access to the nearby shuttle\>

"Good. Can you download and integrate the English language translation routines from the shuttle?"

\<Checking. I have located the routines. I can download them, but I will be required to take a substantial software update from the shuttle. Is that acceptable?\>

\<That is acceptable. Take the update."

\<Updating...\>

Dallitta turned to Bonnie and Jim.

"OK, here's the deal. The AI is downloading an update from the shuttle to bring it up to date. From there, we should be able to add English to its translation repertoire. Then when we communicate, you and Bonnie can use English and I can use Nidarian, but everybody will understand via our internal comms."

"Fantastic," said Jim.

While they waited for the update to complete, they walked around the bridge. The layout was not much different from that of the *Corresse* or any of the other ships of the Nidarian fleet.

But this ship was much larger than the *Corresse*. They

walked back into the crew quarters and counted the bunks.

There were twenty bunks on the ship, not counting four officer cabins which appeared to be one-person compartments.

"This thing is huge, a lot bigger than a corvette," said Dallitta. "This is a damn destroyer."

"Yeah," agreed Bonnie. "Which makes me wonder..."

"What?"

"I wonder if it has weapons, and if those weapons still work."

"Good question," said Dallitta. "We'll soon know."

They checked out the galley. It appeared the crew had cleaned everything out when they departed. There was nothing in the galley except dishes.

"They took everything with them on the shuttle," said Dallitta. "They didn't know if they would ever return. So they took all the food."

"I feel so sorry for that crew," Bonnie said.

<Update complete>

All three of them heard over their internal comms - Dallitta hearing it in Nidarian, Bonnie and Jim in English.

"Wow!" said Jim. "It worked!"

"Awesome!" said Bonnie. "Now we can get to work!"

* * * * *

They spent three days assessing the condition of the *Dragon*. They were pleasantly surprised to find all systems partially or completely functional, except for the star drive. They got the ship pressure checked and it passed, so they brought atmospheric pressure back up and stopped wearing their pressure suits inside the ship.

And to their great relief, they didn't have to shovel the rest of the dirt off the top. The AI informed them there were maintenance bots that could do that. Dallitta dispatched the little creatures, and they had the entire ship uncovered within twenty-four hours.

So now Bonnie was sitting at the flight console, working through a simulated flight with the AI whispering a tutorial in her ear. She had spent hours teaching herself how to fly the ship. Jim and Dallitta sat behind her, Dallitta in the Captain's chair and Jim in the XO chair.

"Dallitta," said Jim via his comm, "I've been thinking."

"Not that again," she shot back.

"I know. It's a terrible habit I'm trying to break."

"So what have you been thinking this time, Major?"

"We're awfully exposed out here right now. We've got the shuttle, the Devastator, and now the *Dragon* all sitting out here for the Singheko to see if they put another picket ship around Mars. And they will. There could be one on the way right now."

"Good point," Dallitta said. She thought for a bit. "We need to find a more protected place to complete *Dragon*'s repairs."

"And I know just the place," said Jim. "The old First Wing Headquarters over at Acidalia Planitia. It was abandoned after the Battle of Saturn. The Singheko already went down and checked it out, we know that. So they have no reason to go down there again."

"Does it have room for all three ships?"

"No; but it has a pressurized working environment big enough to hold the *Dragon*, I think. We can work without pressure suits. We can sleep in full-size beds at night. There might even be food left in the cafeteria reefers."

"Good. Let's move over there. Bonnie - are you able to fly the *Dragon* yet?"

"I can certainly fly it well enough to make it to Acidalia Planitia," responded Bonnie.

"OK. Let's take all three ships over. Jim, may I suggest that you go first and check it out, make sure it's still empty and safe for us to come in?"

"Will do," said Jim, jumping up. He headed for the airlock. "Give me a four-hour head start to make sure everything's OK, then I'll meet you guys there this afternoon."

"Wait!" said Bonnie. She trotted over to Jim and gave him a

kiss.

"Just for luck," she said.

Jim winked at her and went into the airlock. A short time later, they heard the whine of the Devastator as it powered up and departed.

Bonnie returned to her flight console and started checking everything. She had already checked and re-checked every system necessary for flight, but this time it was for real.

They were going to kick the tires and light the fires.

Dallitta had been lost in thought since Jim left. Now she suddenly lifted her head and got a glint in her eyes.

"Bonnie! You know what else we should do before the Singheko put a new picket on this planet?"

"What?" asked Bonnie, turning back to face Dallitta, puzzled.

"Get Arteveld back here with the *Corresse*. We'll need a crew for this ship; we can't get it back to Nidaria without a crew. And Arteveld would be a tremendous help. I think we should get him to come join us at Acidalia Planitia."

Bonnie nodded vigorously. "That's a damn good idea, Dallitta."

Dallitta spoke to the AI.

"*Dragon*. Contact the *Corresse* using my standard code and the comm methods you downloaded from the shuttle. Bring Arteveld up to speed on our status. Tell him we are relocating to Acidalia Planitia. Suggest he join us there to finish repairs of the *Dragon* and lend us crew members for her operation."

<Message ready for transmission>

"Transmit."

<Message sent>

Bonnie looked at Dallitta.

"How long do you think it will take to get a reply?"

"I don't know," said Dallitta. "If they are following standard operating procedure, they'll have placed repeater buoys at sixteen points around the system, such that no matter where they are, they can pick up messages. If they're in the Kuiper

Belt somewhere, they'll get the message about 7 to 10 hours from now. Then we should get a response in about 14 to 20 hours, not counting their discussion time."

"Fantastic. So let's head for the base at Acidalia Planitia."

"Let's," said Dallitta. "I'll go over to the shuttle and get ready to depart."

Four hours later, Bonnie sat at the flight console of the *Dragon*. Of course, the AI would do the actual flying. Bonnie would be monitor pilot in case anything went wrong.

But still... her heart beat a little faster.

Slowly, the *Dragon* lifted out of its pit and into the air. It turned and headed for Acidalia Planitia. As it rose to a comfortable cruising altitude, its speed increased to 1,200 miles per hour. Dallitta fell in behind it with the shuttle.

As they flew, Bonnie was lost in thought.

Two thousand years. And still flight ready. Thanks to the maintenance bots. We need this technology. Humans need this technology now. We can't wait. The Singheko will overwhelm us without it.

Can I give this ship back to Garatella? Wouldn't that be stupid?

* * * * *

They parked the *Dragon* inside the pressurized hangar at the old First Wing Headquarters complex in Acidalia Planitia. It was a tight fit; the only way they could get it inside was to turn it corner wise. The *Dragon* turned out to be 110 meters long. Destroyer-class for sure.

Then they spent two days bringing the hangar back into a pressurized state so they could work in a shirt-sleeves environment. They also pressurized one section of the living quarters on the base so they could sleep inside. Dallitta had a room of her own. Bonnie shared a room with Jim.

At the end of their third day of work, Arteveld and the *Corresse* arrived.

While the Singheko had not yet put a new picket ship

at Mars, they knew it would happen sooner or later. So they reloaded the shuttlecraft back into the shuttle bay of the *Corresse*. Then they moved the *Corresse* under the portico next to the Devastator, out of sight of prying eyes from overhead.

Arteveld and Flo moved into the rooms next to Bonnie and Jim and Dallitta, and the rest of Arteveld's crew moved into the next corridor, glad to get some time away from their small bunk spaces on the *Corresse*.

With the help of Arteveld and his crew, they made quick work of refurbishing the *Dragon* for extended flight. They loaded the iridium brought from Earth into the 3D synthesizer in the *Dragon*. The crew from the *Corresse* showed them how to take the finished product out and stack it in the Engineering space ready for installation by the maintenance bots.

Bonnie and Dallitta had found quite a bit of food left over in the cafeteria at the base. They moved enough into the *Dragon* to ensure it was fully stocked and gave the rest to Arteveld and the crew of the *Corresse*. Then Arteveld assigned a portion of his crew to the *Dragon* for flight test.

After another two days, the AI declared the stardrive fully repaired and ready for testing.

It was time.

Like Bonnie, Dallitta had spent hours at the *Dragon*'s flight console, with the AI whispering in her ear, practicing simulated missions. Now Bonnie took the Captain's chair for their flight test. Jim sat in the XO seat, not sure he would be needed, but ready to lend a hand as necessary. Arteveld and the *Corresse* would act as chase in case an emergency arose.

The hangar was depressurized, and the doors opened wide. The *Dragon* worked its way out of the tight space, then levitated across the apron under the portico until it was in the open area outside.

They had scanned for Singheko ships for several hours and found nothing. Now they executed one more scan. The sky was still clear. Arteveld and the *Corresse* hovered beside them, ready for flight.

"Execute Flight Plan Test-One," intoned Dallitta at the Flight Console.

<Executing Flight Plan Test-One> responded the AI.

The *Dragon* rose into the sky, headed for space. Bonnie kept a close eye on the sensors, still concerned that a Singheko destroyer might be in the area. But she saw nothing. When they were clear of atmosphere, the AI turned them toward the mass limit and steadied down on a vector.

<Increasing reactor to full power. Ready for acceleration>

"Confirm," said Dallitta. "Execute."

The *Dragon* started to accelerate.

And accelerate.

And accelerate.

They passed 255g and continued to build.

But there was no g-force acting on their bodies.

"Holy shit!" Jim swore as they passed 270g.

The *Corresse* was being left behind so fast, it was already out of sight.

And still they accelerated. At 300g, the accel stabilized.

<Stable at Military standard acceleration> said the AI.

Bonnie spoke in a small voice, still disbelieving.

"*Dragon*...this is your max standard acceleration with full compensation?"

<Yes. That is correct>

"What is the maximum speed you can achieve in-system with sufficient wedge deflection to keep us safe from rocks and dust?"

<Fifty percent light speed>

Bonnie sat stunned.

"Say that again, please."

<Fifty percent light speed>

"Don't you mean five percent of light speed?"

<Incorrect. I can maintain fifty percent of light speed without danger>

Bonnie turned and looked at Jim.

"What the hell have we got here, Major Jim?"

CHAPTER TWENTY-SEVEN

Sol System. Outbound from Mars toward Pluto

"Never mind following us, *Corresse*," Bonnie sent to Arteveld. "Return to base. We'll call you if we run into problems."

They were already so far ahead of the corvette it was pointless. Arteveld would never catch them.

Bonnie was a little skittish about letting the *Dragon* accelerate to its rated maximum velocity of 50% light speed, so she had Dallitta stop their accel at 25% light. Even so, they reached the mass limit in seven hours.

Now it was really showtime.

"*Dragon*, set a six-space course for Point Alpha."

<Course set>

"Execute."

The universe went away, and they were in six-space.

"Well, at least the stardrive works!" yelled Dallitta. "Good work, guys!"

Dallitta was peering at the displays. Her eyes grew wide.

"Oh my God," she said quietly.

"What?" asked Jim and Bonnie simultaneously.

"We're making thirty-three light years per day," said Dallitta. She turned in her chair and stared at the two of them.

"Thirty-three light years per standard Earth day. Ten times the current max speed of a starship in six-space."

Bonnie couldn't believe it.

"That's impossible!"

"Look!" exclaimed Dallitta. She pointed to the display. Both saw what she was pointing to and looked at each other.

"We could get back to Nidaria in eighteen days," whispered Bonnie.

"Or," said Jim, a wicked light glinting in his eyes, "We could take out the entire Singheko fleet before they knew what hit them."

"What? How?" asked Bonnie.

"Think about it," said Jim. "We can waltz right up to them, invite them to come out and play. Then we fire our missiles and just run away. They couldn't possibly catch us. We can hit and run without mercy."

"But I'm not sure we have missiles," muttered Bonnie. "I keep promising myself to check weapons, but something always distracts me." She turned back to her console.

"*Dragon*, what is your current weapons loadout?"

<40 standard missiles, 5 ECM drones, two laser cannon, one long-range gamma lance>

"What?" three voices said simultaneously. "What's a gamma lance?"

<A gamma lance is a weapon with the impact of five missiles hitting simultaneously in the same spot>

"Holy crap!" Jim exclaimed.

"*Dragon*, when you say long-range, what do you mean?"

"The gamma lance has a range of 4,500 miles>

The three looked at each other, stunned. Their standard missiles had a range of no more than 2,500 miles. As did the Singheko missiles.

"This is a game changer," breathed Dallitta. "This is an entirely new kind of weapon. Something not seen before."

"And Garatella knew it!" shouted Bonnie, slapping herself in the forehead as it all became clear to her. "That son of a bitch knew it! He didn't send us here to find *Dragon* because of the faster drive! He wanted the weapon!"

<Entering three-space> said the AI. With a slight whine,

they found themselves back in the normal universe. Bonnie took a quick look at the display.

"Where are we?" asked Jim.

Bonnie turned and looked at him.

"Point Alpha. One light year from the Sun."

In amazement, the three of them looked at the display.

Jim spoke first, in a low voice.

"What do we do now?"

Bonnie looked at Dallitta.

"I think we go report to Rita and talk this through with her," said Bonnie.

Dallitta looked troubled.

"We're supposed to take this ship back to Garatella immediately," she said.

Bonnie nodded.

"I know that. But the situation has changed. First of all, we didn't know anything about this new weapon. Secondly, Rita's fleet was pushed out of the system. We didn't plan on that. We've got a whole new ball game here. We need to take this to Rita and talk it through with her."

Dallitta was not happy.

"We are disobeying our orders."

Bonnie looked at her sternly.

"We are delaying the execution of our orders for a good reason, Dallitta. I never said we won't go back to Nidaria. But I want to talk this over with Rita first."

Bonnie turned back to Jim, signifying the discussion was over. Arteveld had provided them with coordinates of a position to contact Rita if absolutely necessary.

"*Dragon*, take us to Point Baker-Two-Four immediately."

<Moving to Point Baker-Two-Four. Ready>

"Execute."

The universe went away again. They were headed for a coded location in the Kuiper Belt, where Rita had assured them they would be quickly found by her fleet.

Sol System. Kuiper Belt

Rita's comm beeped at 4 AM ship time.

"Admiral, we have a priority message from the corvette *Kaimina* on picket duty."

"Read it, please."

"Rita, this is Bonnie and Jim, we got the *Dragon* up and running, we're here and need to talk to you urgently."

That was quick, thought Rita. *And they didn't waste any time getting here.*

"Have the *Kaimina* escort them into our perimeter, Larissa. What's their ETA?"

<30 minutes, milady>

"Very good. Wake Tarraine, read the message to him, and have him meet me in the briefing room when they arrive."

<Wilco>

Rita got out of bed, stretched, and stripped her clothes off. Stepping into the shower, she stood under the water for a good ten minutes, trying to wake herself up. Out of the shower, she dressed and started brushing her hair. As if by magic, her new steward Gakodda entered the room, bearing *nish* and toast. He put it down quietly by her hand and departed.

Now that's a steward.

Rita attacked the *nish*, downing it in a minute. Then she finished brushing her hair and stood up, adjusting her uniform.

This had better be good, she thought. *Four fucking AM.*

Her AI beeped again.

<Commander Dallitta, Major Carter, and Bonnie Page are being escorted from the shuttle deck to your office. They will arrive in three minutes>

Leaving her bedroom, Rita entered the briefing room. As expected, Tarraine was already there. She smiled at him and sat at the head of the table.

"Well, Captain Tarraine, you know as much as I do. I have

no idea why they felt it so important to break protocol and come in person. I can only assume it's worth the risk."

Tarraine smiled. "Let us hope so, milady."

The door swung open and Bonnie stepped in, followed by Jim Carter and Commander Dallitta.

Rita felt a terrible urge to run to Jim and kiss him. She fought it off. She stood. Bonnie walked to her, and for a moment she thought Bonnie was going to embrace her. But Bonnie, recognizing the military formality required of the moment, reached out a hand instead.

"Hello, Admiral. How are you?" she asked as they shook hands, as if they had never been lovers.

"I'm good, Bonnie. How are you?"

"Much better than good, Admiral. And after we tell you our story, you're going to be much better than good as well."

They sat at the briefing table, Bonnie opposite Tarraine, Jim and Dallitta across the table from each other. Bonnie glanced at Jim as if to ask who should start. Jim nodded at her to go ahead.

Turning back to Rita, Bonnie began.

"I really don't know where to start. This is so crazy."

Rita smiled. "Usually it's best to start at the beginning."

"Well, we got *Dragon* repaired and took her on a test flight."

Rita waited patiently, glancing at Tarraine.

"In three-space, she can do 300g accel and 50% of light speed - with full protection," said Bonnie, as if it were the most matter-of-fact thing in the world.

There was a long silence. Tarraine looked a bit stunned. He spoke, almost involuntary as he comprehended Bonnie's statement.

"That's...that's 45g more than we can pull. And we can only maintain reasonable protection up to 25% of light..."

Bonnie and Jim could see the wheels turning in Tarraine's head. Rita kept a good poker face, however.

"What about six-space?" Rita asked.

Bonnie smiled at Jim.

"33.3 light years per standard Earth day."

Tarraine almost choked. Even Rita had difficulty keeping her expression under control.

"That's 10 times faster than our current technology." Tarraine sputtered. "Are you sure? This must be some kind of mistake!"

"No mistake," said Jim. "We tested it out to one light year."

Now Bonnie leaned forward, staring directly into Rita's eyes.

"That's not even the best part," she said. "It has a different kind of weapon on board, something we've never seen. Something the AI calls a gamma lance. The impact of five missiles hitting simultaneously. Range of 4,500 miles."

This time Rita reacted. She rose straight in her seat, looked away and up at the ceiling. They could see the wheels turning in her head. She stood, walked away, paced back and forth, thinking.

"Are you sure?" she suddenly asked, wheeling on Bonnie with urgency in her voice.

"We tested it on three asteroids," replied Bonnie. "It seems to work as advertised."

Rita looked at Tarraine.

"Convene a staff meeting immediately. I think we're going to have a new mission."

Now Dallitta interrupted.

"Milady! Our orders were clear! The High Councilor directed us to locate the *Dragon* and bring it back to Sanctuary immediately! We cannot risk it in a battle!"

Rita gazed down at her.

"Commander Dallitta, I understand. I know how you must feel. But I'm responsible for this solar system now. I must make the hard decisions. We're going to use the *Dragon* to help clear this system of the Singheko. Then I'll decide the next steps."

Dallitta was clearly angry and upset. She started to speak again; Bonnie laid a hand on her arm.

"Commander Dallitta, I take full responsibility for this.

I made the decision to bring the *Dragon* here. All the consequences will be on me," said Bonnie.

Dallitta was not satisfied. She looked at Rita, prepared to continue the debate. But before she could speak, Rita forestalled her.

"Commander Dallitta, your objections are noted. However, the decision is made. Are we clear?"

"Clear, milady," mumbled Dallitta.

"Very good. Bonnie, I propose to draft you into my officer corps, if you'll take the job. Captain of the *Dragon*. What do you say?"

Bonnie looked at the woman standing before her.

This is not the same woman who came out of the medpod on Jade. *The woman who had trouble distinguishing her own memories from mine and Jim's. The woman who cried at night when we were on the moon.*

This is an Admiral.

"I'd be happy to accept that position."

"Excellent. Commander Dallitta," Rita added, turning to her. "Would you accept XO on the *Dragon*?"

"Aye, milady. Thank you."

"Good. Tarraine will help you assemble a crew to move to the *Dragon* and start training. Tarraine, give her the best, please."

Turning to Jim, Rita gave him a grin. She already knew the answer to her question, but she had to ask anyway.

"Jim, would you like a destroyer? I have an opening on one of mine that needs a Captain."

Jim gave a wry smile.

"Thanks, but no. I'm a fighter pilot, always was and always will be."

"Then how about I promote my CAG to the destroyer and give you CAG - Commander Attack Group. You'll be rated as a Commander and in charge of all the Devastators on board."

"Can I still fly?" asked Jim.

Rita sighed.

"Yes, you can still fly."

"Then yes, I accept."

"Good," Rita sniffed. "Then we are done with that, and we can move on to planning what comes next."

"And what is that?" asked Bonnie.

"Killing every Singheko in this system," said Rita grimly.

Earth. Krasnodar, Russia

Tatiana shivered, crying, huddled in the corner of the Singheko holding pen, naked. The huge aliens that looked like some kind of intelligent flat-faced lion on two feet had taken all their clothes and shaved their heads; now they were herding the humans up the ramps onto the slave ship. If anyone resisted, they were shocked with long baton devices that were basically cattle prods.

Slowly the long line of humans moved up the ramp, until it was her turn. Growling, a seven-foot Singheko guard waved his shock-stick at her. Tatiana staggered to the foot of the ramp and took her place at the end of the line.

An impulse made her look across the huge airfield, past the edge of the pentagon-shaped slave ship, to the distant green fields outside Krasnodar.

I'll never see Earth again.

At the top of the ramp, tubes sprayed disinfectant liquid across them. Dripping, she walked into the blackness of the Singheko ship. Following in line, they were directed to a huge wire cage on the right side of a wide corridor.

As she came to the cage door, Tatiana hesitated. One of the big Singheko guards slammed her in the back, knocking her into the cage and onto the floor. She heard the cage door slam shut.

Crawling to a corner, she curled into a fetal position, crying.

Outside the ship, the guards unhooked the ramps from the ship and pulled them away. Then they boarded the ship, sealing up the hatches.

An hour later, the huge pentagon-shaped slave ship rose into the air, accelerating slowly but steadily out of the atmosphere of Earth. Once clear of the atmosphere, it took a vector for the mass limit and accelerated at 20g until it was traveling at 31,000,000 mph. 43 hours later, it reached the mass limit and disappeared into six-space.

Its cargo of 12,000 humans had no idea what fate had in store for them.

CHAPTER TWENTY-EIGHT

Sol System. Empty Space

Three weeks later, Rita's fleet dropped into three-space at the mass limit, a bit over 14.5 AU from the sun. Both Earth and Mars were on the other side of the sun from their position.

"Do you think they'll catch on?" asked Tarraine.

Rita cocked her head a bit.

"I'd like to think we would if the situation were reversed. But let's hope and pray they don't."

She referred to the fact they were almost directly opposite the Earth-Jupiter line. If the Singheko came out for battle, then given the time constraints, the enemy would need to assemble their fleet somewhere between Earth and Jupiter.

Which was good for Rita. Because Mars was just a bit off that line, between her and the place the Singheko would most likely assemble their fleet to meet her - if they didn't snap to her plan.

Her fleet accelerated at 255g toward Earth. After 5 hours, they cut their boost, traveling at 15% of light speed - a bit more than 160 million klicks per hour.

The Singheko picket destroyer at the 10 AU point on their side of the Sun held position long enough to count the incoming ships and classify them - then it ran, and hard. Its job was done - and its survival depended on getting up to speed before the Nidarian fleet caught it.

A half hour later, Rita saw on the holo the remainder of

the Singheko pickets moving at max acceleration back toward Jupiter. At the same time, the cruiser and two battlecruisers at Earth departed orbit on a similar vector.

"Ah. Good. They want to fight," remarked Rita, watching the holo.

"Yes, it seems so," said Tarraine beside her on the Flag Bridge. "Based on their vectors, they're assembling about 1 AU past Mars."

"That'll work," said Rita. "We'll stick to attack plan Alpha-1 unless something changes."

"Aye, milady."

Over the next hours Rita watched as the Singheko fleet assembled. All the enemy ships made for a point just about 3 AU from the Sun, about 1.5 AU on the other side of Mars.

"Designate that point as Point Sierra-1," remarked Tarraine to Larissa.

"Copy."

Rita's fleet started a hard decel as they passed the Sun. They would meet the Singheko traveling much slower, giving their missiles time to lock on target and evade countermeasures.

By the time they passed Earth, the entire Singheko fleet had assembled at Point Sierra-1 and started accelerating toward them.

"They'll meet us about 1 AU past Mars," remarked Tarraine. He turned to Lirrassa. "Designate that as Point Sierra-2."

"Copy."

Rita listened to her staff doing their job, making their calls, setting their consoles, preparing.

She heard Bekerose make the expected announcement to his bridge crew.

"Battle Stations, please."

The klaxon went off throughout the ship. There was an increased sense of urgency to every person on the bridge as they checked and triple-checked everything. It was getting real.

In the missile bays, dozens of crew members ensured every

missile was spun up and the external tube doors were open and ready for launch. All pulse cannon were fully charged, ready to fire.

"All hands and systems ready at Battle Stations, milady," Rita heard from Lirrassa.

"Thank you, Lieutenant."

And that was that. The die was cast. Rita had no illusions about the coming battle. People were going to die. Ships were going to die.

But most of all, she thought, *Singheko are going to die.*

It was as if the fleets approached each other in slow motion. Then, as happens when battle occurs in space, all the time was gone. In front of them was the array of Singheko warships - two battlecruisers, each surrounded by a protective screen of cruisers, destroyers, and corvettes. The Singheko had put on quite a bit of accel, to ensure they weren't standing still when the two fleets met. So, they were coming toward the Nidarians at a good clip, their ships also moving laterally as they positioned for advantage.

Tarraine gave the order and Rita's fleet started moving their ships around as well, to make things more difficult for the Singheko.

"Thirty seconds to intercept," called Tarraine.

Rita watched the holo count down. Then Tarraine started counting out loud, as he always did. Even though they could all see the count on the holo in front of them, it seemed he couldn't resist.

But Rita didn't mind. It was somehow reassuring to hear him.

"Five."

"Four."

"Three."

"Two."

"One."

The battlefield became a storm of missiles and pulse

weapons as the two fleets flashed through each other. On the *Merkkessa*'s bridge, voices yelled in desperation as missiles were fought off with the point defense systems, as ships foundered and died beside them, as a missile hit their front gravity wedge and slammed the ship to the side, overpowering the compensators, and another one hit aft, punching a hole in the ship and killing dozens of crew.

And then in seconds it was over. Ten Singheko and six Nidarian warships had entered the battlefield; as they pulled away, Rita gazed at the holo and counted the cost.

Two Singheko ships were outgassing flames and spinning in space - two destroyers.

But there were also two destroyed hulks tracking along with the Nidarian fleet. Ships once full of life - now just shredded piles of junk. Their ballistic course kept them - for the moment - in formation.

One cruiser and one destroyer. Hundreds of lives lost.

As the wrecks spun silently, bits and pieces flinging off them, Rita felt an urge to add up the crew members of the dead ships and weigh them in the balance against the Singheko deaths.

She resisted.

Do your job. Do your job. Count the cost later.

Behind them, the Singheko turned to give chase, pushing their decel to 260g to make the course reversal. They were determined to catch the Nidarians and bring them to heel once and for all.

Rita pushed up her own accel now. Everyone grunted and labored as the accel went up to first 257, then 259, then finally 260 - 5g over compensation.

But it wasn't going to be enough. The Singheko reached zero velocity relative to the Nidarians and then began coming back toward them, increasing their accel to a bone-crushing 265g - 10g over compensation.

It was a load Rita and her ships couldn't match. The smaller bodies of her Nidarians couldn't tolerate that level of force for any length of time.

The Singheko would catch them at Jupiter.

Sol System. Approaching Jupiter

Space battles take so damn long, thought Rita. *Hours and hours of boredom followed by seconds of sheer terror.*

I think I've heard that somewhere before...

They had been running in front of the Singheko for three and a quarter hours in the asteroid belt, one of the most dangerous places in the solar system for space trash. Rita's fleet was at 10% of light speed now. The gravity wedges at the front of the Nidarian ships sparked madly as they deflected space dust and particles. Behind them the Singheko ships looked the same; neither side willing to slow down for safety's sake. The Singheko had maintained a brutal accel, increasing their speed until they were moving just slightly faster than Rita's fleet.

Suddenly, with a flash like a nuclear explosion, one of their destroyers simply disappeared, no longer in the universe except as a cloud of gas and energy.

The enemy destroyer had hit a space rock too large for the gravity wedge to handle, and too close to dodge.

Finally, grudgingly, the Singheko dropped their accel, coasting onward, still making ground on the Nidarian fleet, but not pushing as hard.

"They finally came to their senses," Rita commented to Tarraine. "Not that it makes much difference. They still catch us in another ten minutes."

Tarraine leaned over to Rita. "Do you think they're stupid enough to fall for it?"

Rita smiled at him.

"I'm hoping there are no limits on Singheko stupidity and arrogance."

"If this doesn't work, we're going to be in trouble."

"We were in trouble when we got up this morning."

Rita stared at the holo, then turned to Tarraine.

"Let's go ahead and execute Baker-Two-Five," she said.

Tarraine nodded, punched it into his console, and hit the confirm button.

On the holo, Rita watched as her fleet stopped all accel and flipped end over end to face the Singheko.

They were five minutes from merge now. They had to survive the full force of two battlecruisers and three cruisers full of pissed-off Singheko for at least thirty seconds after that.

* * * * *

Far behind the Singheko fleet, the *Dragon* was in a hard decel from a maximum velocity of 14% of light speed on her trip from Mars.

She had lain hidden inside the abandoned portico of the old Mars base for three weeks as Bonnie, Jim, and fifty of Rita's best engineers and crew worked madly to meet a deadline imposed by their Admiral.

Fabrication had gone on night and day inside the pressurized hangar. The sound of grunts and curses had permeated the entire space as Jim, Bonnie and the crew tore off the noses and tails of four Devastators and rebuilt them.

Their noses were extended by five feet, giving them an unbalanced aspect that looked ugly as hell to any decent pilot.

But they weren't concerned about looks at this point.

In the rear, they added a second reactor behind the first, kludged together with spit and bailing wire. It doubled output to the weapons system.

They had still been working as the Singheko fleet assembled one AU outsystem of them, as they madly tried to finish the last testing items on a cobbled-up system that might work - or might not.

They had still been loading crew onto the *Dragon* as the Nidarian fleet passed by Mars, on their way to meet the Singheko.

Now, attached to the *Dragon* by hastily built mounts, the

four Devastators looked like ticks on a dog as the ancient Nidarian destroyer finally pulled in behind the Singheko fleet, decelerating at 300g, getting their speed down to battle limits.

"I'm ten seconds behind schedule," called Bonnie over her comm to Rita. "Do you want me to decrease decel a little and try to make it up?"

"No, don't do that," said Rita. "I'm afraid you'll overshoot. Just keep on your track."

"Aye, Skipper," said Bonnie. It was the first time she had treated Rita like an admiral; but in battle, somehow, it just came out.

"Disconnect the Devastators!" Bonnie yelled. She heard the clunks along the hull as the four kludged-up fighters were released from the *Dragon*, floating free in space beside the bigger ship.

"How's it looking, Major?" she called to Jim.

"Hard to be sure," she heard back. "I've got two green lights and two red lights on my weapons console. The second reactor is overheating and shows five minutes to shutdown. This is gonna be a close one."

"Well, get your ass in gear, then, Jimmy Boy," she called.

"That's Major Jimmy Boy to you, Captain," he called back, as he goosed his Devastator toward the Singheko fleet now just seconds in front of them.

"See you on the other side."

"Copy."

And he was gone.

Bonnie watched in the holo as the four Devastators formed up into a loose battle formation and spread out, starting a random weave pattern to evade enemy fire. Even as she watched, the first missiles came out of the destroyers in the rear of the Singheko fleet as the enemy became aware of the threat behind them.

Bonnie pushed all that aside. What happened to Jim and the flight of Devastators now was out of her hands. She had another job to do.

"Stand by to open fire," she called. Beside her in the XO chair, Dallitta nodded vigorously.

"Roger, mum. All weapons primed and ready for release."

"Very good, Commander. You may fire when ready."

"Firing…now," called Dallitta.

With a lurch felt throughout the ship, four missiles left the front of the *Dragon*, and four more departed from the rear tubes, arcing over the ship to take a vector toward the Singheko.

All eight missiles were directed toward the closest enemy battlecruiser, right in front of them. Dallitta waited a few seconds, until the enemy was well engaged with the missiles, spraying flak at them.

Then Dallitta fired the gamma lance for the first time in anger.

Sol System. Jupiter.

Jim saw Singheko missiles coming at him and jinked hard, trying to find a way through them. But they had a good lock on him, and he was in trouble. He spun the Devastator around to the left, spraying chaff, waited for a second, then spun it around the other way, hoping the crazy circle of chaff might confuse the missiles a bit.

It didn't seem to do much good, and he was down to seconds before he was space junk.

In desperation, he hit the newly installed firing switch on the stick, held in place by black electrical tape because they hadn't the time to mount it properly.

The newly built and installed gamma lance in the nose of the fighter toasted two of the missiles in front of him like a marshmallow over an open fire.

"Yes! It worked!" he yelled, thankful to still be alive as he dashed through the gap in the missile spread, evading another two missiles by a heartbeat.

"Tango Flight, use the lance on the missiles, it has just

enough spread to make a hole for you!" he yelled over the comm.

Then he was past the rear guard of corvettes and destroyers and had a big, beautiful cruiser in front of him. He lined up on the warship and said a quick prayer.

"Lord, if you can see your way clear, this one is for Caroline," he whispered as the enemy flak started bursting around him, pieces of shrapnel pattering off the skin of the fighter.

Then he pushed the fire button again.

Nothing happened.

Glancing down, he saw the overheat light from the second reactor flashing red.

"Fuck!" he yelled, punching the button to override it.

He looked up just in time to see a destroyer moving in front of him to block his path to the cruiser.

Slamming the trigger home, he felt the recoil as the lance fired this time. He watched as the destroyer in front of him disintegrated from a hole punched completely through the engine compartment, leaving a wall of parts and pieces for him to fly through if he wanted to get a clear shot at the cruiser.

Instinctively ducking his head as he flew through the mess, with parts clanging and banging off the fighter's gravity wedge, he lifted his head to see the cruiser launch eight more missiles at him.

He had a choice. He could fire at the missiles and save himself, but probably lose his chance at the cruiser, as it jinked crazily away from him and two more destroyers moved in to block his fire.

Or he could fire at the cruiser and the missiles would get to him before the weapon could recycle.

"Well, here's another nice mess you've got me into," he yelled out as he fired at the cruiser.

* * * * *

Rita nearly fell out of her chair as the *Merkkessa* was hammered on the bow, the gravity wedge shunting the blast aside but not enough to prevent the ship from staggering like a drunk.

There was nothing for her to do now. Her life, and the life of everyone on the ship, was in the hands of Captain Bekerose as he fought the ship, jinking, turning, accelerating, decelerating, refusing to give an inch as he fought two enemy battlecruisers toe to toe.

Beside her, Tarraine held on to the arms of his chair with a deathlike grip as he watched the holo.

"The *Dragon* is not close enough to the battlecruisers to take them out," he said, pointing to the holo. "She needs to come in closer."

"Not to worry. Bonnie sees it too. She'll get there in a second."

The sound of the pulse cannon on the hull of Merkkessa made a "braaap" sound that set their teeth on edge each time they fired. The *Merkkessa* lurched again. Something far in the back of the ship exploded. Rita felt the engines change pitch as one of them was damaged.

They were taking a beating.

* * * * *

Bonnie fired for the third time at the battlecruiser on the near side of the *Merkkessa*. It was technically within the range of the gamma lance, but it seemed to have little effect. She was getting frustrated.

"Closer! Get in closer!" she yelled at Dallitta.

"Copy."

The *Dragon* accelerated again, moving in toward the two battlecruisers that were throwing missiles at the Merkkessa with wild abandon.

"Fire, fire, fire!" yelled Bonnie as the lance recycled and the ready light came on.

This time the weapon had more effect. Bonnie saw a large piece come off the enemy battlecruiser, leaving a hole big enough to drive a truck through.

That got their attention. The big ship started to turn, moving to put its front missile tubes on them.

"Jim's in trouble," called Dallitta.

"Not our problem," yelled Bonnie. "Focus!"

Dallitta nodded. The lance light flickered, then came on green.

"Fire, fire, fire!" yelled Bonnie, and the weapon licked out at the battlecruiser just as eight missiles jumped out of its tubes toward the *Dragon*.

And the battlecruiser - and all its missiles - disappeared. In its place stood a monumental explosion of fire and flame. Munitions inside cooked off in all directions as the enemy ship disintegrated, leaving fiery trails in all directions like pinwheels at a holiday fireworks show.

'Scratch one battlecruiser," yelled Bonnie in delight. "Retarget the other one, fire when ready, Dallitta."

"Copy."

* * * * *

In the cockpit of his Devastator, Jim watched eight missiles coming at him. His last shot at the cruiser had taken down his weapons reactor. He had no missiles and no gamma lance.

He was defenseless.

Watching the missiles bore in, he spoke aloud, as he had always done when death stared him in the face.

"Right up to the last second," he recited, the last part of his mantra. His death song, as he thought of it. He wasn't Native American - but he felt he had the right to a death song.

Everybody has the right to a death song.

The missiles were three seconds away.

Right up to the last second, he thought one last time.

Then beside him two Devastators flashed by, both firing their lances at the missiles in front of him. Together they punched a hole in the middle of the group of missiles. Jim felt the urge to duck as he went through the hole in the missile spread with the two Devastators right in front of him, so close he could see the names written on the sides of their cockpits.

Bobber.

Spanky.

And he thought about the name hastily written on the side of his own fighter, just before they left Mars.

Angel.

Pulling in behind the two Devastators, he grinned.

It felt good to be alive.

* * * * *

"Now we're cooking," yelled Tarraine as the last Singheko battlecruiser stopped firing, its missile tubes smashed by the combined force of the *Merkkessa*, the *Dragon* and the three remaining active Devastators. Its engines appeared to be down. It was dead in space.

In the distance, the two remaining Singheko cruisers turned to flee, accelerating away toward the outer system. The remaining Singheko destroyers and corvettes tucked in behind them, all of them making a break for the mass limit.

"I don't want any of them getting away to warn Singheko about the new weapon," called Rita loudly.

"Copy," echoed both Tarraine and Lirrassa. With the survivors of the Nidarian fleet beside her, the *Merkkessa* accelerated toward the escaping enemy.

The *Dragon* passed them by like they were standing still. Before Rita could fully comprehend what was happening, the *Dragon* caught up to the nearest cruiser and fired her gamma lance. The cruiser came apart into two large pieces, both spinning end over end in space. Flame, parts, and bodies poured out of the broken ends into the black.

The remaining cruiser stopped all accel in the universal sign of surrender. A few seconds later, the remaining Singheko destroyers and corvettes did likewise.

CHAPTER TWENTY-NINE

Sol System.

The Singheko corvette sat quietly 35 AU above the ecliptic, with the Sol System spread out below it like a picture.

The big Singheko in command of the small ship spoke harshly, as the delayed light from the battle reached them 4.8 hours after it was all over. Loosely translated, his words would have been:

"Well, that sucks."

His first officer agreed.

"It does indeed suck, Captain."

The captain was a burly Singheko with two vestigial claws on each hand, signifying a member of a prestigious *gens.* He shook his head in disgust.

"Ensure all the recordings are secure and backed up, then plot a course for home and get us out of here. The Admiralty needs to see this as soon as possible."

He stalked off the bridge, too frustrated to stay. As he entered his cabin, he felt the slight shudder and whine as the corvette translated out for its five-and-a-half-month trip back to Singheko.

**In the Slave Ship
En Route to Singheko**

Tatiana had learned how to squat in the corner with two walls of the wire cage on each side and manage a somewhat comfortable position to watch the rest of the women surrounding her: a boring drama of fear, anger, discomfort, and stench.

Inside the cage, day and night became defined by morning wash downs and evening feedings.

Their Singheko captors fed them once a day - some kind of glop that flowed into a trough on the back wall of the cage. It oozed along like porridge - with strange, undefined lumps in it.

The first time it happened, there was a mad rush to the back of the cage, everyone fighting for the food.

Tatiana stayed out of the melee, too shocked by events to move from her corner.

But by the second evening, she was too hungry to let it pass. She stood, watching, as a half-dozen women fought and shoved to get to the food while the rest of the cage stood by.

How stupid! The food is the same for everybody! And there's enough for all!

Then she realized it wasn't about the food.

It was about primacy of place. They were establishing the pecking order. Even in a cage of slaves, someone had to be on top.

A big woman, one Tatiana hadn't noticed before, seemed to win the second battle, pushing and shoving others aside, leaving a few with a bloody nose.

When the more aggressive ones were done, Tatiana and the rest of the women got their food. They had to scoop it from the trough with their hands, eat it with their fingers.

Afterward, Tatiana washed off at one of the two water faucets mounted on the wall.

The next morning a half-dozen of the big Singheko guards came into the hallway between the cages with what looked like a fire hose.

Sure enough, they opened the valve and hosed down the cages, washing away the bodily wastes into a recessed drain at the back of the cage, spraying the women indiscriminately, the force of the water knocking many of them to the floor where they slid to the back.

Tatiana, in her secure spot at the rear corner, was able to huddle down and get clean without getting knocked over.

Thus, their day and night cycles were defined.

Evening was the glop oozing out of the wall into the trough, the hierarchy of the strong taking their turn, followed by the rest of the women, with the weak or sick at the last.

Morning was defined by the hosing down of the cage, washing away the stinking mess of the previous day, knocking down any who were unprepared.

It was on the third day out from Earth that the big woman came to Tatiana in her corner. It was after the evening feeding; the group was settling in for the night, their schedule now adjusted to a cycle dictated by their masters.

The big woman stared down at her. Tatiana looked up, uncertain of her intent.

"I'll take your corner, bitch," said the woman.

Tatiana shrugged, got up, and walked away. She had seen the big woman fight. A corner wasn't worth the beating.

But she hadn't taken two steps before the woman had her in a choke hold, dragging her backward into the corner.

"And I'll take you too, bitch," growled the woman. She twisted, throwing Tatiana back down into the corner.

Tatiana bounced off the wire mesh of the cage wall, and back onto the woman's feet.

It was pure luck; but when she bounced back, she somehow took the big woman down to her knees.

It wasn't good luck. It was bad luck.

Now the woman thought Tatiana had done it intentionally. She piled into Tatiana, all fists, elbows, knees, gouging and scratching, cursing a blue streak, slamming Tatiana up against the wire mesh of the cage over and over.

Tatiana folded up, rolling into a ball on the floor, trying to protect herself. After a few minutes, the big woman finally stopped hitting her and stood up, breathing hard.

"Get your ass in that corner and lie down, bitch."

Tatiana crawled into the corner. The big woman lay down on her and started having her way with her, roughly, punishing her, hurting her.

It wasn't sex; it was a lesson. A humiliation.

Tatiana let her mind go far away, trying to remember the happy times before her life went to shit.

Before she had thought it a lark to smuggle some drugs into their hotel in Odessa.

Before her boyfriend had abandoned her at the first sound of boots on the stairwell, flying out the window and gone, leaving her holding the bag as the police burst into the room.

Back when she had been the privileged daughter of a high-ranking Naval officer, a commander in the British Royal Navy. A man who had fallen in love with her Ukrainian mother, married, had a daughter, given them a kind and loving home - even if he was away for months at a time on sea duty.

Until her mother died when she was seventeen.

Until she and her father were left, bereft.

Until one fell into a pattern, dropping out of college, trekking around Europe with various boyfriends, a pattern of drugs and drink and parties and sex.

And the other one, using sea duty as a soporific from the pain, sending a monthly check while turning a blind eye to the long downhill slide of his daughter.

The big woman grew tired of abusing her, shoved her away, settling down into the corner in Tatiana's old spot, showing everyone she was now queen of the cage.

Tatiana crawled away, as far as she could get, all the way to the other corner of the cage.

Finding a spot next to a couple of older women, Tatiana sat, not crying, not angry, not anything. All her emotions had gone away, somewhere else.

She sat for a long time, unable to move, unable to think. Frozen, a statue of loss and pain.

One of the women next to her slid closer, put an arm around her, leaned her head on her shoulder.

"It'll be alright, dear," she said.

Then the tears came. They came suddenly, without warning. All that she had lost, all the mistakes, everything flooded out of her. She cried, as quietly as she could, until she had no more tears to cry.

Then she slumped into the other woman, a stranger, whose name she did not know, and they held each other for a while.

Finally, they slept.

Earth. Colorado Springs

The conference room was packed. Every chair was filled, and there were people standing around the edges of the room. There were a few who didn't really need to be there - they just wanted to see the Admiral who had saved Earth. And of course, Rita had snuck Jim in, well, - just because. Because he was her support system.

Sitting across from General Raines, Rita glanced over at Jim briefly, then continued.

"First a minor personnel matter, General. I'd like to take Major Carter here off your hands. My understanding is that he is still technically a member of your Space Force. I'd like to steal him for my CAG - Commander Attack Group."

Raines smiled slightly. The relationship between Rita and Jim Carter had already become common knowledge in the group.

"That will be fine, Admiral. Glad to get rid of him. Seems like all he wants to do is fly fighters and shoot things!"

A titter of laughter ran around the table.

"Thank you, General. I'll do my best to get some good use out of him."

Another titter of laughter ran around the table, as Rita's quite intentional double entendre registered on the assembled staff. Jim ducked his head, blushing. With a smile, Rita continued.

"I've dispatched the corvette *Corresse*, with the new drive installed, back to Nidaria. It will arrive eighteen days from now. That will fulfill our bargain with the Nidarians, by giving them the new drive systems. However, Captain Arteveld has been instructed to tell High Councilor Garatella he can have the plans for the gamma lance when we have a mutual defense treaty with Nidaria in place. In the meantime, if he wants it, he can come and take it."

Raines laughed.

"Admiral, please make sure I don't ever get on your bad side."

Rita smiled.

"Thank you for taking charge of the Singheko prisoners from the captured ships. I trust you are making them welcome in their new home in Australia."

Raines nodded.

"They're not too fond of the outback. But they're singing like little birds. We're learning a lot."

"Good," said Rita. "Now. About our fleet. We're converting all our ships to the new drives and adding the gamma lance weapon. Including the captured Singheko ships, it'll take us about six months to finish all the refits."

"And then?"

"And then we depart to take the fight to Singheko. It's far better to fight them in their own system than to fight them here. We'll bleed them there, right in front of their own people - their own government."

"Are you sure about this? Taking on the Singheko in their own system?"

"I am. In two months, I'll dispatch Bonnie in the *Dragon* to the Singheko system to monitor their activities. By the time we are ready to leave, we'll have enough intelligence on the Singheko and their fleet disposition to know how we can best attack them. This is the only way to safeguard Earth, General Raines. We have to keep them on the defensive until they decide to leave us alone."

With that, Rita rose, and her staff rose with her.

"Thank you, General Raines. We could not do this without you."

There was a lot of hand touching, hand shaking, and hugging before she and her staff were able to leave the room.

Walking down the hallway to her vehicle with Jim beside her, Rita was thoughtful, head down. She continued her quiet mood as they drove back to the four-bedroom house assigned as her quarters.

Inside the house, she went straight to the nursery to check on Imogen. Jim stood beside her. Together, they stared at the sleeping child.

"We have one more important task to do tonight," said Rita. She looked over at Jim.

"I know," he said.

* * * * *

Minutes later, Jim sat quietly at the kitchen table, as Rita sat across from him.

Their hearts lay on the table between them, invisible. Both knew they were there, frozen in time. Waiting to beat again - or not. The slightest mistake by either of them, and those two hearts would break, right there on the table.

"Bonnie sent a note for you."

Rita handed Jim an envelope.

Jim laid it aside. He already knew what it said. He could feel it.

It was Bonnie saying goodbye. Telling him she already knew what his choice would be.

"You're sure about going to Singheko?" Jim said, buying time.

Rita nodded.

"I am."

"You'll be fighting those bastards on their home turf."

"Yes. But we either fight them there or we fight them here at Earth. I'd rather fight them there. And fighting them there forces the Nidarians to make a decision. They either have to come in on our side, or take the chance we beat the Singheko without them, and become the new aggressive kids on the block."

"Or lose the *Dragon* technology to the Singheko."

"Exactly. Garatella drew a line in the sand and now he has to stand behind it and fight. Their survival is tied to ours."

"And Imogen?"

Rita paused. Now it came to the rub.

"With me."

"On the *Merkkessa*?"

"Yes."

"You could probably be President of Earth if you wanted it. Every news channel on the planet is calling you the savior of the world."

"No."

There was a long silence. Rita stared at him.

Make your choice, asshole, she thought. *Bonnie or me. Once and for all.*

Jim knew her thoughts. She had his consciousness inside her.

So, he knew what she was thinking as well.

Unbidden, a tiny smile came to curl up the corners of his lips.

"It'll be crowded with you, me and Imogen in your Flag Cabin," he said. "And I have to live with you and Imogen. I won't be relegated to the Bachelor Officer's quarters."

Their hearts began again.

"Then we'll have to get married," said Rita. "I can't have a single officer living in sin with the Admiral. It's bad for morale."

Slowly, Jim grinned. "Isn't living with a lowly Commander just as bad?"

A faint smile turned up Rita's lips.

"I'll take my chances."

EPILOGUE

Portsmouth, England
Three Weeks Later

The pub was nearly empty. Just the bartender, a couple arguing in a back booth, a bored waitress; the usual Saturday night drunk slumped over the jukebox looking for songs that weren't there...

And Luke, sitting alone at the bar, nursing his third pint.

So, he knew something was up as soon as the woman slid into the seat beside him.

There were a half-dozen empty chairs on either side. She could have chosen any of them.

But she didn't. She sat right beside him.

Bloody hell, a damn hooker, he thought.

He stared into the long mirror running behind the bar, expecting to see a worn-out bimbo in a slinky dress, with too much makeup and a desperate look on her face.

What he saw took his breath away.

One of the most beautiful women Luke had seen in his life sat beside him, meeting his eyes in the mirror. Perfect, symmetrical face. An elegant nose, not too small, not too big. Subdued makeup, exactly right. Perfectly coiffed blond hair cut in a bob, falling evenly above her collar, tastefully highlighted.

And green eyes that seemed to go on forever, drawing him in like a man sinking into an infinitely deep ocean - and one any man would willingly sink into - if that's what it took to be with this woman.

Then the uniform registered on his brain...a strange

uniform, deep navy blue, sleeve rings like a Royal Navy captain, epaulets on the shoulders - but a cut and fit not from the Royal Navy.

"And just what the hell do you want, Captain?" he growled. "Another inch of skin off my backside?"

Bonnie Page smiled wryly at the mirror, still meeting his eyes.

"Much more than that, Commander. I'd like to give you a job."

Luke shook his head, threw back his pint, and drained it. He stood up, threw a couple of tenners on the bar, and turned to go.

"Not a Commander anymore, as I'm sure you know quite well, Captain. And I don't need any job that comes with a uniform."

He took a step toward the door, stuffing his wallet back in his pocket.

"Even if it meant you could kill Singheko?" came a voice from behind him.

Luke stopped.

Kill Singheko.

He turned back to the woman.

The memory of his daughter Tatiana came to him, a picture in his mind unbidden, her face as bright and beautiful as the last time he saw her.

Before the Russians threw her into prison.

Before the Russians sent her to the Singheko slave ship.

"Kill Singheko?" he muttered again, staring at the woman. "How many can I kill?"

Bonnie smiled at the man.

"As many as you want, Commander. As far as I'm concerned, you can kill them all. But first, you'd have a job to do, and you'd have to do it my way."

Former Royal Navy Commander Luke Powell stepped back to his chair, stared at the woman for a second, and sat down.

"And what is your way, Captain?"

Bonnie gestured to the bartender, pointed to the empty pint in front of Luke, and held up two fingers. The bartender nodded and started drawing two more of the pints.

Bonnie turned back to Luke.

"No more wild and crazy schemes. No more jumping off into the wild blue without full support and planning. My way."

Suddenly, Luke recognized her.

"You're Bonnie Page," he said. "Captain of the *Dragon*."

Bonnie nodded. The bartender placed two pints in front of them.

"I am," she said.

"So, what do you want from me?"

Bonnie took a long draught of her pint, laid the glass down, and wiped foam off her perfect lips. She turned back to Luke.

"Before you decided to go off and take on the entire Russian army by yourself to get your daughter back, you had a reputation as one of the best and brightest ship commanders in the Royal Navy. That's exactly what I need right now. A ship commander with the smarts to be my XO on the *Dragon*."

Luke was stunned.

"But...the *Dragon*'s a starship! I'm a wet navy puke! How the hell could I do that job?"

Bonnie grinned.

"I don't need an expert on starships, Commander. I have plenty of those already, and the rest of it we can train. What I need is an expert on running a crew. Logistics. Training. Selection of personnel. Maintaining discipline and order. The remainder you can learn on the job like the rest of us are doing."

Luke shook his head.

"Why me? Why a cashiered officer stupid enough to think he could rescue his daughter from the Russians?"

Bonnie looked at him carefully.

"Because you did try to rescue your daughter. Because you were willing to put your life and your career on the line to try. Because you had the leadership skills to put together a team that almost pulled it off. And because maybe I think you got a bum deal from the Royal Navy."

"But I failed," Luke said. "I failed her."

His voice reflected an agony of pain he had not let out for months. It was all he could do to hold back tears.

Bonnie, overwhelmed by the moment, reached out a hand to him and placed it on his shoulder.

"Commander. You did not fail. Humanity failed. We failed to protect our people. But now we have a second chance. A chance to take the fight to the enemy. And maybe, along the way, find our lost people and help them, or even rescue them. I can't say that with certainty. But it's a possibility."

Luke turned away, overcome with emotion. He took the pint, lifted it halfway, looked at it, then gently placed the glass back on the bar.

Quietly, he spoke.

"You should know I've been drinking quite a bit lately," he said.

Bonnie also spoke softly.

"Can you manage it?"

Luke nodded. "Yeah. I can manage it."

"OK. What else?"

Luke knew what she meant.

What else prevents you from leaving Earth and going off to kill Singheko?

"Not a bloody thing," he muttered. "Not a bloody damn thing."

###

AUTHOR NOTES

Thanks so much for reading this book. It was fun to write, and I hope it was fun to read.

Below you'll find a sneak preview of the third book in the series, *The Long Edge of Night*, available on Amazon. Always free if you have Kindle Unlimited!

Special bonus - if you have not already signed up for my newsletter, sign up now and get one of my books for free!

www.philhuddleston.com/newsletter

All the best,
Phil

PREVIEW OF NEXT BOOK

The Long Edge of Night - Broken Galaxy Book Three

In the wee hours of the morning, Tatiana awoke.

Her mind was clear. She had made a decision while she slept.

Maybe her subconscious mind had made it earlier, and it was only just now bubbling up.

Or maybe in her dream state, it had come to her.

But she had decided.

The big woman will come back for me again. She has to have a victim, someone to abuse, to show the others who's boss.

I will not be a victim.

She remembered something her father had told her once in a letter.

Be happy in your life. Live for the joy in the day. But also be prepared for the worst, the unexpected, the danger. By being prepared, you can be without fear, without worry. Prepare for the unexpected - but never let the preparation lead you from joy.

Now Tatiana let those words resonate in her mind.

I will not be a victim here.

She looked carefully at every inch of the cage. Was there anything she could use to her advantage? Anything she could use to defend herself?

Turning, she examined the wire mesh of the cage behind her. She pulled it, pushed it, looking for any weakness.

As she did so, she noticed one of the cage wires had a tiny crack in it, right where it crossed over another.

Pushing on the wire, she saw it move a little. Working it, she thought she saw the crack widen. She continued to work the wire, until an hour later, she managed to break off a small piece of it.

It was not long - maybe four inches in length. By the time she curled it up in her hand to use as a weapon, she had only one inch sticking out.

It will have to be enough. I know she'll attack me again.

Sure enough, after the guards came through and hosed them down next morning, the big woman stood up, shaking off the water.

"Hey! Brytanskyy!" she shouted. "Let's party some more. Come over here and lick me clean!"

Tatiana stood up but didn't move. She just waited.

She knew it wouldn't take long. And it didn't. When she didn't move to the woman, the big Ukrainian started toward her.

"Hey, bitch! When I call you, get your ass over here!" she shouted.

Around her, women scattered as they realized another fight was starting.

Tatiana waited. The wire was curled up in her right hand. Now she turned slightly, hiding her right side, and slowly moved the wire out until an inch of it was exposed, sticking out of her fist.

The big woman was nearly to her, and reached out, intending to grab her by the neck and choke her out again.

Tatiana ducked under the arm and swung her fist, stabbing the wire directly at the woman's right eye. The point of the wire missed the eye directly and hit above it in the forehead. Tatiana pulled it down as hard as she could. The wire cut a raw chasm down her attacker's face from her forehead to her cheek. Blood spattered and the woman fell away, screaming.

"I'm blind!" she screamed. "I'm blind!"

Tatiana stared at her, ready for another assault if necessary.

"Only in one eye, you stupid bitch. Come at me again and I'll take the other one."

Then Tatiana moved her gaze slowly around the room, at the hundred-odd women crammed into the wire cage, all staring at her.

Something happened in her at that moment. Something strange.

Something welled up in her she had never felt before.

We cannot be victims.

She knew instinctively her chance would come only once, and she intended to take it.

"All of you - listen to me. We are being stupid. Fighting among ourselves! Forming up into gangs! This plays right into their hands!"

She pointed at the hallway outside the cage.

"From now on, we don't fight each other! We fight those bastards out there! In here, we help each other. We protect each other. And when we get to wherever - whatever - we fight those assholes with everything we've got!"

Tatiana walked around the cage. People made space for her as she moved. They leaned in, listening.

"Anyone can roll over and die. Anyone can start victimizing the weak, ignoring the threat outside. But we're not going to do that. We're going to form a resistance movement right here - right inside this cage! We're going to organize, plan. When they let us off this ship - regardless of what they do, regardless of where we are - we're going to find a way to take the fight to them. Got it?"

There was a jumbled murmur of agreement from some of the women around her.

"Got it?" she shouted again.

A small cheer went up.

"Got it?" she yelled again.

"Yes!" came a loud, resounding answer.

* * * * *

The big Ukrainian woman had been huddled on the floor for twenty minutes, blood dripping down her face. Periodically she would roll from side to side and moan, or whimper "I'm blind, I'm blind!"

Tatiana walked to her and crouched down.

"I don't think you're blind. I think your eye's just full of blood."

The woman raised her head slightly, looked at Tatiana with her good eye, holding her hand over the other. Blood oozed out between her fingers and dripped off her face.

"Go fuck yourself."

"If I could, I would," grinned Tatiana. "But I don't have the right equipment. What's your name?"

There was no response. The woman lay silent, ignoring her.

"Listen. I have an idea to organize us to fight the Singheko."

"Go to hell."

"No. Let's send the Singheko to hell instead."

There was a silence as the big woman slowly stopped moaning and began to think again.

"Bullshit. What can we do?"

"What can we do if we don't try? And isn't it better than sitting here waiting to die? What's your name?"

After a long silence, the big woman responded.

"Marta," she grunted.

Closing her eye and slumping back down on the floor, Marta turned away.

Tatiana thought she'd lost her chance to get through to the big woman. She sighed and stood up to walk away.

Then she heard Marta.

"And what would I do?" asked the Ukrainian, still facing

away from her on the floor.

Tatiana crouched beside her again, talking to her back.

"I'm not sure. But I know you're the strongest person in this cage. If the two of us work together, we can put together some kind of organization. I can help with the brains, at least."

"How come you'd be the brains?" growled Marta.

Tatiana smiled.

"Who's lying on the floor bleeding?"

After a silence, Marta grunted.

"Point taken."

Then Marta spoke again.

"It doesn't matter. You won't survive another week in this cage."

"What do you mean?"

"Look across the room."

Tatiana turned on her heels, gazed around the room.

In the corner that she had once occupied, and which Marta had taken away from her, another big woman had already taken up residency.

"Her name is Sonja," Marta grunted. "As soon as she gets it in her head, she'll kill you."

"But why?" asked Tatiana.

"Because compared to her, I'm Jesus Christ. She's not as strong as me. But twice as mean."

Tatiana turned back to Marta.

"So again. We organize, we fight these alien bastards. If we have to fight Sonja, we do that too. Why not join forces? You help me, I help you."

Marta grunted, but at least she rose, moved herself to a sitting position. She turned to look at Tatiana, her hand still covering her face, dripping blood.

"I should kill you for what you did."

"Maybe. But that gains you nothing. Joining forces with me gains you brains and something to do - kill Singheko."

Marta thought about that for a bit. Slowly, a wry little smile started on her face.

"I would surely like to kill some of those bastards."

"Then get on your feet, go over to the water, and clean yourself up."

"And then?" asked Marta.

"I heard someone say you were an officer in the army. What were you?"

"Captain," grunted Marta.

"Then you know military organization. That's perfect. Find out anyone else who was in the military, or who knows things that would help. Organize them into a Headquarters unit. Divide the rest into squads and platoons. Get us organized."

Marta nodded slowly.

"You're fucking crazy, you know that, right?"

Tatiana grinned.

"Of course. No sane person would think this is possible."

Slowly, Marta started to get to her feet.

Tatiana stood, reached out a hand, and helped her up.

Marta glared at her for a long moment, and Tatiana wasn't sure if she was going to go clean herself or start another fight.

"I really should kill you, you know," Marta added. "There's a half-dozen women in this cage I'll have to fight to keep you alive."

Then a grin broke out on Marta's face.

"But you just might have the balls to pull it off, you crazy bitch," said Marta.

"Tatiana. Tatiana Powell."

"Ah, right. You're a Brytanskyy - an Englander."

"Yeah. My father was English."

"OK," said Marta, still holding one hand over her damaged face. "I'll help you for now. Until you screw up and I get to kill you."

"Until I screw up," grinned Tatiana.

Marta shook her head.

"I don't think that'll take long," she said, as she turned and headed for the water faucet at the back of the cage.

Continue the story with The Long Edge of Night on Amazon!

WORKS

Sci-Fi, New Books, Hard Science, and General Mayhem
www.facebook.com/PhilHuddlestonAuthor
New books and freebies
www.philhuddleston.com/newsletter

Author Page on Amazon:
https://www.amazon.com/author/philhuddleston

Imprint Series
Artemis War (prequel novella)
Imprint of Blood
Imprint of War
Imprint of Honor
Imprint of Defiance

Broken Galaxy Series
Broken Galaxy
Star Tango
The Long Edge of Night
The Short End
Remnants
Goblin Eternal

ABOUT THE AUTHOR

Like Huckleberry Finn, Phil Huddleston grew up barefoot and outdoors, catching mudbugs by the creek, chasing rabbits through the fields, and forgetting to come home for dinner. Then he discovered books. Thereafter, he read everything he could get his hands on, including reading the Encyclopedia Britannica and Funk & Wagnalls from A-to-Z multiple times. He served in the U. S. Marines for four years, returned to college and completed his degree on the GI Bill. Since that time, he built computer systems, worked in cybersecurity, played in a band, flew a bush plane from Alaska to Texas, rode a motorcycle around a good bit of America, and watched in amazement as his wife raised two wonderful daughters in spite of him. And would sure like to do it all again. Except maybe without the screams of terror.

Printed in Great Britain
by Amazon